A Dragon's Tea

The Dragon Roost Bed & Breakfast Series:

Book 1

Betsy J. Bennett

Ahead of the Press Publishing
St. Louis, Missouri

Library of Congress Cataloguing-in-Publication Data

A Dragon's Tea
The Dragon's Roost Bed and Breakfast Series: Book 1
Betsy J. Bennett / author

ISBN   Paperback   978-1-950392- 12-4
ISBN   KINDLE   978-1-950392- 13-1

Ahead of The Press Publishing
St. Louis, Missouri

TABLE OF CONTENTS

CHAPTER 1

"Andrew?" Lori knocked lightly on the front door, although it stood ajar. She felt oddly hesitant to enter when it was so unlike him to leave his door open, or even unlocked. For the last three months he had been her lover, and while they had casually wandered into each other's apartments, this time felt different.

"Andrew, are you here?"

It was one of his odd quirks that annoyed her, but not enough so she bothered to mention it. He liked his locks secured, no matter what side of the door he was on.

His rented older house stood only a few blocks from the university. Most of the buildings on this block had been converted into apartments but Andrew rented an entire five bedroom house. He said he couldn't tolerate the noise and disruptions of having roommates, although he'd been quite clear he'd adjust, should she move in. It wasn't yet a step she was willing to take.

Lori glanced over her shoulder, expecting to see his familiar compact form, carting the garbage out, or coming up the walk overloaded with groceries, any normal excuse for leaving the front door ajar. She scanned the empty street and caught no sight of him.

The neighborhood was silent. She'd even say appeared deserted. At three o'clock in the afternoon, children should be playing kickball in the streets or college students walking from the bus stop lugging heavy backpacks. She should be able to observe cats eyeing oblivious robins, or gray haired retirees spending their golden years stooped over lawns, trying to get a handle on the dandelion encroachment. Lori saw nothing but silent homes. If she'd walked into a painting, the street couldn't have looked more uninhabited.

Feeling panicked, Lori looked around. She didn't even see a mosquito or housefly. You're imaging things, she whispered to herself, realizing as she did so she was also spooking herself, and creating premonition for disaster built on years of watching horror flicks and reading suspense novels.

"The sun is shining, for heaven's sake," she mumbled, looking through the open door, expecting, and not seeing, blood spatter, or other signs of a home-invading assassin.

The hallway was spotless. Another of Andrew's little quirks. He didn't tolerate dirt. What had he said when she'd mentioned that little detail? "Dust can interfere with my spells."

Spells, like Harry Potter. When she said so yesterday, his reaction was instantaneous and violent. He grasped her, one hand at her throat, tightening his fingers until she couldn't breathe, the other on her arm, painfully digging into her flesh.

"Don't you ever compare me to that miserable fraud!" he'd ordered, while she frantically struggled to breathe. "My power is real."

Then he must have realized he'd gone too far, for he released her with an abrupt shove, clearly without apology. He mumbled she'd caught him off guard. He continued his spin control, citing a perfectionist mother and strict upbringing.

Following his lead, she countered, mentioning the newest dusters being marketed which were supposed to make housecleaning a delight. While rubbing the tenderness at her throat, she added that she could see him dancing to hard rock while dusting, and Andrew with obviously no idea what she was talking about, agreed, seemingly relieved. Lori only remembered the sudden flash of violence, the feeling of betrayal since he was so obviously lying, and the fact he believed he was perfecting spells.

Spells. She thought back to her doctorial thesis, approved that morning, where she stated, no, proved there was no such thing as a man of power. All power was securely in the capable hands of women. Men, she wrote, were frauds, masters of slight-of-hand, showmen. Women knew the herbs, the techniques, had the empathy to be considered real magicians.

She had stepped back after his abrupt—and inexplicable—assault, putting distance between them, while trying to swallow with a raw throat. She looked at him differently, knowing this was the beginning of the end for them. She would not stay with a man who'd attack her violently for any reason. She'd always wonder what might set him off next. She thought back, realizing there were other equally unexplained facets of his personality she had accepted as quirky. Now, bathed in the bright sunlight of an early spring morning, they seemed sinister.

Last night, disguising her distrust, she stayed for dinner, and Andrew salted his words with charm the entire evening, overly gracious, wishing her success on her oral defense of her doctorate the next morning.

Last night Lori could have left for her apartment, put in another hour or two of prep for her oral defense, but she knew in order to be clear-headed for the exam, she needed to take the evening off, avoid anything to do with anthropology in general and with her thesis specifically. If she'd left after his abrupt attack, she would have been worthless, wondering what prompted it, churning over their relationship, her future and fretting about her coming educational ordeal. So while her flesh crawled and she thought of slimy things that liked the dark, she stayed, leaving before she would feel obligated to spend the night between his sheets.

This morning after her defense of her thesis, she wanted to celebrate and do something fun. She felt drained, mentally and physically, even though she had succeeded and the pressure was off.

"You're looking at Doctor Lori Larwick," she would say to him, to inform him the morning had gone well. Then he'd hug her, and they **would** swirl together in dizzying circles until neither could stand. Perhaps the rest of the afternoon and evening, even the rest of the week, they could spend entwined in his bed.

But his front door stood ajar.

She tried to remember if she'd arrived unannounced before. Of course she had, hadn't she? She'd been here dozens of times, but thinking back, every time she'd come, he was with her, after class, studying, or dinner out.

"Andrew?" she called again, then fearing for his safety, stepped inside. "Andrew, I'm coming in. I just want to be sure you're safe, and your notes haven't been touched."

As far as she knew, his research was the only thing he had which could be valuable to anyone else, and he guarded it jealously. It was such a secret, she didn't even know the topic of his thesis. While she'd freely expounded about the successes and failures in her research, he had kept his own council, never divulging details. He didn't seem to spend as much time in the library as she did, but that meant little. She was under the impression most of his research took place in a lab.

She debated calling the police because the house felt unnatural, as if someone else had been inside, but she knew he would never forgive her if she did. She pulled her cell out of her purse, and instead tried his phone. She couldn't hear an answering ring, and eventually it went to voicemail. Either he wasn't home, or his cell was off. Inconclusive evidence. He still could be here, hurt, bleeding, or murdered, his research stolen.

Lori pulled in a deep breath, tried to calm her nerves, which were starting to quiver. She wished her imagination wasn't so keen, pleased that she wasn't wearing a thin negligee, heading downstairs holding nothing more than a quivering candle, as all femme fatales did in horror movies while thunder rumbled in the background. She repeated to herself that she was an educated woman, a scientist who really needed to get a handle on her emotions. Traditionally she did not chose panic as a first course of action.

The front door opened into a long hall with doors on both sides. To the left was his living room, filled with typical grad student furniture: a lumpy couch, scarred end tables picked up at garage sales, and a very expensive entertainment system containing a flat screen television with all the latest gadgets to provide perfect reception and ideal sound. Nothing looked like it had been touched at all. Lori realized there were no magazines, no half-finished pizzas in greasy boxes, no school books or even a television guide. He didn't spend much time here, although on dates with him, they'd often spent pleasurable hours entranced with the latest videos. This room, she decided, was just for her, to make it look like he lived a normal grad-student life. This room was a decoy.

Lori didn't like these thoughts, and cursed herself for a fool for thinking them. He was just a normal guy she had a crush on. She doubted she would ever marry him and raise children, but for now, he satisfied her, a fun man with similar interests, who was frequently available to show her a good time.

His bedroom was on the right. The bed was made, covered with an old-fashioned white chenille bedspread. With an entire house of his own and another floor above this one, it amazed her that he had chosen a ground floor room for his bed, and not used the space for an office. It would have made more sense to her. She stepped inside. The room was empty, not a speck of dust visible on the hardwood floor or on the dresser. There was nothing of a personal nature visible, not a picture on the wall of someone he knew or a crazy stunt he had performed caught on film. There wasn't even a handful of change, a crumpled receipt, or some half-scrawled messages piled on the dresser. Nothing. Odd, that when they'd been here together, making love, she hadn't noticed the room's emptiness.

She thought quickly of her own room with traces her life all over it. Books, with socks, combs or other odd things acting as bookmarks were piled six or seven deep on every available space. Remnants of the field research she'd done, the tools of her trade, and mementoes of friends she wouldn't part with rested everywhere. There were pictures of her family, even the family dog. Her favorite quilt, almost as old as she was, and starting to fray where she had rubbed the edging as a child covered the bed. Empty yogurt containers, computer manuals, pencils, a phone charger, and enough earrings to wear a different set every day for a month decorated the nightstand. This room felt empty and unlived in.

But he did live there. She'd spent hours in this bed, sleeping, and doing athletic things with his naked body as counterpoint.

"Andrew—" she called out again, feeling the voyeur in his bedroom without him. "There isn't anything wrong," she muttered. Annoyed for letting her imagination run away with her, she opened the top drawer of his dresser, expecting to find socks, shorts, a year's supply of condoms, but there was nothing. The drawer was empty.

Was it possible he had moved out without telling her? After all, she had been here only yesterday. He knew how important today was, and she would need him to celebrate or to console. They'd all but made plans, more detailed than "I'll catch you later," less specific than "two o'clock at the clock tower," for she hadn't known how long her defense would take.

There was nothing in the other drawers, not pants or a t-shirt. She ran for the bathroom. There at least was evidence of life. Her toothbrush and his, toothpaste, mouthwash, and soap. They'd spent hours entwined in that shower. She blushed thinking back on it, but still curious and annoyed, she opened the cabinet under the sink. There were towels, but nothing else. No additional bars of soap, razors, floss, or headache remedies. Post grad students usually went through a lot of Excedrin.

Then it hit her. He must only use the downstairs bedroom, the downstairs bath, when she was visiting. On the nights when she didn't stay over, he must sleep in another bedroom, keeping his private life private.

It made sense. He'd never allowed her up the stairs, and for one reason or another, had kept her so occupied that she just realized she'd never been on the upper level.

She reached the laundry room next, and felt relieved. There was open detergent, dryer sheets, and a pile of lint, carefully bagged, indicating this room, at least was used.

"Andrew?" she called again, putting her hands on the rail leading upstairs.

It wasn't bravery which had her heading up the stairs. Bravery had nothing to do with it, or did curiosity. She had wanted to celebrate, now she only wanted to know if he were okay.

The stairs didn't creak. Funny how it was the lack of sound that disturbed her, rather than the reverse. It was an old house. The stairs should creak. Thinking that, she looked down, and caught sight of something she hadn't noticed before. A dark blot of something, just a droplet she instinctively assumed to be blood was on the tread. The impulse was strong to dip her index finger into it, sniff to see if she could identify the substance by scent alone. She thought maybe she should call the police after all. The cell phone was still clutched tightly between her fingers, but it didn't have to be blood. It could be anything.

Even if it were blood, he didn't have to be murdered. Andrew could've cut himself shaving, stubbed a toe doing mixed martial arts exercises, or snipped a fingertip with a carving knife slicing onions. The average human bled occasionally and there was no proof yet the police were needed to intercede.

She sped past the blood droplet, not wanting to know. If DNA analysis were needed later, the sample remained mostly undisturbed. That too she got from horror movies and reading suspense novels. Leave evidence undisturbed. The first room at the top of the stairs was a bedroom, obviously used. Jealousy reared its ugly green head, until she noticed nothing feminine in the room. So he wasn't keeping a wife or another lover.

"Just as well he doesn't," Lori said. She was scared—for him—and wouldn't be comfortable until she knew he was all right.

There was no need to check the dresser to know the drawers would be filled with clothing, or to look in the bathroom to determine he showered upstairs when she wasn't with him. The facts left her with a problem. He obviously had a secret he didn't want her to know. Why else the subterfuge? What did he have up here that he didn't want her to see? She thought she knew him, thought there wasn't any more to him than the superficial secrets college students kept from each other, even college students who were lovers.

The next bedroom was empty. Stepping inside, Lori saw not a dresser, not a packing box or a resting place for his exercise equipment. The hardwood floor was dulled, but obviously clean, dust free. Dark curtains covered the windows. This room faced the front of the house and the street. So, if he did anything in here, it couldn't be observed from outside, but she suspected the room was exactly how it appeared, unused.

She stepped back in the hall, about to return to her apartment and call her parents to share the good news about her thesis defense, and then perhaps take herself out for ice cream and call Andrew in the morning. She would shut the door behind her, the least she could do.

Except she saw a second drop of the substance she suspected was blood further down the hall. Two feet from that one were several more, not a pool by any definition, but enough that whatever had been bleeding had to have rested there while something else happened.

"What?" she asked aloud. The drops were in the middle of the hall, with no obstructions around them. Whoever or whatever had bled, assuming it was blood, should have kept moving and not stopped where it did. Lori decided an injury hadn't occurred here. No, she was certain in her active imagination she had never trusted before, that the victim had been carted upstairs and had rested or been restrained here.

"Why?" she asked this time, her voice for the first time exhibiting the tiniest quiver. She added "Who?" wanting to cover her bases. She was a scientist and this was starting to look like a mystery. She couldn't forget that the open door was totally uncharacteristic of Andrew.

She looked up, and realized why the droplets were there. Above her head was an access panel and a long rope that delayed the bleeder or his captor. There was an attic above her. Without thinking, she tugged the rope, and the panel opened easily, dropping a set of stairs silently.

Lori shoved her phone back in her purse and climbed. She didn't think to call out. She went, not knowing what to expect, but assuming it would be like any other attic, cobwebbed with decades of spider homes, layered in dust, old boxes of forgotten Christmas ornaments, clothing and furniture long unused.

Instead she found his laboratory.

What else could it be? The room went the length of the house, and was taller than she would have imagined judging from her impressions from the sidewalk. It was well-lit. Perhaps a dozen wall sconces burned cleanly, torches flickering without smoke.

She caught the sharp stench of herbs or incense, and the underlying copper smell of blood. She continued up the attic stairs, until she stood on the slate floor. When she was fully in the attic, she noticed Andrew.

They were about the same height, which made him five foot five or so, but here he seemed taller, more imposing. He was stark naked with his back to her, and he worked over a small black pot of something on a tripod suspended over a burner, which was the source, Lori suspected, of most of the stench.

Meat was her first impression of the massive chunk of skinless flesh at his feet, but upon looking closer, swallowing bile, she wasn't sure that was accurate.

She must have made a sound, gasped or gagged or even started praying those abrupt phrases which come at times of high stress like Mother of God, for he turned around and faced her.

The man who met her gaze wasn't the kinky, sexually aggressive Andrew she knew. This was another facet of him, a deeper, viler version; the evil-twin, Mr. Hyde version he kept carefully hidden from everyone.

"You practice the dark arts," she said, pleased her voice didn't shake and she sounded so normal. She was an anthropologist. A large portion of her thesis had been on a specific primitive tribe's method of idol worship and most of the facts she had uncovered had not been discussed in literature before.

"Lori," Andrew didn't seem surprised to see her, nor, with the twitch of life from his groin did he appear disappointed. "This is very, very sensitive, or I would come over there and welcome you properly. How did your dissertation go?"

It was so abnormal she wanted to scream: A naked man in an upstairs lair, working arcane spells over something bloody, asking casually how her day went.

"What are you doing?" Her voice, while controlled, hit a higher pitch than normal.

"It's a surprise," he said, "and it's not quite ready. Another ten minutes before I can leave it. I don't suppose you'd be willing to sit, quietly mind you, so I can finish this up?"

"Devil worship?"

"Nothing quite that easily pigeonholed," he answered, and his grin looked snide more than evil. He turned his back to her, continuing to stir. "I know you like wizards, you did mention a fascination with fictional ones, but real wizards don't use wands. We access our powerstrands with spells, domination, and control. Power is tapped from the universe. I won't bother using technical terms I doubt you'd understand."

He turned back to face her, eyes alight with insanity, but it was his erection which made her gasp. Whatever he was doing was clearly turning him on.

"Yes," he answered, noting where she looked, "after I finish my experiments, I usually have residual power to release. You've been quite helpful, even if you've never believed men can control power."

She felt lightheaded and her stomach rolled.

"You're insane." A dozen less-complementary words flashed through her mind, but she had the presence of mind to bite them off before she further enraged him.

"Before you think of running back down those stairs, what you need to know is although I appear unarmed, I am really quite capable of defending myself."

She studied the bloody carcass at his feet. "And the … meat?"

He shrugged casually, touching his hip, leaving a long bloodied bloody smear. "Research. I am looking for something. I haven't found it yet, but I'm a closer than anyone else in my field."

"You're really insane. You need help." She looked at her hands, realized she wasn't defenseless herself, for she had her cell phone. "Let me get you some help."

"I haven't got time for this." He set the ladle down, then twisted his hands as if attempting the motions of a particularly involved game of charades.

She watched, forgetting the need to dial 911. Less than ten seconds later she felt something crawling up her legs, something definitely serpentine slithering around her calves, heading for her knees. She looked down, saw nothing, yet the feeling of a cold, reptilian invasion persisted.

"Stop it!" she screamed, "Stop it!" she reached down, tried to dislodge whatever it was which was now past her knees, tightening and holding her in place.

He returned to the caldron, chanting words she couldn't understand, whether because he mumbled them or because they were another language. She screamed, then felt the invisible force sliding up over her throat, cutting off air, slithering over her mouth, preventing speech.

"I promise you, I have need of you," he said, over his shoulder, then his work resumed once again.

She struggled, and somehow, through luck or fate or blind ability, managed to get free, to escape whatever invisible menace he trapped her with. Without knowing why, she inched up behind him, abruptly kicking the cauldron, toppling the tripod, spilling the contents.

Andrew roared, heading toward her, continuing his odd hand gesticulations.

Lori fled down the stairs, out of the house, and into her car before he could pursue her. His vile curses rang around her, although she blocked most of what he was saying. In the melee, she'd dropped her cell. She continued driving until she reached the airport. She wouldn't go back to her room, wouldn't go to her mother, and it wasn't until she saw a flight listing for Albany, New York that she remembered her Aunt Jan. She would be safe there. Andrew wouldn't find her.

From the airport she called the police, giving her name, her address, and her impressions of what she'd seen. The meat she noticed had been skinned. It also had a human foot.

CHAPTER 2

Lori Larwick steered the car cautiously down the main street of Au Sable Forks, a small upper New York town two hours due north of the state capital. It was approaching ten o'clock, and for the most part the town slept, the parallel parking slots empty, and the shops dark and shuttered. Exhaustion flowed through her, residual from the panic which fueled her escape from the house of horrors that morning.

She drove carefully, hoping beyond hope for an open gas station, and someplace, anyplace to ask for directions. Her aunt lived in this area somewhere but her address book was in her phone and her phone was three time zones away and likely key evidence in a newly opened murder investigation.

The car twitched, as if with a mind of its own, a recalcitrant Mustang, not the Detroit steel it actually was. The steering wheel turned of its own volition, initiating a hard left which had her fighting the wheel to negotiate a blind turn between buildings into a small parking lot behind a row of stores. It was as if the car itself didn't want to go any further, and would rather stop here than continue on to somewhere safer. Perhaps there was a force-field in place, an invisible barrier she needed to penetrate using only gumption and the last of her energy reserves.

"I'll have you know I'm in charge here," she said, tightening her fingers around the steering wheel. After the disaster this morning, and the fact her rear view mirror had remained mercifully empty the entire trip, she needed someone to talk to. Panic never seemed so out-of-control when you were with someone.

"We're not staying here," she said, as if in warning. She did not want the car to get too comfortable.

The engine pinged once, a cooling sound, so she removed the key from the ignition, and held it up, as if in warning, to herself or it, she had no idea. "Ok, I'll get out and walk, but if I'm mugged or attacked in any way, I'm blaming you."

The car didn't seem to heed the implied threat. Lori had no idea when she had developed this odd habit of talking to Detroit machines, but somehow in the last hour or two the Mustang became her partner. She wished it no harm.

Her legs were stiff from the cramped plane trip, compounded by the long drive up the Adirondack Northway. It felt good to use them for something other than the gas pedal or brake, and as she walked back through the dark alley to the main street she breathed sharp, clean air deep into her lungs. Still, as she stamped her feet it was for more than getting her blood flowing. She was annoyed, for she could have parked right in front of any store on the strip. For an instant, Lori wondered why the car had forced her into the back, as if it and it alone were responsible.

Warm yellow light contrasted against the black night drew her attention, for deep shadows hung in the alley she passed through. The first shop was a clothing store, clearly closed, with security lights shining on their display window, but the next was better lit, so pushing through her exhaustion, she kept traveling.

This was a jewelry store, and the succinct one word sign on the door clearly stated 'open.' She paused for a moment to view the stunning display of necklaces, earrings and other fabulous bling through the glass. It was a small store and clearly a tourist trap, for she doubted the hard working independent people of this one-traffic-light town could afford this degree of affluence frequently enough to keep the store in business. The front window displayed wealth beyond her wildest daydreams. For long seconds she stood spellbound.

Lori mentally analyzed the window, small compared to the stores surrounding it, not much bigger than seven feet by four feet. Due to the artistic display it looked far greater. The store owner had designed a castle with battlements and turrets, so lifelike she felt she would be questioned by armed sentries if she decided to cross that drawbridge into the main bailey.

In one corner, about four foot high stood a crystal dragon, wings unfurled, his jaws wide, defending the treasures that were draped almost negligently over the castle walls. Lori studied the incredible array of breathtaking jewels: diamonds, rubies and emeralds which sparkled as if lit from within. The work was intricate, and each necklace and bracelet was more stunning than the next, so much so that to choose a favorite seemed impossible.

Two men stood arguing in the store, a tall, thin man with shaggy dark hair behind a display case and an older, gray haired man facing him. Although the door between them remained firmly closed, Lori could hear them as if they spoke through microphones.

"Why do you deny what you need?" the shopkeeper asked. His voice held an old world accent, maybe Germany or Austria, tempered by time, or perhaps the need to blend in. His 'w' had the slightest trace of a 'v' sound.

"You think I would take from you?" the older man returned, his accent thick with an English brogue. His silver hair was styled short and he wore a manicured beard. "I've killed your kind."

Before Lori could shiver, think on the events of that morning, the younger man laughed. "Perhaps we're well rid of them." He held his hands out, palm up, as if to show he was unarmed. "I offer what I offer with no strings."

The older man shook his head, turned as if to leave, but didn't quite follow through. "There's always obligation. Don't you think I've lived long enough to know that? I'm not sure I'm willing to let you have that much power over me."

"Yes, because dying is so much wiser," the shopkeeper said, dripping sarcasm. "And you're so easily replaced." He leaned on the counter now, and Lori thought he reeked sincerity. "Take what I offer freely. It's not something I provide just anyone."

"Don't I know that." There was something biting in his response as if this boon had not been offered when it would have been the most useful, and now it was too little, too late.

The younger man came out from behind the counter, his movements lithe with an athlete's grace. "It will help. I know we disagree but we fight the same battles."

The old man hiked an eyebrow. "Do we? Perhaps now—" He let the sentence drift off, and somehow Lori sensed deep abiding regret. When he spoke next, it sounded like a threat. "One day, Old One, you'll be betrayed by a woman."

The shopkeeper appeared unconcerned by this turn in the conversation. "You've taken to fortune telling then?"

"No, I just want you to understand what I've gone through, the pain of love, that burns down to the soul."

"It's just as well then I've no soul."

"But you've a heart, and it will be broken soon enough."

Embarrassed to be eavesdropping, having places to go and people to see and all that, Lori entered the shop, her arrival announced by the tinkling of a small bell above the door. The interior was decorated to look like a medieval common room, with rushes on the floor and a scarred oak table, set with dented pewter steins and plates. In one corner stood a full suit of armor, and everywhere dragons: ceramic, marble, carved oak, wrought iron, hulking or whimsical, enraged or relaxed. One wall held a standard jewelry shop glass fronted case, and it was here Lori was drawn. "And I thought the jewels in the window were spectacular." For these were truly breathtaking.

She looked up, met the jeweler's eyes, for he was very tall. "Hello, I'm sorry. I know I'm intruding. You're still open, aren't you?" she asked, in case the sign on the door was an oversight, and hadn't been flipped to indicate the store's true status.

"We're open as long as we need to be," the shopkeeper said, coming toward her. "How may I be of assistance?" But then his nostrils flared as if he got a good whiff of her, and whatever friendliness he had approached her with vanished with a nearly audible 'poof'.

The gray haired man watched the shopkeeper, then when he turned to look at her he smiled, took her hand with such gentleness that Lori couldn't help but think of charm and courtly manners centuries out of date.

"Please, indulge an old man for an instant and tell me what you think of the display?"

Lori blinked, tried to keep her mind on task, which was difficult with the warmth of his hands. "I, um, only came in to ask a question. The rest of the town seems closed—"

"This will only take an instant."

Before she could finish her request, he turned her around to face the castle and dragon scene she had witnessed through the glass while standing out on the sidewalk.

"I don't know that much about precious stones," Lori hedged. She had never been greedy, never known desire for gold as she felt now. She wondered if it were a flaw within her, or if somehow the jewels themselves were possessed and had inexplicably become addictive.

"The wealthy come from all around the world to shop here. They stay for a while, skiing in the winter, enjoying the leaves in the fall, but what draws them are the jewels. He—" with a notch of his head toward the shopkeeper, "doesn't part with many, that's a fact, and sells them dear, but once you've worn dragon's gold, it spoils you for anything else."

The old man pointed to a diamond solitaire ring with a matching gold band, a wedding set. "It's said that a marriage sealed with dragon's gold will never dissolve, not through all eternity."

Lori dragged her eyes from the gems, looked over at the older man and noticed a visible trace of melancholy about his eyes, as if he had loved not well and still grieved over its loss. He looked like he needed a good cry, and perhaps a houseful of grandkids to remind him that life was worth living.

"I've never heard of dragon's gold. Is it a new way of refining the metal?"

"That's what it is, lass. Brew sells them, significant in and of itself. No other dragon has ever relinquished jewels, and believe me, I've studied them all. He uses what he earns to help those in need. It takes money to do that."

"I'm sure it does."

He laughed, as if she had supplied the punch-line to a joke he had been setting up, but before he could offer an explanation, the shopkeeper appeared at her side.

"My Lord," he said, speaking to the older man but his tone was somehow less respectful than the words should have demanded. He kept his gaze locked on her and there was no friendliness in his eyes.

"Byron," Arthur bowed his head in what honestly looked like subservience. "I am showing your lady—"

Byron snarled, a sound a pit bull probably taught him, coming from low in his throat she felt as well as heard. Without knowing anything else about him, she knew then that he was capable of great violence.

"I'm not anyone's Lady," Lori insisted, feeling threatened, not by the Lord, whatever that term meant in this day and age, but by Byron the growling shopkeeper. She gently extracted her fingers from the stranger's grasp. For he was old, his fingers callused, but his grip had been warm. "I just need some directions. I'm relatively certain I'm hopelessly lost. I've spoken to the car, but if it knows, it's keeping information from me."

"Cars have a habit of doing that," the younger man said, and if he were mocking her, she could not tell by word inflection alone. "I am Byron, but I suspect you already know that."

"Why would you think that?"

He kept his face emotionless. "Call it more than a hunch."

Finding him rude in the extreme, Lori turned back to the older man. "I'm very sorry to bother you. The car came with a GPS. I mean it's a rental, so of course it did, but I've forgotten the exact address. I know I'm in the right area, but I've got to narrow it down a bit."

"I've lived here quite a long time, so if your friend can be found, I'll find him for you."

"Oh, it's my Aunt. Jan Pikorski."

The older man laughed, and Byron snorted, an action clearly fueled by distrust. She had no idea why he had taken such a complete and utter dislike to her.

"Ahh, You're interested in getting invited into the Dragon's Roost Bed and Breakfast?"

"If that's where she lives."

"It is."

"My name is Arthur," the gray haired man said, "and I am a great fan of your aunt's. When you see her, please state that I asked after her health."

"I'm sure you could do so yourself," she said.

Arthur shook his head and looked regretful. "Before I go," the older man said, "I'd like to test out a theory, if you'll indulge me for a moment."

"My Lord," Byron said, his snarl clearly a dismissal the old man did not heed.

"Please hold out your hand, no not your right, your left."

She wore no ring, for more often than not she found herself leaving jewelry in odd places during field work, and discovered it easier to keep her fingers unadorned. Arthur dipped his fingers into the treasure trove in the front window and brought them back holding the wedding set she'd drooled over. Before she could respond, he slipped the two-ring set over her third finger.

Byron stepped back, as if he had been shocked into a heart attack, and Lori knew exactly what he was experiencing. When Arthur slipped the gold on her, visions flashed across her mind, a thousand images passing so quickly that she didn't catch a fraction of them, but in each one she and Byron, this stranger she had only met ten minutes before, stood together in spring, summer, fall, winter. Sometimes she was pregnant, sometimes there was a dark eyed child with her. She had visions of running along the shore, hand in hand with him. Laying beside a roaring fire, their feet entwined, both wearing only smiles and a fine sweat. Walking under a sky with so many stars that God must have imported a couple hundred just for them. And always love, passion, and yes, eternity.

Byron rubbed his chin, the stubble there giving off a scratchy sound. His eyes had turned gold, blurred, as if he too had been witnessing dark haired children and beaches. "This doesn't prove anything."

Lori had no difficulty at all hearing the snarl in his voice.

"No, it proves nothing," Arthur agreed, but if there was a way she could read his mind Lori would state he was pleased for the exact same reason Byron was annoyed.

"Yes, I suppose that was what I was thinking," Byron muttered, clearly speaking to himself.

"What?" She found it difficult to breathe, almost impossible to speak. She held her hand out, away from her body, admiring the way her fingers looked far more complete with the promise the wedding rings imparted. The large diamond was not ostentatious, but obviously flawless, for it sparkled with flashes of red, blue, and orange. If he told her it was sentient, she would believe him. The gold warmed to her finger immediately and the jewel glistened as if proud, as if saying, "Finally! I've waited so long for this."

Lori leaned against the cabinet, still staring at the rings, a bit sad since the transient images had vanished. Now there was only a jewelry store, a jeweler, a man she could easily consider a friend and a heavy pressure in her heart that must have its origins in the unfamiliar weight on her finger.

"What do you think, Old One?" Arthur asked Byron, as if the younger man carried far more years than he did.

Byron pursed his lips, then shook his head. His eyes remained unfocused and laden with golden highlights.

"It means nothing."

CHAPTER 3

"Yet the gold …" Arthur said, dropping the sentence off as if there was something about the precious metal Lori did not need to know.

With another shake of his head, which dropped a particularly unruly shank of hair into his eyes, Byron reluctantly answered. "I will give you directions to the bed and breakfast, but whether or not you can get there, I leave to you."

"I don't understand," Lori said. She had tightened her left hand into a fist, cherishing the feeling of the rings which seemed to be far more than rare stones and priceless metal. They seemed to be pulling significantly at her heart strings, a feeling that before this moment she had never believed in. This wasn't love at first sight, this was something far more sinister and seductive. This was almost marriage at first touch, for these rings clearly felt like they were hers, and she wasn't going to relinquish them easily. They had molded themselves not to her skin, but to her soul. She wanted the completion of love and the vows of marriage to make these rings hers in truth.

"How much do they cost?" Eventually she would find a boyfriend, a lover, a man who would ask her to share his life, and she would have the rings, even knowing traditionally the man offered the jewelry.

"They're not for sale."

"This is a store, isn't it? Of course they're for sale."

"You couldn't afford them."

"Byron," Arthur said. It was the first time she heard an edge in his voice.

The shopkeeper shook all that shaggy hair like a dog coming out of water, or rather, she decided, as if it took an effort to pull himself out of whatever daydream he'd been transported to. "I created these last year, knowing I would not sell them. They are to be given to complete … well that doesn't matter. I'd like them back." Byron's words were clearly enunciated, as if he needed to be careful what he said, as if affected by the surprising intensity of the rings as she was.

"I'm sorry if I've caused a problem," Arthur said, clearly more enchanted than sorry. If he were a leprechaun, he'd be dancing. "I wanted to see what they looked like on your finger."

Lori pulled them off, suddenly fumbly, embarrassed by the thoughts she had entertained, the visions she had experienced. "They're lovely.

They will make someone a very beautiful bride." Someone, not her. Her nails were bitten, the pads of her fingers rough. These rings needed a superstar's hand, and based solely on the events of that morning, she obviously had horrendous taste in men. Andrew was a murderer, if not a cannibal, for he had been cooking the flesh. It was entirely probable that kill had not been his first. She had stewed during the long plane ride trying to analyze his reactions. She was positive Andrew's cocky assurance, his arrogance was not the way a man hovering over his first murder would react.

Lori looked down at her hands, realized although she had taken them off, she had not completely surrendered the rings. She still held them, no, she caressed them or perhaps possessed them. With whimsy, she thought of Gollum, wondered if she should start calling them My Precious. The band which went with the solitaire was etched with a cleverly wrought spindle design, elf writing she thought, a nearly invisible decoration. It took no effort at all to remember Arthur's comment that marriages sealed with dragon gold lasted throughout eternity.

Lori coiled her fingers around the gold and diamond rings, infusing them with her body warmth, and with a silent, unspoken prayer she was not even aware of until that moment: "Please, let them be mine."

"I should give these back to you. They really are lovely. You create miracles here. And I apologize if I've caused any disagreement between you two." She was rambling andknew it. When she held out her hand, Byron closed his warm, inviting fingers over hers. She expected him to mock or scorn, for something about her clearly set him on edge, but when he spoke this time, there was tenderness, or perhaps simply understanding. "Don't be ashamed. The gold has that effect on people. And don't be afraid of what you felt."

Lori swallowed. Her mouth had gone dry and her stomach tightened. She tried to recall the images for she never had been clairvoyant before. "I'm not sure what I felt. And I am not afraid."

Lori realized there wasn't much light in the jewelry store, only what beat in through the display window. There was nothing happening here that exhaustion and hunger couldn't explain.

Arthur rubbed his beard, spoke to Lori, although he clearly watched Byron as you might watch a sleeping Doberman. "In all the worlds, do you know what the one thing to be afraid of is?"

Byron's hands were still wrapped around hers, and he was so very secure. She couldn't think, not when he'd moved closer, not when his lips were inches from hers and between them they held a set of wedding rings. "Death?" she asked.

"No," Arthur continued. "There is never a need to be afraid of death, and many times," sharpening his glance at Byron, "it's welcomed. You reap what you sow. Humans are promised heaven; certainly that should be a welcome reward. No, the only thing to be afraid of is missed opportunity."

"I don't understand."

"Sometimes you can't go back and make something right. Sticking with clichés, opportunity doesn't always ring twice. If you had a chance, and for whatever reason you pass on it, you could easily regret it the rest of your life."

She smiled, recognized as she did so that her bottom lip quivered. "That sounds like such a tragedy."

His eyes turned distant, and the gold around his pupils muted back to copper. "Sometimes if you let the right woman out of your arms, she is gone and there's no getting her back."

"I'm sorry if I've brought up unpleasant memories," Lori said to Arthur, trying to pull her hands away from Byron.

He was firm, but gentle, then almost with an audible snap, he released her and accepted the rings she all but dumped into his palm. Lori wandered the store, finding it impossible to settle and regain the comfort she had while she branded by his token.

"Have you missed many opportunities?" Her back was to both men, and she studied the window display, getting a different perspective, viewing it from inside the store. The crystal dragon really was magnificent.

She expected Arthur to answer, but it was Byron's voice she heard. "One or two, but now, looking back, I see things quite a bit differently. Things I thought were missed opportunities might have been preparing me for something unexpected."

Although she heard no gentleness in his statement, only regret, his words wrapped around her, imparted warmth, like his hands had, and her body flushed. Lori felt hot and cold, moist and dry simultaneously.

She reached out, caressed the filigree of a necklace so intricately wrought it should have graced the neck of some Etruscan princess. "You must be very proud of your work. These are all exquisite."

She refused to turn around, but felt his gaze as if it were tangible. She was certain his sweet breath caressed her neck. "I like to surround myself with beautiful things." He laughed, and the intensity of the mood was diffused. "It is something of an occupational hazard."

They waited without speaking while the old man left, moving surprisingly quickly for one who appeared so old.

"The directions?"

"Directions?" Byron asked, as if he'd lost track of the conversation.

"To Jan Pikorski's house. My Aunt. I'd like to see her."

"Is she expecting you? No, don't answer that. Who knows who or what Jan expects from moment to moment?"

"What does that mean?"

"You don't know?" He laughed, again she thought it more of a snort. "You play the innocent so well. But maybe they didn't tell you that my nose is sensitive. You'll not be catching me off guard."

"I have no idea what you're talking about."

He moved back behind the counter, started locking up. "You reek of evil."

"Oh, oh." The first came as a surprise, but by the second, she understood and it was an acknowledgement.

"Yes, oh!" he laughed again, this time showing real humor and teeth that looked far too long for his face. "Whatever perversions you ply will not get you inside the inn. It's guarded by more than a dragon. In case your masters didn't tell you, its magic is, I'm sure, rather more than you can handle."

"You're suffering from delusions, and I think you're a lunatic. Now I'm leaving, and I hope I can find someone else to give me instructions, someone who clearly doesn't have a straight-jacket reserved with his name on it."

"No. I will take you. No one else could give you precise directions."

"I don't think I trust you."

"That's certainly wise on your part, but perhaps not so wise telling me. If you thought to beguile me with your charms, stating you don't trust me is a real mood killer. Not that there was any chance I would have trusted you anyway, not with the stench of evil about you."

"I can explain that."

"I'm sure you think you can. I'm not easily fooled."

"What are you doing?" she asked as he grasped her wrist.

"Shutting the store, taking you to your aunt. I've an interest in seeing if she'll welcome you."

"I'm not going anywhere with you. What do you think I am, naive?"

"Actually yes, although that is not the first adjective that comes to mind." He pulled her though the back of the store, out toward the back alley and her car.

"Aren't you going to lock the door?"

"It's locked. There are not many who can get through the door with the ease you did."

"That makes no sense."

"I agree. I thought the door would at least give you pause."

"Doors that let only certain people in?"

"Yes, and if you don't believe me, you're in for a rude awakening at the inn. Now unlock the car. I'm coming with you."

"I don't think so."

"It's dark and the mountain roads are poorly marked. You won't find your aunt—if she is your aunt—without me."

"You're probably an axe murderer," Lori growled under her breath, loud enough that she had no doubt he heard her.

He stared at her over the hood of the car, and for a moment, she was certain his eyes glowed red. "Axes were never my favorite weapon, but the imagery is close enough, and that's about all I'm willing to admit to you."

Lori jiggled the keys in her hands, trying to come to a decision, knowing although she might have been in top form for the defense of her dissertation defense earlier that morning, too much time had passed, and too many weird things had happened. She didn't trust him, but she didn't not trust him, a distinction which would have sent her screaming if her mind had been clear. "I'm tired, I'm hungry, and I've had enough of your insane insulations. I only want to see my Aunt."

"Why didn't you call her?"

"I left my phone at a murder scene."

"Ahh," he said, and she almost expected those eyes to glow again, although they remained dark, unfathomable.

"You don't seem surprised."

"With the way you smell, I was expecting something along those lines, although I will admit, I never expected you to confess."

"I am not the murderer!"

"So you say."

"There's no blood on my hands." She almost held them out, showed him how wrong he was, but as soon as she started to move her arms, she remembered the feel of the rings and the sharpness of the image returned. The vision flashed in her subconscious then that she had a lover and a child, and it was him, and for some reason, although it hadn't happened yet, a significant part of her believed it would, or at least should.

Byron studied her over the hood of the Mustang, and she wondered if this interaction with a maniac was what the idiotic car wanted when it made her park here. If so, she'd have to have a long talk with it once they got rid of the jeweler.

"I can get you to the B&B, but I cannot get you inside."

"What does that mean?" Lori wanted to scream, then find a Holiday Inn or any of a dozen hotel chains, and spend the night in safety. She could just as easily look up her aunt tomorrow.

"Unlock the car, Lori. I will take you to your aunt."

"How do you know my name?" She couldn't be certain, but she thought she hadn't introduced herself.

"Jan has only two nieces, and I've met Brenda."

"You know how she smells?" Lori asked, hoping to be snide.

"Yes," he answered, and if she had to guess, she'd say that was exactly what he meant.

She fiddled with the car keys again, found herself unlocking the doors. "You won't kill me?"

He slipped into the passenger seat, his long legs folding up. "That remains to be seen."

She refused to look at him as she drove, instead she followed his directions and realized if he'd tried to explain them, even written them down, she wouldn't have found the turnings, and remained lost. What she found worse was they passed no other open store where she could have asked for instructions and no hotel, although she suspected the latter was because he was working some magic on her mind so she didn't see them.

"Turn here."

"Where?" All she could see was uninterrupted trees.

"The opening there. We're here," Byron said. She made the turn, and wondered if her aunt's bed and breakfast ever had any customers, for who in their right mind could find the place? She settled her foot on the brake and shifted the car into park. He exited the car as if he couldn't wait to be away from her, and she wondered if she did smell badly, for he rode with his window down, and she had to keep the heat blasting, since the temperature had dropped significantly. These mountain evenings were cold.

Lori put her hand over her mouth and blew out, no bad breath, and raised her left arm and sniffed her pit, finding only the healthy trace of flower scented deodorant.

"I do not smell," she muttered to herself.

That check of personal hygiene done, Lori stared out the windshield. Her initial thought after she turned off the engine and sat paralyzed, her hands still white-knuckled on the steering wheel was: "I'm safe. Andrew can't find me here." It was the first time she'd thought of him since Byron got into her car. Those statements were followed quickly by an analysis of swathe view through the bug spattered windshield. "Aunt Jan lives in Buckingham Palace!"

The house was not at all what Lori expected. Her Aunt Jan was considered eccentric, but in the past that always meant mismatched earrings, crazy-toe orange and green socks and uncombed gray hair, so Lori expected the place where she lived to be an extension of that. The vision in her mind was so sharp, Lori almost demanded to see gutters sagging under the weight of maple seedlings already over a foot tall, and peeling paint laid down by some homesteader who lived in Paul Revere's time, but the house she viewed through eyelids sagging with breathtaking exhaustion.

Of course it was possible that this wasn't her aunt's home. Perhaps the jeweler had led her somewhere where he could murder her uninterrupted.

Well, it was all a bit unexpected now, wasn't it?

She finger-combed her shoulder length streaked blond hair with hands that shook. Slowly, methodically she filled her lungs, holding the air trapped for a three-count before releasing it. Relaxation wasn't that easily accomplished, but at this point anything would help, even running, screaming, panicked into these verdant green woods and never being seen again.

Her breathing regulated. Her fingers grew limber, although in preparation for what, Lori had no idea. She opened the car door slowly, slipping out from behind the steering wheel.

Byron had disappeared, but that didn't matter, for the house commanded her attention. The B&B sprawled for as far as she could see, and had at least three floors, judging by windows layered one on top of another. There was no telling how deeply it dug, rooted in the sturdy Adirondack soil. Lori had no doubt there was a basement. Years ago, her sister Brenda had mentioned monsters chained in a dungeon. Odd, Lori hadn't thought of that in eons. At the time, she'd written it off as Brenda's overactive imagination, fed by separation anxiety. Now, even though she was an intelligent woman with the best education, she was about to whisper "I do believe in spooks. I do believe in spooks."

She almost asked the car if it did too.

One thing was certain, she would stay away from any stairs which led down. The tiny hairs on the back of her neck itched as if they knew something she didn't, and for the tiniest of seconds Lori felt the trees were talking about her in some interwoven mishmash of sign language and rustling leaves. While she suspected they were not saying, "Phew, she's finally here, we can stop worrying," she hoped they were not muttering, "Man battle stations! Prepare to repel all boarders!"

Constructed of gray fieldstone and mortar, the house gave the impression it had been layered like a jigsaw puzzle, each piece fitting precisely where it belonged. One or two of the windows were lit, and the building had almost the look of a cozy Thomas Kincaid painting.

The double doors, a commanding presence at the top of ten stone stairs were painted Federal Blue and looked like uniformed, armed soldiers standing at attention. She wondered if she should salute or retreat.

To the left of the double doors, the building was graced by a mammoth wreath of pinecones and dried wildflowers. Hanging from it, a small plaque written in archaic calligraphy, "WELCOME ALL WHO COME AS

FRIENDS."

She gave this greeting a good pondering. Lori wondered if many who approached this portal did so armed to the teeth and intent upon assault. For a welcome sign, she decided, it was not all that welcoming.

The air was thin, and pragmatically Lori decided that was why she was having trouble catching her breath. She was high in these endless mountains, and oxygen was at a premium. But the air was also filled with the tantalizing scent of burning apple-wood, and raising her firm, stubborn jaw she noticed wisps of smoke coming from at least one of the visible chimneys. That was a good sign. Someone was home. There would be food.

She left her two suitcases in the trunk, not having the strength to lift them, and was surprised to find she held her purse, for she had no memory of having picked it up from the center console. Lori pulled the strap up onto her shoulder, and made her first tentative step toward the monstrosity of a house.

The plan of arriving without warning on her aunt's doorstep had seemed like a good idea three time zones away, and her luck at finding an available airline seat on a direct flight no less, and at a price she could afford, seemed to validate her impulse. Andrew, drat his scurvy hide, had her mother's address and phone number, which meant going home had not been an option. He didn't know she had an Aunt Jan, let alone how to find her, and that had been her primary consideration.

"Hi, Aunt Jan, remember me?" Lori was surprised she had spoken aloud, for it was only thought, but her breath had taken form in the rapidly dropping temperatures, and the echo of her words swirled around her. Compared to the majesty of the enveloping mountains, the speech sounded hollow. The birds stopped their endless chattering with her speech, as if they had hoped to catch bits of wisdom lacking in their shallow lives, but started up almost immediately, louder, more invasive than before. The trees had not paused their sign-language. Without being facetious, she decided they had not only decided to ignore her, but they'd taken a vote and were making every effort to drown her out.

"The very least Byron could do would be to walk me to the house." Her statement was more of a growl than a true complaint. She needed something, someone to blame for the uncomfortable situation she found herself in. Besides, he might be an axe murderer. No, not an axe, he'd denied that, certainly, but he hadn't quite denied the murderer part, now had he? Sticking with clichés, as he had, she wondered if the saying she should be considering now was 'out of the frying pan into the fire'.

Lori moved a bit, more stretching of cramped muscles than any forward progress. There had to be a hotel with a vacancy somewhere close.

The need for a strategic retreat gained prominence. The house, the mountains, the guarding trees and the long vanished sunlight created a daunting overall image. She reconsidered the welcome-wreath on the door, which could just as easily stand sentinel as a warning. "I've come as a friend." Perhaps she hoped to convince the rental car that it, too, could rest for the night, but the car didn't seem to mind Byron, did it?

She shifted forward, climbing the stone stairs almost at a jog and rapped firmly on the thick, solid oak door. If a doorbell lay hidden, she didn't see it. "I am a friend," she repeated. It didn't bode well to think of herself as a refugee.

The house was absolutely silent as if her knock had been consumed by the immensity of the fieldstone, and Lori swallowed, and wondered if the trees had really been that close to the car ten minutes before. She hadn't thought so. They seemed to be encroaching.

Without warning, the door slipped open on well oiled hinges, and Byron faced her, his dark, slightly stubbled face illuminated by a snarl.

"You've made it this far. Did you think to be invited in?"

CHAPTER 4

"What do you mean, Lori's here?"

Byron snarled. He really wanted to dig his talons into flesh, feel the satisfaction of the kill, give into primal urges he hadn't allowed himself in centuries. Oh, over the years he'd killed, but he hadn't relished it, hadn't enjoyed the elicit thrill of hot blood on his scales. That's what he wanted.

Because he felt his blood heating, because the woman he faced was not his enemy, he paced, his long legs making short work of traversing the kitchen. "She says her name is Lori, that she is your niece, and that she'd like to visit you. She's outside, wondering, I'd presume, if she has enough magic to get in."

"You didn't invite her in?"

"Why would I do that?"

"Byron, she is family. That gives her special treatment."

"No."

"Why? What's your problem?"

His problem? The fact that some ancient warlord, he wouldn't give Arthur the dignity of calling him a king, put his rings on her finger and they fit? Because when he saw how those rings completed her he knew, for the first time in more centuries than there'd been Homo sapiens that he wanted her for his wife, to mother his children, to understand for the first time the meaning of love. Because all that was impossible.

"Because she is a wizard."

"Wizard? Hardly!"

"Or a witch. They smell the same to me."

"I've watched her grow. She's my sister's daughter. I know Lori. There's no wizardry about her. Now go to the door. Oh, and Byron, when you get back, I want tea."

"No."

"Yes." If his word was stamped out in anger, hers was soft, but held no less command.

"No."

Jan wasn't much older than fifty, less than a child compared to his ancient age, although in all items that mattered while he was here, in her kitchen, she outranked him. He could leave, but it remained to be seen if he would. But he knew Jan well enough to know she'd make sure that he didn't defy her.

"When Lori is in this Inn, you'll serve her tea."

No dragon liked bowing so completely to another's will. "I'll not be murdered so casually."

"It is not your death I want Old One, it is your hospitality. Your tea is the greatest honor you could bestow."

She had never ordered before, never asked. It was his duty. His gift.

Byron bared his teeth as he thought again of the rings and of a dozen other worlds where he'd be welcomed. And he thought of the work Jan did here, and how she respected him. He hated that she was putting him in this position, when she had never endangered him before. "Then let me keep my honor and my life from the wizard."

Jan turned her back to him, returning to the large pots she had simmering on the stove. She picked up a spoon, stirred, and Byron found the action soothing.

"You're keeping her waiting. She's up the stairs."

"But she's yet to knock. She's afraid."

"Maybe she's exhausted."

"She'll bring trouble."

Jan grinned, but kept her face turned so he could not see that she knew that she had won. Byron understood her well enough to allow her her petty victories. "Neither one of us are afraid of a little trouble. We've both had our share, haven't we, Brew?"

"Trouble avoided is—"

"Trouble you'll have to face another day," she finished for him, although that was not what he would have said. "And I promise you whatever trouble Lori brings, together we can handle it."

"I'll open the door," Byron said, the words punctuated with more of a growl than she was used to hearing from him, "but if she destroys me, know you'll have to till your own garden."

"I am not worried Brew, about my niece or the garden."

Byron heard Jan's last statement for his hearing was excellent, but he was already more than half way down the long corridor, about to open the front door.

He heard the knocking and opened it immediately. He had fire at his command. Many other weapons as well, but fire was his favorite. She would burn nicely, but he closed his eyes against a phantom pain, and remembered the visions brought about by dragon's gold.

He stared at her a long moment, then looked past her, as if expecting an armed force of goblins, before returning her gaze when he realized she was alone. "You made it this far. Did you think to be invited in?" he asked.

Lori folded her arms across her chest and looked about as defiant as a June bug. "Is Janet Pikorski here?"

"Yes. She's waiting for you, if you can cross the wards."

"Wards? What the hell does that mean?" Lori asked.

Byron looked down at her. He towered above her by a foot, the height difference magnified by the fact that he stood inside, a step above her. For a heartbeat their gazes met, held, but before he had a chance to deal with the visions flooding his consciousness, he spoke.

"The door's open. Come in if you can."

"Is there a joke here I'm not catching?"

"Oh, you'll catch it alright."

"Jan Pikorski lives here?" Lori seemed to be repeating herself, but Byron could see by the way she lowered her eyebrows that not much of this conversation was making sense to her.

"Here, there, other places. Location nouns don't mean a lot once you step over the threshold, but you'd know that, wouldn't you?"

"I clearly have no idea what you're talking about."

He held his hands out, not quite in welcome, yet not holding a pitchfork and a burning torch either. "Ok, let's just call this testing a theory. Enter if you dare."

"Let me see my aunt first."

He spread his hands wide, as if the proper host. "Try to get in first."

"I'm tired and hungry and more than a little annoyed, so with that, I'll state I'm through with playing games."

Byron didn't like his quixotic emotions. He was not one to be swayed by a pretty face, but since she wore his rings, he couldn't wrap his mind around the evil of her scent with his desire to get her alone for a seduction a bit less violent. He hated being played for a fool.

He bowed slightly from his narrow waist, keeping his head raised so he watched her at all times, and his grin—showing sharp white teeth—added a touch of mockery to his words. "Enter then. Jan Pikorski is just down the hall. She has dinner ready."

"I am—" she started, but before she finished the thought she pushed past him and entered.

"You got in."

"Sorry to disappoint, but you did say my aunt is here."

He gave her points for the sneer, but her entrance had him flabbergasted. "You didn't have any trouble."

"I'll trip. Would that make you feel better?"

Her smile was brisk, completely without warmth. He was about to toast her to an indistinguishable crisp to see if that would help and decided he would enjoy every second of the act. Dragons, on the whole, were not known for tolerance.

But if he did that, he would annoy Jan, and from experience Byron understood that must be avoided at all costs.

Byron breathed deeply through his nose, trying to control his rising temper. "Where are you going?" Without thought, he reached out, grabbed her slender wrist. Shock waves traveled through him, like when she wore his rings. The warmth he felt was completely unexpected and equally unwelcome. What was it about her that had him wanting?

Indignant, she pulled away, her features confused as if she were innocent and still half-terrified that she had made a colossal mistake in coming here, with no proof she was in the right place. This witch was good. He had to give her credit for that.

She locked her gaze with his and with a snarl, Lori rubbed her wrist. "Down the hall. I'm tired. I'm hungry. I'm frustrated and I hate to keep repeating myself, but you did say my aunt was here."

Intrigued with her pitiful show of defiance, Byron rested his free hand against the door, double checking, as if sound weren't enough, to ensure the lock had firmly latched. "In case you're wondering, you're in my territory now, and you're playing by my rules. Whatever game you think you're running, the odds, as always, are in my favor."

"How nice for you," she said, dismissing him by turning and sprinting down the long corridor.

Oh she was dragon fodder. And this time when he exhaled, there was clearly steam visible.

***

He caught up with her in about five steps and stepped in front of her, blocking her from moving further down the corridor. His legs were massively long. Well muscled. Mercy, what that man did to a pair of jeans. For a second, when he touched her, she felt the need to wrap her legs around his waist, her arms around his neck, to mate her mouth with his. This was insanity. Lori understood she must be far more spooked by Andrew than she thought.

Byron exhaled and modulated his voice to appear friendlier. Lori would have felt considerably more at ease if she realized such a change in his attitude hadn't been accomplished with quite so much deliberation.

"What's your hurry?"

She studied the hall, found it dark, punctuated with sporadic pools of quivering white light offsetting its length, leaving Byron's face deeply shadowed. She could see his features only dimly now, as if he were fading into the woodwork, vanishing, Cheshire Cat style, an impression heightened by his too-white teeth and the fact that she thought his eyes glowed red for just a second. His hand where he touched her had been very warm, almost unnaturally so. Lori wanted to believe her own fingers were so chilled from the drive that his felt feverous.

He bowed again, and as before, kept her fully in sight. He would not have looked out of place wearing a floor length black cape and shiny knee-high black books with a heavy claymore belted at his waist. She would have been more comfortable in the nearest Motel 6. She could always greet her aunt tomorrow.

Lori gave herself a good solid shake, and cursed Brenda for her tales of monsters and her own flawless memory which was great for pursuing advanced degrees, but at the moment quite the hindrance.

Without waiting for her answer, he moved two, three steps down the long corridor, then stopped, slid back when he realized she hadn't followed at his heels like a well trained puppy.

"I am," he started, but Lori could see there was obviously something bothering him, for he did not finish.

"You are—" she asked, breaking the question off, fishing for an answer to any of a dozen questions she had boiling in her mind. It might be best if she knew his role in this place before she continued with her well defined fantasy involving silk sheets, lazy mornings, and a porch swing— the latter in another fifty years or so. She thought it would take them that long to deal with the first two items on the list.

"I am," he repeated, and for a second she thought he would end there again. "I am," as if he needed no other introduction. But Byron showed those long teeth, clearly indicative that he was not pleased, "ordered to make tea."

The sound of his voice was so deep and seductive that it took her a moment to analyze what he had said.

"Tea?" Not much of this conversation made sense, but for all that, it was clearly saner than the fantasies her libido constructed.

"Tea," he answered firmly, pulling her down the shadowed hall.

"Why tea?" With nothing to go on beyond first impressions and a bubbling imagination, Lori suspected that having him prepare tea would not be her choice for putting him to his best advantage.

"Making tea is," he paused, this time searching for a word or phrase, as if English were not his native language, "perhaps why I was born."

He snarled before she could respond, and the hall rippled with his anger. "Do you think to find me vulnerable?"

"In case you're wondering, I have no idea what you're talking about." As a matter of fact, if Lori were being honest with herself, nothing had made sense since that morning, facing a naked man cooking over a tripod. For all that, things hadn't really gotten weird until she had tried on his rings. And she was annoyed with herself because just being with him had her pulse tripping. His warm hand sent feelers of unspoken invitation throughout her body.

"Vulnerable? Because of the rings?"

"Rings?" He snarled, looked taken-aback. "Is that what this is about?"

She was about ready to scream. "I have no idea what this is about."

Byron leaned closer, whispered seductively, "Do you like tea?"

She swallowed, felt like she had fallen down some silly rabbit hole and wondered what would be the most appropriate response. "I don't know. I haven't had your tea."

His nod indicated her answer pleased him. Air puffed from his nostrils, with a clean, crisp scent redolent of strawberries, apricots and seduction. "Exactly right." He encroached closer, rested an arm on her shoulder, proprietary and possessive. "And, if I may be as bold to ask, how do you feel about dragons?"

She shivered once, had no idea if it were anticipation. She liked the way his hand, on her shoulder now, moved with her. It was most defiantly a caress. "Dragons? Like the ones at your store?"

"No. Those are statues, representatives of dragons, merely works of imagination. This is the Dragon's Roost Bed and Breakfast, which means that at least occasionally a dragon comes and roosts."

Lori was a modern woman, had been raised to fight her own battles. Over the years she had allowed her sister Brenda to teach her some basic self-defense moves. She knew the power of a 911 call, and what her legal rights were against two-legged swaggering predators, still she fed into the fantasy he was building. She did everything but bat her eyes, wave a non-existent fan. "If a dragon appears, will you protect me?"

Byron's scent wrapped around her, fuelling her fantasies of tangled legs and mutual surrender. Just looking at his square, scruffy jaw and those full lips set her mouth watering. Considering the events of the past twenty-four hours, she felt like she needed protection.

His long, slender fingers reached out as if to cup her chin, but dropped back to her shoulder before they made contact. "You think you need protection from dragons?"

She met his gaze directly. "Don't I?"

He stroked her chin with long, tapered fingers. "Time will tell."

He moved casually, his legs long, his stride confident proving he was no stranger to this house. If her aunt did live here, Lori wondered if she'd taken a young lover, and contemplated why she felt a painful stab in the center of her heart. Following him, Lori forced her gaze from the snug fit of his jeans and took the opportunity to study the inside of the magnificent house.

There wasn't much to see. The floor was slate, comprised of flat, oddly cut shapes of red, purple, blue or green stone set together in an interlocking mosaic. If there existed a pattern, she could not make it out in the dim corridor illumination. The coldness of the stone was eased only occasionally with a woven rag rug. Their footsteps made no impression on the overall silence, and Lori felt things might have seemed a tad less unusual if they had.

Her eyes were wide and her breath came quickly, far more rapidly than it had while she rapped with the knocker. There was just a tinge, a subliminal background annoyance, that there were things hiding in the dark corners that she should be frightened of. Perhaps she'd made one hell of a mistake in appearing unannounced.

She was encouraged to hurry down the long corridor because he seemed unwilling to compensate for her shorter legs and slow down. They passed more than a dozen rooms; some with their darkly stained doors shut with a do-not-trespass air, some with their doors open, revealing cold, lifeless interiors of which she could infer nothing, for all were shrouded in darkness.

He turned, stopping so abruptly that she almost plowed into him, which considering the width of his chest and the way his jeans fit his slender hips, would have been the highlight of her day.

Within a step or two they reached their destination, a huge kitchen, the one attached to Lori's university dorm couldn't have been much bigger. Slate still comprised the floor, but the rock pieces were smaller, tamer, as if they were more civilized than the stone in the hall, and the colors were brighter, but that might have only been an expected byproduct of the fact that the kitchen was well-lit, almost glowing.

To her left a solid oak table with six mammoth chairs took up residence as if they had grown there and had been carved in situ, with roots still buried deep into the Adirondack soil. It was there the strange man with the stranger eyes dragged her.

She didn't make it to the table, for her Aunt Jan came bounding in from her right, and wrapped her in an immense hug. "Saints alive, child. It's so good to see you." There was a trace of Irish whimsy in her speech, a rolling, lyrical song which Lori's grandmother, Aunt Jan's mum, had never lost, even in the seventy years she had been in this country. Lori's own mother spoke with a flat New York accent, topped by broad Yonkers vowels and clipped consonants.

"Rest your weary bones here," Jan said, "and I'll bring you some nice stew." But before Jan let her go, she kissed Lori once lightly on the top of her head. Of course, how could she have forgotten Aunt Jan's kisses on the top of the head? For safety from the evil spirits, her aunt had whispered once when she was wide-eyed enough to believe in ogres and faeries and things that go bump in the night. In some subliminal place, Lori found herself still enchanted with the possibilities of protection achieved at so little cost.

"I can see you've gone too long without food," Jan continued, making Lori wonder if her hearing was acute, for her stomach loudly protested the enforced starvation.

With such an invitation, how could she refuse? Lori settled herself into the roomy oak chair, and studied her aunt, who looked no different than she had nearly a dozen years before. Slightly overweight, giving her a soft, roundish look, she wore a floor-length yellow print house dress, one which wouldn't have been out of place on a Renaissance housewife. Her feet were clad in shin-high work boots Lori was certain, she had seen advertised in an LL Bean catalogue. Her hair was a blend of gray and sliver and wove down her back in a neat plaited braid.

In her hands Jan held a child's tea service, small bone china plates, slightly larger than half-dollars and minuscule cups, with tiny handles some Barbie doll could hold. Jan went back to plucking them from a large potted tree growing just inside the door to the corridor they had entered through. Oddly enough, the plates and cups were soiled. Someone had recently eaten off them.

"Sorry," Jan continued, dropping what was probably a service for eight gently into dishwater. "Unexpected company. They won't bother you tonight, I promise."

"Company?" It made no sense. "And they eat in the tree?" Off plates which would not comfortably hold an Oreo.

Jan shrugged, went back to the tree, discovering a additional cup she had missed. "Oddly enough, wood sprites only eat in trees. I've been trying for decades to get them to sit at the table like other civilized beings."

"That's your problem," Byron said, his voice sounding distant. "Wood sprites prefer not to think of themselves as civilized."

"My job would be considerably easier if more creatures could consider themselves civilized." She gave the word 'creatures' an odd inflection, and he laughed at her words. Clearly her remark had been aimed at him.

"And were you going to make tea?"

"I live to serve," he answered, and Lori, looking at her aunt, wondered if there was sarcasm there, but Jan's expression did not alter.

"Aunt Jan, I hope I'm not interrupting anything important."

"Saints above, no. You're always welcome." Jan turned from Lori, studied the floor. In a spotless kitchen, there was the tiniest hint of crumbs on the floor, obviously dropped heedlessly from the plates. "If I don't get this now, then grumble…grumble will get it. Well, I suppose just this once won't ruin their diet."

Even straining her ears, Lori could not make out the name of the recipients of her aunt's largess. She scanned the floor, looking for puppies, kittens or even, heaven help her, some creature of the rodent persuasion, but nothing lurked, shifted or scurried.

When Jan moved back to the stove, Lori returned her gaze to the furniture. The table was set for two: two spotlessly clean straw and twig woven placemats, two mugs, two bowls, two forks, two spoons. The silverware was heavy, sturdy, looked at least a century out of date, and Lori half suspected if she ever saw the knife which completed the set, she would have a hand dagger which would serve her well should she ever need access to a weapon to fight whatever nepharious beings she was protected from by the kiss. The bowls were large solid stoneware affairs, probably thrown on some local potter's wheel, for each was charmingly unique, and slightly off-round. Their glaze was crisp, bright copper, complete with moldy green colored patina, but when Lori snapped a fingernail against hers, she found it was not metalwork but stoneware.

"Where's—" she tried to ask, turning around in the smooth chair to study the kitchen, her feet restless as she looked for the dark-eyed jeweler. Byron couldn't have disappeared that quickly. It was not possible. The hug and the kiss and the foolish discussion of wood sprites hadn't lasted that long.

"Byron will be back later, I promise." Her aunt spoke with a twinkle in her Irish-hills green eyes. "There's something he had to do first."

"Make tea," Lori said, hoping she wasn't sounding idiotic.

"And make tea he has." Jan took a potholder and lifted an immense teapot. It had obviously been steeping, but not too long, for it was fragrantly hot, and steam rose seductively from the surface, as Jan poured first Lori's cup, then her own. Lori breathed deeply, finding the scent honestly welcoming, not like a brass band and a huge banner, instead like melting into a comfortable armchair after a long, exhausting drive.

She wrapped her fingers around the mug, adsorbing the warmth as she inhaled the fragrance. It reminded her quite clearly of the powerful heat from Byron's hand, and she was all the more delighted because of that. The teapot itself had an unusual shape, and it took her a moment and several times blinking her eyes to be sure they could be trusted, before she was able to analyze what the shape was. It was a dragon, wings folded back, tail arched to form the handle, and an open mouth grin complete with sharp white teeth, which formed the spout.

"A d-d-d-dragon?" Lori stuttered.

CHAPTER 5

Lori had never stuttered in her life, but the situation somehow called for it. Her eyes must be tearing, from exhaustion or something, for she was half-convinced the one eye from the teapot which faced her, once Aunt Jan put it down, had smugly winked at her.

"It's a delightful pot, isn't it?" Aunt Jan said. "An old friend allows me to use it on occasion." She rubbed her hands lovingly down the wings, as if following thick fur of a favored dog. Lori had never once considered dragons might have fur or that they would like petting. She never thought she belonged to a family concealing a relative who would caress a teapot. On the whole, all the people she was related to were far more pragmatic.

"The tea is marvelous, isn't it?" Jan continued. "Nothing in it will hurt you, nothing will keep you awake, either. I can see by the look of you you've burned your last inch of candle."

Lori preferred coffee. After five years working on her graduate and post-grad degrees, she lived on that brew almost exclusively, but the time didn't seem quite right to mention that. Maybe in the morning. Before she had a chance to take a sip of the tea, her bowl was whisked away, and returned almost immediately, filled with a thick, luxuriously scented stew. Beef was in abundance, huge chunks of tender meat which came apart at the mere approach of her fork. In addition the stew contained fat potatoes, small round onions, carrot slices, some kind of squash, perhaps acorn or butternut, and a thick gravy, heavy enough to hold a spoon in a standing position. Aunt Jan then gripped her own bowl, and came back with it near to overflowing as she had with Lori's.

A timer dinged at precisely that moment, a sharp high interruption, like an anachronism, and Aunt Jan opened an oven door, there were at least two ovens, and with a potholder, removed a cookie sheet filled with golden brown, yeasty smelling rolls each as big as her fist. She removed about half a dozen, there were probably twice that many still on the sheet, and brought them to the table in a towel covered basket.

Jan sat beside her, and pointed with her spoon. "The butter is fresh this morning." Lori looked, and sure enough there was a trencher with a slag of pale yellow butter Lori, obviously overwhelmed with everything else, hadn't noticed before. Beside the butter was a small pot with a wooden handle sticking out of it, and lifting it, Lori found honey. She watched the slow-moving, amber colored sweetener, and licked her lips. Without a pause, she envisioned fields exploding with yellow or orange wildflowers, assisted by fat, hardworking bees. Although a simple pleasure, the honey dripped of decadence.

"Tea's fine enough without it, I think, but try a sip. If you need a wee sweeter, there's nothing better than local honey."

Local honey. People who kept bees called it local honey. She'd seen roadside stands with mason jars bright with overflowing radiance. "Over one million employees," one sign had boasted. Bees worked hard. That's why it was a proverb.

She set the wooden honey scoop aside, and concentrated on her stew. She was far too hungry to ignore the bounty any longer. Lori found it rich, hot and filling, as individual flavors from the meat and vegetables exploded on her tongue. This stew had not arrived by the simple expediency of opening a can.

"You must have been preparing this all day."

"Cooking is one of my favorite tasks here. I always enjoy it when I can spend an entire day preparing vegetables and breads. Not that I'm complaining about the other tasks," she added quickly, as if someone listening might take offense.

Lori ate until her spoon scraped the bottom of the bowl. She slathered the dinner rolls with butter and feasted on them as well. College food was generic, what it had in quantity it generally lacked in flavor. Lori supposed that was why the stew and the rolls tested so delicious. It had been a long time since she had had a home-cooked meal. Occupying the seat to her right, leaving the chair at the head of the table vacant, Aunt Jan matched her bite for bite.

While Lori leaned back in the massive chair, breathing slowly now that the impulse of desperation-feeding had passed, Aunt Jan collected the plates. She dropped them by a sink, then stirred the stew with a long handled spoon, which might be useful if she ever was stranded on a river and needed an oar. The pot itself was large enough to be called a caldron, immense enough to boil a half-grown piglet in, and was, from the way the spoon moved, still full. For all they ate, they hadn't made much of a dent in the contents. Jan turned the flame off from the gas range, then rubbed her hands together in a job-well-done motion.

"So, this is what you were after," Aunt Jan said, but it clearly looked like she spoke to the dragon teapot, so Lori let the comment pass, pretending she hadn't noticed. "We'll have to have a talk about this, you and I," Jan finished, and drat if it didn't look like the dragon eye facing Lori blinked again.

"I am so sorry to barge in on you like this, all unexpected," Lori started, but her aunt held up a hand.

"It wasn't unexpected, was it? I had tea on." She made no mention of the stew. "It is my pleasure to welcome all who come here as friends."

Lori had the sense the plaque which guarded the door, (guarded the door, what an odd thought) was more than a token piece of whimsy set there for decorative purposes. It was not so much a welcome as an implied threat.

Before she could form her twisting thoughts into sentences about being expected, and who or what exactly constituted a friend, Lori stopped as Aunt Jan wiped her hands on her apron, and pasted a huge smile across her lips. "You look all out, so I'm sending you up to bed."

If Jan expected to be overruled, Lori had no idea, but now that her hunger had been assuaged she could only think of sleep, and wondered if she had enough strength to make it to a bedroom. "I should help with the dishes, with the clean-up," she protested stifling a yawn, but it was more of a token offer, and neither of them expected her to be taken up on it. Besides, there was no need. Except for the bowls, the mugs and the silverware they had just finished using, and apparently the miniscule set of eight collected from the tree, the kitchen gleamed. Not a speck of dust, not a crumb overlooked.

"While there is nothing I would like better than to sit by the fire and chatter the night away, catching up with your life and with that of your family, I think that will have to wait for another time. Come, child," Aunt Jan said, lightly taking her hand. "The bed is ready for you."

"Should I take my tea upstairs to finish it?" The brew, although delicious, had left her with odd and fleeting impressions, so she hadn't drank more than a token sip or two.

"Oh, heavens no. It's never a good idea to grant him access to your bedroom this early in the relationship."

Him?

"Gracious, if you like it," Aunt Jan continued, with a girlish laugh both forced and natural, "there will probably be more tea at breakfast, and we'll talk then, when all of us will have clearer heads."

Her head did need clearing, Lori thought, for Aunt Jan hadn't said when both of us have a clearer head, but all of us, as if there were far more than the two of them sharing tea.

A heavy lethargy stole through her, and Lori couldn't think to ask how the bedroom could be ready, how she could have been expected, when she hadn't known herself until that morning that she had to escape. In addition to the door from the main hall she'd entered, the kitchen had a back door, which led to what looked like a mud room overflowing with boots, hoes and all kinds of abandoned flower pots. From there, it undoubtedly opened to the outside. There was another door, Lori just knew led down steep wooden stairs to a root cellar, where quart jars stood in rows like foot soldiers, filled with testimonies of summer: pickles, beans, peaches and applesauce. In dark corners potatoes would reside in bins, pears wrapped in newsprint, and squash in sawdust, enough to feed a conquering army. Although Canada was probably less than twenty minutes away, there didn't seem to be much need for such incredible preparations. Canadians were really quite harmless on the whole, so Lori shook her head, ignoring the whimsy. After all, what she faced was a shut door. She really had no idea what lay beyond it.

And of course there was another door, the door which led downstairs where Brenda had stated monsters were kept chained.

Aunt Jan directed her toward the mudroom. This door appeared miniscule, except when Aunt Jan passed through it. Lori saw it was the exact size a door should be, and by comparison the others were huge.

As Jan passed the boots and the gardening implements, Lori gazed at them, thinking they looked unfamiliar. She was not a gardener, and locked in a university library for the better part of the past seven years had little exposure to rakes and hoes, but somehow these looked invasive, somehow malevolent, instruments of torture, kept there to repel invaders who avoided the welcome sign because by entering the house through the rear.

Jan patted Lori on her shoulder, and Lori shook the image of stacked weapons from her mind. "This is the back staircase. The main staircase you passed, though I doubt you noticed. It is quite near the front door, and of course there are others, to our east and our west, but this one is convenient to the kitchen, so I suppose that's why I use it the most."

Past the gardening tools or whatever they were which were stacked in readiness, Lori entered a small landing fronting the door to the outside. Off to her right a steep staircase rose, its red woven carpet scrupulously clean but worn. Before Lori reached the first step, she noticed a broad, uncurtained window, deeply recessed. What was on the other side of the glass could not be determined, for there was nothing to see but blackness and her own half-startled, exhausted refection. On the window ledge, a cardboard box reading Crannings Baking Powder rested and inside, on a hair matted blanket, an ebony cat nursed half a dozen blind kittens while she dozed, eyes lidded with contentment.

"Happened three days ago," Aunt Jan said, pointing to the kittens. "Genevieve is a good mother, experienced I'll tell you that, and she'll let you touch her kittens with no problem, but save it for the morning, for you need rest now."

Lori said nothing, for it was exactly as if Aunt Jan had read her mind. "Oh, what's her name, and when where they born, and would she let me touch them," the kind of flashing, confused thoughts that rush around chasing their own tails when faced with the small everyday miracle of a mother cat and her litter of soft, milk-round kittens.

"And who knows who the father is—" Aunt Jan said, starting up the narrow staircase. "There's no end of possibilities." Lori could see that, for the kittens resembled their coal black mother not at all. Not one looked like another, except for size and deportment. One was an orange tortoise shell, one a gray tabby, one blindingly white, one calico, one a pale, creamy Manx. "Five?" Lori asked.

"Six. Traveler's probably buried in there somewhere. He likes to be laid on, or so it seems."

And so it did seem, because there was a trace of a long, narrow tail between the Manx and the calico, not immediately apparent, because the Manx itself had no tail, but this tail, in this light, looked green and somehow more reptilian like an iguana not a kitten. Lori swallowed any comments, and silently followed her aunt up the stairs.

They stopped on the second floor, which was good, for Lori felt her strength not only waning, but completely eradicated. The stairs cheerfully carried on, another flight at least. The light was dimmer there, as if it couldn't quite bother to put forth the effort of any greater illumination when it was obvious anyone traveling this way would most likely stop at the second floor.

"No," she said, suddenly paralyzed by the thought, "I've got to get back to the car, and get my suitcases." Although she had put on her one talk-to-the-department suit that morning, she couldn't face sleeping in it, or in any of the under-clothing she had donned two thousand miles away.

"Awk, that's taken care of. I've got your luggage brought up and ready for you."

Lori would have asked how, for she was certain Aunt Jan couldn't have done it herself—even if she had left long enough to have completed the task, but decided to save the question for the morning. Her brain, at top form for her oral defense this morning, wasn't quite working at warp speed any longer. And if there had been another person in the house, how did he, she or it, get the trunk open, for she was certain she'd locked the car before she made her brave foray toward the front door.

"Your room is here, first one off the staircase," Aunt Jan said, opening a door. The wood was painted a high gloss white enamel, and the hint of fresh latex paint lingered in the air, as if the job had been completed recently. "You've not got a private bath. Well, you do, for there's no one else on this floor. At least no one who will bother you, and it is here, across the way."

Aunt Jan passed two closed doors before she opened the third, and Lori found a bathroom well enough appointed to serve an emir's harem. The tub itself was nearly big enough to practice the backstroke, and there was a separate shower with multiple heads, a toilet, and a broad marble-veined counter with modern conveniences, including, Lori could see, her own hair dryer and brush.

"Towels reside here, in this linen closet," Aunt Jan said, opening a door just off the bathroom, a walk-in big enough to be another bedroom, stacked to overflowing with towels, washcloths and sheets, some of which although folded, looked broad enough to use as sails on an eighteenth century clipper ship. The linen closet smelled like lavender, a scent redolent of spring, and the towels seemed to complement each other, brilliant pastels and deep rich hues, a rainbow panorama. "They like their privacy, so, after you take what you need, be sure to close the door."

"Privacy?" Lori asked. Her tongue thick and her eyelids drooping. All around everything was looking fairly fuzzy and she knew she would be asleep on her feet before too long. She'd pulled enough all-nighters to know when she had reached the limits of her endurance.

"Please, use what you need. The yellows are pushy. They seem to think they should be used first, but don't mind them. If you've an interest in any color, help yourself. I don't mind speaking to the yellow ones if they bother you." Jan rolled her eyes, long suffering. "Believe me, I've done it before."

And while Lori was digesting that, it did look as if a row of towels from creamy butter to a brilliant, almost blinding sunflower, inched back a bit, so they were not so overwhelming. The cranberry towels beside them looked smug.

"There's a linen chute here," Jan continued, pointing to a small latch-covered hole in the wall just inside the closet. "It leads down to the laundry room. Of course, that might be why the yellow towels are so pushy. They seem particularly enchanted with the drop, but that's neither here nor there. There's plenty of hot water, soaps, and shampoos, whatever you need, in the cabinet."

Lori had to finish a long, broad yawn before she could speak. "I'll be fine. You've been most generous."

"I do so like entertaining," Aunt Jan said, which on some level Lori found surprising. As far as she knew, other than her sister's one visit long ago, no one in the family had ever been here. On the odd occasions when Jan had arrived at family gatherings like the death of her grandfather, for example, or the blessing of a baby, Jan had appeared and disappeared without any advance notification, and extended no open-ended invitations. She probably felt honor bound not to leave the yellow towels pining for a long drop down the laundry chute.

"A bath sounds heavenly," Lori said instead. "I would love to soak.

But I think I'll save that for morning."

"Right you are then," Aunt Jan said, shutting the linen closet door snugly, backtracking toward the bedroom just off the staircase.

"Before you go, I saw a man named Arthur in Byron's shop."

"Did you now?"

"Yes. He said to tell you he asked after your health."

"That man," Jan said, but didn't elaborate.

"I wasn't sure if Byron would tell you."

"He wouldn't. Byron and Arthur go back a ways. Byron can hold a grudge a good long time."

"But Byron was offering him something. It sounded like an honor."

"Really? I'll have to speak with him about it in the morning. Nothing can be done tonight."

Jan kissed her again on the top of her head, then gave her a firm shove toward the bedroom before disappearing before Lori could even think to say Good Night.

Lori stepped further into the bedroom. The bed was a sturdy four poster, with cherry wood pillars taller than she was. It was covered with an airy film canopy from post to post as if some parachuter had landed here and left his accruements. The bed was big enough to use as a wrestling arena and when she sat on the bed, Lori found it firm, yet comforting. When her mind evoked images of a wrestling match this time, it was not the kind that would be televised, nor the sort involving bashing, hitting and thumping.

"The altitude must be getting to me," Lori mumbled as she trailed her fingertips along the soft, smooth surface of the pillowcase. She allowed fantasy to curl around her, aided and abetted by candlelight and the soft scent of spring flowers. In spring, a woman's heart turns to…

"So, you had no trouble getting in?"

Lori jumped, startled. She had thought herself alone, fantasizing and enjoying imagination, but as she turned, she faced the tea-making intruder. Wrapped in emotions, and suffering under a day with far more confusion than she was used to, her responses were unreliable. She didn't want to be interrupted—and she did.

He stood outside the bedroom door, which Jan left open foolishly, and Lori had negligently forgotten to bolt. She never would have been so foolhardy in any public hotel.

His fingers were long, tapered, an artist's hands. Without much difficulty, she could see them creating his magic with gold and diamonds, or pleasuring a woman's body. Her impulse, which she had to deliberately bite her bottom lip to prevent herself from following through with, was to reach out, touch him. Lori wanted see if the warmth was still there, and if it would compliment the coldness within her she had not realized existed until the first time she touched him.

Hands. Yes, she had realized how much hands could be used for seduction, but Andrew hadn't been one for touching. At the moment she was desperate to be caressed.

The light in the hall was indistinct, muted, but Byron radiated a glow, seemingly created deep within him. His teeth glimmered, shining, as he parted his lips.

"Yes. I got in. It didn't seem all that difficult."

"Yet, for some it is. I thought you—"

"What?"

He shrugged, ran his hands through his too long hair. "I don't often misjudge people, but at the moment, I don't know what to make of you. You carry the stench of an evil one, yet you waltz in here without a second thought, and drink the tea ignoring the teapot. Something is seriously not adding up here."

She wanted to be coy, seductive, but realized, swaying on her feet, she'd have to settle for blunt. "I suppose I should say I'm sorry I'm confusing you, but I'm not."

He pulled in a deep breath which she watched as his chest expanded. She'd bet he was stunning without a shirt on: all washboard abs and sexy pecs. "Not going to say it or not sorry."

"Both, actually."

She hadn't noticed how attractive he was while in the jewelry store. She had been hungry, anxious to get to her aunt, and suffering residual effects of shock compounded by seemingly endless travel. Now, having eaten and feeling safe, she saw him a bit differently. What she had noticed as slender was honed muscle, and his hair she had considered shaggy was soft, oddly inviting.

"I must be more tired than I thought."

"What?"

"Nothing. Talking to myself."

"Did you enjoy the tea?" Although there was a bite to it, as if an accusation, his voice wormed through her seductively, as if it were morning, and their bodies were both sweat-soaked, and they had not yet gotten their breath back, and he had murmured, "did I please you?" knowing from the flush to her breasts, from her uninhibited response, that he had.

"The tea?"

"At dinner. I made tea."

"I ... um ... didn't notice." She was too tired, and suddenly, too disorientated, for he, while definitely human, was also something else, a figment drawn from loneliness, a siren from mythology, come to entice naive innocent maidens like herself. She wondered, fleetingly, if this were still residual from the rings or if there had been some hallucinogenic in the smoke in Andrew's loft.

Byron stretched, with cat-like grace, all long, sinuous muscle, up the doorjamb. She could almost hear him snarl. "I will find all your secrets," he said, making sure she understood the underlying threat. "You won't get what you want. This inn is too thoroughly protected."

"I'm sure it is," she answered, her tongue suddenly far too dry. She really had no idea what he was talking about, had no concept how the tea of all things fit into the menace he exuded, and why, even though there was clearly a threat, there was also inexplicable, sexual interest on her part.

A fireplace stood in regal honor against one wall, and the fire within it had died down to nothing more than faintly glowing embers. The comforter had been turned down, and her bathrobe unpacked and rested at the foot of the bed. If he came in, they wouldn't need the robe, and the room was plenty warm without having to stir up the blaze.

She was not a woman who indulged in casual affairs, and she was still bleeding from psychological wounds received from her previous relationship. It had lasted months, but now she knew it had been based on fantasy. After Andrew she might never trust a man again as long as she lived. It was time for a long, hard dose of cold-shower reality.

Lori, needing distance from the enticing bed, walked to the door. "Is there anything else you wanted?" She let the tone of her words sound threatening, she hoped, as if she were formidable, not exhausted and, admittedly, entranced.

His eyes softened. He lowered his chin, tilted his head to a rakish angle. "Oh, yes, a great many things, but they will have to wait until morning."

"Morning," she echoed, not sure, even to herself if her response were a promise or a threat.

"Morning," Byron echoed but his sounded like a warning. He coiled back into himself with a cat's haughtiness, the unspoken gauntlet thrown down between them.

With an offer, with a look, her evening would end differently, but she was finished with men. All men. Except Lori realized she was rubbing her third finger where she could remember an etched gold band and a flawless diamond. She looked at him again, at the way his jeans hugged his narrow hips. He had such large hands. Yes, she was through with men. At least for tonight.

"Byron, wait!" That wasn't what she meant to say.

He didn't answer verbally, instead he turned slowly, until he faced her, and settled his hands on his hips, as if that was where he wanted to draw her attention.

He had her attention alright. Mercy, what that man did to a pair of jeans should be illegal. Of course, she had his attention as well. "What is there fun to do around here?"

Who was this woman who had taken over her body, and was using her voice to say all kinds of things she only dreamed she had the boldness to say.

"Fun?"

"Besides drinking tea, I mean."

His chuckle started low and rumbling, like thunder building in intensity. "My tea is probably all the fun you can handle." Seductively, he rubbed his long-fingered hands down the front of his leg, as if his palms had suddenly grown moist. "Perhaps I'll offer again when you're not exhausted. But then again, depending on the answers I get, maybe not."

She darted a bold glance toward the pillow and the draped bed. "Tea is the best you have to offer?"

His eyes flashed, angry, and she had no idea how she had insulted him, when she wanted to intrigue him, then

slam the door in his face, feeling her own power.

"Your master did not train you well for this assignment, did he? Do you think annoying me will make me serve you again?"

"Serve me?"

Lori stumbled for the bed, barely having the strength to stand. She tried to remember the taste of his tea, but it wasn't taste her memory invoked, but a clear recollection of that teapot winking and mixed impressions of antiquity and danger, and yes, arousal as the liquid swirled around her tongue and warmed her, down her throat, past her tingling breasts, deep into the very center of her. His loving would be like that, Lori imagined, and gave into the impulse to delight herself with speculation of potential future encounters with the tall, invasive stranger on this wrestling mat of a bed.

CHAPTER 6

Andrew heard sirens before he was finished. The bitch had kicked over his pot, destroying months of planning, but he struggled on his hands and knees trying to save something. Unfortunately with the sirens, he had to gather his books, dress himself and disappear. Oh, and one additional thing: there could be nothing left in this lab to tie him to these experiments.

He stood, and twisting the powerstrands in his hands, wished himself dressed. The clothing appeared, the slacks, the button down Oxford shirt he preferred, the tie, worn loosely at his neck. He liked to look powerful, successful, and why shouldn't he, when he was both?

He called a golden powerstrand. It hesitated, recalcitrant. They were not sentient, but some had, for want of a better term, 'attitude' and had to be called to heel. He was a master wizard. It would obey. His movements became sloppy as the sirens drew closer. He could hear the police cars racing down the street. He had less than a minute. Reluctantly the gold obeyed. He used it to open a portal, a transfer point not on Earth, but by definition not anywhere else either.

Andrew locked the gold in place, then grabbed a handful of peach colored powerstrands. On the whole they were weak, but plentiful. With them in his hands he called a few other colors, azure, navy, lime, saffron, and knotted them together. As the police entered through the front door Lori had left open, he spoke a single word of power and the powerstrands ignited in a loud, explosive tangle. Liquid super-heated fire whooshed, traveling across the floor, up the walls, around the ceiling. He had planned for this eventuality. In fifteen minutes, there would be nothing left of the house except a few bricks from the fireplace. And nothing left except dental records of the police officers who didn't make it out.

He would have to kill her. That was always the plan, but now he'd have to move her death up. Oh, he knew where she'd run. He'd hoped to use Lori to get entrance to the Inn, but no matter. He'd get in. His plan would culminate with her death, and the death of the dragon.

With a grin, Andrew stepped through the portal, and disappeared.

CHAPTER 7

Awake, Lori slipped out of bed. Her toes curled as she stepped onto the cold floor, although the room itself was warm. The fire had died long before, and she scratched her chin, trying to dig for the memory—no not memory, a shred of her dream. Byron had been there, sitting in that chair, watching her sleep, but more than that, it was as if she were the orchestra and he the conductor and with the firm strokes of his hands, with the powerful thrusts from his baton he had directed the dramas her sleeping mind played.

Trying to shake the images, Lori padded across the cold floor, felt the seat of the chair, where in dream he had been sitting. Oddly, she found it warm. Startled, she felt the other chair, its identical twin in every way, and found it cold.

"Imagination," she said, wiping her eyes where dream images still flirted. "Nothing but imagination."

She rubbed her palms down her arms, trying to recapture a caress, and could not dismiss the dream that readily. Mercy, her sister came here and found monsters in the basement and she discovered what, some nocturnal Don Juan? If so, she certainly had gotten the better deal.

Lori stared back at the sheets as she returned to the bed and shoved on her slippers. She found the sight of the gold dragon pattern comforting and recalled a half-forgotten childhood desire to see real dragons. With a grin, she realized it had been deeper, more complete than a wish to simply see dragons aloft, breathing flame and protecting their loved ones. She had wanted to ride one, command and understand one. Oddly, she had never hoped for a handsome prince to slay a dragon in her honor. Not when she dreamed of taming one with honey.

Putting the foolishness from her mind, Lori pulled clean clothes from the dresser, although last night she had been too exhausted to unpack. It nagged at the back of her mind that no one should have been in the room to do it for her. Seconds later in the bathroom, after the barest moment of indecision, she pulled a towel from the linen closet and showered quickly, deciding to save a decadent bath for later.

She thought of Byron and dreams as she unzipped her makeup bag. She dabbed on some lip gloss and added the lightest trace of mascara to give her light brown eyelashes some definition. Her face looked better, she decided. The haunted, black circles under her eyes had vanished, undoubtedly the result of having her thesis successfully defended followed by a good night's sleep. The fear she had seen in her own pupils yesterday was gone. Her aunt's kiss undoubtedly protected her, but there had also been the dragon. He would defend her; or rather, they would fight together against joint enemies. Her dreams had been so vivid she trusted the unmet reptile completely.

In the bathroom's bright light, her eyes were clear, shining. She hardly recognized herself. Lori smiled at her reflection, fluffed her hair to give it a touch more wildness and decided she felt ready to face the day and the adventures surely waiting.

Lori opened the door and ran smack into the solid wall of Byron. Although she had worked with the blow dryer and a styling brush, her hair was still slightly damp, and she clutched her nightclothes to herself, suddenly shy that he should see her pajamas, even if she wasn't wearing them.

"Were you waiting for the bathroom?" she asked, trying to step back to give him room and finding it impossible. When she had crashed into him, he had reached out, steadied her, and his hands no longer offered support. His touch now indicated something quite a bit less sturdy, if the weakness in her knees were any indication.

"Bathroom?" he tipped his head, as if the thought had never occurred to him.

"You are waiting outside the door. You should have knocked, if I were taking too long."

"No, I—" he mumbled, and she knew anything he finished the sentence with would be a lie. He had been waiting for her, perhaps even stalking her. The thought, and its resultant power, gave her an illicit thrill. She hoped he had suffered, waiting for her to exit, as he had waiting during his long vigil in the chair beside her fireplace. She moved back gaining some distance, but no equilibrium. He stood too close, was too masculine and too invasive. Mercy, the man crawled into her dreams for heaven's sake. How could she hope to find peace when he towered six inches away?

Was it peace she sought when she was with him?

The light in the hall highlighted the depths of color in his hair. What she had viewed last night as dark enough to be black, was streaked with traces of auburn as if this color hid during the evening hours, afraid to be caught without the sun's protection. He gently shifted his hand from her shoulder, and while she thought he was going to caress her cheek or perhaps dip a bit lower, instead Byron rubbed the damp towel between his thumb and index finger.

"Yellow?"

Although from his expressive copper eyes, past his firm, lilting smile, down the long length of his leather clad legs, he was stunning, something about him made her edgy, so she answered foolishly. Lori went to the linen closet and shoved the damp towels through the chute. She could almost imagine them saying "Wheee!" as they fell. "My Aunt Jan said yellow towels like the drop."

He didn't mock her, although perhaps agreeing with her was mocking enough. "So they do."

He leaned against the door jam, for all practical purposes imprisoning her in the linen closet for she would have to push past his broad chest to gain her freedom.

"You smell different this morning."

Certain she was being insulted, Lori tried to push past him. "I think that was the purpose of the shower."

"No. The stench you had yesterday is usually not so easily removed."

"I have no idea what you're talking about."

"You're right. I can see you don't. Innocence and evil. I've never known anyone who can float so easily between the two."

"I'm neither innocent nor evil, and you're bothering me."

He wore flannel again this morning, the shirt a blend of green plaids, the top three buttons undone. Although his presence annoyed her, seeing his chest was enough to have her salivating, hungry for her dream which had ended rather intimately. He looked more formidable than last night: dangerous, as if his humanity were only a costume. His eyes sparkled and she thought, held a trace of warning. No longer annoyed or frightened, a step beyond aggravation, Lori could not quite decide on what emotion he evoked within her, couldn't compartmentalize him as she yearned to. She rolled her tongue along her inner teeth and decided that would only make her pleasure more complete when she brought him to his knees.

Byron fingered a strand of her damp hair, rubbing it gently, like, she assumed, a silk merchant judging quality. As his voice dropped to sensual levels he met her gaze. "Shall I tell you what the blue towels like to do?"

She watched as he licked his lips, brought her hair to his nose and flared his nostrils.

She didn't speak, move, nod, or shake her head. He grinned, slowly and seductively, which left her feeling very warm. His grin started in his eyes, and his lips only curled as if in afterthought. Feeling a sharp awareness of her body, Lori realized something she hadn't a few minutes before. She had woken up hungry on those soft, dragon covered sheets, but her body craved something far different than breakfast.

Byron shifted closer, until there wasn't but a breath between them. She could sense the back of his knuckles against her temple, and with that movement, Lori understood the yellow towels got off easy.

Their faces inches apart, his scent reminded her of the tea she had been too tired to savor the night before. "The blue towels love to roam along a woman's wet body. The love to soak up the moisture she has at her neck, her shoulder and especially her breasts." He released her hair. She followed his expressive hands as they marked her, in the identical places he had mentioned. Lori felt his light touch in the muscles tightening between her legs, in the beading of her nipples, in the way her breath hitched.

Encouraging him had to be exactly the opposite to what she wanted, trapped in a linen closet, but the opening he had given her was so rich, she couldn't resist it. She lowered her voice. "Then the next time I'm here alone, I'll make a blue towel happy."

He laughed, his eyes crinkling at the edges. "If that's what you want, you'd find far more pleasure with me. All you'll have to do is lay back, close your eyes ..."

She wouldn't allow him to finish. Casually she reached out, as if to touch the broad expanse of his chest, before diverting her hand at the last moment, and landing on terry cloth. "And what makes the green towels happy?"

He stepped back and Lori breathed for the first time in minutes. "Green towels are boring. They like spinning in the washing machine. They are a little like the yellow towels in that respect. They don't mind getting dirty, because they know after they do, they can have what they really want.

"And you—" Byron continued, flashing her a look that stripped her naked. "Do you mind getting a little dirty?"

She understood clearly the emphasis he put on his final word, but Andrew had made her feel filthy, and she was no longer in the mood to continue this foolish game. She shoved him and he moved so easily she almost fell, since she was expecting resistance. "No. I don't."

He let her go. Lori realized she could have left any time, because he would play with her only as long as she wanted. She tossed her nightgown into her room and fled down the stairs. She stopped at the landing, not out of breath so much as out of control.

She had let him rile her. She had played to his taunting when she knew better. It was a mistake she would not make again. After Andrew, after that ugliness, she was finished with the male gender. Let them ply their torments on someone who wasn't wise to them. She would build her walls and defenses so high it would take a dragon to breech them.

The mother cat, Genevieve, was awake, giving her brood a good tongue lashing, washing them between the eyes and under the tail, rubbing the fur this way and that. From what she could tell, only five kittens lay in the basket.

"Good morning, ma'am," Lori said, not at all shocked to hear herself talking to a cat. After all, she had made a towel's day just a few minutes before, and perhaps was planning on going back later to see if she could make a blue towel feel sensual.

"You've a lovely family there."

Without looking up, she could see Byron sauntering down the stairs, with a controlled, arrogant gait. He was all legs this morning, lanky and delicious. He wore a large silver filigree belt buckle, which drew her attention exactly where she was sure he wanted it. She hadn't been drawn to bad boys before, but for the first time understood their attraction.

He stopped behind her, close enough that she could feel his breath flaming the soft hairs at her neck, yet his gaze was the only way he touched her.

The calico mewed, raised her nose high and with blind eyes sought attention. Ignoring Byron, Lori plunged her hand into the baking power box and removed the infant. It was feather soft, so tiny it almost felt unreal. Lori caressed its soft fur against her cheek. "I hope it's all right with you, momma," she said, purring herself as she let the fur tickle. The kitten was soft, like the sheets last night, like the feel of Byron's breath against her neck.

Genevieve didn't seem to mind. But there was shuffling in the box, movement as one kitten after another was disrupted, as if something under them was tunneling deeper into the blanket. "I hope this one hasn't had its bath yet, so you can get my scent off it," Lori said, replacing the kitten, but the black mother cat sniffed her daughter with approval and continued bathing her white sibling.

She found herself trapped for the second time in as many minutes, for Byron had his long arms spread out on either side of her, resting his weight on his palms. His hips were close to her bottom. Should she shift back a fraction of an inch, she would have no trouble gauging his desire, but that would be inadvisable. Inexplicably she understood what he was feeling more clearly than what her own body felt. A bit off-center, Lori continued to stare into the baking powder box, trying to find the composure she had woken up with.

"Do you like cats?" Lori asked. She swayed slightly, foot to foot.

"The enemy of my enemy is my friend," he answered.

"What's that supposed to mean?" She felt a bit claustrophobic, for the air around him was scarce, and she could only see him, smell him, and sense him. She couldn't think at all.

So quickly she didn't catch the movement, the mother cat reached out and raked her claws across Byron's left hand, leaving several long scratches beading blood.

Byron put his hand to his mouth, sucking at the wound before she got the impression it wasn't red at all, but some other color she couldn't analyze.

"No, I don't particularly like cats."

Genevieve returned to bathing her kittens, as if the abrupt assault had ever happened. Her ears which had arched forward shifted back, and her claws completely disappeared. The tiny creature under her tongue rumbled with pleasure.

"You've a protector," Byron said, lowering his hand, rubbing his right thumb over his left wrist.

"Two," Lori answered, remembering the kiss from the night before.

His eyes darkened, and his voice lost its velvet and took on a hard edge. "Neither of which will keep you safe from me. I take what I like."

Lori turned around, she didn't like that he was behind her and she couldn't see what devilment brewed back there, but immediately realized her mistake. Her breasts brushed his arm as she moved, then touched his chest. "Are you threatening me?"

The copper in his eyes flashed. "You might feel better imagining yourself a victim, but I'm like the blue towels. I like to rub against a woman's wet body."

Remembering the lesson learned upstairs, before she could succumb to his invitation, she pushed past him, and rushed to the kitchen. Cookware rattling and what sounded like conversation brought her back to the fact that she was hungry, a seeming impossibility after the feast she consumed the night before. Jan was just backing out of what had to be a walk-in refrigerator Lori hadn't noticed the evening before. She expected to see another person in the kitchen, but Jan was alone.

"Am I disturbing anything?"

"No, dearie, not at all."

"But you were talking to someone."

With the back of her wrist, Jan brushed a stray hank of hair from her face. "Just the yeast in the sourdough starter. You'd think by now they'd learn they really can't win an argument with me."

"You talk to the yeast?"

"Someone has to. They don't mind fermenting. Of course they don't. They all get a little drunk. But the kneading they can't abide, and they get in a huff when I remove a chunk to make bread."

Lori didn't know how to make heads or tails of the conversation. "Should I talk to them?"

"That's not necessary. At the moment they're behaving."

Lori breathed deeply, a heavenly aroma that had her thinking of flowers blooming by the thousands on fruit trees as she wondered if this were insanity, making towels happy, arguing with bread leavening. "Do they mind baking?" It had occurred to her live yeast would be killed by the baking.

"No, far as I can tell, that's never bothered them."

She looked to Byron, an odd ally after this morning's encounters. He was sprawled more than sitting to her right at the head of the table, his booted feet crossed at the ankles, leaning back in the chair. He watched her, no doubt of that, but he had dribbled golden honey against his index finger and stuck it his mouth and sucked. It felt as if he were acting out her earlier thought, that she would tame a dragon with honey. He seemed to be saying dragons like honey well enough, but they're not easily tamed.

Lori cleared her throat, finding her mouth dry. "Is this conversation making any sense?"

He gave his finger one last long lick. "Yes. But the yeast does not argue with me."

"They cringe in terror," Jan said, and swatted him on his shoulder with a large wooden spoon, so he righted the chair back to all four of its legs and brought his long, narrow hands up to the table.

Feeling powerful, since she had evaded him twice, Lori teased, "Yes, he is quite terrifying."

"You've no idea," Jan said, sounding both indulgent and long-suffering. Byron opened his mouth, then audibly snapped his teeth shut, a wordless 'bite me.'

"Well, it does look like you've slept yourself out," Aunt Jan said looking her up and down with a sparkling grin of approval. Then Jan recognized the high color staining Lori's cheeks, and Byron licking his wrist.

"Run into some trouble this morning, Brew?" Jan asked.

"A challenge more than trouble," he said with a negligent shrug of his shoulder. "You know how I like a challenge."

"She wouldn't fight you if you didn't bait her. You are after all, on the same side."

An eyebrow hitched. "We are?"

"And stay away from Lori. You promised you would never harm blood kin of mine."

He laughed and lowered his hand, where there was no sign of the scratches. The skin was unblemished, as if there never had been a wound there. "You know I can't be trusted when I see something I want."

"If you didn't—" Jan said, but looking at Lori, didn't bother to finish.

"But I do, and you know it." He sat forward, straight and still, all his careless swagger gone. He looked like a young boy at the principal's office. "Shall I leave, Majesty?"

Jan folded her arms, and although holding nothing more lethal than a long-handled spoon, looked deadly. She lowered her brows, a "hairy-eyeball" look Lori's mom used, but never with this intensity. "It might be for the best if you made yourself scarce for a week or two."

"And your garden?" he asked casually. He stretched out, reached down the length of the oak table for a speckled antique-appearing blue teapot, and poured tea into a waiting mug.

"Do you bargain with me, Brew?"

"No. I obey you," and he inclined his head, a bow which lacked the mocking Lori expected. "And I will see to your garden."

"Just make sure that is the only thing you stick your talons into today."

He grimaced as if the tea he had just tasted was vile, but he kept the mug cupped between his hands. "I feed where I like."

Quite a different statement, Lori thought, than his earlier one, that he took what he liked.

Jan turned back to her stove, where a dozen burners were busy. She threw her comment over her shoulder. "Then feed somewhere else."

But his laughter and draining his tea cup were his only answers.

Ignoring Byron, Jan turned from the stove, and cupped Lori's chin in her palms. "He can't enter your bedroom unless you invite him. That's not much protection, dear, for he has full reign of the house and all the exits, but you'll be safe in your room or here in the kitchen."

"I can handle him," Lori said, breaking the contact. She didn't like the depth of Jan's gaze, as if she were seeking secrets deeply buried in her soul even she didn't remember.

"She can handle me," Byron said, but it wasn't quite agreement.

"Brew, you've behaved yourself for decades."

His laughter rang through the high-walled kitchen. "Then maybe it's time I was bad again."

Lori was intrigued or perhaps entranced. She thought of blue towels, but it wasn't terry cloth she imagined against her skin.

"He will be civilized." The accent on the verb made it an order rather than a promise.

Byron stretched his arms, first the left, then the right, a slow, provocative action that looked exactly like a bird, arranging its feathers before flight. "Becoming civilized has never interested me."

Jan chose to ignore him, instead putting her hands on her niece's shoulders. "I can see the sleep did you good. You don't look quite as transparent as you did yesterday when you first entered this kitchen. Whatever you're running from, this is a good place for sanctuary."

"I, um…" she started, and she covered her eyes with her palms and shook her head, as if those simple superficial gestures could clear an image of carnage from her mind. She lowered her hands, looked around. "Where did all these pint jars come from?"

"What do you mean, where did they come from? I've been canning all morning. It's peach jam. Sit, girl. We were talking about how you looked so exhausted yesterday, and you were running away from something. But first, tell me how you slept."

"I don't think I've slept so well in my whole life." She sniffed the heavenly scents from the kitchen, "and I had such marvelous dreams."

"Dreams, did ya say?" Jan asked, inclining her head toward Byron.

He raised an eyebrow, and it looked like he might have nodded his head, but then he raised his tea cup in salute to Jan.

"Warm, deep-sleep dreams," Lori said, sniffing the huge caldron which last night had contained stew. "You know the kind, impressions more than anything. I think it was because of the change in time zones, and finishing my oral defense."

"That's ok," Jan answered. "This is a good house for dreams, but some," here she looked pointedly at Byron, who met her glance without any visible response, "don't quite know what to do with dreams when they've got them."

"I dreamed of dragons," Lori said, wondering why she had felt such an urgency to confess.

"Dragons?" This from Jan.

"Dragons I controlled."

"No one controls a dragon." Byron lifted the honey ladle, let the liquid dribble back into the jug without tasting it. "Many try," he said, as if he spoke of something as mundane as trying to teach a Labrador to fetch or a macaw to speak. "Few succeed."

Lori felt empowered with no idea why. "I will."

"It might be best if you find some other project to interest you," Jan said firmly. "You wouldn't want to get burned."

"Dragons don't burn everything."

Jan's response was to raise a silent, disbelieving eyebrow.

"Your aunt has been quite remiss," Byron said, standing up, offering a hand, "in not formally introducing us." He sauntered closer, as if what had occurred in the linen closet and again by the baking powder box had never happened.

"Since you don't seem to be leaving any time soon," Jan said without any of the animosity present in her vocal inflections, "I certainly will, if you give me but a moment with this jam."

Pint jars were lined up, sparkling clean, perhaps two or three dozen. Golden, enchanted peach preserves bubbled merrily on the stove, from five or six separate pots.

Lori shut her eyes to concentrate on the aroma. "I can't imagine I've ever smelled anything that delicious," she said. "Really, I can see you're busy. Is there anything I can do to help?"

"Everything here is in order. Sit. For the moment I'll let Byron entertain you. I don't think he can get in much trouble as long as I've got an eye on him." She turned her back to them, concentrating on the jam, making Lori wonder if she was giving the tall stranger permission to do just that.

Reading her mind, Byron grinned. "Oh, she's still watching. Eyes in the back of her head," he said.

"Must be a family trait," Lori giggled. "There were times when I swear my mother had them too."

"I thought you were going to introduce yourself to the lass," Jan said. "Be careful not to leave anything out. She probably needs to know all about you."

"Forewarned is forearmed," Lori answered, feeling lighthearted, for this is what she hoped for as she bounded down the stairs, to continue the sparring they had initiated in the linen closet. "And get on with it, will you? I want to take a long soak, and I am planning on using the blue towels."

Byron choked, as if something had gone down his throat wrong, and Jan turned, holding her spoon out as if it were Excalibur. "What have you told her about the blue towels?" She turned her makeshift weapon to her niece. "You leave the blue towels alone. At the moment I think they're far more than you can handle."

"Oh, I doubt that," Lori said, savoring the feeling of power.

"Do you like playing with fire, little girl?" Byron asked, and there was nothing of the pest about him now, but instead a predator. He smiled, and she witnessed those too-long teeth, almost feeling them at her throat, or other, more intimate locations across her body.

She leaned back on her heels and met his gaze. "I like playing in the water. I've learned it puts out fires," she taunted.

"Not mine," he responded.

"Byron, sit! You're frightening my niece."

He kept his gaze locked on Lori. "She doesn't look frightened to me."

To show she wasn't intimidated and didn't know why she should be, Lori let her eyes sparkle. "I didn't really get a chance to thank you last night for your tea."

"We were quite honored by your tea, Brew," Jan said, but instead of the familiar baiting Lori expected between the two of them, this time the tone of her voice indicated the tea service really had been an honor.

"Byron MacLauchland at your service," he said, offing a short half-bow with gallant courtesy, and she accepted his handshake, thinking nothing of it beyond courteous social contact. Instead of a perfunctory greeting between two strangers, when her flesh met his she felt again such a jolt of recognition she was nearly knocked off her feet. If it had been the equivalent of poking a fork into an electrical socket, it couldn't have stunned her more. His flesh was warm and inviting, as if by taking his hand she had knocked on a door she only had to open and pass though to find all kinds of unexpected and amazing miracles. Warmth flooded her, and traces of her dream flashed across her retinas. She would bring him to heel, but before then she would let him play with her, let him whimper.

Why should the blue towels have all the fun?

CHAPTER 8

He was certain there had been evil about her yesterday. Over the centuries he had come across the stench so often he could not deny it. Yet it was gone this morning. She smelled fresh, innocent, and regardless of the fact she thought he meant sexually innocent, he meant innocent of the perversions of the evil ones. She had smelled of wanton slaughter yesterday, and today she smelled of orange blossoms.

That kind of evil was not so easily discarded. It got into the marrow; flowed through the blood. It was not defined by what you did, it defined who you were. And she had crossed the wards of his shop without thinking. She had entered the Inn with no idea there was a barrier in place.

Jan, who had been given immense powers by all creature of faerie to fight against the evil ones, welcomed her, offered her tea. His tea. Clearly Lori had no idea what she swallowed.

She was doing something to him he hadn't felt in decades. No, in centuries. She was making him crave.

Byron lowered his eyes, trying to determine if she were as affected by the handshake as he was. This desire, which had hormones bubbling he'd all but forgotten, had to be magic. But, the question was, and to quote an old favorite movie, he needed to determine: "Are you a good witch or a bad witch?"

    * * *

He was tall, the top on her head only came to his shoulder, but she had always been attracted to tall men. Lori looked up at Byron. For a fleeting second she thought she saw sparks, realized her imagination, which she usually kept tight rein on, was in overdrive.

"Brew—"

"Yes, ma'am," he finally said, disentangling their fingers. Then, when he spoke to Lori, his eyes twinkled. "May I pour you a mug? The tea is freshly steeped. Peppermint, this morning."

"I was looking forward to seeing the dragon teapot in the light. I think I was too exhausted last night to appreciate it, but I do remember it was beautiful."

"You'll see it again soon. This tea is not as good as what you got last night," Jan said, "but occasionally we have to make due."

Byron bowed toward Jan. "I try my best to serve."

Lori forgot she wanted coffee, as she got lost in his mesmerizing glance. He was young, she imagined, not much past mid-thirties, certainly not yet forty. His hair, richer even than it had looked in the shadowed linen closet, showed different hues in the bright kitchen light. Now it seemed lighter than a black, not quite mahogany. It curled in wild abandon around his shirt collar, and looked far more disreputable than it had last night. If he owned a comb, he certainly hadn't used it in recent memory. He had shaved, for his cheeks were soft, but unconsciously she missed the masculine bad-boy look of heavy stubble.

"Your eyes," she said.

His irises were copper. At first she thought they were brown, but that did not describe the subtle shift of hues, and red was too abrasive a term and orange had too much yellow in it. Copper, with a deeper ring of weathered bronze around the edge.

"It's a draconic trait," Jan said, ladling peach jam into jars, not bothering to turn.

"Is that why you put me in that bedroom?" Lori asked, and Byron whispered "bedroom?" to no one in particular.

"What about the bedroom, dear?" Jan asked. It must have been important, for she turned around, holding a spoon drooling sticky peach nectar to the slate floor.

"Because of the dragon sheets."

Byron raised an eyebrow in sardonic amusement, as if he got the punch line, but her aunt spoke matter-of-factly. "I'm sure that was the reason."

Under Byron's heated perusal, her knees felt weak. Lori backed blindly, not breaking her gaze from his, until she reached a chair. She sat in the same seat as the night before, and he bent beside her, pouring the tea into her mug. Steam rose, hot and fragrant. She cupped the mug in both hands and inhaled deeply. "I think I could get used to tea."

"Aye. Anyone can get used to tea," Byron said.

"Anyone with brains," Jan amended. "There's—"

"I know," Byron said, "I will take care of it," and he vanished to the stove for moment and brought Lori a mushroom and cheese omelet. It was perfect, hot and fluffy, and how it could have been ready at just that second, she had no idea.

"Is this yours?" Lori asked, pointing a fork at the omelet, feeling self-conscious.

"No. I ate hours ago. It's really quite late for me."

"Quite late, indeed," added Jan, who continued ladling peach preserves into pint jars by the thousands. "Don't you have something you need to be doing?"

"I'm not in much of a hurry," Bryon said. "I can stay to see to the lady's breakfast. After all, you asked me yourself."

"So I did. You'd think I'd learn." Jan set the ladle aside and started wiping the rims of the jars, placing canning lids and rings around them, ready for a water bath.

In addition to the omelet, Byron supplied three fat link sausages, still sizzling, and fresh white bread. It had a yeasty, beer smell and was still warm. He won Lori's undying gratitude when he stole a small bowl of peach preserves from the huge caldron, moving quickly to avoid Jan's lancing spoon.

"You'll be sorry when winter comes and you're hungry because there are no preserves," Jan said, her voice taking on the dire tone of warning.

Winter? Lori wanted to protest. It was only April, and winter seemed so far away, but she kept her own thought.

"Then I shall feed my stomach with memories of making a beautiful woman smile," he said, and offered Jan a half-bow. Lori wondered if it was mocking or respectful. The pair seemed to volley between those two conditions, as if there wasn't a shred of difference between them.

"Eat, or it will get cold, and drink your tea. For all it's just tea," he said, as if what she had swallowed the night before was far more. "It's good for what ails you."

"There's not much ailing me at the moment," Lori said, swallowing a forkful of omelet, and finding it delicious. The mushrooms were plump and spongy, as if freshly picked. They tasted of woodland glens and dark, secret places. Suddenly she wished she could remember more specifically what her night's dreams had been about. "Everything is perfect."

"Perfect is exactly the word I was going to use," Bryon said, winking at her, and flashing his incredibly long, dark lashes. His teeth didn't look quite so feral in this light, but his legs appeared longer, if that were possible. The pants he wore fit him just as well as they had yesterday.

"Wherever did you get peaches this time of year?" Lori asked, her mouth full of warm bread she had slathered with the preserves. "This is so incredible. I bet you could sell it and make a fortune."

"See," Jan said, all but sticking out her tongue. "There's some who appreciate my talents."

"We all appreciate your talents," Byron said, lifting his tea in salute.

"I just dug them out of my freezer. When they were fresh, I was up to my armpits in other projects. I had to save them for a day when not so many things were pressuring me."

"So," Byron asked, not so much questioning as teasing, "does that mean less things are pressuring you now?"

"If certain people," and she gave the word an odd inflection, "would leave me alone, I might be able to get this job finished before moonrise." She continued filling the jars, one after another, while a batch bubbled in a hot water bath.

"I do miss the dragon teapot from last night."

Byron stood. "I could provide it."

"Sit," Jan ordered. "There's nothing wrong with that teapot. It's experienced."

His hands around the teacup looked delicate, but with his clasp, she had felt strength and calluses. Who knew being a jeweler was such hard work? On his left hand, his ring finger ended in a stub before the first knuckle and his pinkie had been amputated.

"Accident?" she asked, indicating his hand.

"I occasionally get careless. It could have been a lot worse."

"An old injury?"

"No, new enough. I am not quite used to fighting without two of my claws, but I still manage."

"Brew!" Aunt Jan snapped sharply, and he pulled his hands back and rubbed the stub of his ring finger with the palm of his right hand. She hadn't noticed the missing fingers when the cat lashed out.

His eyes turned dark black, fathomless, and when he spoke they sparkled with a different appreciation than when he spoke with her.

"I was hoping to get some hiking in today," Lori said, pushing her plate away with a satisfied moan.

"You'll have to wait a bit. There's snow."

"Snow?" she asked, and ran to the back landing and opened the back door. Her aunt was correct, snow had fallen thick and heavy during the night, obscuring the entire backyard. The snow glistened, as snow was wont to do under a brilliant, low sun, and the yard was undisturbed.

"It won't last long. By tomorrow we'll have you out walking."

"Can I tour the house? I hate to be a bother, but the rooms look so exciting."

"What rooms?" Byron and Jan asked at the same time. "You didn't look in any of the rooms, did you?" Her aunt forced casual tone.

"No, I slept soundly, then when I woke, I showered and came right down. But this is an old house, isn't it?"

"Ancient," Brew said, grinning, and Jan, who held the thick spoon, held it up in mock threat.

"The house is old enough," Jan admitted.

"Then there must be dozens of interesting places to explore. The basement, the attic—"

"Both should probably wait for another day," Jan said, ladling preserves with renewed vengeance.

"Then the rooms on this floor. There must be something I could dust, or old drawers I could empty, anything?"

"How about if you can sit there, and update me on your life. As I recall, last I heard from your mother, there was a young man you were rather interested in."

Byron stood, offering her a tempting muffin. Lori shook her head sadly.

"If I keep eating like this, none of my clothes are going to fit, and I'll return home looking like a blimp."

"You'll not put on an ounce of fat while you eat at this house," Aunt Jan said, speaking over her shoulder as she continued canning.

"Aye, that's the truth. It's part of the magic of the place." But he said it to get a rise out of Jan, for the older woman snorted, and he laughed out loud.

"Really, Aunt Jan, is there anything I can do to help? I need something. Can you find me a diabolical chore? Can I clean the basement?"

"There are things chained in the basement," Byron said. He had lowered both his voice and brows, and the copper was back in his eyes. He spoke conspiratorially, but the older woman obviously heard.

"There are not," Jan growled. Her actions as she filled canning jars went became more forceful and abrupt.

"You let them go?" Byron chuckled.

"No, I didn't let them go. This conversation is pointless," Jan said, lifting the sealed jars from the water bath.

Lori clapped her hands. "I would love to see things chained in the basement. I've always wanted—"

"Brew is perhaps not the person to tell the things you've always wanted."

Byron raised that dark, mobile eyebrow of his again, as if he had a suggestion he'd loved to offer, if only to set off Jan, but her back was to him, and, unless she had the eyes in the back of her head he mentioned earlier, she missed the expression.

"If you're really bored, of course you can help. I've a bit of potatoes in the sink that need peeling."

"Great," Lori said, feeling relieved the task offered was actually something she could manage. She was hopeless at cooking and useless at cleaning. Too many years in a library or doing her field research had kept her from learning any more practical domestic skills.

The morning passed quickly. Aunt Jan kept her busy, working up to lunch, then through most of the afternoon with a thousand little chores. After she finished the potatoes, there were a ton of onions to be peeled and diced, and a sink full of carrots. "More stew for dinner tonight?"

"Goulash," Jan answered. "It's similar to stew, although the seasoning is quite a bit sharper."

"A hundred people couldn't eat all this food."

"We'll see," Jan answered, noncommittal. After the goulash was simmering in a poignantly scented paprika sauce, she spent four hours pitting cherries, while Aunt Jan canned them, jar after jar, filled with fruit beautiful enough to use as a table decoration.

"So tell me," Lori asked as she carried a large colander filled with cherries she had just rinsed back to the table, "what have you got chained in the basement?" She didn't believe for a second the statement was true, but her imagination was tickled with the image. And her sister Brenda certainly had believed there were monsters.

"Brew talks too much."

Byron had left immediately after Lori finished breakfast, before she set peeler to her first potato, as if him staying around would result in his conscription into mess hall duty. Without saying anything, his glance promised he'd see her again, then he'd grabbed a jacket and headed out the back door.

"Why do you call him Brew?"

"Many reasons, mostly because it's appropriate. Tell you the truth, I've been calling him Brew so long, I'd almost forgotten he had another name."

"So can you tell me about the things in the basement?" Her eyes sparkled with whimsy. "Should I run them down some table scraps so they don't starve?"

"It's unlikely they're going to starve, and this conversation isn't for you. You're an adult now. You certainly should have put such imaginative images from your mind by now."

"Why? Isn't imagination more, not less, important as you age?"

"Not to hear most people talk."

"Aunt Jan, I'm not interested in most people. I care about what you think."

"Aye, child, imagination is important, but not as important as facing facts. That said, tell me why you came all the way across country to see an old lady."

She sat down with a thump, wiped her bangs back from her eyes. The day had turned warm, and in the afternoon sun most of the snow had vanished. Beyond that, the kitchen, with so many burners on the range going at the same time, nearly reched sauna temperatures.

"My mother was right. There was a guy, and for a few months I was serious about him, but things turned weird, then they turned crazy, and when I had to get away, the only place I could think to run to was here."

Steam whistled through the narrow spout of a kettle, and Aunt Jan turned off the gas and started brewing yet another pot of tea. "Just make yourself comfortable and tell me all about it."

"Thanks. I need to talk. Tell me, do you believe in wizards?"

* * *

Byron didn't appear at dinner, which disappointed Lori, nor at breakfast the following morning, or outside her shower when she had been expecting him. If her aunt noticed her frustration, she didn't mention it, and knowing she probably wouldn't be staying much longer, Lori didn't ask about him. There didn't seem to be much point.

On her way upstairs after breakfast to straighten her room and organize her thoughts, Lori noticed Genevieve, the mother cat, meowing at the back door, needing out. When she opened the door, she saw the ground looked dry enough for a short, exploratory hike.

"Do you mind if I walk around outside?" Lori asked as Aunt Jan appeared behind her. "My legs feel a little stiff."

"No problem. Take a coat. The breeze is apt to be a might chill. Do leave out the front door, though, won't you? Off to your right as you exit the house is a trail. You can see it from here, beyond the stump. It's well marked, and you should have no trouble finding your way."

"Why can't I use this door?" The cat she had let out only moments before was nowhere to be seen.

"It's safer to use the front for all comings and goings around here. You'll never know who or what you'll run into if you leave through the back." Saying that, Jan shut the door firmly.

"That's absurd. I'd only have to walk all the way around the house. It's more direct this way."

"I thought you wanted to walk," Jan said dryly.

"All right. I'll leave from the front."

Lori zipped her jacket, wishing she'd brought her winter coat. She turned when she reached the edge of the forest to study the house. If anything the Inn looked even more massive from this direction, and she thought perhaps she'd been mistaken, and there were at least five floors, maybe as many as seven. The first chance she got she was going to make Aunt Jan, or better yet, Byron, give her a tour of the monstrosity. They could play hide and seek, she thought with a grin, determining she would not be difficult to find.

She walked for about an hour, strolling leisurely, realizing for the first time in as long as she could remember, she didn't have anything pressing. No obscure fact she had to research for her dissertation, no class she had to teach, and no lectures she had to audit. She thrust her chilled fingers into the deep pockets, enjoying her own thoughts and the freedom to think nonsense.

Trees and bushes encroached on the path, and a heavy layer of freshly unfurled fern fronds tried to obliterate it. For all that, she had no difficulty following the winding trail deeper along the mountainside. Yesterday's snow had vanished, and in its place rose the sharp scent of early growth. Spring had its own aroma.

She heard rustling all around her, indistinct noise coming from what she suspected were clever white-tailed deer and small mammals: chipmunks, squirrels, raccoons, and skunks. She saw nothing beyond an occasional darting bird.

Lori debated whether or not to return as she popped through some heavy brush and entered a clearing. Surrounded on all four sides by the tall pines, maples and all manner of bushes with blood-seeking thorns, she found the clearing unexpected. It was as if someone had posted signs, Stay Out! The forest obeyed, and even the grass knew better not to grow taller than three pillowing inches here.

The clearing was massive enough to play a soccer game if goal posts could be erected at either end, except in the exact center was a huge, broad trunked tree so massive a half dozen people couldn't span it. Lori arched her neck, finding its top branches invisible to her gaze. The tree was not yet in leaf, although tiny green buds promised that situation would soon change.

Forming a ring around the tree, as if planted equidistantly, thick eight inch high ecru mushrooms with broad red-spotted caps sprouted. Enchanted, Lori hopped over the massive fungi into the center of the circle. She twirled for a moment, dizzying spirals, and jumped, startled, when she sensed movement behind her.

"What did you say?" she asked, surprised she faced Byron. She felt foolish for her whimsy of acting like some mad dervish deep in Upstate New York, and wondered if a blush coated her cheeks.

"It's a faerie ring," he repeated, stopping outside the ring of mushrooms. "And you're intruding."

CHAPTER 9

"I beg your pardon?" She found her mouth dry at the sight of him. He held his shirt, but she noticed his broad chest was covered with sweat and dirt. She licked her lips for all it was a good twenty degrees too cool for Lori to perspire.

"It's a faerie ring, and you're intruding."

"A faerie ring?" she asked, liking the imagery of magic and perhaps hedonistic indulgences. "And what do you do in a faerie ring?" she asked.

He grinned, a lopsided smile. "When you're invited?"

"Ok, when you're invited."

"Dance mostly. There is usually some feasting, some ritual, but dance is the priority."

"Come join me!" She threw back her head and laughed, returning to her dizzying circles in crazy spontaneous steps of her own devising. Byron looked like something stolen from the depths of time, and with the enchantment and the magic from the morning, she wouldn't need a band to hear music they could waltz to.

"It's a faerie ring," he repeated. "I'm not welcome inside unless I'm invited."

With enough degrees to paper a small bathroom she did not like being taken for a fool. Andrew had done that and worse, and this was idiotic. He would start spouting about Bigfoot next, or alien landings, laughing at her gullibility.

She tried to pull air into her lungs, surprised she was so breathless. "Faerie ring? With real faeries?"

"This is an old forest. There are many creatures that roam here, stolen out of time and kept safe by me and mine."

Me and mine. "You believe in faeries?" She gave the last word an odd inflection, as if indicative of something which might or might not have sexual connotations. Faeries: there were other, uglier names for the same thing.

"Do you believe in the literal power of myth?" he returned, shifting her question as darkness crept in around his irises, making his eyes blacken, and his voice deepen with accusation. "Do you believe most, if not all, legends and faerie tales have their basis in reality?"

She was an anthropologist. There was only one way she could answer: "Yes."

With her acknowledgement, Lori looked around at the tree specifically, using the same intensity Byron had. She could almost see something ethereal, with light adsorbing wings and tiny feet. Creatures of imagination or unclassified life forms.

Byron slashed his hand, an angry movement, oddly not directed at her, but something, if her eyes did not deceive her, residing near the trunk. While Lori had no doubt many of the tree's roots went deep, she could see several shallow ones, and they crept, serpentine-like along the inside of the faerie ring. It would be an uncomfortable and hazardous place to dance. She could imagine herself tripping over those thick roots, spraining an ankle. She could also accept that faeries, with their light steps, would have no trouble at all.

"Do you believe in Darwin?"

"Darwin? Charles Darwin, survival of the fittest? Voyage of the Beagle?"

"Yes, that Darwin."

"Yes, of course."

"Then you understand evolution. But note this: not everything that walks in this forest can trace ancestry back to this planet's first primordial goop. Not everything is direct kin to what you consider normal. If DNA is the building block of life, it is important you know it is not the only construction material available. Creatures of faerie," me and mine, her mind whispered as he continued, "come from completely different processes."

Lori shook, suddenly cold. She rubbed her arms with palms all but numb with shock. She felt something almost pushing her, trying to force her from the faerie ring.

Lori wrinkled to nose to show her distaste. "Thanks for the genetics lecture."

He picked up her sarcasm. "Then you're one of those people who think simply because you don't understand something, it doesn't exist?"

"I am one of those people who stopped believing in things that go bump in the night years ago. And perhaps if it can't be seen, can't be taken apart under a microscope, it doesn't exist."

He nodded, not conceding the point so much as deciding she wasn't worth fighting with. "You could at least apologize to the tree. You can see the tree, can't you?"

"The tree?" she scoffed. This had gone on far enough. "I've insulted the tree?" Why had something which started out so fun, so freeing, turned into a mockery?

Byron stepped closer, did not cross the line marked by red capped mushrooms. "You know different cultures have different rituals?"

"Yes." Lori no longer wanted to dance. She wanted to strangle something tall wearing leather pants.

"And many cultures worship trees. Do you know why?"

"Because so much of their livelihood depends on trees."

"That will do as well as any other explanation," he said in a tone of voice which suggested she missed the point, but he would give her credit for trying. "If a culture worshiped trees, and you bounded into what they considered sacred territory, what would you do?"

Lori interrupted before he could finish. "Any tree? Or this specific tree?"

"This specific tree."

She looked at it, a massive oak, beyond huge, it was majestic, and it did appear that with the forest beat back, to be standing in what could be considered a sacred grove. "I would apologize," she mumbled, when she realized that was exactly what he wanted. "Then I'm intruding." She felt suddenly reticent.

He shook his head and all that shaggy hair brushed his shoulders, making her knees weak. She had been close to him, in the linen closet, by a mother cat bathing kittens, but she didn't believe she had touched his hair, and wondered how stupid she was, that with all her education, she had made such a phenomenal blunder. Some things should not be put off.

"You entered in ignorance, and the faeries are quite used to the foibles of mortals who enter their rings without thought to consequence. I, however, don't have the same latitude. I'll stay here."

Faeries, is that what they were still talking about? Somehow, watching his hair, checking his naked chest for imperfections and coming up without any, she had lost the trace of this conversation.

Carefully Lori stepped over the mushrooms, moving swiftly to his side. She didn't believe in faeries, not for one split second, but she liked the excuse to be close to him, a rationalization to reach out, take his hand. Byron however was staring at the center tree, his eyes unfocused, as if he conversed, telepathically, with those she could not see.

"Have I done any damage, in entering?"

"No," he said, finally giving her what she had been seeking when he took her hand in his mutated one. "But if you would like to offer apology, they are listening, and will not take offense."

She would have scoffed, wanted to, but for two things: first, he was serious. Whatever she'd done concerned him. Second, if she expressed disbelief, she'd have to break physical contact with him, move back emotionally as well, and it was too glorious wrapping her fingers with his. The contact this time was not as visceral or as invasive, but there was something warm, and for want of a better word, complete.

"Then they're watching? The faeries?"

"Yes. They guard this tree closely."

Her eyes widened and she searched deeper into the dark, hidden recesses, of which there were an endless number. "Faeries?"

"Most certainly. This is their part of the forest."

She scanned under mushrooms, into the lower limbs, and any other place which might conceivably hide a faerie. "Can you see them?"

"Yes."

"Can I see them?"

"Of course. When they make themselves known to you. At the moment they have no reason to trust you, and if the truth were known, no reason to trust me either."

"But you've been here, dancing?" She had no idea why it was so important to her to establish that.

"Yes. I'm known as quite a good dancer, when I care to be."

She squinted her eyes, looking at him askance, tried to imagine what he would look like, dancing under a full moon in a faerie ring surrounded by faeries, and other than a rather licentious image of him entertaining ethereal women who wore little beyond translucent wings, she came up empty. "And you supply the tea?" she asked, not knowing where the question came from.

"No, my tea is generally only for mortals, and to offer my tea to faeries would be the gravest of insults, for they are famous for their hospitality."

Lori looked back over her shoulder to the faerie ring. "Do you think I should apologize?"

"It is not for me to say, but you certainly may if you wish. You never know when you'll need a favor from a faerie."

Not knowing what served as an apology for violating a faerie ring, but liking the thought of the creatures listening, she swept into a curtsey, and spoke to the base of the broad tree. "I apologize for bounding so thoughtlessly into something obviously not meant for me. If I have caused you any pain or inconvenience, I am most humbly sorry."

"Was that all right?" she asked Byron.

"That was enchanting," he answered, stepping away with her, heading back to the path.

"May I walk with you for a moment?" she asked.

"It would be my pleasure."

He bent down and picked up his shirt, using it to wipe his sweaty brow and shoulders before putting it on.

"I thought you were in your shop, working in gold, creating your miracles. Why are you in the forest?"

"A garden, a rather large one, needed tilling before it could be planted.

You aunt will see to the seeds and the cultivating, but I'm glad to help, because most of the food she grows helps those I care about."

Me and mine. Again the thought left a sharp stone in the pit of her stomach.

"Is there something wrong?" he asked a moment later, after they'd walked in what amounted to uncomfortable silence.

"You're married?"

He raised an eyebrow. "What gave you that idea?"

"Your family. You said my Aunt Jan grows food for your family."

"No, I'm not married, not now and never before. But there are many beings your aunt feeds."

"Is the growing season at this elevation long enough for vegetables to ripen?"

"Jan manages. I haven't pushed my luck to ask her how."

"Is the tilling finished?"

"No, but I can get back to it later. I've earned some time off for good behavior. Besides," he laughed, "the boss isn't looking."

He reached out to take her hand, when without warning he was knocked aside by a huge snarling creature. For a second, Lori had no idea what happened, then she screamed and instinctively stepped back as the monster—whatever it was—attacked Byron. It was at least the size of a grizzly bear and the weight from its huge paws pinned him to the ground. From her angle, she could only see massive shoulders, a fur covered back and claws … long, bloody claws.

Its elongated teeth snapped closer to the exposed skin at Byron's neck. Muscles bulged in his forearms as he wrapped his hands around the creature's throat.

Monster and man rolled along the grass carpeting, Byron on top, then the beast, then Byron again as he fought to subdue it. His face reddened with effort.

"The faerie ring," he yelled, sparing a glance for her. "Get back into the faerie ring."

"I want to help—"

"They might protect you," he said, but any further words were torn from him as the beast renewed its attack. She stood, paralyzed, watching the battle, trying to identify the animal. Although large enough to be a bear, something about the way it moved was definitely not bear-like.

Lori tried to shift her brain into gear. It was probably a feral dog, but even stronger was the impression that what he fought was a gorilla, for its forearms were long, and she it had clawed fingers, not paws, but even that was not precise. Its mouth was long, a snout, with sharp, visible teeth, now stained with blood.

Gaining leverage, Byron kicked the creature, and it went flying high into the air, landing with a thud and a yelp close to where Lori stood. For an instant it stood, then turned on two solid legs. Slowly its gigantic head turned, its nostrils flaring as it caught her scent. Crimson blood dripped from its fangs.

It took a step toward her. Then another.

Unarmed, vulnerable, Lori turned and ran blindly back toward the faerie ring leaping the mushrooms and entering it. The creature followed, but stopped outside the mushroom barrier as if it had run into a brick wall. Ugly, vicious teeth snapped so close she could almost reach out and touch them, but the monster would not enter the ring. Her heart thudded. She hadn't run that far, but she had never felt such terror.

Facing her, growling, it dropped down to all fours, but she was certain it ran on two legs with long arms hanging down, with clawed fingers curled under. Its eyes were black on black, without a discernible iris and pupil, and it snarled, trying to get at her, only to slam again into that invisible force field, marked by red-capped mushrooms.

"Byron--"

He sounded breathless and in pain. "You're safe in the faerie ring."

He knelt, his back to her, huddled into himself as if without the ability to stand. Her heart thudded high in her throat, her breath came in loud, staccato pants. "No, I mean, are you alright?"

He struggled to his feet, turned slowly to face her with his left arm cradled in his right. She could see no sign of his wounds, but he limped forward slowly.

"Lori, I need you to listen to what I say."

She nodded, moving left, then right, the beast shadowing her but still unable to cross the invisible barrier.

"I'm going to draw it off. Stay in the ring."

"No. Don't leave me." She couldn't bear the thought of him alone with the monster, hurt or even killed while she waited in safety.

While it concentrated on Lori, Bryon retrieved a stout branch, and somehow, for she couldn't see a match or a torch, set it ablaze. He swung it with deadly accuracy, and the creature snarled, retreated, and finally disappeared altogether.

He watched for a while longer, sniffing the air before he spoke. "You can come out now. It's safe."

"It's gone?"

"Yes." He bent down, rubbed the stick in the dirt until the flame died, then covered it with soil to prevent it from it reigniting. Seconds later, he pulled his shirt from his shoulders and wrapped the shredded material around his forearm.

"You're hurt."

"It's no matter. I'll be healed momentarily." He grinned, showing no residual effects from his battle, beyond a make-shift bandaged arm, and rapid breathing.

Lori stepped through the mushrooms, moving to his side. "We've got to get that looked at."

"No, really, it's fine. From this wound I will heal." He turned toward the faerie ring and bowed, low. "For the sanctuary you offered my lady, I humbly thank you." There was no mocking in his words, and she knew something had stopped that monster, preventing it from attacking her, for the creature had been unable to enter the faerie ring.

Lori took her cue from him. "For the second time in almost as many minutes, I find I must apologize for barging into your sanctuary, but you have my honest and sincere thanks for your protection."

She found she was trembling from eyelashes to toes, residual from the attack she hadn't felt while the creature had fought Byron. He wrapped his good arm around her, held her tightly until the worst of her tremors subsided.

"What was that thing? It couldn't have been a dog." She was certain of that, although she let her voice inflection rise on the last word, making it a question.

"You don't have to worry. It's gone now, I promise. And while they have been known to travel in packs, there seemed to be only one this afternoon."

Lori put her hands on his shoulders, her eyes wide. She had a hundred questions, a thousand. "How badly are you hurt? Have you seen that thing before? Should we call someone? How did the faerie ring stop it?"

Byron stopped her the most expedient way possible. Abruptly, he pressed her against a broad, stout sugar maple, his body bridging hers, his arms on either side of her, his hands resting on the bark. That didn't matter in the slightest, for he moved his hips forward and their bodies touched. Through the heavy material of his worn jeans, she felt the hard length of his interest. He moved closer, then back again, letting a small distance appear between them, before sliding back against her. Lori breathed deeply, all her senses at the highest alert.

The air, clean, cold, and smelling of pine only a few moments before, sizzled and smelled of musk, lilacs, and fresh strawberries.

"Hush," he whispered, inching his lips toward hers. "Shhh."

She hadn't been about to speak, had no idea why he was trying to shush her for her brain was too busy processing sensations to form words or even thoughts. Warmth surrounded her, like blankets, fireplaces and life-giving sunlight, and the air now smelled of lust.

Lori allowed herself be charmed, knowing as she leaned her slender back against the rough bark of the broad trunk tree, that it was her decision. Beyond the clear seduction, any time she wanted, she could push him away. She had done it before, and the knowing gave her power, not to escape, but to submit.

Within this magic moment deep in a dappled forest she only wanted him near with a compulsion she could not understand. She wanted to be absorbed by him, swallowed as she had swallowed tea, taken completely until there was no difference between them. Her pulse, which had spiked with the creature's attack, had no time to relax, for with his lips against hers, it started tripping again.

"Byron," she whispered, the name sounding foreign and distant, her mind sluggish, as if as her sensations had become heightened from his nearness, and her mind had slipped into neutral. "By—"

"Let me," he said, pleading, as if she had the fortitude to deny him anything. "I only want a taste."

Lori rested her forehead against his shoulder while his arms wrapped around her back. His hands became restless, caressing her from shoulders to buttocks, igniting fires of passion everywhere he touched, molded, massaged.

She breathed deeply, and found within the strawberries and lust the clean, honest-work male scent of soil and sweat was pleasant. If he had been bitten by the monstrous black creature, and she was certain he had, the wound no longer bothered him. She must have given him a subliminal clue for with her arms wrapped against the strength of his back, they danced with primal movements of ancient mating.

In slow motion, he lowered his lips, dragging out the time between the start of his gentle assault and the first incredible touch. Silently, he met her glance, and in the black on copper of his pupils and irises, she read many questions and she answered all of them with a nod. *Yes, I'm ready. I think I've always been waiting for this.*

Lori's hunger grew. Her lids drifted open again, only to find him slightly out of focus, as if too close or not close enough. During the battle her eyes had also been unreliable. Too much of what she had seen, or thought she had seen, was impossible. When she could think again, maybe she'd consider getting glasses.

When he had fought, there had been something savage about him, as if his humanity was a carefully developed shield he dropped when faced with danger. She had been frightened, for him, and by him, but now her emotions were totally different.

This assault she welcomed.

CHAPTER 10

Hungry for his taste, desperate for his touch, Lori wound her hands along the broad muscles of his arms to his shoulders, then with single-minded intensity dug her fingers into his firm muscles.

"Byron—"

As her body responded, all she could think of was the contrasts of hard and soft. She found him such a delightful hodgepodge of contradictions. His lips were softer than anything she could imagine. The closest she could come was 'kindness' but instinctively she recognized there was no kindness in him, so that analysis had to be wrong. And hard: his muscles, the strength of his jaw, the intensity with which he matched her kisses.

Her heart pumped with increasing fervor, doing more than moving blood and oxygen. It was as if her heart were connected to his, and because of their union of lips, her blood heated, setting her on fire from the inside. She burned out of control, but without pain. Light and heat consumed her. It occurred to her his kiss was the most incredible aphrodisiac she had ever experienced. Within this seductive form of internal combustion she could easily die of happiness.

Ripples of pleasure traveled through every secret inch of her. Her skin became sensitized, throbbing for his touch, and Byron kept his hands busy: touching her cheeks, her eyelids, her shoulders, her breasts, everywhere. The terror she had felt when the beast attacked mutated. Her emotions didn't lessen in intensity, but they changed, from overriding fear to unbelievable, undeniable pleasure.

Lori kept her eyes shut, but that didn't stop rainbows of colors from flashing against her lids. She thought she saw, a beast of incredible majesty flap his wings, take to the sky. A beast, but unidentifiable. Too many of her senses were locked on the new experiences surging through her to give attention to transitory visions.

She did not know Byron. He remained a stranger to her. At the moment he was a half-naked man who might have saved her life from a monster, who believed faeries built rings around trees and tea solved all the world's aches, but she did not know anything about him.

No, Lori corrected herself silently, there was something significant she did know about him: he kissed like the devil.

She couldn't get enough. Her mouth fed hungrily. He made her ache in her breasts and her pulse points. Kissing him became a food and she was starved for. At his lips she fed. And Lori realized something else. She wanted more than intimacy with him; she wanted everything.

Byron spoke her name, gave it an odd inflection, making it sound regal, making her feel honored, then he spoke a word or two in a language she didn't recognize. The draconic image solidified behind her eyelids and the majestic creature bowed, lowering its wings and its long sinuous neck. She felt cherished. Too many dates from her past had only taken, or groped, or followed a hidden agenda, so this experience was new and heady, even if only imaginary. Perhaps it was only the result of the pressure of his lips against hers, the transmutation of fear into adrenaline, and likely the lack of oxygen to her brain.

Her emotions swirled kaleidoscope fashion, until she found it impossible to settle on one. Lust was there, the driving force for all the rest including daring, pleasure, enchantment, and a trace of something silly which tickled her, tapped into her whimsy. While she felt trapped by his kiss, by his proximity, she also felt liberated.

She giggled, raising her chin, letting her pleasure escape into the late afternoon forest. That provided him exposure to the long, white expanse of her throat. Byron bit and the rough abrasion of his teeth against her skin created a thousand sensuous impressions each more improbable and more erotic than the last. Lori had never felt so bold, never wanted to experience the whole man as much as with this copper eyed stranger with lean hips and massive shoulders and a mouth that tasted like sin.

"I've got things to do," Byron said, the sound rumbling from deep in his throat. Before Lori could analyze the statement to decide if it meant he shouldn't be kissing her because he should be about other more important assignments, or he meant he was working on the only major task he had left unfinished, his lips connected with hers again.

She had never known such pleasure.

Throughout, he kept her pinned against the bark, imprisoning her with his quivering hips and his mouth which both promised and delivered paradise. She could have been floating ten feet in the air for all the awareness she had of her personal space: she knew only pleasure not location.

He cupped the cheeks of her buttocks, used his talented fingers to knead her flesh until she felt boneless. His hands were firm, experienced. He knew what he was doing and the effect was not lost on her. She wiggled her hips back and forth, found it impossible to remain still under this charged sexual massage.

"You've got too many clothes on," she whispered, her fingers at the snap of his jeans. She smelled lust wrapped in sweat, rich planting soil…and tea.

He scratched his roughly stubbled chin against her cheek. She laughed again, moved her jaw deliberately so the experience could be repeated.

"In all the centuries, never once," he said, "never once," not finishing the sentence, not leaving her a functioning brain cell to even realize she had no idea what he muttered. If this passion was the anticipated result of the assault, she would silently pray for another beast to appear nightly.

The dense forest canopy added an uncivilized dimension to the seduction answering an unspoken need in her. Primitive peoples had always called to her on some instinctive layer, and only now, with his hips rubbing desperately against hers, did she understand why.

He was not a man who would make reservations at a five star restaurant, dress in black evening wear, approve the wine with a small, analyzing sip, ask for an aperitif, a soup course. This was a caveman who would take what he wanted in the forest, and leave them both breathless because of it. She had been taught 'savage' was less attractive than 'civilized', but now, wrapped in molten lava, Lori realized she had that notion backwards. If she could rewrite her doctorial thesis, perhaps she would now arrive at different conclusions. One sensual assault and her universe had shifted.

Eager to please him as thoroughly as he pleasured her, she rubbed the contours of his ears, felt his forehead and the ridges of his eyebrows. She found him familiar, as if her hands knew the route from extended practice, as if they had been doing this for ever so long.

"We've got to stop," he said, "before I cannot stop." She admired his honesty and strength, for at the moment she had neither. It didn't matter that it was too cold for what she wanted, or they were in the middle of a forest and whatever attacked him might return without warning. She had few lovers in her past, but she was used to lovemaking on sheets in uninterrupted privacy, unless a roommate, pounding on the wall, yelled an abrupt, "cut it out, you're rocking the pictures off the walls."

"Lori? Lori, are you all right?"

It took more than a moment to rub her fingers against her own face, as if by her movements she could recapture the magic. It took even longer to regulate her breathing and force her eyes to focus. Her sight was unreliable from the kiss-induced traces of the monster she could not recall, except it was of an ancient age, and not human, nor even mortal. It was a lovely fantasy, aided and abetted by his embrace.

"You're not still frightened, are you?"

"Frightened?" He had not been rough only thorough, and by the same token, incomplete. She must have lowered her brows, started to form her question, for he explained.

"Of the ... dog."

She had not forgotten the hairy black creature, but instead started thinking of it kindly, as if it alone was the catalyst for this kiss.

Her eyes twinkled. "No. I'm not afraid of the dog." She would use his word, although they both knew the monster had been no dog. If she were afraid, it was only that he wouldn't kiss her again and she would have only memory to bring passion to life.

He shifted, removed his hands from the tree. His lips were swollen. It pleased her to know she had held her own during the kiss. It empowered her to see the tangible proof.

"Can you stand, on your feet I mean?"

The only thing keeping her upright was the support from that tree, and she wanted to carve something into its bark, the date, then some obscure "It happened here," coming generations would read wondering what disaster or miracle occurred, and never come close to understanding its magnitude. It happened here. Yes, that would work, even if what had happened between his lips and hers was only a prelude.

"Am I still breathing?" she asked.

He smiled, devilish, a grin of self-satisfaction and male superiority. "Yes. Did you think you had stopped?"

"I think while kissing you, I didn't need air, for—" she let the statement fade.

Sound returned to the forest, the symphony of hidden birds, the drone of distant insects and the chattering of warm blooded creatures with four legs and long tails. It was comforting, especially when she thought on how much an animal's vocal expressions were deliberate seduction techniques. She was not the only one looking for a mate.

"You're hurt. You should get to a doctor." She would drive him herself. It was a small car. She would be compassionate, as she pumped him for information starting with his birth, working from there. She would learn all his hidden secrets, make sure she faced no rival for his affections.

He didn't give his forearm a glance. "I will be fine."

"Aunt Jan will blame me if your wound gets infected."

Laughing, Byron shook his head. "Jan will know where to place blame. She won't be pleased if her garden is not tilled."

"She can't expect you to work after you've been bitten by a…" she paused, made sure he knew she used his word, "… dog."

He stretched, a movement a bird might make when straightening its feathers. "I'm made of sterner stuff. Are you ready to go back?"

Back? Her eyes glazed as her anticipation rose, but she realized almost as quickly he meant the Inn, the safety of walls, floors, doors, not back to the magical fantasy where he had transported her when his lips seduced hers.

Lori could not be sure of anything, especially whether or not she wanted to face her aunt while still experiencing residuals of what had to be the most explosive kiss on record. "Will you be there?"

He shook his head, shrugged. His long hair was tousled, and she wondered if she were responsible for some of that sexy look. "Tonight, if I can make it. Now I've got to finish the garden, but you should return."

Lori found herself listening with extreme concentration. Was he adding the tiniest push to the sentence, making it a command? It didn't matter. She tested her powers as a woman. "I'm not ready to leave yet. I've still got some things I need to think through."

She met his gaze, hoping for approval or even better, a match to rekindle flame. She wished she'd dressed more provocatively, for even hiking gear could be seductive, but the clothing she wore had been selected for comfort not enticement. Her heart still tripped, and her pulse showed no sign of slowing, not while Byron stayed close. "If it's safe, I'd like to walk a while longer."

He touched her, gently, the fingertips only of his ravaged left hand to her swollen lips. "Take your time. It won't be true dark for another few hours, but mind, before the sun starts to set, I want you inside."

"Why?"

He grinned. "The temperature drops."

Lori recognized the lie, but because it was Byron, she would accept his fantasy.

She reached out, brushing dirt and debris from his chest. He rolled on the ground when he'd fought the creature, and had been dirty even before that.

"I've forgotten the way."

The copper returned to his eyes as the gold faded. "Whenever you come to a fork, keep to the right. That will see you back to the Inn."

Lori rubbed her lips yet again, knew the action bulls-eyed when she noticed his nostrils flair, his pupils dilate.

"Is it dangerous to take the left fork?" After that kiss, she was ready to experience a little danger.

He leaned forward, brushing his nose against hers. "If I told you yes, would you try it, just to spite me?"

She grinned, felt daring. This afternoon, after being attacked by a monster and perhaps kissed by one, anything was possible. "Probably."

"You're not likely to find another faerie ring to give you sanctuary, and I might not be around."

"The creature wasn't after me." Of this she was certain. While it had chased her, she knew it had only been because she had been available.

She lowered her eyes, returned to her earlier investigation of his naked chest, pleased when she realized his breathing wasn't quite regular. His muscles stood out in sharp definition, his stomach washboard flat, his hips narrow. There was a trace of hair on his chest, and a darker mark on his left shoulder she suspected was a scar. He cupped her chin, raised her eyes until they met his. "Just because it wasn't after you this time doesn't mean it won't be next time. I've put my scent on you."

"Byron, should I be frightened?"

Around them the forest cackled. He tilted his head, his eyes losing focus as he listened to something she could not hear. Grasping her hand, Byron pulled Lori away from that lifeline of a tree, forcing her to stand. "I've changed my mind. I don't want you wandering alone. Get back as quickly as possible, for there are things in this forest even I do not wish to face after dark."

She nodded, stepped closer. There were things she would like to face tonight, even if this fragile relationship between them was moving too quickly.

"Will I see you for dinner?" She licked her lips, watched a muscle at the side of his neck throb. Pleased with his unconscious response, Lori reached out, touched him on his forearm, above the wrapped shirt.

"I'll make tea tonight. It will help you sleep."

It wasn't exactly sleep she was craving—or tea—but Lori let him go. "Just keep to the right forks." Byron turned away with that warning ringing in her ears, and ignoring his own advice took a left-hand fork. He whistled, swinging his narrow hips in a devil-may-care swagger, which had her hungry all over again. He still wore his shirt wrapped around his left arm, but gave no indication at all the wound underneath the makeshift bandage pained him.

Lori stood paralyzed for all of ten seconds after he disappeared into the overgrowth, while she imagined she could still sense him. Then, she started for her aunt's home with a spring to her step. She remembered how he had tasted when she kissed him.

Yes, maybe she could get used to tea after all.

CHAPTER 11

Byron hesitated as he pushed through the brush, his hands on the branches. He smelled blood. The air was tainted with it, sweet and familiar, and just a bit off. Something had been attacked and killed here. His fingers twitched, preparatory for the changes mutating through his body. Well, whatever it was, he wasn't going to catch it unawares.

He made enough noise so whatever was there would be aware of him. Lori wasn't around and he would not be so vulnerable this time.

He concentrated, and his body changed, his neck elongated, his teeth grew pointed, and on his back, high at his shoulders, ridges appeared, rapidly transforming into wings. The talons at his fingers sharpened, coiled. Seconds later he stood eighteen feet high, a massive golden dragon.

He stomped through the brush, bellowing his roar of dominance with no need for stealth. As a dragon, he really did like to make an entrance.

Arthur stood over the start of a bonfire, heavy black smoke rising through the canopy overhead, the blaze weak; it hadn't really caught yet. He used his sword as a poker, attempting to keep the fire alive.

"Ah, Old One. I've been expecting you." He laughed, looked down at the pitiful blaze and back to the dragon. "I suppose as a point of honor, you want a piece of this?"

The dragon sniffed the air, and Arthur moved back as a rush of liquid fire caused the pyre to explode in a massive burn. Byron recognized the scent, little needing the question or the answer. *What have you got*

"Garntz. Five of them. One got away, but it returned five minutes ago. I've added it to the collection."

With a thought, the dragon disappeared and Bryon faced the old man. "I was with someone. I wasn't able to kill it."

"Without giving away too many secrets? So, she really is Jan's niece?"

"Yes." Frustrated, he ran his hands through his hair. "I still haven't figured out if I should roast her or—"

"Kiss her senseless?" Arthur finished.

"Then you saw?"

Arthur rubbed the blade on the grass then sheathed it with the efficient movement of someone who has done the same hundreds of times. "I was looking for the fifth. I have no need to spy on you."

"Aye. My Lord, she is—"

Byron studied the flames, the red, blues and golds burning together in their ballet of destruction. As a dragon, fire was his element. He sighed, the sound long, drawn out. "There is no need to tell me what she is. I know she is a mortal. And I know the curse of my kind."

Arthur straightened, shifted the weapon at his side, more an excuse to avoid looking at Byron than to find a more comfortable position for it. "Actually, if I may be so bold, the curse of all mankind as well."

"I think not with the same degree. But my heart is not engaged."

"Is it not?"

"I will walk away before it comes to that."

Arthur straightened, his voice becoming mechanical as he recited something stolen from darkest antiquity. "Should one of the Old Ones mate with a partner not his species, his lifeforce will be drained by the very one he's come to love."

"I have not come to love her."

"No?"

Byron recalled the kiss, doubted he would ever forget it. "She is a wizard. I know enough to keep away from those who practice dark arts."

Arthur chuckled, realizing he was nearing an arbitrary non-interference line between them. "Not all wizards are evil."

"Enough that the remaining few good stand no chance. I will walk away from her."

"Will you?"

"I must. The Caretaker has already warned me off her."

"Jan would welcome you to the family. I think it's what she wants, a way to carry on the bloodline."

"And you would know, because you've had such success with bloodlines yourself."

Arthur grimaced, acknowledging the hit. "I had a wife I loved but no child from that union. Have you ever thought how different history would have been if she'd been able to give me a son?"

"The fates are rarely kind."

A nod. "It is why over the years I have decided I have no reason to live."

The bodies of the monsters coiled in the flames, their destruction both grotesque and oddly beautiful. "There is always a reason to live."

Although Arthur did not kneel, he shifted in supplication, approached the dragon who now walked as a man. "Ancient One, while you are strong, kill me, I beg you."

"I have done enough killing."

He pulled his sword, the action quick and instinctive. He stuck the blade into one of the burning garntz, the black creature that hunted this mountain for those it could slaughter, the action so smooth as to almost give lie to his words. "I have not the strength to do it myself. The years weigh heavy."

Byron laughed, seeing irony. "Many years I would have gladly killed you. You should have asked me then. Now, I'm starting to like you. I could almost call you friend."

"It is not your friendship I want."

"You were given immortality for a reason. I do not know what it was, but perhaps the purpose has not yet come to light. And," he said, looking down at the carcasses slowly disintegrating, "you have your uses."

"Killing garntz? You or any number of your allies could do as much. I thought that was fairly obvious. Although now I'm destroying any evidence. Still, the battle would have gone better if I'd had Excalibur."

Byron chuckled. "Although I confess friendship, I don't feel with you is its safest location."

He rubbed the sword hilt, the action just short of a caress. "It is my heart. My soul."

"Be thankful you have a soul."

"I kept it safe for almost two thousand years."

"Now I keep it safe. But what are you doing in the forest? You could not have known the garntz would be hunting tonight?"

Arthur stepped back out of the smoke and rubbed his beard. "Jan wanted me to check on the garden. You know how she worries when she can't break away to see for herself."

Byron pulled the branch and started poking the fire himself, his laughter ringing around the clearing. "So, Jan actually spoke to you?"

"No, alright, no. But I know her well enough to know she is worried about her garden."

"I have never let her down."

"And I will pay repentance as long as I live."

"Which should be a couple more centuries. The Good has need of you yet."

"No. I'm tired. I was hoping—"

"To kill yourself against garntz teeth?"

"Yes."

"Lucky you are too trained a fighter. Five would be hardly enough to do you in. Not when you have slaughtered mature fighting dragons."

"Never as many as my reputation claims. And no longer."

"Now if you've nothing else pressing—" Byron said, then a full five seconds later the dragon stood, *I've got to see to the garden. You may tell Jan I am making progress*

With a slow gait borne more of depression than weariness, Arthur turned away. "I'll leave you to your work." He rubbed his sword hilt, and his soul felt unsatisfied.

CHAPTER 12

Looking down the basement stairs, Lori couldn't see anything. It was that black. The kitchen was empty when she arrived, no bubbling cauldron, no rows of fruit recently preserved. Her aunt was nowhere to be seen. At first she was annoyed, because she wanted to share her happiness. Then she was concerned Aunt Jan did not answer her call. Now she felt a creeping tinge of panic: the door to the downstairs stood open.

Andrew, she thought as fear ripped through her. Gathering her courage, Lori hoovered at the opened door, her knuckles white against the frame. She had no idea what she faced, a staircase or a Black Hole into the abyss, even some temporal distortion that might lead to the Cheshire Cat and Wonderland. What would she do there? Nibble on cupcakes? Swallow potions labeled "Drink Me?"

The feeling of danger and evil swamped her. Her pulse raced, she could feel her heart throbbing in her fingers, hear it as if it were magnified, loud enough to curse Edgar Allen Poe. Lori coughed, found it difficult to breathe.

"Aunt Jan?"

The words were swallowed. She had no sense that the noise traveled further than her vocal chords or her own ears. She remembered the kiss on her forehead, given when she had first arrived. How long did that protection last? Did it have an expiration date? Had no one thought to kiss her Aunt Jan on top of the head? Would she forever grieve because she had thoughtlessly avoided protection so vitally important?

Unlike the vacant kitchen, there was a sharp, distinct odor coming from the blackness at the bottom of the stairs, where jokingly Byron had mentioned there were monsters chained. Lori found the scent dank and vile, and had no idea if that were her imagination or reality.

"Aunt Jan?" Why wasn't there an echo? "Aunt Jan?"

Something moved toward her, black and indistinct, and Lori filled her lungs with air, preparing to let out an ear shattering scream when her aunt appeared coming up the steep stairs, wiping her hands on her apron. "Goodness, child, what happened? You look like you've seen a ghost."

She hugged her, spontaneously, relieved, yet still fighting residuals which had caused her heart to thump. "I'm sorry. I got spooked." She held her tightly, rested her head against her chest. "I know it sounds silly."

"Not silly at all, child." Jan broke the embrace, but before she could get away, Lori reached out, cupped the back of her neck, so she could kiss her on the top of her head.

"You must have been really frightened."

"I thought I felt something." Left-over adrenaline still pulsed through her.

Jan tightened her eyes and looked around the kitchen, as if about to give a tongue-lashing to the refrigerator for acting up or to the ovens for annoying her. She shook her head slightly at an empty corner as if to say, "I'm not done with you yet," but then she turned toward her niece with a friendly smile.

"It's not silly at all. This house can sometimes be daunting. I can't tell you how many times when I first moved in that I felt something watching me."

"Something evil?" Lori asked.

"Something without my best interests at heart," Jan answered. "Let's save the word 'evil' for times when it's appropriate. It doesn't lose its force that way. Also, and it's important you know this, true evil cannot enter this house without an invitation. Now I can see beyond this kitchen something is bothering you. What happened?"

Lori moved, surprised now at how friendly the kitchen felt, how welcoming. She remembered the assault in the forest; she would not belittle it and call it simply a kiss.

"Before you start your tale, let me scrub my hands and change my apron. Then I can put on the kettle, and dig out some of those cheese Danish from breakfast."

Courageous now that she felt safe, and embarrassed she had overreacted, Lori waited until Jan had her back turned, water running and soap bubbling over her hands before she inched toward the basement steps, reaching for the doorknob.

Lori jumped, startled, as a hand rested on her shoulder. "Now child, I don't think there's anything down there to interest you."

She swallowed, tried to come up with something not a lie, but which wasn't the truth either, a middle of the road excuse. "I would like to see more of the house."

"Another time might be better. I've already got the kettle on."

"What's downstairs, Aunt Jan?"

"Dust and cobwebs and jars of canned fruit no one got around to eating."

"Are there monsters?"

"Brew really should have his mouth washed out with soap. If there were monsters down there, why were you so spooked up here? No, don't answer that. Come," and gently, but firmly enough so she offered no resistance, Jan directed her to the table. She pulled out the chair she'd been using. "Sit. I'll serve the tea."

"Byron said he would make tea."

Jan dipped her head in acknowledgement, considering implications. "Something must have happened. He's rarely that generous with me."

Lori kept her eye on the doorknob to the basement, as if something would creep up if she didn't maintain her vigil. "Is there anything that could hurt me in this house?"

"What kind of absurd question is that? You haven't been afraid when I've been here."

"Please just answer the question. If you had come to my apartment, I would say, 'feel at home, there's nothing that could hurt you.' Can you say the same here?"

"I run a bed and breakfast. As long as you are with me, and under my protection, you'll be safe."

"Under your protection?" Lori tried to digest the odd codicil. She thought again of the coldness of the doorknob, coldness which hadn't been present when Jan was on the stairs.

"Perhaps I misspoke." She ran water from the sink into an old fashioned, heavy, whistle-type tea kettle. "You will be safe as long as you are a guest in this house. You have my vow."

"But in this house there are things which might do me harm, or might not have my best interests at heart," she insisted, feeling peevish.

The kettle whistled, loud and shrill. Jan poured water into the fat blue teapot and the familiar tang of summer rose gardens scented the air. "Tea is ready. Why don't you tell me what happened on your walk." Jan brought Danish to the table, as well as the huge mugs she had seen at dinner when she first arrived.

"I want the dragon teapot." She hated sounding petulant, but her annoyance was finding form.

"That will have to wait Dear. I can't serve dragon tea without Byron's approval. This is rose hip tea. Very good for you. It has all kinds of vitamins, and a lovely taste. Sip, tell me what you think."

And Lori let herself be distracted, from her interest in the basement, from her fears, imaginary or not about the house.

"It's delicious."

"I thought you would think so. Now, you wanted to tell me something, I believe?"

"Byron kissed me."

"Saint's alive. Did he now?"

She cupped her aunt's hands in her own. "I don't have words to explain it. It was wonderful. You can't imagine what it was like."

"Aye, lass, I'll be betting that's the truth."

"My fingers are still tingling. My toes are still curled." She laughed again, enraptured, stood and twirled unrestrained. "I never thought a kiss, a single kiss, could have such an incredible impact."

Kindly, firmly, Jan grasped her, returning her to her kitchen chair. "Well then, why don't you start at the beginning? I thought the monster was out harrowing my garden for me."

Lori read no connotation into the word 'monster' beyond a light endearment. "Byron was working in your garden. I'm sure he was, for he was smattered with dirt when I met him. His shirt was off and he was covered in sweat." She supposed in retrospect, that was the catalyst, sweat and naked pectorals. What an incredible aphrodisiac. Add his boyish charm as well, maybe not believing in faeries so much as spilling their yarn … of course she had been more than ready for his kiss.

Jan busied herself at the stove, her back turned, pulling out who knew what from cabinets and drawers and hidden fastnesses. "A dragon's usually so fastidious about its appearance," she continued, speaking over her shoulder. "So, tell me more. I can see you're aching to, and if I have to whack him on the snout for misbehavior, I'd rather have all my facts straight."

Lori chewed over that, enjoying the image it evoked: Jan, a rolled-up newspaper in her hands, doing battle against Byron, treating him like some misbehaving puppy. Lori felt her own jubilation rise a notch. She would set the stage, enjoy her afternoon a second time. "I was walking alone in the forest when I stepped into a faerie ring."

Jan reached for a towel, drying her hands. She turned back, leaned against the sink, and raised an inquisitive eyebrow. "And lived to tell about it?"

"A faerie ring? You know faerie rings?"

"A bit," Jan replied dryly.

Lori giggled. She'd been in school far too long, had forgotten girlish chats and laughter, and more importantly, giggling. But she remembered. Byron hadn't been laughing when she stepped into the ring, hadn't been teasing or taunting. He'd been serious and oddly respectful when he refused to enter the ring himself. She sobered a notch, tried to recall if she had missed some vital fact or put a lighthearted spin on something important. She felt the need to defend herself, knowing as she did so ignorance was no excuse. "Byron said I was in no danger, but did make me apologize."

Jan replaced the towel on a hook beside one of the ovens. "So that's what brought him in from the garden."

"What?"

"Faeries can be noisy when their rings are disturbed. You didn't knock down any of the mushrooms, did you?"

"No, I stepped over them."

"Always your best bet when wandering into a faerie ring. They may be small, but they always find a way to revenge even imagined slights. A faerie can carry a grudge for centuries."

Lori lowered her brow and she tweaked her head to an odd angle, trying to make sense of where this conversation had gotten off-track. "A grudge?" was all Lori could think to ask.

"Not that faeries are ever really malicious, like some creatures. They are more jokesters, putting salt in the sugar bowl, that kind of thing, but it can get pretty annoying when it goes on for so many years you reach for the salt shaker when you need a tablespoon of sugar. I can't tell you the number of pies I've ruined."

"Aunt Jan, what are we talking about?"

Jan laughed, and the talk, heading toward too-serious suddenly lightened again. "I believe you were telling me why Brew kissed you. We left off when you stepped into a faerie ring."

"Then we were attacked by a monster, or rather Byron was attacked."

Jan sat down heavily beside her, her expression suddenly haggard. "Do describe the monster."

Lori shivered. So much had happened since, she tried hard to remember what it had looked like. "It was black and gorilla-like, but it wasn't a gorilla. At first I couldn't determine if it were a wild dog or a bear. That was what I expected to see, something normal which might conceivably be in a forest. But instead I think it was a person in some kind of Halloween costume."

"Why do you say that?"

She added her revised impressions of the beast walking upright, of the long-fingered hands complete with opposable thumbs. Still, a person in a costume didn't quite fit. Had it been she was certain Byron would have treated it differently, laughed it off, spoken of mountain-men, drug addicts or something along those lines. He fought it like a wild animal. Besides, there were other facets of the creature which didn't add up to the costume theory: the way it snarled curling its upper lip to expose fangs, the way it left a bite mark on Byron's arm not from human teeth.

"I was frightened." She was professionally trained, gave estimates of height and weight, added descriptions of how hair had hung low from its chin in a gross goatee, how it had rumbled as it moved.

"And did Brew do anything? Anything unusual?"

"What could he have done which was so unusual?" Lori asked.

Jan rubbed her hands on her apron, nervous now, for her hands were clean and dry. "Mercy, with that man, anything's possible. Still, I'm listening. Finish your story."

"He fought it off with a burning branch."

"That's always best. Garntz don't like fire. Was he hurt?"

"Garntz? You know what it was?"

"Sure, just a type of wild dog which runs around here." Jan looked Lori directly in the eye, as if to underscore her sincerity.

"Garntz are wild dogs?" she said it with disbelief, adding, "and they walk upright, and have thumbs?"

"You didn't answer my question. Was Brew hurt?"

"He was bitten on the arm. It didn't seem to bother him. I couldn't get him to go to a doctor."

"Well, he'll be in a mood when he appears, but I suppose it could be much worse. He doesn't use his foreclaws for tilling."

"Aunt Jan, what are you talking about?"

"Nothing much, except I doubt I'll ever taste dragon tea again, although how he could blame this on me, I have no idea. Rest assured, he will. That boy can hold a snit a good long time. Still, as I believe I mentioned a second before, it could have been much worse. And you weren't hurt?"

"No, I hid in the faerie ring."

"Not something I would have suggested, but it seems to have done you no harm. Now I suppose I'll have to make them some caramel apples, for the inconvenience."

"Make who caramel apples?"

"The faeries. It's their favorite."

Lori shook her head. This conversation was going from weird to weirder, without much of a pause. "You've actually seen faeries?"

"Of course. There are days when you can't move around here without tripping over a dozen. Especially when I'm making caramel apples, but that's neither here nor there. So, I take it that's when Byron kissed you?"

"Yes, and it was magnificent."

"I think perhaps I'm not keeping that boy busy enough. I may have to think up some additional chores. As if I haven't got enough to do. And I suppose I'll have to think up some work for you as well, to keep you out of trouble."

"Will I get in trouble if Byron kisses me?" The thought had possibilities.

Aunt Jan laughed, a sharp pulsing expletive. "More trouble than you can imagine, and I don't mean something which can be solved as easily with caramel apples, either."

"I'm an adult now. I can handle myself around men."

"I think if you believe that, you're a shade too naive to stay here. I might have to send you packing."

"Oh, Aunt Jan, you wouldn't do that, would you? I know I've been a bother, and undoubtedly more trouble than I'm worth, but really, don't send me away, not yet. Not until I know more about Byron and the way he kisses. Has he had a lot of women?"

Jan reached under a cabinet, pulled out a large bag of sugar and ferreted around all sorts of cabinets for a pot until she found one which pleased her. "There's two ways I could answer that. Byron with women, huh? Well, to answer the question I'm sure you're asking: no. For all he's good looking as a human, I doubt he's been with many women at all."

Lori sighed, long and dreamy. "Then how'd he learn to kiss like that?"

"That," Jan said with a huff, "is something I don't even want to speculate about. Now help me," Jan said, and proceeded to keep Lori so busy she couldn't even formulate questions, let alone ask any.

Two hours later, Jan set the last of the caramel apples down on a sheet of waxed paper. She looked pleased with herself.

"Can I have one?" Lori asked.

"No, I need every one."

"Twenty-five?"

"Well, faeries are odd creatures, and like their treats in odd numbers." Jan handed her the all but empty pot she'd used for the caramel, and the spoon, and Lori had to be content with licking those. "I'm not sure they actually eat them. From what I've seen it's more likely they roll on them, covering their bodies and their wings with sticky sweetness, and then there's this massive org—well, we'll call it a party. Best to stay out of the forest tonight, not that I was going to let you go anyway. I suppose it's dark enough now." She lifted the tray. "I want you to take this to the stump in the backyard. You know the stump?"

"Yes, sure."

"Just leave it there."

"And the faeries will come get them?"

"Never knew a faerie who could ignore a caramel apple. You hurry right back inside, ok?"

"Sure."

"And Lori," Jan said as Lori was slipping into her jacket and heading for the back door, "better leave through the front."

She grumbled about taking the long route. Why go all the way around the massive house when the back door stood a good three feet from her and offered a more direct route, Lori had no idea, but she grabbed the tray of caramel apples and obeyed.

It was dusk, and the colors were fading into shades of gray when Lori set the treats down on the stump. She wasn't sure if the temperature had dropped, or if the chill she felt was from the breeze, for a strident wind had picked up. She shivered, zipping her jacket closed to the neck, but the action didn't bring comfort. Lori felt she was being watched.

"These are from my Aunt Jan," she said to the forest, and the rattling trees, and whatever else might be listening. "But I want to thank you again, first for not taking offense when I bundled into your faerie ring, second for offering me your protection. I hope you enjoy your apples."

It was almost completely dark, even the stars were keeping their distance, and she started to feel uneasy. As she headed back for the house, something small darted under her feet, the size of one of the blind kittens, but it was no kitten. Although Lori didn't get a good look at it, it was reptilian and scaly, and disappeared under some rocks. When Lori straightened from almost falling from surprise and nearly stepping on the creature, she realized she was no longer alone.

"Good evening."

The words, sounding friendly from connotation, were grated and rough and when the shock wore off that she had company, she knew her idea of a good evening and this interloper's would be two completely different things.

"Good evening," Lori responded. She squinted, trying to determine through the misty dark who spoke. For a second she thought she imagined the voice, for she didn't see anyone, just the house a few dozen yards in front of her, the forest and the stump behind her, and the rattling of tree branches, which seemed much louder than before.

"Hello?" Lori called out, about to dismiss the greeting as a fabrication of her imagination, when she noticed movement, and the stranger slowly came into focus. She didn't so much move closer physically as it seemed like Lori's eyes were finally able to bring the image into clearer view. Her caller was an older woman, late seventies to early eighties probably, but in this age of face creams and cosmetic surgery, who could tell with any degree of accuracy?

She was dressed plainly in some type of woven gray slacks, that might have been wool, and a light plaid cape of muted earth tones which came to her fingertips and hid most of her body. There was a prevalent scent too, without sweetness, like a perfume, not invasive, just distinct. It seemed to fog Lori's thoughts then disappear, for she didn't notice it any longer.

The woman stepped closer, pasted a smile on her lips, the type offered by strangers to young children they hate when they think them not intuitive enough to notice.

"I've been out walking. It's a beautiful evening, don't you think?"

Conveniently forgetting the creature which had attacked them, and the warnings about this evening, first from Byron, then from her aunt, Lori only recalled the incendiary kiss. "Yes, it is beautiful."

"I like to walk, been doing it all my life," the woman continued. "Not for exercise, or any cardiovascular benefit, but simply to enjoy the scenery."

"I don't actually walk far enough or fast enough to get any aerobic benefit myself," Lori said, but blushed when she pleasantly recalled just what had her pulse racing.

"I just bought the place about half a mile down the street," the stranger continued, pointing with thick, stubby fingers, the fingernails bitten to the quick and the cuticles pulled and red.

"It's a lovely area."

Lori was annoyed at the interruption of her solitude, and annoyed with herself that she was annoyed. She should be friendly. What was wrong with chatting with a new neighbor? Yes, she'd come to get away from everything, including her own life, but that didn't mean she had to be antisocial.

"So, you've left something there on the stump."

"It's a gift, a surprise."

The stranger didn't look convinced of the idea, but other than a sharp downturn of her puffy, purplish lips, said nothing.

"Do you think there is anything dangerous in the woods?" Lori asked, a prelude to introducing the subject of dogs or faeries, or handsome, shirtless men.

The old woman cackled, there was no other word for it, and although it spoke of pleasure, instinctively Lori knew it was not something she would find pleasure in.

"Oh, yes, there is quite a lot in the forest that can harm a young innocent, but I am quite at home there. I am not easily bothered."

"I've been in the woods," Lori said, forcing her voice to remain friendly. "You don't happen to own a dog, do you? A huge black dog?"

"Over the years I've had many animals call me master, but none at the moment. Why? Have you seen a wild dog?"

"Not a wild dog," Lori said, not wishing to explain her encounter, not understanding her own reticence.

"It is best to watch out for them," the woman replied cryptically. Although the light was indistinct, Lori tried to study her features, but each time she tried, they seemed to have changed, subtly, yet substantially. First her nose was narrow and thin, then wide and short. Her eyes were green, then blue. Her chin pointed, then round. Her neck narrow, turkey-like, then broad. Without giving it much thought, Lori rubbed her temples, as if she had a headache, and didn't look the woman in the eyes again.

They walked, the woman matching Lori's long-legged stride effortlessly, although she was considerably shorter. "You're not the new Caretaker, are you?"

"Caretaker?"

"Jan. She die?"

The question sounded just a tad hopeful, so Lori answered quickly. "No, my Aunt Jan is fine. She's inside."

"Ahh. Sorry. You live here long?" Her voice was sandpaper rough, as if from long-term smoking, deeper than it should be, and made the small hairs on Lori's forearms stand at uncomfortable attention.

"Oh, I was certain I mentioned I've only been here a few days. I don't live here at all. I am visiting. I needed a break before I faced my life again, and what better way to do it, than to stay with family?"

"So you're staying at the Reptile's Roost?"

They were almost completely around the house and the front door was closer. Perversely, Lori hoped this woman would take an unspoken hint and vanish.

"Reptile's Roost? Reptiles don't actually roost, do they? Not like chickens and pigeons." Without understanding why, she felt the need to be contrary.

Walking beside her, the woman chuckled, with a particularly grating sound. "The larger reptiles do, like dragons, for example. But I was referring to the big house. That's what it's called."

"Yes, that's where I'm staying."

"I've always wanted to see the inside."

"I wouldn't mind seeing the inside myself," Lori muttered.

"I don't suppose I could trouble you for a cup of tea?" the woman said. They had reached the turn-off for the driveway and Lori recalled the welcome sign. This was a small, undoubtedly close-knit community. Her aunt wouldn't want her to be rude to neighbors and surely would welcome a guest with the same friendliness she welcomed Lori herself.

"Of course, come in. There's probably tea brewing already."

"That's what I'm hoping, dearie."

The doorknob shuddered in her hand, but Lori attributed that to exhaustion, and rubbed her palm on her jeans as she allowed the woman to precede her. She had no idea what she would have done if the woman had wandered into the dark rooms along the long corridor, or tried to enter any of the closed doors, but she traveled directly, single-mindedly, toward the kitchen, as if she were familiar with the layout of the house.

Lori looked at the woman again, finding her different again, this time attributing the darkening of her hair, the recessing of her eyes to the lighting in the hall. "Aunt Jan, I brought company."

"That's lovely, dear," Aunt Jan said, her back to them, working diligently at the stove, as if she hadn't moved six inches since this morning when Lori left her. Lori didn't see the pot the caramel had been cooked in, and she had no idea how Aunt Jan could have become so deeply involved with a new canning project, when the kitchen had been spotless just a few minutes before. It hadn't taken long for her to drop off the caramel apples, meet the neighbor and return. Certainly not long enough to fill the several dozen pint jars which rested on towels, their lids already sealed, waiting only to cool enough to be put in storage, even if their contents had been simmering earlier.

Jan turned around slowly, a smile on her face, and dropped the spoon she had been holding, a large metal affair which crashed loudly to the floor and echoed as it settled against the slate tiles. Her mouth dropped open, as if she had clearly seen a ghost, or something equally undesirable.

"And your dear, sweet niece welcomed me in herself. Those were her exact words. 'Please, be welcome.'"

"This is," Lori said, then broke off. "I'm sorry, I didn't catch your name."

"I didn't offer it, dearie."

Jan kept her attention riveted on the stranger. "That's all right, Lori. I know exactly who she is."

The woman smiled, a broad grin, too wide and clearly artificial. "I'm pleased to be welcomed inside after all these years. Now that I'm here, I've decided to have a nice cup of tea."

She sat beside Byron, putting her hand on his knee, her fingers curling as if they dug deeply into his flesh. "You will be a dear and make the tea, won't you?"

Byron swallowed slowly, his eyes wide, and started to stand, but Jan settled her hands on his shoulders, forcing him to remain seated. "Stay," she ordered.

The woman laughed, an odd cackling sound. "Now, you know he cannot refuse an honest request for tea. That's in the rules, isn't it? You can stand there until hell freezes over, but he will make the tea."

Lori shifted with no idea what was occurring. "Of course we'll have tea."

"Please, don't get involved," Aunt Jan said. Her voice strident, as if she were experiencing a sharp, unexpected pain.

"Yes, she has done enough damage for one day, hasn't she? A nice full bodied tea would do me so much good. My throat, you know."

Byron struggled to stand with increasing desperation but Jan continued to put pressure on his shoulders, keeping him rooted to his chair.

"Oh, and look at your poor fingers," the woman said, taking his unresisting left hand into hers. "I really thought the injury would have been far more extensive. Well, it will probably be much worse in a moment or two, for I really would like tea now. Janet, the worm cannot refuse me."

"There's no way I'm going to let you practice your vile, murderous arts in my own kitchen."

"Let's let him tell us the rules, shall we? What do you say, Ancient One, do I get my tea?"

Byron swallowed again, this time with more difficulty. His pupils were wide, his eyes dilated. In the forest he had faced a monster without fear, but looking at him, Lori recognized his terror.

"The rules are quite clear. Of course I will provide you tea."

"And I shall savor the brew. Unfortunately, teapots are such terribly fragile things, aren't they? It will be such a tragedy if it breaks."

"Jan," Byron said, a fine sheen of sweat popping up against his upper lip and his forehead. "You've got to let me up. I cannot refuse."

"I'll not let him die. You'll get your tea, but I'll pour."

The stranger cackled. "You think that will save him? It is such a pity he is so vulnerable. If it is any consolation to you, Old One, I have been waiting for this opportunity for years. Still, I know you have friends who will mourn. And I will have to find a new goal, something to give meaning to my life, when there are so few of your kind left. Unfortunate too, for I really would like the fangs."

"Kill him this way, and you won't get any."

"Considering the sacrifice our dear Byron is willing to make, being disappointed in this is such a small flaw. Now, I would like that tea."

CHAPTER 13

Slowly Jan removed her palms from Byron's shoulders. Her fingers tightened in fists and her eyes mutated to slits. "I'll hunt you down," she growled. "If it's the last thing I do, I and those who answer to me will find you. You won't have long to enjoy your victory, and I will make sure you suffer."

Belinda laughed. "Perhaps. But first I will enjoy the tea."

Byron stood, raised his chin, straightened his shoulders, looking like a man going to the guillotine with dignity and resolution. He looked at Lori, one long glance, and she had never seen despair so vivid, hopelessness so tangible.

"Won't you enjoy a cup with me?" Belinda asked. Her features had stopped shifting, as if now, in getting her wish, there was no need to maintain pretense. She looked both ugly and petty, Lori thought, and more than that, she looked evil. "Perhaps the lass would like a nice cup as well."

Byron swallowed, and placed his hands against the chair back, his knuckles white.

"Byron, don't do this!" Jan begged.

"I have to." The despair was so real, Lori wanted to cry out, but she had no conception of what the problem was.

"No!" Lori shouted, having no idea she even intended to speak. Something was happening with undercurrents she couldn't understand. She refused to look at Byron or her aunt, for she suspected they would blame her for the brewing disaster, which seemed to involve far more than hot water.

"You don't want any, dearie?" Belinda asked sweetly, her features shifting again.

Lori stood, oddly enough thinking of their woodland kiss, the beast which had precipitated it, and the caramel apples given in thanks. "I will get your tea. As you are my guest, here at my invitation, I shall play hostess in my aunt's kitchen."

Byron met her gaze for a moment, and she saw fleeting hope, and Lori had no idea what caused it, nor how to encourage it, but she continued. "Now there is a lovely blue teapot around here somewhere, you know Aunt Janet, the one we've been using for breakfast tea?"

"No!" the woman muttered, grasping Byron's hand with fingers now elongated and clawed at the tips.

Jan released him, springing forward. "I think the blue teapot is an excellent idea, child. It's here in this cupboard." She reached in, grasped the teapot like a life preserver thrown to a victim floating down a flood ravaged river.

"No! I want the dragon tea!"

"I don't believe you specified anything beyond a full-bodied tea, and Lori is right, as her guest, she should be allowed to serve you. Here, let me put the water on. It will only take a second. I have some fabulous loose tea, a peppermint and honey. Just the thing for warming cold bones after a chilly evening walk."

Jan filled the huge kettle with water from the tap, then adjusted the flame under it. Faintly Lori heard what might have been Jan whistling, a hard juxtaposition considering the terror of only a moment before.

"I demand the dragon tea!"

Still having no idea what had caused the tension, nor her aunt and Byron's abrupt release from fear, Lori said, "There are some delightful cheese Danish somewhere. Would you like one with your tea?"

The woman stood, her hands fisted at her sides, looking like she was about to have a stroke. "I don't want any of your miserable sop. I want—"

"If you'd be reseated, this will be ready in just a moment," Jan said, stuffing loose leaves into a tea ball.

"I'm leaving!"

"Really, Belinda, what is your hurry? The evening is still young." Jan laughed. "You could even stay for supper. I promise, there is plenty."

"I'll get him yet. I'm telling you, Janet, you may have won this time, but there will be a next."

"And we'll find some way to foil you then too. Byron, if Lori's guest is leaving, would you please escort her to the front door?"

Byron who had been standing pale and terrorized, laughed and bowed deeply to Lori. "My pleasure."

"I'll leave from the back."

"No, you came in the front like a proper guest, and like the proper host, I'll see you leave the same way. I'm even willing to call you a cab, since I know you have such a long way to travel to get where you belong."

Lori waited while Byron walked the woman to the front door, biting back a hundred questions. She was so disorientated, even her confusion made no sense. Byron was back within minutes. He picked Lori up and swung her around the kitchen in a spontaneous dance, his laughter ringing around the tall ceilings.

"The blue teapot. I don't believe it. You were so brilliant." He smacked her a hard, wet kiss against her lips, not as devastating as the kiss by the tree earlier, but still sent her pulse racing.

"Brew, put the girl down. Sit. The tea has steeped."

He swung Lori around once more for good measure. "I never thought I would be grateful for mortal tea. You really were brilliant. Even if I had thought of it, and I hadn't, it wouldn't have made a difference. I thought she had me."

"Brew," Jan said, making it an order, "drink your tea."

"I might as well," he said, laughing, "as you said, there's plenty."

"It was the dragon teapot you were protecting?" Lori asked, trying to put the pieces together. She toyed with a Danish, but at the moment it was answers she was hungry for, not food.

"If you'd like dragon tea now—" Byron said.

"No. You're to sit. You had a close call, closer than I care for, actually, so as punishment, you're to drink this tea."

"I think I can handle that," Bryon said, still smiling. As if to prove he didn't mind, he had two cups. Lori waited patiently, enchanted by Byron, who managed to tell one pointless, yet humorous tale after another. She laughed under his banter, but she knew what he was doing, distracting her so she would not remember the questions about their visitor which still bothered her.

Whistling, Aunt Jan returned to her canning. She filled dozens of jars with a thick, tangy spaghetti sauce. Then she cleaned the rims and tightened the lids. With that complete she shoved them seven at a time into one of four hot water baths she had going. A few minutes after the jars were removed there was a satisfying 'pop' as the lids sealed.

Aunt Jan must also have been cooking, for Byron placed veal parmesan in front of her, the veal lightly breaded and tender, the pasta covered with the a rich oregano flavored tomato sauce. Beside her plate, Byron set a tossed salad, and soft breadsticks, the latter delightfully light with a hint of garlic.

"You're not having any?" Lori asked Byron, as Jan placed a second plate down and started to eat.

"Pasta isn't good for my digestion," he said.

"Watching your carbs?" Lori asked, and Byron, who clearly didn't understand what she was talking about, shared a look with Jan, who answered for him.

"He takes most of his meals elsewhere, as I don't allow him to make a mess in my kitchen."

"I am not always messy when I eat," he said, but it was a taunt, and both Lori and her aunt recognized it as such.

"He's always messy," Jan finished.

"Well, now that's established," Lori said, pouring herself another cup of tea, "I've some questions. You obviously had met that woman before."

"Belinda."

"Yes, Belinda. What can you tell me about her?"

"There are some things, some people," Byron corrected, "that are evil. She is one of their leaders."

"Actually, Brew, she's more misguided, but serves as an assistant for those who have earned the title evil."

He brought his hand to his mouth, as if to bite off the missing tops of two of his fingers. "You're really going to have to give up that disgusting habit of finding good in everyone."

Jan rolled her eyes, more in tolerance than aggravation and continued. "She is not extremely powerful, not as such things are measured, but she draws powerful people to her, and therefore should never be overlooked. And as you can see, she occasionally gets lucky."

"Lucky," Byron scoffed. "One day I'm going to eat—"

Jan coughed loudly, and Lori never got to hear what he intended to eat. Lori found she had no trouble believing Belinda evil. She twirled pasta around her plate with her fork, changing the pattern, almost as if the secrets they were discussing could become visible in spaghetti graffiti. "Belinda seemed, I don't know, to change shape. Every time I looked at her, she appeared different." She looked to her aunt and to the handsome man sitting beside her, expecting to be ridiculed for such a statement, but Byron nodded agreement.

Jan took over the conversation. "Yes, she does, and it was perceptive of you to notice. Not all mortals can, you know. She has to keep adjusting her appearance because the shape you saw her in was not natural to her, and because she was so confident she was going to get what she wanted from Byron, she let her guard down a bit. She allowed her image to slip, but is not usually so careless. However, that is an excellent way to identify the evil ones. It might help you recognize her, if she ever crosses your path again."

Lori stabbed a piece of veal with her fork, slicing it, with no intention of eating it. "I know what she looks like now. She won't catch me unaware again."

"She won't necessarily look the same. Also, she has no ancestors. This is another way to discover the evil ones. Most of them have no family tree."

"What does that mean?" Lori asked. Jan had removed the plates to the sink, and was back at the range continuing with her canning. To occupy her fingers, Lori shredded a breadstick into a small crumbly mountain.

"She had a family, of course she did, born the normal way, from a mother and father and probably uncles and aunts and cousins, but after a while, those who are evil lose their connections to their blood-kin."

"I'm not sure I understand."

"Why do you think the Good Book spends so many verses, so many chapters on the 'begets'? Most every established religion has some form of maintaining bloodlines and genealogy, if you prefer. They become so corrupted, it's easy to think the evil ones have no fathers, as most of them were created not born."

"Most, not all," this from Byron, but Lori ignored him.

"Mind you, most of the evil ones create themselves. They have the same agency as anyone and choose a road most of us refuse to take."

Jan leaned over, wiping the table where they had eaten. "If you find someone you think might be evil, you should ask about their family. It gives them away every time."

Lori shivered, remembering something Andrew had said when she asked casually if he were inviting his family to graduation. "I have no family, you idiot." Then he apologized, spoke of making it on his own, but she had been more sad than annoyed. At the time she was hoping for a future when she was addressing wedding invitations.

Remembering the tripod, she could believe he had no family far more easily than the fact that she had been so taken in by him.

Still, Lori refused to be sidetracked by Jan or her own mental wanderings. "We were talking about Belinda. What specifically did she want with Byron? And don't say a full bodied tea, because I won't believe it. There was something sinister going on. You both were terrified."

"Sinister," Byron said, tasting the word as if he liked its flavor.

"Brew, I know you have things to do, and when you come back, could you bring my tray back in? It's on the stump. It should be empty by now."

He grinned, looked very young. "And I suppose I'll be tripping over apple cores."

"Just don't trip over anything else, and keep yourself out of trouble."

"Tonight I feel invincible," he said. Standing, he kissed Lori, gently on the top of her head. "Who could hurt me now, when we've got the blue teapot?"

* * *

Jan ignored Lori's questions for the remainder of the evening. Every time Lori brought up the subject of what specifically Belinda had been after, her aunt found something else to occupy her. Lori spent hours running bushels of fat ripe tomatoes through a strainer to remove seeds and skin, so Jan could continue making spaghetti sauce, not going up to her room until she could no longer keep her eyes open. Upstairs, alone, Lori found herself restless, and knew she wouldn't sleep. She bathed in the huge tub, not so much soaking for the hour she spent in there, as trying to come to grips with her life and her confusion. A PhD in anthropology wasn't the most marketable of degrees. She supposed she should get busy and start sending out feelers to every university and college potentially in the market to increase their anthro staff, but the idea of teaching after spending her entire life in a classroom held little appeal. Field work was impossible to come by and she didn't have the patience to catalogue a museum's collection, even if she had the interest. She had loved her coursework and had been good at it, but it was almost as if now that she had her degree, she didn't want it.

Her fingers and toes were crinkled when she finally exited the tub, although her body, as she glared at it in the mirror, had a healthy glow. The water, for although she had been soaking a good long time, had miraculously stayed hot. There was no need to drain a few inches out, and replace it, one of the most annoying aspects of a standard tub.

Lori sang as she dried off, starting with silly childhood tunes subtly mutating to torch songs of love and longing. While her voice was fair, it was untrained. She never had much interest in singing and having the nakedness of her emotions made public through someone else's words and melody. She had been drying her toes with the towel when she realized her emotions were strong, bubbling to the surface and she could no more keep them unspoken than a wave could calm itself during a tsunami. She considered herself a scientist and an observer of other people's emotions, preferring to keep her own feelings hidden. Lori wondered if this overwhelming passion for song was a residual from the tea, the kiss in the forest, and the spontaneous, joyous one in the kitchen. With a flash of whimsy, realized there might be a more pragmatic answer.

She continued drying her knees, her thighs, hips and breasts. Earlier, before she stepped out of the clothing she had been wearing for a walk in the forest, before she had turned on the faucet to a water temperature just about steaming, she had reached for the yellow towels, realizing tonight she didn't want to play safe. She wanted to feel sensual, if only for a reaffirmation that she was a woman. She wouldn't call Byron, but she would sleep, dreaming of him, and that would be enough for now.

"You're doing this, aren't you?" she said, holding the towel up. She would not let a towel make her feel like a fool, but she was enchanted with the impression that with soft, absorbent abrasion alone could make her feel feminine.

Lori felt decadent, deciding not to wonder why she was so susceptible to Byron's suggestion. As she dried the moisture from her thighs, she thought of what he had said, how the blue towels love rubbing against a woman's body, and although she had been enchanted when he said it, she hadn't believed it for a second. Not until she brought the towel, which was thick and soft and adsorbent, to her flat stomach, then higher, to her breasts.

The earlier music vanished from her mind, and instead she found herself captivated by sensuality. She'd never owned a sex toy. Lori never wanted one, but had an idea none could be as fulfilling as her imagination responding to Byron's suggestion. It was just a towel. She had dried herself off with the like almost every day of her life. She lifted it behind her, pulled it against her shoulders, down her spine, to her buttocks.

If this were just a towel, then she needed severe psychological counseling or a night spent wrapped in a man's embrace. It was just a towel. And Lori found herself responding as if she were being caressed by a lover with talented fingers, a man who knew how to touch her and where. It was impossible to describe, even in her own mind, so she shut her eyes, enjoyed the sensations that erupted along her pores. It was as if the towel did more than dry, but also massaged like the taunting kind between lovers which left no one relaxed. Her body responded to the blue towel's caress, to its possession. Her nipples hardened, erect and yearning for a man's gentle invasion to pinch and roll and torment. She tightened her legs, feeling moist there, but not from the bath.

When she was dry, when she could no longer pretend there was any residual water on her body, she released the towel down the laundry chute, muttering under her breath that she needed to get out more if she were this susceptible to suggestion.

She rubbed her fingers along her arms. It was as if the towel had anointed her body with expensive scented lotion, for her skin felt softer and there was a deep trace of something not particularly floral, but definitely primal in the air.

Her toes curled. Her pulse points throbbed. She had only been drying off, not doing anything to please herself. Still, she felt wanton. It wouldn't take more than a man's touch to bring her to an explosive climax.

She slipped into her nightgown, a sheer, low cut, floor length she had bought several months ago, and never got around to wearing to bed. She stared at herself in the mirror, noted with a woman's pleasure at how her breasts stood poised, high and firm, with the nipples slightly darker. She noted how slender her waist looked, and her legs and her back had good muscle tone, a firmness as if she had been working out. What surprised her was the flush of color on her cheeks.

That color had to be the result of hot water and heated imagination. She thought of aphrodisiacs and tea and silently vowed to give the blue towels another opportunity to please. She had been relaxed while she had soaked. She wasn't relaxed now. Her dreams, she suspected, would be explosive.

With her hair wrapped in another blue towel, Lori made her way down the quiet corridor to her room, hoping to see Byron. He had waited for her outside this bathroom door before. The nightgown covered nothing, more alluring than if she were naked. She would tease him, let him look his fill. She would flirt, bat those eyelashes of hers, which in the mirror had looked fuller, darker, more enticing. She might allow him to inch closer, to drop his innuendos, to suffer.

He was not in the corridor. She cursed, annoyed at her imagination, and at his lack of foresight and inability read her mind. She wanted to call him, but how could she be subtle then, how could she act coy? She had never been a flirt. So she would suffer tonight, only meaning the next time she exercised her possession of the blue towels, she would be better prepared. Oh, the power of suggestion. It has his fault for telling her of the towels, making her believe something so ridiculous. She would hang him out by his toenails. He would suffer too.

Although she was annoyed, Lori was pleasantly surprised when she opened the bedroom door. Flames crackled cheerfully in the fireplace grate. Although Byron had not met her outside the bathroom, someone had read her mind, for this added to the romance of the evening, and Lori knew she didn't have the energy to start a wood fire. The room was toasty warm, scented slightly, with a trace of mountain pine.

No other lights burned, leaving the large bed and the remainder of the room in deep shadow. By the chairs, the fire cast enough light to read by. She dropped the blue towel on the carpeting then tossed her head until her hair fanned around her shoulders. She would let it dry naturally.

With a feline grace she had never experienced from her own body, Lori moved to one of the upholstered chairs and settled in. On the small side table beside her, sat the dragon teapot, a single mug and a book of ancient folktales, the kind any anthropologist wouldn't be without.

"Thank you," she whispered, "to whoever did this," and darn, if it didn't look like that silly dragon teapot winked again.

Lori found the chair remarkably comfortable. She pulled her feet up, under her, and considered herself content. Without a thought she cherished the warmth on her skin. She poured tea, took a moment to savor the bouquet before taking a sip. The first time she had tried it, she'd been exhausted, hadn't really noticed the subtle layers of flavor. This time it tasted reminiscent of woodland glens and strawberries. The sexual edginess she had experienced in the bathroom mutated, becoming more sensual: an awakening of all her senses.

She tried to concentrate on the folktales, discovered her mind wandered, so she sat, sipping tea, letting her thoughts flitter around to why Belinda wanted dragon tea. Although it was marvelous, she had no idea why it would frighten Byron and Jan, who had managed all evening to side-step her questions. Mostly she thought of the kiss, and after finishing her second cup, she went to bed, wondering if she'd be able to sleep in the huge bed alone, but she passed out before her head hit the pillow.

He came to her in dreams. A dozen separate dreams, and in each one he seduced her, in each one she responded, stroked like Michelangelo working in oils or Beethoven over a keyboard. First was a vision when they flew together, on what she couldn't be certain, for she doubted it was a magic carpet, but that was the only thing that made sense. She could see majestic snow capped mountains below, feel the wind in her hair, knowing the clouds hid them, while Byron was between her legs. She held on tightly to him, grasping him with her thighs, the rocking up and down motion exhilarating. His hands played with her breasts, and taunted her in the sensitive spots of her woman's fastness, causing waves of pleasure to ripple through her almost endlessly.

There was a fragment of dream where they walked through a virgin rainforest with trees so tall the canopy covered the sky. She heard water flowing and the call of unknown birds. He was naked and she nearly so, and when he stopped, he pushed her against a tree, kissed her senseless, until she lifted her legs around his hips, and he thrust himself home, deep within her. Again, the rocking motion made her scream, but with pleasure, and when he threw back his head and laughed his teeth were white and too long, and then he brought his mouth down, to feast at her breasts, while he continued his possession.

For a while they ran along a white sand beach, primal and undisturbed. Waves lapped at the shore, but there was too much purple in the water, not enough blue. Tiny creatures scampered out of their way as he chased her, allowing her the illusion of freedom, knowing as she knew, that he could capture her at any second. She looked back over her shoulder, laughing, and he dove, crashing into her, until they fell arms, legs, and endless kisses into the water. It was warm enough to be bathwater, buoying like salt water, but it didn't sting her eyes. With long, perfect strokes, she pulled away from him, but when she stopped and looked back she didn't see him. The beach was deserted, white sand as far as the horizon but no sign of Byron, until she felt something grab her foot, pulling her under, and while she feared monsters, being forced down by an undertow, it was him. His erection was hot, thick, invasive. He kept her underwater, filling her, possessing her. She did not need to breathe so much as she needed the climax ripping through her body, passion intensifying with each thrust.

In one she walked down Michigan Avenue in Chicago, window shopping amid stunning Christmas decorations. It was cold, for snow fell thickly, and the streets were crowded, but no one noticed her. She was looking for something specific, and she searched the shelves, the store interiors, and the people in the crowds who jostled her. And then she saw him. He waited inside a bus stop shelter, stark naked, with his erection proudly jutting forward, an invitation she could not refuse. She ran to him, jumping into his arms, and they completed their union. Where thousands could witness she made love with Byron and it was magical, for the only thing which mattered was the passion they made together.

Other snippets of dreams proceeded, one after another, and in addition to their love making, all the dreams had two things in common: she was still wearing the sheer blue nightgown she wore to bed, and each time there was a large golden dragon which looked exactly like the teapot, except it was alive.

CHAPTER 14

"Where did you find that?" Aunt Jan asked the next morning as Lori carried the dragon teapot and the mug down the stairs. She wiped her hands on a towel laying on the counter before she gingerly reached for it.

Lori shrugged. "I thought you left it for me. It was in my room."

Because she had wanted to stroke the teapot last night and for some reason hadn't dared, and because she would soon be relinquishing it to her aunt, Lori rubbed the dragon's wings, as she'd seen Jan do. She raised her hand with a startled 'oh!', then handed the teapot over, gently.

"Something bothering you?"

Lori wished she knew her aunt better, wished she knew the history of old teapots, so she wouldn't feel like such a fool. "The teapot, right now, when I caressed it—" she let the sentence drop off, deliberately shutting her mouth, which she was certain hung open wide enough to attract bees. While she pet it, she distinctly felt the teapot shudder, as if it enjoyed her ministrations. The ceramic ... it had to be ceramic, didn't it? wasn't cold and lifeless, like it should have been after spending the entire evening on her nightstand. It felt leathery, almost suede soft, like it was a living being. It was warmer than it should be, for her room this morning had been decidedly chilled.

If it wouldn't have made her look like an idiot, she would have snaked out a hand, in order to touch it again. She didn't have words for the feeling, and after all it had only been an impression, but there was something almost sexual about its response—or at least that was the thought bubbling up from her over-active imagination. Had it been a cat responding to a caress, Lori could have ignored it; that would have been normal, expected.

Lori shook her head, wondering if she were in a trance, or if the tea from last night had been drugged and she were still living through the hallucinations in her dreams.

Jan accepted the teapot, put it carefully on the only available clear spot of counter, then laid her hand gently on Lori's arm. "Tell me what you felt." There was such compassion in her statement, such understanding, that Lori didn't think to lie.

"I always thought dragon scales should be hard," she said, trying not to sound so completely like an idiot. "Like a turtle."

"Then you believed the old storytellers?" Jan asked with a chuckle. "Oh, don't get me wrong, dragon scales are hard, perhaps the word is impenetrable, but that doesn't mean they can't be soft to the touch, when he wants them to be, that is."

"I believe you're as batty as I am, Aunt Jan."

The lines at the corners of her lips, and those radiating out from her eyes, deepened. Laugh lines Lori would call them, for her aunt was clearly enchanted by the statement, which easily could have been misinterpreted. "Oh, more so," she said. "Far more. Although if you stay here, I can't promise you won't get battier as time goes on."

"That still doesn't answer my question." Lori was a scientist and she had had enough of this nonsense. She was desperate to find a subject to talk about which wasn't something boy scouts on an overnight camping exposition would chatter about by flashlight, long into the night. "Who put the teapot in my room?"

"It must have been Byron," Jan said with a twinkle to her eye. "It is the kind of thing he would do." Then she turned her head aside and laughed, as if she had a joke she had no intention of sharing. "The teapot actually belongs to him."

"It does? I thought it was yours."

"Not this one. I've got a dozen others, but nothing that compares to this brew. When I'm lucky, he lets me enjoy its tea."

"It is marvelous tea. Does Byron live here or does he have a place in town?"

The timer dinged. More bottles out of hot water. More in. "The easy answer is that Brew lives where he wants."

"If I were interested in the hard answer?"

"I'm not trying to be evasive. It's just that explaining where Byron lives isn't possible."

"How can it not be possible? I only want an address."

"A clear cut address isn't possible."

"Isn't possible? He does live in a physical place, not a metaphysical one, right?"

"That's not an easy question to answer. He's got a place locally, and of course he's around when I need him, especially at planting, for all he complains he's awfully good at helping. Then he'll disappear for months at a time. He doesn't like to leave the store untended, and of course the gold and the jewels call to him, so he always returns."

"Jan, I know you think you're trying to be clever, and perhaps even protect him from me, but I'm not a stalker. All I want to know is where he lives."

"No one is accusing you of being a stalker. Trust me, that's the furthest thing from my mind. To tell you the honest truth, as far as I know it, he lives here and there."

She shook her hands out in front of her, giving physical manifestation to her frustration. "That sounds like a Dr. Seuss line. Next you'll tell me he lives on a boat or with a goat."

"Lori, don't worry about Brew. He can generally take care of himself."

"Ok, since you won't tell me where he lives, tell me what you know about him. He's awfully thoughtful, isn't he?"

"This tea was his way of thanking you. You may not realize it, but you did save his life yesterday."

"Save his life? From an old lady who wanted a cup of tea? Is that what you're referring to? I don't suppose you'll explain?" Lori asked, lifting the lid from a kettle Jan had bubbling merrily.

"Since the tea is hot, would you like a cup for breakfast?"

"Hot? It's been sitting on my table all night."

"Oh, I just made a fresh pot," Jan said, clearly lying. "Really, here, sit. There're flapjacks this morning," and as Lori sat, Jan turned her back for an instant, then returned and put a large plate of pancakes, a bowl of fresh blackberries, and a pitcher of maple syrup beside her.

"Will Byron be joining us this morning?"

"Of course," Jan said laughing, "you'll probably see him later." She stroked the dragon's wings then poured the tea. It was fragrantly steaming, filling the large kitchen with its rich aroma, of cinnamon and orange blossoms and perhaps even early morning magic.

"How did you sleep?"

Lori chopped off a great chunk of light pancake, stuffed it in her mouth. She spoke around it as she chewed. She felt hot color highlighting her cheeks, and felt it a ridiculous time for an educated woman to feel maidenly. "I'm not certain I slept at all."

"Oh? The tea kept you awake? How much did you drink?"

"Only two or three cups. It was so delicious, and I was feeling so …" lonely wasn't the right word, and wanton wasn't a word she wanted to share with her aunt. "… so comfortable, that I sipped slowly, but I was in no hurry to get to bed. I didn't come anywhere near to finishing the pot."

"No, it takes quite a bit more than two or three cups to empty this pot," Jan said, stroking the teapot again.

"Then I dreamt, dream after dream, one after the other. And in each one I was making love with Byron."

Jan shook her head, sharp abrupt movements indicating her disapproval. "I can see I'm going to have to talk to that miserable reptile. If he thinks he can come in here and seduce you…"

Lori laughed, and put a comforting hand on her aunt's forearm. "But I liked it." She had almost expected to be sore as she woke, her legs weak and her breasts tender from the night-long assault. But there was no indication what she experienced was anything more than a dream, no matter how real it felt. Still, she had handled the blue towel gently as she tossed it down the laundry shoot. No sense asking for more trouble. "And it was just a dream."

"I'm sure," Jan said, back to stirring the green, slimy, noisome concoction on the stove.

Lori swallowed, stabbed another chunk of pancake, spoke this time with it suspended half-way between plate and mouth. "I soaked in the tub and that relaxed me, and I did grab the blue towels—"

"I suspect that's what gave him the idea," Jan grumbled, her back to Lori. "Not that he isn't fully capable of coming up with trouble on his own. Still, it might be better if you stay away from the blue towels for a while."

With hedonistic indulgence, Lori finished her breakfast, then picked up her plate and brought it to one of the kitchen sinks. "I know you said this was a bed and breakfast. Why isn't every room filled? Anyone would pay big bucks, just to eat breakfast this fabulous. You need to do a little advertising and hire some help." Once the idea struck, Lori found she liked it. Probably not the best way to put an anthropology degree to work, but she latched onto the idea of staying here, entertaining guests and helping out. Although she wouldn't admit it, she wasn't ready to face the real world so this seemed like an idea solution.

Lori took a sip of tea. Because it was marvelous, because every taste was just a little bit different, a shade richer, she savored the impressions bursting on her tongue before she swallowed. "Did you send all your guests home because I was here?"

"No, many of my 'guests'" Jan gave the word an odd inflection, obviously using it only because Lori had, "are shy, but don't worry about them. Every room on all the top floors is occupied at the moment."

Lori considered that unlikely. She had passed no one thumping up the stairs, heard no shoe drop to the floor above her.

"So what is that you're cooking?" It had been yellowish green, and full of all sorts of lumpy looking things, few of which Lori recognized. "I don't suppose it's the gruel you feed to the things chained in the basement?"

"It's mustard pickle, if you must know. It's really delicious."

"It smells," she tried to find a politically correct word, "unusual."

"It might be an acquired taste."

She sipped the tea again, and decided to go for whimsy. "And the things chained in the basement?"

"You think I would waste something as delicious as mustard pickle on them?"

* * *

Lori missed Byron. After she went back to her room to straighten up, and raced back downstairs, Jan told her he had come and gone, left to finish tilling the garden.

"Will you show me the rest of the house today? Your mustard pickle looks like it needs to simmer for a while yet."

Jan straightened. She'd been bending down, pulling quart jars by the handful from a box, and setting them on the counter. The woman must have an endless supply of clean quart jars. "I would love to, but I've seeds to start and that cannot be put off another day. You could help me, if you're interested."

"For the garden Byron is tilling?"

"Yes."

"Then I would be glad to."

Jan put on some heavy work boots, which looked like they started life with Davy Crocket, and took her not out the back door, as Lori expected, but again, out the front, and around the house. Lori passed her rental car, sitting where she left it. She patted it on the hood as she walked by.

"Don't worry about him. He's doing fine."

"Him?" Lori parroted.

Jan's voice softened as she looked back over her shoulder to the Mustang. "You have no idea how hard an existence a rental car has, always putting up with different drivers, going almost every minute. He's enjoying his vacation almost as much as you are."

"I'll have to take your word for it," Lori answered, not much for anthropomorphism, but having to admit the car did look rested and content.

Jan led her past the driveway, along the side of the house, along a narrow trail, for lilac bushes had encroached, and the two women had to bend under or push past heavy branches. The bushes, far taller than she, were laden with old fashioned purple flowers, dynamically scented.

"I could stay here forever and just breathe," Lori said.

"Then we wouldn't get any planting done, and you did say you would help."

"I will, but don't you love the scent?"

"I do. There is something healing about lilacs. These are rather fond of Brew. They're probably blooming for him, to show how glad they are that he escaped yesterday."

"Don't they always bloom this time of year?"

The clumps of dripping flowers looked more like wisteria than lilacs, and were massively fragrant. "They bloom when they feel like it. All Byron has to do is mention he would like flowers and poof, lilacs all over the place. They draw bees, but that is no bother. Honey is always better with a little lilac. We're almost there."

Overgrown with vines and saplings, the old greenhouse was invisible until she was almost upon it. It didn't look that big from the outside, but Lori wasn't disappointed to find her impression wrong.

She stepped inside, than did a three-sixty, turning in rapture. "This place is incredible." She started revising her plans for the B&B, incorporating fresh flowers in every room, greenhouse produce available for purchase and at meals.

The light was excellent, especially considering the abundance of greenery, both outside and along the walls inside. The center was filled with over two dozen oversized tables, each holding perhaps a hundred trays, each tray packed with empty, small round peat containers.

Lori pulled in a bracing lungful of air, rich with potential and with life, as if all these plants were sending vitality into the air as they did pollen, and that energy was hers just for the cost of a deep breath.

Jan, all business, grabbed a small peat container, waved it under Lori's nose to get her attention. "The growing season is short. I'm glad you're here to help."

The ground under her feet was dirt, but springy and soft, and, she hesitated to admit, well behaved. It didn't seem to cling to her shoes, or rub off on her jeans. Lori stripped off her jacket, since the temperature was far warmer than outside.

"Are you ready to work?" Jan asked dryly.

"Sure." Lori stopped spinning and touching leaves, forced herself to pay attention. Jan showed her where the potting soil was piled, just outside the greenhouse, huge mounds of the stuff, dark brown, rich with humus. She filled a bucket, handed it to Lori. "Go, start filling the little pots. I'll provide the seeds when you're ready."

"Ok." Lori was eager to get to work. She found something primordial about digging her fingernails into soil, which pleased the anthropologist in her, for so much of the survival of diverse civilizations had to do with how they grew and gathered food.

"If you see Genevieve, don't bother her, for she likes to hunt here. Suits me just fine, as she keeps the area clear of vermin."

With that, Jan left, and Lori found herself working for hours by herself. There was a seemingly endless supply of tables and little potting-cups to fill, but she worked steadily, refilling her bucket dozens of times, making little dent in either the mound of soil outside the greenhouse or the pots yet to fill. Time passed quickly. She let her mind wander to rituals ancient civilizations developed to ensure a good harvest by placating their restless gods. She didn't see Genevieve, but more than once out of the corner of her eye, while she was concentrating on something else, she witnessed the scamper of different colors, making her wonder if the tiny blind kittens were old enough for hunting lessons from their mother.

The exact second she was wondering if she'd have to go back up to the house to ask, Aunt Jan appeared with a heavy tray loaded with both lunch and seeds. Jan stayed and ate with her, overstuffed egg salad sandwiches, said her mustard pickle was coming along well and she was starting to can it, but that she could take the time to help finish the plantings.

The dragon teapot rested in a spot of honor on the tray, but there were no mugs, and to drink Jan supplied tall glasses filled with tart raspberry lemonade, which in the increasing heat of the greenhouse was no trouble at all to drink.

While Lori plopped two seeds into each soil-filled cup, Jan 'watered' them with liquid from the dragon teapot.

After about five minutes, Lori stopped, brushed a loose strand of hair out from her eyes, with dirty hands that left a streak on her forehead. "Aren't you going to ruin the teapot, filling it was planting nutriments?"

"This isn't fertilizer, it's tea. The tea is so healthy for both people and plants I haven't added anything to it. I adjusted the temperature a bit, as the seeds can't take the drinking temperature."

Lori said nothing, but occasionally gnawed the inside of her cheek, for although she planted thousands of fat, oval seeds into the cups, Aunt Jan never had to go refill the teapot. It just kept flowing as if it had an endless supply inside.

* * *

Later that evening, Lori bathed, soaking until her skin wrinkled. When she drained the tub, she suspected there was enough dirt to fill another cup, for it had been a messy day, but remarkably satisfying. She liked the timelessness of planting the seeds; it made her feel kin to hard-working, bent-back women from thousands of ancient tribes since the beginning of time. Because she was exhausted and worked so hard, she reluctantly passed on the blue towels and grabbed a red one, wondering as she did what made a red towel happy.

Dinner was a quiet affair, just the two of them. It was simple: hard crusted bread, chunks of three or four different types of cheese and thin sliced summer sausage. The meal was rounded out with fresh fruit, nothing so simplistic as apples, bananas, or oranges but a dozen other kinds, a few she didn't recognize, and the blue tea pot put in an appearance with a herbal tea mixture tasting pleasantly of peppermint. Lori ate with good appetite, and realized she would probably ache in the morning, for although it wasn't strenuous work, it was repetitive and she had worked diligently.

"I have to finish canning the mustard pickle," Jan said, clearing the table, "but would you take this to the red living room?" She held out the tray which had first made its appearance that afternoon with sandwiches.

"Red living room, which one is that?" Lori asked, gratified she was being given the opportunity to explore more of the house when she had the distinct impression that particular pastime was off-limits. She was pleased her restrictions were being raised, at least a little. On the tray, Jan placed a heavy mug filled with a steaming broth, but what kind of broth, Lori had no clue, for it had an odd aroma, some of the bread and cheese from their dinner, and the blue teapot.

"Byron should be there. He'll complain about the tea of course, that's ok, you can let him. It makes him feel superior, but make sure he drinks. He needs to replenish his fluids."

"Is he sick?"

"Let's just say he worked harder than you and I did, and you know how much work we put in. And if he'll drink more, by all means come back and I'll get you anything he wants."

"What about the dragon teapot? You said it was good for replenishing what ails you?"

"That will have to wait for another time." She smiled as if something had just occurred to her. "I left it out by the greenhouse, and I haven't got time to go get it now."

"I'll get it."

"No you won't. I'd rather you didn't go out after dark. Take this to Byron. And Lord amighty, don't tell him you want dragon tea."

"Ok, I won't."

She wished she had paid more attention during the times she traveled this corridor, for without proof it seemed, that some of the doors previously menacingly shut were now open, and some of the open ones were now forebodingly closed. It wasn't difficult to find the red living room, for it was the only one with light showing through. As she entered Lori noted the light came from a fire in the massive fireplace and about a dozen randomly placed fat pillar candles. She didn't detect Byron at first as she settled the tray on a high table to one side of the fireplace, until he moved, shifting one arm in a weak wave to gain her attention. He lay on the couch and didn't have the strength to hold up his own head.

"What happened to you?" Lori asked, rushing to his side.

"I overdid it today," he said with a pitiful grin. "I haven't worked that hard since," he paused to consider, "this time last year when Jan needed the same done. You'd think I'd learn to tell her no."

"She swears the broth will do you good." Lori had to support his head up to get him to drink, and he did grouse about the blue teapot, but drank several cups.

After a while his eyes drifted closed, and she tried to juxtapose the vibrant man who had kissed her in the woods with this one, clearly suffering from more than just exhaustion. His eyes had deeply recessed, as if from prolonged illness or starvation, and his wrists and fingers, the only other part of him visible, were far past slender and looked skeletal. Curious and caring, while he slept, she reached for his wrist to check his pulse, and found it strong, belying his appearance. She stroked his hair tenderly, finding it impossible to keep her hands to herself. With her actions he stirred and moaned, and Lori suspected she disturbed his sleep, so she dug her hands into her pockets and studied the room.

There was no red in it, nothing that would make her call this the red living room, beyond the fire which seemed to burn redder than normal. A stack of wood rested against the hearth, but the fire burned hot and did not need replenishing so she left it alone. A tapestry filled one wall, a huge thing, which would have dwarfed any normal sized room, highlighting its immensity. Lori stood with her head tilted and studied the patterns woven in it, mostly flowers she thought when she looked at it directly, but with the hint of winged dragons when she studied it at an angle.

She circled the room, her footsteps silent. Deep, rich mahogany paneling covered the walls, and heavy, weight bearing shelves filled the remaining three sides of the living room. She would have placed tons of books there, but with the exception of the occasional knickknack, they were completely empty even of dust. Lori couldn't imagine when Jan found time to dust between all her cooking.

"There's a secret passageway behind the fireplace," Byron said, his words startling her, for she thought he was asleep.

She turned slowly, found him looking stronger. "Really, where does it go?"

"One of the lower levels of the house. I'm not sure which one."

"How many lower levels are there?"

"Just the basement," he said, but she knew he lied, and from his tone, she knew he had spoken deliberately so that she would.

"You probably should eat more," she said, returning to his side. She wanted to reach his wrist to feel for a pulse again, or to touch his forehead and check for fever, but knew if she did either of those it would be for a completely different reason. It was not so easy being bold now as while he had slept.

When he didn't complain and didn't move, she ordered him to stay put, and she took the empty tray and hurried back to the kitchen, where her Aunt Jan ladled some additional broth and made another pot of tea.

He hadn't moved in the time she'd been gone, and she was half afraid he'd fallen back to sleep, but his eyes fluttered opened as she walked in. As before, she fed him.

Although it obviously cost him, for he was weak, Byron raised his hand until he was able to caress her cheek with the back of his knuckles. "You have the most amazing eyes."

"And you're going to make me spill this broth."

"Pabulum. How the Innkeeper can expect me to eat this, year after year, I have no idea."

"To keep your strength up."

The look in his eyes darkened, except, she was certain, for a transient flash of crimson. "I have no difficulty keeping my strength up." His fingers moved from her cheek to her neck. "I can raise up when I need to."

How quickly the conversation changed. Lori, who hated her porcelain fine skin, blushed.

He caressed a wisp of her hair which had escaped the band she wore. "Fire hair."

She shoved a tea cup against his lips, to shut him up, but then spoke, as if in apology. "It's an annoyance. It doesn't keep a curl. It frizzes. When I wear it short, it looks like I stuck my finger into an electrical outlet."

"Fire hair," he repeated. "It is said no dragon can resist."

"Dragons," she said, craning her head to reinspect to the tapestry. He was the one with the magnificent eyes, with the dynamic hair and she felt like a fool.

"Don't you believe in dragons?"

"As a symbol of good ... or evil?"

"Yes, we do have that reputation." He released her hair, lay back against the couch, his eyes shut, his breathing again shallow.

The fireplace, unlike the one in her bedroom, was brick, not fieldstone. The floor was not slate, but hardwood, polished to a sheen heavy enough Lori wondered if she took her shoes off, she could run and slide the length of the room on her socks. It was the kind of floor any five year-old would cherish. Two couches formed an L, both longer than normal, for there was still room at one end one of the one he occupied. The room was populated with a dozen thick chairs loitering around haphazardly, as if they couldn't bother talking to each other. There were no clearly defined conversation areas in this living room, no reading lamps, nothing beyond the candles and the fireplace to provide any light. Still the throw pillows were soft and it wasn't the furniture which intrigued her.

Lori rubbed a napkin against his bottom lip where some of the broth had dribbled, knowing he didn't have the strength to manage himself. Then she sat back on her heels and looked around with fascination. "Are you sure I can't drive you to a hospital or get you some pain pills or something?"

"I'm not in any pain, and I promise I'll be right enough in a day or two."

He snapped his comment, so Lori tried a different tack. "Why do they call this the red living room?" she asked.

Byron struggled, finding enough strength to rest the weight of his upper body on an elbow. "Well, the yellow living room and the blue one and the green one had already been taken. It would be confusing if it was called any of those."

"Really," she said exasperated. "Why?"

"I haven't been living here long," he said, "and the history of the house goes back a long way."

"There is no red at all in this room. Was there at one time?"

He chewed, she had soaked some of the bread he hadn't managed to eat earlier in some of the broth, and he had finally managed to eat it.

"If you must know there was a particularly gruesome murder here a long time ago, and the floors and walls were covered in blood. The red comes from that."

"Do you know the story?"

"Yes."

"Would you tell me?"

"You'd have nightmares and I won't be around to alter your dreams."

"Is that what you do, alter dreams?"

"When I wish."

"It must be a great gift."

"It's more of a fancy, a parlor trick. If I could change the course of worlds, that would be a gift." He growled, a sound deep in his throat, "I really need to go kill something."

"Would that make you feel better?"

"Infinitely better."

Lori sat on the end of the couch, raised his feet so they rested on her lap and wondered if he had personal involvement in a particularly gruesome murder. "Could you tell me the story about the dragon teapot? My Aunt Jan said it belongs to you."

She rubbed his feet, finding it both relaxing and sensual. His toes were long, clean, and the action warmed her almost as much as his caress of her cheek.

Byron shut his eyes, and Lori wondered if he were drifting back to sleep when he spoke, his voice strong with a rich storyteller's cadence. "Long ago, on a world far from here, dragons filled the skies the way birds fly here. There were hundreds of different species. Some of the dragons were small, as small as a fruit bat, and some were huge, about the size of a blue whale."

She grinned.

"What is so funny?"

"I am trying to imagine a blue whale with wings, flying. It's not an easy image."

"Not the shape of a blue whale, the weight and the length of a blue whale." He looked exasperated.

"Do all dragons have wings?"

His complexion had lost the pasty look of the invalid, but he still had little strength. "All true dragons have wings. There are several species of serpent who were once dragons, or rather, shared common ancestors with dragons. These creatures are without wings, and if you'd never seen one before, you could easily be confused, and think you were seeing a true dragon, but all of them have wings. Not all dragons fly. Some species have taken to the water and their wings are mere vestiges and some have disdained flying, so they couldn't even if they were being chased by witches, but to answer your question, the easy answer is yes."

"I'm glad."

"Dragons have the ability to cross worlds. Not to fly among the stars, like astronauts and other types of space explorers, but to find portals and cross worlds. They did so for centuries, and for the dragons, it worked out well. They would plunder a world's wildlife, then, when they were hunted in earnest, and they were always eventually hunted, they would slip through another portal and start their feasting somewhere new. Over the centuries, they sort of stopped reproducing. They were territorial, but mostly proud, and when they found a particularly good hunting world, they would tell no other dragon, for they grew greedy."

"Greed is a common theme in most folktales."

"It's a fairly universal emotion. It doesn't matter what you have, as long it is more than someone else has, you feel possessive over it. Portals last centuries, but eventually they get, for want of a better word, tired, and they close, preventing anything to travel through them in either direction. Some creatures can open portals, but dragons cannot. The dragons found themselves trapped on different worlds. At least I assume the others were trapped different worlds. Several were left here on Earth before the rise of humankind, during the periods of the dinosaur. The dragons here managed to keep out of nearly everyone's way, hunting, and maintaining their distance even from their own kind. Then the change came. Centuries passed. Many of them forgot the portals and what it was like to cross worlds. The dragons were hunted here, but on the whole they were safe from anything a human brought against them. Not immortal, for they can be killed, but nearly invulnerable, which meant if they were not hunted by those who knew their weaknesses, they could live practically forever. With the advance of humankind, the rules changed. In order to stay on this planet, the dragons were required to benefit man."

"Benefit man?"

"I'm not being sexist. I mean man in the sense of people, mortals."

"I know, go on."

"One by one, the dragons chose how they would help mankind. One chose to be an anvil, used by a blacksmith, for example. Another became a sword. You get the idea."

"Of course. And one brave dragon, younger than the rest, decided to be a teapot?"

"I don't know if he were younger than the rest, he was fairly old by then by any estimate, but yes, he became a teapot, required to serve tea to anyone who asked, at any time."

"The teapot came to you."

"Yes."

"Passed down to you from your great grandfather and your grandfather and your father, for generations unnumbered."

"Nothing quite that linear, although in case you're wondering, I do claim a family."

"That wasn't a trick question. I know you're not evil."

"Back to the story. While this dragon could regain his form anytime he wanted, when asked, he had to serve tea."

"Is there a problem with that?"

"Yes, for the portals opened again, and some of the creatures which hunted dragons entered this world. When they were serving mortals, the dragons were vulnerable. Humans didn't think much when an ancient sword shattered. Weapons break all the time. And the anvil, there wasn't much call for an anvil anymore, was there? So when that dragon was killed, no one noticed for years."

"And the teapot?"

"Your aunt does her best to keep it safe. You can see there are witches on its trail. Yesterday was the closest to losing it I've come in a long time."

"You would have allowed that witch tea?"

"Yes, and as she drank it, she would have broken the pot. You heard her."

Something wasn't making sense here, for all it was fantasy, he was weaving in events that actually happened and she wasn't following when he left fiction and started on fact. "Why didn't you just say no?"

"The witch, Belinda, is human."

"So she wasn't one of the things that crossed portals to hunt dragons."

"No. The significance is I cannot deny a request from a human."

"On pain of death?"

"Obviously death would be preferable."

Disconcerted, Lori asked, "Are you feeling better?"

"I'm still exhausted. It's getting late. Why don't you return to your room?" It sounded like he was offering her a reprieve, so she could run upstairs like a good little girl and be safe, or she could stay and take her chances with him. Lori thought of blue towels and fantasy dreams and decided she had been playing it safe far too long.

"Would you tell me what the red towels do?"

"And then you'll go?"

"Perhaps."

"Red towels heal. Not massive, mortal wounds, but shallow cuts, and help the body to heal after surgery."

"And if you're not bleeding?"

"They're like a normal towel. They don't do any good or bad, but if you've used a red towel, don't worry about it. Now, say good night."

"I'm not ready to leave," she said.

He slid around the couch, moving beside her where she rested, his movements slow, for she could see he was still drained, but they were deliberate for he was setting the parameters of the seduction. "I can't stop thinking about you."

"I keep thinking about that kiss," she whispered, "about how you tasted and how you made me feel."

His grin started slowly, at his eyes, reached his lips with agonizing precision. "Would you like to see if I could do it again?" Byron asked.

CHAPTER 15

"If that's an offer, the answer is yes." An unfamiliar huskiness seeped into her voice, wrapping itself around her with timbre she did not recognize. Lori felt the need to clear her throat, to try again, but recognized the sound was not regret or insecurity, but passion, and passion had been missing from her life for a long time.

Byron raised an eyebrow. She knew it for a question and Lori did not hesitate to locate the answer from deep within the secret internal places of her body now secreting joy. She remembered the vivid dream, and her concern was for his strength for they had been vigorous.

"I want…" she said, uncertain if she stopped because that was her full answer, "I want," or if she were waiting for him to fill in the details, to anticipate her desires. Byron slid his hand around her neck, turning her ever so slightly to face him. Other men had touched her, and she had been repulsed, or stoic, or had tried to dredge the enthusiasm he created so effortlessly within her. His actions were seductive, matched exactly what her body needed.

She watched him, his eyes turning molten gold as he studied her with an intensity making her feel cherished. Gently, he combed his fingers through her hair, as his dream-double had done on more than one occasion. He cupped her neck, a caress which had her leaning closer to him. His movements had her scalp tingling, her body screaming for completion.

She would let him set the pace, and at the moment, slow suited her just fine. Long, ebony shadows crept along the walls, as if unwilling to miss her seduction. She could almost feel sorry for them, since they had to get their thrills vicariously.

Across the room, in the hearth which dominated an entire wall, the fire burned brightly, but somehow Byron remained in darkness, becoming ethereal as if his long, expressive body was too weak to accept illumination.

Lori blinked. She was having trouble seeing him, for her eyes were unreliable, but she had no trouble feeling him. With his palm at the nape of her neck, he caressed her ear, lightly, a tickle, a foray. While the action was not specifically sexual, it was one of the most sensual feelings she had ever experienced.

"Your hair is incredible," he said, his voice awed with discovery. He pulled strands through his fingers, in a long caress. It fluffed about her shoulders, down her chest, toward her breasts. He reached out again, rubbing tendrils against her clothing. "Soft doesn't begin to describe it." She thought of blue towels, and how they had made her feel wanton, but the towels had just been fabric and the anticipation of this moment had caused her blood to burn.

She lowered her lashes, looked to the pulse point at his throat where she could see his blood throbbing. "It needs a cut. I should hack the whole mess off."

Working on her research, then through the long months of pounding out her thesis, other than a daily shampoo more for emotional sanity than hygiene, she had basically ignored her hair. She had let it grow past the saucy chin length style she preferred. It now hung beyond her shoulders, and she constantly had to sweep her bangs from her eyes, for they were not quite long enough to behave themselves and stay behind her ears.

"Soft," he said, pulling a strand toward his nose, sniffed it, rubbed it against his gaunt cheeks. "I love the feel of it. Dragons aren't much for growing hair. I think that's why we like it in others." He highlighted his words by dropping a chaste kiss along the tips which somehow she felt. The air all around her was suddenly scented with strawberries.

Byron left her hair, rubbed a tender index finger along her brow, then across her lids. "And your eyes, they're green."

"Aye," she said. "Not as dynamic as yours." Really, copper eyes that turned gold with passion? They had to be contacts.

"Green, the color of life."

"They wash out, when I wear different colors." Lori wasn't certain she knew how to accept a compliment from him.

"Green is the rarest of the eye colors," he insisted. "Think how much of the world has dark eye color. The East Europeans, the Asians, all those of Latino and African descent. Green eyes are rare, should be cherished."

"My mother's parents were Irish."

"Ahh, the little people."

"No, my father was quite tall," she countered, deliberately misunderstanding.

"It is said people with light eyes can see through the veil easier."

"What veil?"

"The wall between this world and the next. The one that guards not only the dead, but the faeries as well."

He did not smile. He was not teasing her, not dealing a hand of seduction in this game of strip poker. The veil. A lot of anthropology dealt with primitive people's death rituals and their way of answering the questions the separation of death always raised. But with him so sick, she had no interest in thinking about death. Instead, Lori let the image tickle her fancy.

Her eyes sparkled, and she felt a flush rising against her cheeks. "Then you're saying I've been faerie-kissed?" she asked.

"Aye," Byron agreed, his look of deep, thoughtful intensity mutating to the trace of a smile. "You have been and you're about to be again." He lowered his head slowly, indicative of the mixture of his exhaustion and his enchantment with her. "Not that I am, strictly speaking, a faerie."

His fingers a moment ago had been cold, now, against her skin, she could feel them warming, as if she were providing him with more than heat and by her presence she offered him life itself.

The fire blazed hotter, as if it also fed off the emotions they generated. The light undulated in strange dancing patterns that aided and abetted the surreal quality of the room. The shadows danced. She stole a glace to the huge tapestry on the wall. This time she could see a portal through which winged dragons could cross worlds, and those dragons, a dozen or more, soared with their wings unfurled, catching the morning breeze. Besides the dragons, other items, previously invisible, filled the tapestry: an anvil, shaped like a crouched dragon, wings folded tight to his body, a sword, again decorated with a dragon motif. There was a bridge, over a steep canyon, and a ladder, tall and stately, up against a silo. Finally, in the corner, the familiar dragon teapot rested. Her hand twitched, remembering the suede feel of the crockery, the way it had been warm. It had shuddered under her caress, had all but purred. Then Byron captured her lips and she thought no more of teapots or veils, for she needed all her senses to capture the pleasure he offered her.

His eyes were gold again and they sparkled. Pallor still marked his features and his eye sockets were still pronounced indicative of his weakness, but his lips, when they twitched, spoke of desire, and Lori was beginning to recognize: inevitability. She would be tenderly assaulted whether she wanted it or not.

And she did want it.

"I shouldn't be doing this. I really haven't got the strength for it tonight." Although his voice was a whisper, it held urgency.

Lori rubbed her nose against his, a teasing prelude.

"And I shouldn't be doing this. I barely know you. Regardless of what you think, I don't usually throw myself at strange men."

He laughed at that, and Lori hoped it was because she enchanted him, not because he found her amusing. But he explained, returning his fingertip to rub against her eyebrows, her chin, and across her full, pouting bottom lip. "I am strange. You need to know that. By any definition of the word, I am strange."

Lori closed her eyes and leaned closer, pressing her forehead against his. "Then make me strange too," and then she was lost in an incredible fantasy of desire and passion and heat.

At the tree in the forest, after they had been attacked by the beast, there had been wildness and desire, and perhaps relief they had survived and needed to let off a little adrenaline. They had no such balm this time, but the kiss was just as explosive, just as invasive, just as complex.

Lori felt her heart trip-hammer, as her breathing increased and her skin felt both hot and cold and sensitive. With his kiss, the colors in her mind reappeared, fireworks exploding against the inside of her eyelids. As her tongue danced against his, she tasted unexpected things, strawberries and peppermint, and something sharp, like the bitter tang from the caffeine in black tea. Then before she was ready for the kiss to end, Byron broke away, shutting his eyes, leaning his neck against the back of the couch. She tried to straighten, found she lacked functioning muscles. His kiss had empowered her, stopping it had left her cold and bereft.

She was about to moan, complain that what he had offered her was not enough, only a temptation and he could not leave her throbbing, unsated, when she noticed his breathing, shallow and irregular, and his color, now practically non-existent.

"Are you all right?"

He didn't open his eyes, as if he didn't have the strength to, and his voice came out as a whisper, as if all his energy had been transferred to her through the kiss. His response was so slight, she could not understand it.

"Byron, answer me. Are you all right?"

Several long seconds escaped before he responded. She measured time in the way her pulse throbbed, for she could no longer see the vein pulsing in his neck. "No, I am not. Not for what I want to do with you, to you, all night, tonight and every moment for the rest of your life."

While he sought a deep breath, she reached out, touched his hand, when she found it freezing, she brought it to her lips, hoping her breath, her prayers would give him strength. The bite mark, residual from the beast in the forest, marred the back of his arm, although barely noticeable, a scratch, healing without a scar. For some reason she didn't comprehend, identifying it didn't make her feel better. She hadn't seen the wound when new, but had imagined it deep and painful, leaving him with months of shooting pain every time he tried to flex his fingers. Perhaps the red towels had been busy.

His lids were closed, but he must have watched something she could not envision, for she saw his eyeballs bounce, trace their movement. "I'm in you, Lori. You might not realize this, but I am: heart, body and soul. You have tasted me, enjoyed the nectar I have offered. It is more than just tea. It is my lifeblood."

She waited, feeding on his poetry, his declaration of love, although he didn't use the word, it sounded like he spoke of far more than desire.

He tightened his fingers around hers, a confirmation he would survive, as well as an acknowledgement of her attempt to succor. "Go upstairs now. I cannot give you what you want tonight, and you cannot give me what I need."

"What do you need?" Even with the squeeze of his fingers joining her own, she was scared. "Should I call an ambulance? Should we get you to a hospital?"

His eyelids cracked open, mere slits, and his eyes were dark now, black, deep and bottomless. "There is no need for worry. It's only exhaustion. I overdid it today, working for your aunt. I need sleep and fluids. I can promise you in the morning I will be recovered. I will rest here."

"Can I get you more tea, more broth?"

He shook his head, and it was as much a thanks for her offer as it was a negation of her request. "I'll hunt again in the morning, if I can get my wings to sprout."

She smiled, enjoying the image. "I'd like my wings to sprout. You'll have to tell me how you manage."

His voice droned low, sounded like it came from far away. "Leave me now. Your aunt wouldn't let anything happen to me. You saw how she protected me when the witch was here."

"Byron," she started, but when she didn't know how she was going to finish the sentence, she let it drift off.

She stood, her own legs shaky, a combination of worry for him and a latent desire to finish what they had started with the second kiss. He had been sitting, but when she relinquished her position on the couch, he stretched out, and she could tell, was already asleep. She looked to the fire, saw it burning cheerily, enough to keep him warm without a blanket. The shadows looked disappointed. They did not get the show they were expecting.

She hoped whatever was chained in the basement wouldn't break free, use the secret passageway up to this room and disturb him. Because the image of something dark creeping through long forgotten passageways was so clear, she kissed him gently, once, on top of his head. Gripping the tray with the empty bowl and mug, she left.

She dropped the tray off in the kitchen, but as she was about to climb the back staircase, Lori decided she wouldn't sleep well unless she checked on him one more time, so she ran down the long corridor. She stopped, disorientated when she reached the front door. She back-stepped, one door, two, confusion creeping through her. It should be here. The living room was right here.

But it wasn't.

Carefully, Lori went up and down the corridor, trying closed doors, peeking into dark, cold rooms when the doors were ajar. And she couldn't find the red living room. She backtracked all the way to the kitchen. Told herself she was being ridiculous, blind, fanciful. It must be there. It hadn't been ten minutes since she left it—or him. It was as if the red living room had vanished, it was so completely gone. All of the rooms with open doors were cold and dark, no candles spaced throughout the expanse, no fire barreling out massive amounts of heat. All the rooms with closed doors were inaccessible.

"Sleep safe, Byron," she said, to no door in particular. Shaking her head, she went back up to her room, hoping the bedroom fire there would be lit and the dragon teapot waiting, but the room was cold, dark, and the table was empty.

* * *

The kitchen smelled yeasty the next morning when Lori ran downstairs, a warm, homey smell of fresh baked bread that had her mouth watering. Of all the comfort smells possible throughout history, one of the most enduring had to be fresh baked bread. Lori pulled up a chair to the table, where her breakfast waited, a calzone stuffed with gooey melted cheese, rich spicy sausage and firm sweet egg. The pastry was light, flaked at the approach of her fork, and the filling was steaming hot. She chewed thoughtfully, wondered if she'd ever tasted anything this good before.

Jan looked up, grinned as Lori sat down. She was up to her elbows kneading dough on a floured counter, occasionally muttering, "You may think you're getting away, but I'm wise to you. Back you go."

"Is that the sourdough starter, the one you were fighting the other day?"

"Yes. They're such a trial, but I suppose it's their last hurrah, so I let them enjoy themselves."

"Have you seen Byron?" Lori had convinced herself she had been more tired than she thought the night before, and there couldn't have been any foolishness like a living room disappearing, but she hadn't quite managed to go down the main corridor this morning and check.

Jan spoke lightly, clearly unconcerned. "He was gone this morning when I awoke. I suppose he's out hunting."

"What does he hunt?" Lori asked, half afraid it was young woman, a different one every week.

Something must have tickled Jan's fancy, for she answered, "At the risk of resorting to cliché, he hunts anything he wants."

Annoyed, and interested in redirection, Lori ate silently for a few moments before she spoke again. "What are you making today?" A clear glass pitcher of apple cider rested on the table, fat condensation dripping down the sides. No teapot was in evidence, dragon, blue or otherwise. She was starting to crave tea.

"Travel cakes. They are not exciting but they store for years and are nutritious."

She poured herself some cider, then peered over Jan's shoulder. Lori giggled. It looked as if a piece of the dough bulged out, before Jan kneaded it back into the mess. "It really does seem to be giving you trouble."

"Wouldn't you try to escape, if your only option was the ovens? But no, don't worry about them. They don't seem to mind the baking."

Lori took a long swallow of tart cider. "It's alive?"

"Of course it's alive. It's made with sourdough yeast. How do you think bread rises?"

Lori looked at the raw dough, bulging now in a dozen different spots, and suspected there was more to it.

The kitchen overflowed with piles of baked travel cakes brown and glorious. There had to be hundreds, not including stacks off in corners of the expansive room. The deep boxes scattered around, Lori guessed, were stuffed with travel cakes already packaged for storage. "Aunt Jan, who eats all this food? People at your bed and breakfast?"

"No, most of the creatures who come here I feed fresh meals. Do you like the pasty?"

"It's marvelous. You could make a fortune marketing this alone. I suppose it's got about a thousand fat grams, but don't answer that, and don't get me off track. Someone must eat this food. Do you feed the faeries?"

Jan wiped her hands on her apron, grabbed a pot holder, reaching into the oven and pulling out two trays. She set them aside and slipped in two more. "Faeries? What would faeries want with travel cakes?" With a spatula, she lifted the bottom of one of the freshly baked loaves, checking to see if it were brown.

"Aunt Jan, there's no such thing as faeries are there?"

"I wouldn't tell them that. Besides, who do you think ate the caramel apples?"

"I am an adult and I would like a straight answer. Who eats the travel cakes," she continued, ticking off her fingers, "and mustard pickle and beans and spaghetti sauce and cherries, and the ten thousand other things you can and preserve?"

Jan cleared the tray, putting the baked loaves onto a cooling rack. "Faeries are fairly self-sufficient this time of year. I admit, I've had to help out a bit, some of the creatures of faerie and their friends."

She pointed her finger at the dough, a clear warning to behave, that she was watching it—or them—then she sat down beside Lori, and pouring herself a glass of cider. "Do you have any plans for today?"

A string of perversity rose within her. "I want to systematically go through every room in this house, all the closed doors and the dark corridors. I want to explore the basements and attics. I want to look in cupboards and closets, and I want the history of anything I come across like the broad tapestry in the red living room, and the knickknacks on the shelves."

"I need help in here. How are you with a rolling pin?"

Lori was in no mood to be misdirected and set to doing fifty projects, even if it did help her aunt. "Actually," Lori continued, as if her first statements had been merely whimsy, "I was thinking of driving into town. The walls feel like they are starting to close in on me."

Jan clapped her hands, poofing up a small cloud of flour. "Shopping would be an excellent idea. If I got you a list, would you pick up some things for me?"

"I would be glad to. Are you going to stay here, and finish making your travel cakes?"

"No, the rest of these have to rise for a few days before they can be baked, thank heaven, for I have far too much to do to worry about travel cakes. No, I am going to plant the seedlings we started yesterday. Byron has the garden tilled and they should be tall enough to survive even the storm arriving tonight."

"Tall enough? They shouldn't even be germinated. We only planted them yesterday."

Jan ran water, washed her hands with bubbles, which like the bulges in the travel cakes seemed alive, bent on escape. "They're tall enough to plant. Would you like to see them? Then you can get on your way."

Lori set her fork down. Her plate had been all but licked clean. "Sure."

Ten minutes later, Lori stepped into the greenhouse, and stopped, shock still. In twenty-four hours, the plants, all thousand trays of them, were about eight inches high, and root bound in the little peat cups. The stems were thick, the leaves were broad and overpoweringly green. The scent in the greenhouse had altered, a verdant aroma, redolent of contented growing things.

"Overnight?" Lori asked, wondering if she had slept for a week or two, or if she had somehow been brought to an identical greenhouse, where the plants were about five weeks older. "Or does time move differently here?"

Jan lifted a tray onto a kind of flatbed wheelbarrow and did not bother to turn around. "No, here time moves normally."

Lori didn't understand the distinction, as if there were other places where time did indeed move differently.

Jan reached out, patted a plant with firm, direct thumps as if it were a golden retriever with a Frisbee between its teeth. "With the fertilizer Byron supplied yesterday, they grow quickly."

"What are they?" Not a gardener, Lori wouldn't have recognized them if they were as common as tomatoes or green beans. The leaves were not smooth but had small, almost invisible hairs and the edges were serrated and looked sharp. If they kept growing, they would need a barber in a week or two.

"Halchatze. Purple halchatze, to be more precise, not the gray ones, which I've found to be tough."

"And you eat halchatze?" Whatever halchatze was, it was not a grain or vegetable name she recognized.

"Sure, why not?" Jan answered, giving her a firm thump on her back. "It makes good eating. Now run off to the store. Here's the list. You should have no trouble finding everything, but if you do, give me a call."

"Give you a call ..." Lori groused as she left Jan in the greenhouse, "how can I do that when there doesn't appear to be a phone in this entire B&B?" Hoping that meant she wouldn't run into trouble, Lori ran back inside for her purse and jacket. She was set to waste the day with a disappointing trip into town all alone, but when she bounded down the stairs, she saw Byron leaning against the Mustang on the passenger side, looking better than the evening before, but not fully recovered. His pants this time were a rich brown leather and looked soft enough that Lori had to curl her fingernails into her palms to prevent herself from reaching out, touching them, to see if they were as supple as they looked. His feet were encased in low boots and he sported a leather jacket a shade darker than his pants. It looked worn at the elbows and stress points, making him appear disreputable. Stubble sprouted thickly from his cheeks dark and menacing with bad-boy overtones. He would have looked healthy, except his eyes were deep seated, and she could see he still suffered from the exhaustion of the night before. He had looked better bare chested in the forest, but he did some rather nice things to leather. Lori found her mouth watering.

"Mind if I hitch a ride? I'm afraid if I stay here your aunt will find something diabolical for me to do."

"That's why I'm leaving," Lori said pulling her key into the ignition, reaching over, to unlock the door to her right. "I'd love the company. You can act as tour guide."

Byron settled in, shifting uncomfortably for a minute and mumbling under his breath. When she looked over, it was as if the car had grown to accommodate his size, for he no longer looked cramped. She shook her head and decided she was imaging things.

"Did you get your wings to sprout?" she asked as she shifted the car into drive then pulled out of the gravel drive onto the road. The morning air was crisp, but smelled clean and she felt enlivened, as if magical things were happening all around her.

"No. I really did overdo it yesterday and flying takes a lot of energy. I found something to eat though, and I should be able to handle anything which comes up."

"Are we expecting trouble?" she asked, her concentration riveted on the narrow, windy mountain road. Since approaching traffic appeared non-existent, the only trouble she could imagine would be precipitated by his kisses and the effect they had on her pulse.

When he made no response, not even a shrug, Lori decided to dig for conversation. "What can you tell me about the dream I had the other night?"

Byron grinned slyly, and the slow, deliberate way his lips curled up on one side showed her he felt rather pleased with himself. "Did you enjoy it?"

"Is it getting warm in here?" Lori rolled the window down a fraction.

He laughed, then folded his long fingers together over his stomach. "Let's just say the dream was an experiment that worked out well for both of us."

CHAPTER 16

So, how did she respond to that? Was the creep saying he manipulated her dreams?

As if.

"Are you a voyeur, Mr. MacLauchland?"

"If I were, could you blame me?" The twinkle was back in his eyes and some of his pallor had vanished, as if he fed off her. "But I am out of practice, for want of a better phrase, in making love to a woman. I needed to know what would work."

Lori rubbed her hand around the inside of her collar. "Trust me, whatever it was you did, it worked. Did you manipulate my dream?"

Clearly sensing he was on thin ice here, he laughed. "Is that possible, Ms. Larwick?"

"I'm not drinking any more of that dragon tea until I've had a chance to get it analyzed. Are there drugs in it?"

"That tea is my heart and essence. Nothing more, nothing less. Have it analyzed if you wish to know the internal workings of a dragon."

"Dragon? Why is it every time I ask a question around here, the answer seems to be wrapped around a dragon?"

"That's not surprising. A dragon lives in, at, over, or near the Inn."

"What? Not through?"

His laughter was his response.

The further from the bed and breakfast she drove, the more spring seemed to have taken control of the landscape. Trees exploded into full leaves, and the quaint, well spaced houses were decorated in rainbow hued tulips, vibrant purple hyacinths and crocus, punctuated with flaming yellow forsythia bushes and the occasional warm-looking fuzzy pussy willow.

It was Lori's time to raise an eyebrow. "Ok, then, let's back up a bit." Her fingers tightened on the steering wheel. "In, at, over or near the Inn? Could you be a little bit more specific?"

He shifted, turning in the seat to more fully face her. "The choice of preposition depends on your understanding of doorways."

"And I suppose the dragon doesn't live under the Inn because that's where the things are chained. Unless it's the dragon that's chained?"

"I believe I mentioned no one chains a dragon."

She set her teeth and growled, looking at him askance as she kept her eyes on the windy narrow roads. "I suppose you're doing that just to drive me crazy."

Byron ran his hand through his straggly hair, a seductive movement which had her salivating. "The thought had crossed my mind, and I don't have to give you any tea to accomplish the goal."

"So, which would you chose? In, at, over or near the Inn? For if there is a dragon, I want to be as far away from him as possible."

"Do you now? Why?" Casually he moved his hand until it rested on the back of her head rest, then proceeded to tickle her ear and caress the back of her neck.

"Dragons are nasty, smelly things, aren't they?"

"I'm sure your aunt would agree." His accent thickened, but he was obviously amused. And, he didn't stop his sensual assault.

Lori curled her nose. "And knights seem to be in short supply to kill the thing." This was as ridiculous a conversation as his discussion in the upstairs linen closet, but since then, she certainly had an increased appreciation of the blue towels.

"Knights, maybe, but there are enough creatures hunting this dragon that if you seek his death, you might not have long to wait."

"Are you saying it's a good dragon?"

Byron tugged on her earlobe, a slight movement that shouldn't have had her thinking of warm beds and pleasure. "Good is clearly a conditional word. If you want my opinion..." he waited, and she nodded, to show she did. "I think it's a grand thing having a dragon close by. You don't have to worry about little pesky things bothering you, for they keep their distance."

"I understand your logic. You would rather live next door to a grizzly bear than have to worry about the occasional fox, badger or wolf?"

"Of course. Especially if you know how to handle the grizzly."

"And how do you handle a dragon, Mr. MacLauchland?"

"It's not difficult. Dragon's are sensual creatures. If you do something he likes, he'll tell you."

"And if you don't, he'll eat you."

"There's always that possibility." But his eyes darkened, and rich gold appeared around his pupils. "I don't think you have to worry. And to answer your earlier question, I know enough about doors that I could make an argument for each of the prepositions."

"In, at, over or near," she finished correctly.

"Yes. And trust me, you're going to be so close to a dragon soon, you're not going to have to be concerned with syntax."

"A real fire breathing dragon?"

"Yes."

"Then at least I'll sleep warm at night."

For the second time in almost as many minutes, his laughter rang through the small car. "That you will. That you will."

The town of Au Sable Forks was a small, thriving upstate community, with a Catholic, an Episcopal and a Methodist Church on Main Street, neatly ironed sidewalks that catered to tourists and anyone else with a need in town.

At the single blinking red traffic light Lori brought her car to a complete stop to look around. She passed the American Legion, the liquor store, and the bank on her quest to find a parking spot, before she got lucky, and slipped into one in front of the ice cream parlor. She made a mental note to check it out before she left. Although Jan's food was tremendous, Lori decided she needed some good old fashioned junk food clogging up her arteries.

"Should we split this up?" she asked, showing him the list. "We could get this done faster."

"If you don't mind, I've got something to check in my shop. Stop by when you're finished, and," he said reading her mind again, "I'll buy you an ice cream."

"It's a deal. I'd love to see your shop in the daylight. I was so exhausted when I was there before." She hoped he wouldn't notice she was unconsciously rubbing her third finger, left hand clearly remembering wedding rings. "I'll see you when I'm finished."

He pulled his long, lanky frame from her car, and as he strode away, Lori renewed her appreciation for leather.

Lori waited until he disappeared into a building several doors down, then realized the list would have to wait. She had to call her mother. She didn't want to call from Aunt Jan's house, which seemed ridiculous, since Jan was a relative and so far denied her nothing, but Lori was pleased when she found a payphone inside the ice cream parlor.

"Hi, Mom. I'm just calling to check in." Throughout her college years, Lori had tried to keep in touch at least once a week, figuring they both felt better after a call.

"Andrew has been calling here every day looking for you. What was I to tell him? I didn't know where you were. I started worrying. He said he thought your oral defense didn't go well."

"It went fine, mom. It was approved. What have you been telling Andrew?"

"He's such a nice young man. I told him you'd be sure to call him as soon as you could. Are you sure you're all right?"

"I'm fine. Listen, please promise me you will not tell him where I am. Promise. He's a—" how was she to finish that, when she had no proof? He's evil. I think he's killed. I think he wants to hurt me? None of that she had any basis to say, and for a long time, nearly half a year, she had thought him wonderful, had thought herself falling in love with him, had imagined spending the rest of her life with him. Now she was afraid of him: of what he thought, of what he did, of what he was. "We broke up and I'm not ready to face him."

"He'll probably call again."

"I know. Don't tell him I'm at Aunt Jan's. It's important to me. I'll probably come home in a few days, and deal with him. For now, just tell him you haven't heard from me."

She quickly hung up, checking the first item on her list. "Hardware store. Right you are," she said, as she scanned the street. This was a proper tourist town, catering to out of town visitors with money to burn. The stores she passed were mostly upscale, with sale signs to clear the ski-trade winter merchandise sprouting up. Catching sight of her goal, Lori hiked down the sidewalk and opened the heavy door. A bell rang as she entered. The store was stuffed wall to ceiling with paint cans, shovels, canning jars, bulk seeds, and every imaginable hand tool. It smelled thickly of fertilizer, and reminded her strongly of her youth, trailing behind her father on an occasional Saturday when he needed to putter around the house. Big box hardware stores were too generic, too sanitized. This was how a hardware store should look. She passed a young man with sandy hair and healing acne stocking garden tools with the precision of a librarian shelving best sellers, and went to the salt and pepper haired clerk lounging by the register.

"Hello, welcome. What can I help you with?" His voice was gravely, with a trace of accent, French Canadian, perhaps, and she found herself missing Byron's 'w's that sounded like 'v's.

Beside the register were clear glass gallon jars each filled with a different treat: fire balls, root beer barrels, bubble gum and taffy. If she hadn't been still stuffed from breakfast, if she hadn't been anticipating hot fudge while feasting on Byron, she would have filled the small red-stripped paper bags to overflowing with this bounty.

"This is such a delightful town." It was so decidedly different from her university town, where all the students, even the international ones, were generically fighting for common goals.

"We like it." The clerk was friendly, in the mood to chat. His eyebrows were long, curled a bit, and there was dark hair sprouting from his ears. Lori decided she could spend the day here, catching up on the latest gossip. After the pressures of university life, that sounded relaxing. She had spent too much of the preceding years doing research, hadn't imagined she could feel so comfortable in an old fashioned hardware store.

"My aunt Jan Pikorski told me to pick up some packages for her," Lori said. The clerk shared a look with the stockman, changed the tone of his voice, and said, "I've got it all ready."

Ice dripped from his words, and mentally she took a step back. "Do I owe you for them?"

He held his hands out, worn palms facing her, as if he wouldn't stoop so low as to accept her money. "No, that's all taken care of."

From a dusty shelf behind him, he pulled five packages, each wrapped in brown paper, tied deliberately with string. One small package was exceptionally heavy, as if it had lead in it. The largest package was so light, she wondered if left out alone it would float up to the bare-bulb ceiling. The weirdest thing was one of the packages squealed, like there was something alive in it.

"What is this?" Lori asked, afraid to touch that one.

He ground his teeth together, giving her to wonder if he suffered jaw problems, if his dentist had prescribed a bite splint for nights. "I'd appreciate it if you would just take these and leave."

Lori filled her arms, but was loath to leave without an explanation. "I don't understand."

"This is a God fearing community, and while we are taught tolerance to all with different beliefs, there are some who cross the line."

The package squealed again, but stayed stationary, not at all indicative that the creature inside was trying to escape. "My Aunt Jan is one of the most loving, giving people I know."

"So she would have you believe."

"I would like an explanation, if you don't mind," she said, trying to keep her question light and inquisitive without being invasive. "She is a caring woman, who, I am certain, would do anything for this community."

"Yes, that may be true, but can you honestly tell me since you've been there, nothing unusual has happened? Things didn't disappear or appear out of nowhere, or some creature didn't shimmer, just out of your line of sight?"

Lori was too stunned to answer. "I'll take the packages. I'm sure my aunt appreciates all the work you've done on her behalf."

She got to the door, found she couldn't manage with her hands filled, and waited while the stockboy opened it for her. His eyes darted, looking back toward the register before he spoke. "Be careful if you walk in the woods. There are things…not right…there, particularly after dark."

"I'll be careful." Lori hefted the packages. Fighting her confusion and wishing she had Byron with her to answer her questions, she returned to her car. She deposited the packages in the trunk except the squealing one, which she set on the back seat, leaving the window down an inch, so it would get some air. She worked her way down the list, meeting the same response at the post office, the grocery store, the bank and the lawyer's office: open friendliness until she mentioned who she was and what she wanted, then each expression changed to a wary caution, and usually they offered a vague warning about things that wandered around the old house and the woods after dark. It occurred to her that was why Byron didn't accompany her. He knew the reception she would receive, and he didn't want to provide her explanations or evasions, since it was more than likely he was one of the things sulking around her Aunt Jan's property after dark.

An hour later, the trunk of her car was filled, and the backseat nearly overflowed with her aunt's packages. She was about to go hunting Byron, for she had worked up an appetite and had questions she was certain he could answer, if he would. Lori realized she rarely got information from him, only evasions and comments about syntax and ridiculous statements about dragons coming and going. She discovered two other squealing packages and Lori had handled them delicately. As with the first, she'd been afraid to leave them in the trunk or to pile other things on top of them, so she put those three packages in the back seat, and told them, "I'll be back soon," feeling like a fool. Although she probably was imagining it, her words seemed to calm whatever was upset in the packages.

"I wouldn't open those, if I were you."

Lori looked up, startled, so see a wizened old man beside her. She was a bit miffed she hadn't heard him approach, hadn't been aware of him until he spoke.

She smiled, tried to pretend he hadn't startled her. "I wasn't planning on opening them. They are so well sealed." She wasn't sure if Jan would mind if she took a peak, but decided after the first stop that perhaps she didn't want to know the contents.

"I saw you in the hardware store. It was a bit of luck on my part that I came into town today. I don't usually, and Jan usually picks up her supplies herself."

"You're Arthur, aren't you? We met the first day I came into town in the jewelry store."

"Indeed I am, and indeed we did."

She recognized friendliness in his tone, a welcomed contrast to what she had experienced that afternoon.

He cleared his throat, then looked over his shoulder, in the direction Byron had disappeared. "In case you don't remember, I'm a friend of the dragon's. Jan doesn't think much of me, although I've never meant her any harm. But I've spent some hours with him, and while I do have a reputation as a dragon-killer, I would do anything in my power to help him."

Her throat felt dry and she couldn't swallow. It was bad enough joking with Byron about a dragon, but this man was a stranger who could not know of her fantasies. "What dragon?"

"You've got his mark on you girl. More than just the tea, although I can see by the glow you've had quite a bit. No, if I were to be so bold to say, I'd guess he's kissed you a time or two, knocked your socks off, by the look of you, but don't tell me, for it's not my place to know."

Friendly or not, Lori decided she wanted to find out more. "Listen, there's an ice cream parlor right here. Can I buy you a cup of coffee or a sundae? I'd like to find out what you know."

The stranger ran his fingers down his short, trimmed gray beard. "There's nothing I know that can help you."

Lori wondered if batting her eyelashes would be overkill. "If I told you I don't have any idea what you're talking about, would you tell me any more?"

"Trust the dragon. He obviously trusts you. And remember, your aunt is a good woman. The old creatures have been hunted nearly to extinction, but that doesn't mean they're completely gone or shouldn't be saved. Your aunt is one of the few creating a haven for them."

"Them?"

"The elves, the faeries, the leprechauns, the sprites and the pixies. She's even tried to befriend a troll or two, not that I think much has come from that. She does good work and she needs someone she can trust to carry on the vocation. Someone of her bloodline."

Lori exhaled with a puff. "This conversation would make more sense if she wrote fairy tales."

His face was rough, craggy, as if he were trying to look more disreputable than he actually was, but when he smiled, his features lightened. This time when he moved, he shifted his right hand to his left hip as if seeking the familiar comfort of a sword hilt.

"Fairy tales. I could tell you a thing or two. But no, that's not for the sunlight or an open street. Heed me, some things can only be continued through bloodlines. Have you ever wondered why kings and other peers spent so much effort trying to secure succession? Some important matters can only be passed along a paternal or maternal lineage. Of course, recent kings have forgotten, and see succession as merely keeping the money and the power in the family. It's more than that. Much more."

He looked around, checked over his shoulder, as if suddenly paranoid. "There's evil sulking nearby. Don't forget that. It will have your scent soon enough, especially with you closely allied with the dragon. Take care, and if you walk the forests, it might be best to stick to the right turnings."

"Mr.—"

"You may call me Arthur. It is important you realize not everyone who lives in Au Sable Forks is against the crusade your aunt mounts. Many hope she succeeds. It's a hard battle she fights, made easier with the dragon on her side. Hard to lose a battle with a fighting reptile beside you, and Ole Brew has seen his fair share of battles."

To be perverse, she wanted to ask him what his father's name was, and to ask him to tell her about his genealogy, but Lori didn't believe for a moment the really evil ones had no father, no mother.

"I will walk you to the store."

"Thank you for your aid, but I will have no trouble finding it."

As she was about to enter Dragon's Gold, the door opened and a handsome man exited, patting his pocket and looking pleased. Lori realized she knew him. He was a rock star and she loved his music, but he slipped into a small black sports car and was gone before she found her voice.

"Was that—"

"Yes."

"And he bought Dragon's gold?"

"Yes, actually about ten years ago. A wedding set, a man's ring, an engagement ring and a matching woman's band. I was afraid he was going to offer it to the woman with him at the time, some super model, but he left it here until this afternoon."

"A marriage sealed with Dragon's gold never dissolves, isn't that what you said?"

"Yes. Don't worry. He chose well."

"I'm glad. So, have you been working on anything here?"

"A couple things. I've got a buyer who sends me unique gems, and I try to do them justice."

Idly, without realizing what she was doing, Lori strolled to the inside front window and checked, just to be sure the wedding rings she had tried on, "her" wedding rings, had not been carried off by some former child superstar.

For a second she did not see them, was about to cry out, even knowing they could by no definition be considered hers, but she saw them and her heartbeat changed from panic to throbbing welcome, a love-at-first-sight happiness. They were there.

Byron slipped up behind her. He had to know what she was thinking, feared, and wanted, for she had no doubt every single emotion was visible in her expressive eyes as he cupped her chin with his sensitive fingers. She opened her mouth to speak, but he prevented her with the simple expediency of a kiss. There was no prelude this time, no hesitation, no angling his face to fit more properly against hers. He turned her with one quick motion, swooping down, hawk to prey and attacked her, lips ravaging hers, tongue doing battle to gain entrance to her mouth, hands assaulting the high, pert pony tail she had worn until the rubber band popped, spilling her glorious hair out along her shoulders. As he had at the maple, he arched his hips along hers, rubbing, pressing, making obvious the extent of his desire did not end with a desperate need to kiss her mindless.

Lori, weak and lightheaded, swayed, but only enough so she could be swallowed in his passion, consumed by his desire. The taste of strawberries returned, ripe and bursting with flavor, as did the lightning flashes of vibrant colors, but this time it was as if she knew what they portended. She had seen her future hadn't she, when he had marked her with dragon's gold? She had witnessed them together throughout eternity, sometimes passionately alone, sometimes sharing their love with dark eyed children who looked exactly like miniature representations of their father.

His too-long teeth nibbled against the fullness of her bottom lip. With boldness she should have fought but instead celebrated, he brought his palms against her straining breasts. Her nipples tightened so firmly in response it was almost painful. She wanted to wrap her legs around his waist, wanted the out-of-control passion to burn to its obvious conclusion right here. She throbbed not only with desire, but a heady dose of love.

She was fully clothed, and they stood in front of a shop window, where any local could see them, where any tourist could enter after being enticed by the illusive promise of gold.

"Byron, I have, I want, I need …"

"Yes," he mumbled as he continued his tender invasion against her neck, her ear. His hands were large. He moved one from its massage against her breasts and cupped her thin, narrow chin until she looked at him, locking her eyes with his. "And we're going to have to do something about this very soon. I don't care what your aunt will say, for I am going to have you."

He broke off the kiss, holding her, for Lori found herself dizzy and incomplete, and without his support would have melted into a puddle in the middle of his store.

"Could we …" she asked, not wanting to be crude, but desperate to go back where she was when his body had been pressed against hers.

"Yes." His voice was low, graveled. She imagined the beast in the forest, and thought herself captured. "There will be no escape for you. But not here in this town, where not all who pass are friends."

She shook her head, trying to clear cobwebs and fanciful images, instead felt the swish of her hair against her shoulders. She was not used to wearing it down, and the feeling was seductive.

"Are you ready?" Byron asked. He took her hand, led her unresisting to the sidewalk, then turned around and did nothing more devious than locking the door to his store.

"Yes, I guess. I've got all of Aunt Jan's packages."

"What do you say to hot fudge?"

"I never turn down hot fudge." The truth of the matter was at the moment she was hungry for strawberries, and he laughed out loud when she told him.

While Byron secured a table and ordered she thought of forever and promises and drinking tea long into the night by a fireplace, and she grew warm again hoping her face hadn't flushed.

"You're an anthropologist?"

"Yes." She shook her head and tried to avoid looking at him. She had never considered eating ice cream part of a seduction, but he alternately bit the confection on his spoon or licked it sensually. Watching him eat was without a doubt foreplay.

"What is your specialty?"

"My dissertation was on medicine men." She had ordered a strawberry sundae and the whipped cream was real, heavy and intense. The plump, succulent strawberries in the topping almost made her swoon. "I found a compact aboriginal tribe in the Australian outback and studied their medicine men through their oral histories. I thought of studying the wise women, but I found they were the ones with the actual ability. They knew the herbs to stop bleeding, the plants to use as bandages, the techniques to ease the pain of childbirth. The men used their 'powers' to intimidate and control. I liked the fact that they were seen as all powerful when really they were but smoke and mirrors. The real work was being done behind them in the huts."

"And if a patient died or a laboring mother did not survive childbirth, the men could blame the women, and remain all powerful."

"Exactly."

"Do you think those men had any true power at all?"

"Of course not. There is no such thing as wizardry."

His eyes twinkled and he took a long, slow taste of ice cream before he spoke again. "I beg to differ."

"You can't honestly think men can wave their arms, throw some powder on a fire and the spirits will come to call?"

"Actually, I do. I have extensive experience with wizards … none of it good, mind you. It's a bit more involved than simply waving their arms and muttering mumbo jumbo, but do not dismiss wizardry."

"I suppose you're a wizard?"

"Ah, no. My powers are significantly different. But the power is there. A lot of it has been lost and forgotten, but there are still some who practice the arcane arts with authority."

"Black magic?"

"And white. As with all power, wizardry can go either way."

Lori had been looking out the window, for she was nearly finished with her sundae, watching about a half-dozen people loitering on a bridge she could see through the front window of the ice cream shoppe. "Bolt counters" her aunt had called them, people lacking a life, so they spent their time on the bridge, smoking, doing nothing more than taking up space.

Two people joined them, spoke a while, then meandered toward the town, and the ice cream shoppe.

One was Andrew, and he was talking to Belinda, a 'witch' her aunt had called her. The woman who, somehow, had been trying to kill Byron.

"Be quiet. Don't make a move, and don't do anything to draw attention to yourself," Byron ordered.

"The witch—" Lori said, but her attention was locked on Andrew. Even if her mother had told him where she was, he could not have arrived so quickly.

"She has no dominion in this town," Byron assured her, "but do not let that relax you. Her powers are real. As are his."

Her spoon dropped, clattering against the glass. "Do you know him?"

"No, but I know what he is. He reeks of it. He's a wizard and at a guess, the powers he controls are far more significant than hers."

"I suppose it's too late for me to update the conclusions in my dissertation," Lori said dryly. Andrew and Belinda turned, disappearing down a side street.

"They're gone. We should get back to your aunt."

They didn't speak during the ride back to the Inn, for Lori could see something was bothering him, something which started when he noticed Andrew. Something was bothering her as well for she had hoped the police stopped him.

Byron helped her tote the packages inside. "I was beginning to worry," Jan said. "You were gone so long."

"Lori, there are things I must do now, but with your permission, I would like to bring the teapot to your room tonight."

The promise had her heart tripping. "I would like that. We could sit by the fire and talk."

Jan interrupted before Byron could speak again. "I would appreciate it, Lori, if the teapot does show up, don't drink much. A cup or two should be fine."

"Why?"

"Let's just say it is too precious to drink foolishly. Now go back to the car and bring in the rest."

Jan waited until Lori disappeared. "Byron, I think I'd like a long talk with you before you ingratiate yourself in her room tonight."

He rubbed his head. "Do you threaten me?"

"No, but I would like to make some ground rules clear regarding my blood-kin."

"Perhaps, if I have the time later we can talk. There was a new wizard in town. I would like to investigate his intentions. Oh, and maybe you should ask your niece about her thesis. It seems she is an expert on men of power."

"What?"

"She has been researching shamans. Her conclusions are that men have no real power, but all ability comes from women."

"Then she wouldn't be far wrong, would she?"

His eyes darkened, and he pulled straightened his shoulders, raising his chin. "Perhaps I should show her what a man of power is capable of."

"No. Stop that. No demonstrations. You keep your wing ridges where they are. And I really don't want you in her bedroom."

"I am only offering tea tonight."

"Then make sure that is the only part that gets inside her tonight."

"Phew," Lori said, dropping the last of the packages down onto the kitchen table, oblivious to the tension between her Aunt and Byron. "Now, if you have a few minutes, I'd like you to tell me what is in all these packages."

"I'm sorry, but I'm afraid that's going to have to wait for another time." Jan kept her so busy she didn't have time to ask questions or even realize she was not getting the answers she desired.

CHAPTER 17

Her watch called it six o'clock in the morning, but there was no going back to sleep. Not that she really slept. It had been a hard night. Byron had promised the teapot and talking long into the night. Although she waited expectantly, he never showed. She made her way downstairs several times until Jan, busy doing something Lori could not figure out, finally sent her off to bed.

Finished in the bathroom, Lori caught a flicker of herself in the mirror. She turned back to face her image, startled, for just a moment, because she had thought a stranger faced her, someone she did not recognize. As she cursed herself for a fool, she stared deeply at her reflection. She wouldn't be at her best. After all, she hadn't showered or even brushed her hair.

As she moved, securing her hair with a tieback, the mirror image shadowed her, matching her actions, except there was a significant discrepancy. She looked different. What she saw indicated not only physical changes but deeper than skin deep, emotional, social, psychological differences.

The strange feeling flooded her that she should ask "Who are you?" or the more insightful "What has happened to me that I look so different?"

This Lori Larwick knew something she did not, had been exposed to traumas or heights of pleasure she didn't remember. This doppelganger had altered in fundamental ways that Lori, pinching her own cheeks, could not comprehend.

Some urge was pressuring her this morning to get moving, but before she could heed the impulse she forced herself to take the time to see what physical changes manifested themselves.

The mirror indicated change, no doubt, even as she tried to deny it. Didn't she recognize the sweater, the way she always wore her hair pulled from her face? Same nose. Same cheeks, although under Aunt Jan's marvelous cooking, they were starting to flesh out, look a bit fuller, quite a bit healthier. Those last few months while she finished the thesis, while she prepared her oral defense, she had eaten almost nothing, drank little beyond gallons of cold, stale coffee. She could argue the trip here was worth it for the food alone. The change which so startled her wasn't her cheeks, or her lips, which she thought vainly, looked a bit fuller since Byron's kiss. She smiled at that memory and the image almost transformed back into the Lori she knew, the one she expected to face in the mirror.

It was almost like she had lost her innocence, not in a sexual sense, for that had happened a few years back, but the type of innocence that kept her denying the presence of faeries, creatures chained in the basement, and things science did not accept. It was as if having denied Santa Claus all these years, she now realized he was real, a force to be reckoned with.

A line from the stranger Arthur returned. It haunted her at the time since she had no idea what he meant. "You've got his look about you girl, not just the tea, although I can see you've had a bit of that."

He had been speaking of a dragon.

She had been thinking of Byron.

It was Byron's tea, wasn't it? If it was, how did he make it so personal, so intensely his?

Lori returned to her investigation of her mirror image. This stranger facing her, wearing her clothes, echoing her movements, definitely knew something she didn't. It was etched in her eyes. She reached out, slowly, touched her lids, the soft skin above her cheeks, the lashes winking down. She watched as her reflection did the same. Her eyes were wider, the green of her pupils darker and shadowed. Her complexion was better, the bags under her eyes had disappeared with sleep, fresh air and exercise, but her eyes themselves looked haunted.

Eyes. What did poets call them, windows to the soul?

Lori left the mirror, annoyed. Windows to the soul indeed. What was that nonsense? She was a scientist. A researcher. Not a silly moon-June-spoon word-hack. Still, as she turned her back on the mirror, as she left the bathroom, she could not deny there were severe alterations which had manifested themselves as differences in her eyes. She was changing.

Shoulders back, head high, Lori decided she would work on that analysis another time. Right now she had worlds to conquer. That thought too, made her smile.

She stopped back into the bedroom, ignoring the unmade bed and the mess she'd made with last night's clothing. She looked for the teapot hoping she had overlooked it. It was not there, and it had not been last night. Byron had promised it would be. She had gone to bed disappointed, and had grieved, wishing for the taste of his magical tea. Thinking herself foolish, wanting only him to satisfy her desires, she would not go downstairs to ask for the pot. It was after all only tea.

Lori had no dreams during the night, but her mind had fought the rebuttal of Byron and her aunt's comments that men of power did exist, and shouldn't be trifled with.

She bounded toward the stairs, fully intending to thump down to breakfast and see what new culinary marvel her aunt was canning this morning. Maybe she would seek out the dragon teapot, to prove to herself it was not enchanted.

She was almost to the third floor before she became aware she had gone up, not down as she had planned. For a fleeting moment she wondered if she had fallen into an E.C. Echker drawing where up was down and down was up and corridors dead-ended, then magically reappeared elsewhere, coming out of a solid wall. She turned, fully intending to sidle back down to pancakes or cheese omelets and conversation. But she knew instinctively this wasn't a morning for normality. Hadn't her eyes told her that much?

Firming her resolve, and this time making a conscious decision, she planted a booted foot on the next step going up. She grasped the handrail. She needed something to hold on to. Really, when common sense was gone, she had to grip something. Her sanity had clearly skipped town. Hadn't her eyes said that as well?

As she continued upwards, ignoring the third floor landing without a glance and continuing up toward the fourth, she thought maybe the mirror shouldn't be trusted. Maybe the fault didn't lie within her own eyes but an enchanted mirror. That was a common theme in fairy tales: enchanted mirrors popped up in all kinds of places. In a second floor communal bathroom? That Lori doubted. If it had been in the one bedroom Aunt Jan had chosen for her out of seemingly hundreds of other empty rooms, it would have been worth considering. Not the second floor bathroom. Such a thing wasn't done in fairy tales.

She passed the fourth floor landing without slowing. As she headed toward the fifth, she decided when finished this adventure, (what else could she call it?) she would check her reflection with the mirror in her purse, one she was certain wasn't enchanted. Lori chuckled, pleased at the whimsy. When had she started believing in enchanted mirrors again? She was certain she abandoned that particular belief at least fifteen years before. She puffed out a breath and fluffed her bangs. Well, just goes to prove, you never know.

She continued up, thought this landing was the sixth, although it might have been the seventh. She had lost track, although the tightness in her thighs indicated she'd been climbing for a while. It would be nice if they put numbers on each floor, like she found exiting hotel elevators to reassure visitors they weren't exiting at the wrong location.

She giggled. If she wanted adventure, she should have headed down. After all, wasn't she dying to see the things chained in the basement? Really, if she did that, she should take Byron with her for emotional support. He had experience fighting monsters. If he were eaten by the things chained in the basement, would Aunt Jan let her have his teapot?

No, she still had plans for him that didn't involve his becoming an appetizer to some voracious creature.

She reached another landing and determined to continue up she tightened her grasp on the handrail. She'd pull herself up if she had to. Breakfast would taste all the sweeter when she returned to the kitchen. From the outside, it looked like the house had only three, maybe four floors. With her new insight, there appeared to be another floor added every time she looked. Perhaps the house itself was enchanted. Not just the mirror: every room, every hall, even the staircases. She could be climbing these stairs for eternity, forever higher, never reaching her destination.

Another landing. Then a few minutes later, with her heart thumping and her lungs screaming for oxygen she reached yet another.

"I don't know how many more floors there are but I'd like to reach my destination," she gasped, speaking to no one and nothing, except perhaps the house itself. Lori realized a significant fact as she continued. Her 'goal' was not the attic, which would have been logical, but rather it was her 'destination', which made more sense. Her goal was only adventure, and there was a strong likelihood if she investigated any of these floors she could find that.

Then, and she was positive it hadn't been there the moment before, the stairs above her ended at a landing and she realized she'd reached the top.

"Thank goodness," she said, huffing out a breath of hot air, pulling herself up the last few stairs.

"Goodness had nothing to do with it."

Lori jumped, startled, no, more like scared out of her skin. It was a good thing her hand clasped the handrail, for if it hadn't, her fall would probably have ended on the next lower landing or even the one below that.

"Byron, you startled the life out of me."

He loitered there, his back against the wall, feet crossed at the ankles, casually studying her. From his far too roguish smirk to the undeniable twinkle in his eyes, he studied her with a devil-may-care look that should have had her common sense saying "Run" instead of her pulse tripping to "Oh, yeah!"

Why in heaven's name did her palms suddenly feel moist?

Stubble darkened his chin, rugged, longer than yesterday's and more than a shade uncivilized. Should she kiss him, she would definitely get lip burn. Why was she thinking of kissing him? Why did abrasion sound so incredibly sexy?

His arms were folded against his chest, poised, she decided, as if he practiced in front of an enchanted mirror himself, to give off the proper look of annoyed tolerance and sexual availability.

His clothing was standard. No leather. Only jeans, work boots, and a flannel shirt. If masculinity were sold on the open market to anyone with a

Y chromosome, part of the package would definitely be jeans, work boots and a flannel shirt with a side of damned annoying arrogance.

Staring at him, she felt a bit light-headed. It was possible this high the oxygen was thinner and the reason she was having trouble catching her breath. It also occurred to her perhaps the reason she went up this morning, instead of down to breakfast, was her suspicion on some unconscious level that Byron waited for her here.

"If I thought you were a woman who took advice," he said showing long, overly white teeth she was certain indicated she amused him, "I'd tell you to turn around and head back down these stairs before you get yourself into trouble you can't handle."

Lori felt boldness surging through her, awash with the force of a tsunami. "Ahh, I can handle you."

"I'm sure you think so. You might be surprised when you find out there is more to me than tea."

She licked her lips, sauntered closer. Although she had not dressed for seduction, she felt feminine beside him. "Shall we try some tea now, and see which one of us comes out the victor?"

His eyes narrowed, and the copper of his irises vanished, leaving black and shadow. "Is that a threat?"

"No. A promise." She walked her fingers up his granite hard chest, starting just above his belt, a slow seduction she maintained until reaching his chin. Byron was clearly affected, betrayed by the throbbing of the pulse at his throat, the way he set his too-long teeth as if he wanted to ravish her—or rip out her throat.

"Your Aunt Jan will worry about you."

"She won't." Pleased with his response, she rubbed her fingertips along his clavicles, until she met his shoulders. "She knows I am with you."

He laughed, abrupt and mocking. "All the more reason for her to worry. You see, she knows all about me."

Lori had come too far to be timid and never known to be reticent, she pursed her lips and cocked her head, knowing the fall down the stairs might be a lot less painful than the fall she might experience if she thought she could create a position in his life. "She knows all of your secrets?"

His smile vanished and his eyes remained dark, unreadable. It was as if the light, coming from no discernible source, suddenly dimmed, draping his face in shadow. He appeared less substantial, although she stayed close enough to touch him.

"She knows all of my secrets. Not much gets past her."

Then her eyes went fuzzy and she had an inner vision of long dark winter afternoons, followed by longer, darker, colder nights: Aunt Jan and

Byron seated in the red living room, drinking tea or beer or wine or a heady potent liqueur while he unburdened his soul in sharp, painful confession. She granted absolution by taking his sins, and planting them in chests to wait in the darkness.

She could see her aunt doing this for two reasons—so the sins might not be a burden and so she could have a hold over him, if she ever needed a garden tilled, or some other more uncomfortable favor.

He must have read her mind, or perhaps he had planted the vision in her gray matter, for he said, "I don't have a soul. Perhaps one day I'll share what I do have, but for now you must realize I don't have a soul. Whatever you think of me later, whatever happens between us, I want it clearly understood up front I told you that, and I tried to make you accept it."

She nodded as if she believed him, whereas if she had spoken she might have said, "Yeah, sure," in sharp sarcasm, but her eyes had caught the door.

"No," he said, stopping her before she reached for the handle. "You're not going in there."

She would, she decided, live dangerously. Hadn't she decided that earlier? "No soul?" she asked, for she could be subtle as she planned her assault past him into the attic secrets beyond that portal.

Byron exhaled slowly and Lori watched tension peel away. She knew what he was thinking, liked the thought that she knew: Yes, she can be reasonable. No doubt it was a comforting thought for him, especially since being reasonable was the furthest thing from her mind.

"No soul," he agreed.

"You've destroyed it, with your cruel and thoughtless actions?" she taunted, for while he spoke, he displayed no remorse, no begging for forgiveness, nor the opposite aura of prevalent evil.

"I never had one." Byron leaned against the door casually, as if explaining would take all the time in the world, and Lori silently cursed. She had hoped by distracting him, she could slip past and into the attic.

"Regardless of what you might think, not every creature has a soul."

Her breath heaved in her lungs, and she became aware of fabric rubbing against her breasts, of warmth flooding her bloodstream, and a tightening coil somewhere below her navel. "I've come this far to discuss religion with you?" She let her incredulity show from her tone of voice and her slender raised eyebrow.

"I don't think it's religion you're after," Byron taunted, playing her game. "I've learned many things in the years I've lived on Earth, and one of the least accepted is aptly described by the cliché: Little girls who play with fire get burned."

"My aunt won't thank you if I come back charred."

"True. She will accuse me of pulling you up the stairs by your hair, to ravish you in the dark."

Lori felt the need to drool. She remembered a tree and a kiss, the shop and the kiss and a monster who didn't frighten her as much as the coldness of his manner now. But, she added wryly to herself, it was a completely different type of fear. "I will tell her I wanted answers to my questions."

If she had thought Byron seduced she found herself mistaken, for when he spoke his words were sharp with accusation. "So you can report back to your master?"

"Master? I have no idea what you mean."

"Don't you? The innocent maiden act is wearing thin. Didn't you think I would investigate the new mage I saw in Au Sable Forks yesterday?"

"Mage?"

Byron looked taller, darker, far more lethal than he had only a moment before. The amused tolerance was gone, in its place was building a towering rage. "Mage, wizard. Man of power. Did you think I wouldn't discover your relationship with him?"

"Andrew? You're jealous because of Andrew?"

"Jealous, darling," he spit the endearment out, "is the least of what I am feeling right now. Did you plan to bring him the teapot last night? Did I play into your hands when I offered it? How you must have celebrated to think I was both foolish and gullible."

"Byron, why would Andrew want the teapot?"

"So, he hasn't told you of the powers it contains? Looking at your reaction, I suspect he has not told you I cannot change when held in mortal hands."

"Change what?"

"Change into mortal form," Byron said, his teeth clenched.

"Why would he want the teapot?"

"For the same reason the witch did, although I doubt he would be so callus to destroy it, not when it is a much greater prize he is after. Did he mention fangs? Blood?"

She thought of rabbit holes and her confusion mounted. How had they gotten so far off-track? They had been working on seduction, not sedition. "No."

"Yet you knew he was a wizard."

"No."

He shook his head, seeping rage like uranium spewed the poison of radioactivity. "Lie all you want. You knew. I was with you in the ice cream parlor. I witnessed how you rose, how you tried to draw his attention as he and the witch walked by. I wouldn't have been able to fight him there, in the city. Did you think that would make me vulnerable? That manform is my weakest shape?"

Lori was deeply frightened, at the menace she saw in his gaze, at his rapidly venting anger. "Byron, honestly, I knew he was insane, and I wasn't trying to draw Andrew's attention. I was trying to hide."

"Insane? Is that what you think?" His laughter had her skin crawling.

"He killed a person. I don't know who. I found him cooking something in a pot in the attic of his house."

"That's where you got the smell."

"The smell?"

"That I detected when I met you. And while I don't deny the likelihood he is, tell me why you think he's insane?"

"He said he was a wizard. He said there were spells he knew and that he was powerful. Isn't that insane?"

"You study men of power and you have no idea what he is? You are his lover. You've had me as your lover in your mind. I suppose you intend to argue that you wouldn't turn me over to him, that you just wanted the experience. What is your goal? To seduce all the great creatures of power? If so, I may have to get my talons on your thesis. It must make titillating reading."

"No. I'm a scientist. Women have the power!"

"Really? How your Andrew must have laughed when you told him that. When it comes to the sexes, men and women are fairly evenly matched for control. Although, his goal is to be a Lord, one of the great masters. A goal, I might add, he could come very close to achieving if you gave him the dragon teapot."

"The teapot is just a teapot."

"How sad he has kept you in ignorance. The tea is a gift. A gift of immense power. Your lover—"

"He is not my lover! He was. I can't deny that. I found him doing something vile." Lori's pulse tripped, and cold shivers wrapped her in revulsion, reliving the terror of her memory. "Will you listen to me? Yes, Andrew and I were lovers, off and on, and I thought he was nothing but a little eccentric. Post grads usually are. It's the pressure. After my oral defense, I walked into his house. He was there, and he had killed a man, chopped him up for some perverse pleasure." She gasped, oxygen was precious here. "It wasn't just murder. It was… experimentation. I called the police, ran out of the house and hopped on a plane for here. I didn't even stop at my apartment for my computer or cell. I didn't dare. I've been here since, and I'm terrified he will find me."

He crossed his arms against his broad chest. His muscles stood out in stark relief in a body so perfect, Michelangelo could have used him as an ideal. There would be no finger-walking between belt and neck now.

Byron's laughter rang around the landing. "Yes. I have no trouble believing that. So he shipped you here, to your aunt, who believed you innocent enough of evil to serve you dragon tea, and after you washed the stench away I was intrigued, until I did my research last night."

"No. I am afraid of him. I came here to hide."

"There's no hiding any longer. Run back downstairs to your aunt, maybe she can protect you from me, but I doubt it."

He grabbed her sweater, dragged her closer until his lips were inches from hers. "Then return to your lover. You won't be welcomed here again. This Inn is protected, not in the least by the dragon on this floor. Go. Go now before I slaughter you, and I promise you, I will not regret it, and I will not pine for the magic I thought we could make together. My tea and my love are not for the likes of you. Not for spies who serve evil."

"Byron, I don't know what you're talking about. You're a jeweler. I am only here to see my aunt. I am not a spy."

He released her, but immediately thought better of it, for he grasped her again, pulled her to him, matched his lips to hers with a violence not painful, only abrupt and shockingly sexual. Her body responded to his, instantly with a sharp, incredibly thorough arousal. She would melt there, at his feet, but first she wanted the feel of him, in her, over her, through her. She begged for completion of the building explosion his kiss had ignited.

Lori desired him enough to plead. "I want you."

"Oh, yes," Byron laughed, large, aroused and very powerful. "I have no doubt. But I do not play pawn to a mortal wizard."

"You ..." words failed her. She groped, her hands outstretched, for she could not understand his reaction, but she certainly did her own. She wanted him with desperation bordering on insanity. "We made love the other night, in my dreams."

"Yes." He would not deny it and the answer was growled out on a snarl. "And that is all you shall ever have from me. I had plans for last night, to complete what we both yearned for, but before I found out where your loyalties lie."

"I do not work for Andrew, and I do not love him. I am terrified of him."

"You should be terrified. When he finds out how you have let him down, there will be another sacrifice in his attic room. Your aunt will grieve, but I will laugh."

"Byron, please, I will tell you everything, but don't hate me, and don't make the mistake that I serve Andrew. I didn't know love until I tasted your kiss by that tree."

"Did you send the garntz to distract me? Well it worked but your evil will get you no further."

"Garntz? I don't understand this conversation! I am not evil."

"Shall we discuss this over tea?" he asked, and it was ugly, accusatory.

"Will you make it?" she countered.

"You still think to control me? How little you know. To show you I am not afraid of you or your lover, if you want," Byron responded with a slight bow, "I am willing to accommodate you, but if that's your desire, you'll have to get your answers from Jan, for I won't be able to speak. I can give you dreams," he amended, "but if you want answers, you'll have to get them from Jan or forego dragon tea and ask me." He held up his hands, palm outward, as if refusing to let her speak, although she had no thought to interrupt him. "I am not denying you tea, merely offering you options."

She thought, had an insight. "You're never around when there's dragon tea."

He laughed. This thought ticked his fancy and there was no mocking to it. "I am there."

"If I ask for tea, any kind of tea, we'll head back down these stairs and talk in the kitchen."

He nodded, and on one level looked relieved. "In this house the kitchen is the best place to talk, although," and here his eyes took on a devilish gleam, "I suppose we could ... eventually ... have a lovely discussion in your bedroom."

Lori felt her face flush and for a second experienced heart palpitations. Yes, she had definite plans for exploring the option. At the moment she had another goal in sight. "I look forward to that—" she made herself clear, "at another time."

She lowered her lashes, hoped he read invitation, not cowardice before she raised them again, looked him in the eyes. When had he grown so tall, or had she shrunk?

"I am not ready to go back down. I've come such a long way. I want to see what I've set out to see."

"Does Andrew not know about the cave?"

"This has nothing to do with Andrew. I am interested myself. I would like to see what's behind that door."

"Pandora," Byron said, with a casual amusement, "learned not all boxes should be opened."

Lori felt her own power. "Pandora also learned once a box has been opened, shutting it too quickly, before it is fully investigated, is perhaps worse than opening the box in the first place."

He bowed again, this time a shade deeper, a touch more respectful. Still he kept his head raised, his eyes locked on her. "Your point," he said. "But, it would have been better in the long run, for her, if she hadn't opened the box at all."

"For her," Lori answered, a distinction he could not misinterpret.

"You'll have to take my advice on this," Byron said, his tolerance slipping a notch, "some things are best left alone."

Lori stepped closer, felt the heat radiating off him—fires burning deep within. She thought again of the huge bed she slept in alone. "Step aside, or are there things chained in the attic as well?"

"No." He shook his head, but his next words carried the tightness of a threat. "The monster which roams this attic is free to do as he wants. This is his lair and he has dominion. You will have no power here. Even asking for tea won't save you."

She didn't understand, but she didn't want to understand. She wanted, no she anticipated, being foolhardy.

"Step aside." This time she made it a command.

Byron offered a final warning of his own. "Remember what I said: I have no soul, so I will not, cannot regret anything which happens to you inside. This is my domain. To a large degree the laws of Earth do not exist here."

Lori forced a laugh to cover an increasing nervousness. "Is there a monster?" she asked, but the question he answered was significantly different.

"I am a monster," Byron said. Then he stepped aside and opened the door.

***

Andrew quirked his lips to one side, then quickly scraped the straight razor against his chin, removing shaving cream and stubble with one fluid movement. It made a dry, raspy sound he liked almost as much as he liked holding the weapon. The action was quick, almost thoughtless, and considering the length of the razor and the fact it had been honed to deadly precision only moments before, was decidedly fool-hearty. He looked into the mirror, decided that was an ineffective move, then turned around slowly, to study his companion. "You said the woman is here?"

"Of a certainty," Belinda said. She stood away from the mirror, off to one side, and beside him, she looked short, frumpy, for he was tall, slender, muscular.

He twirled on his heel, returned to his shaving, finding it slightly unsettling that from the mirror's perspective, he was alone in the room. Her kind held no reflection, and while he knew, and on one level reveled in it, he still hadn't gotten used to this quirk of witch nature which voided what he had learned in high school physics. Andrew knew mirrors made her uncomfortable, so his shaving, now was done in slow motion.

"You saw her?"

"I spoke with her myself. She welcomed me into the manor."

"Really?" An eyebrow hiked. "I thought you couldn't get in."

"I can't get in unless I have an invitation. I caught her unaware. She won't be so foolish again."

His lips curled, slowly, and the blade scraped along the patch of skin under his nose. "You were foolish to call attention to yourself. To have such an unprecedented opportunity and fail should invoke some penalty, don't you agree?"

She shifted, uncomfortable. While he could not see her, he sensed it from the rustling of her clothing. "Even you could not get in without an invitation."

"How sad," he mocked, continuing. "I have no intention of going in. What I want is easier hunted outside."

She shifted again, this time, in acknowledgement of his prowess. He lowered his brows, thought, it really was a tragedy the fool failed. "And what did you see of the Inn?" He would not give it the dignity she had and call it a manor.

"The dragon was there."

"Of course the dragon was there," he snapped. "The dragon lives there. This is not news. What other … creatures…did you see we should prepare for?"

Belinda cleared her throat, delaying.

"Well?" he asked. "Do you have an answer for my question?"

"Nothing. I saw nothing. The doors along the corridor were mostly shut, the rooms dark. Besides, I wanted to catch the dragon unaware, and I could not disguise my presence by creeping through their closets."

"But you did not catch him unaware."

"I did. You should have seen him. He was practically groveling, knowing his death was unavoidable."

That was, perhaps, a poor choice of words on her part for he scoffed, and she knew it for mocking. The blade scraped again, the sound a screech like fingernails on a blackboard, or a fan-belt in need of tightening. It was an unearthly sound. "You warned them of your intentions, gave them time to prepare, and got nothing in return."

"If I had killed the dragon, it would have been worth it." She spoke defiantly, but it was bravado. He knew it and she knew it. She backed away a step, for she saw the flash of anger in his gaze.

"But you didn't kill the dragon. Even if you had, you wouldn't have gotten the fangs. Haven't I told you I have plans for the fangs?"

"And none of our plans will come to fruition if the Ancient One is alive to meddle in our affairs. I was close enough to touch him. I had my hand on his knee. I had him quivering to make tea. Even that other harridan was worried, mindlessly making her soups and her stews, knowing the rules favored me, and she was powerless to stop me. Oh, I tell you it was a heady feeling!"

"Heady?" The blade clipped his chin, a deep nick. Blood pooled, then ran, too dark to be considered red.

Belinda watched the blood meander slowly down his chin, saw the droplet huddle, then fall. She licked her lips, seeing the puddle forming on the sink edge.

"If you had him under your power, why isn't he dead?"

"The girl interrupted." Her eyes were no longer on him, or avoiding the mirror. She watched the rapidly increasing blood pool and felt herself grow hungry.

"Didn't I tell you there was more to Lori than meets the eye? Hadn't I told you I had been investigating her for almost a year? Did you listen to nothing I said?"

Belinda swallowed before she answered, for her mouth was moist. He rubbed his left hand against the cut and it magically healed, leaving no scar, no indication there had ever been one. He ran his hand over his entire face, and the lather and the stubble he had not gotten to yet disappeared, leaving him clean-shaven.

"I have been intimate with Lori, buried deep within her body, and yet not able to touch her."

"She has no magic."

"She has her aunt's protection. I would not be so sure she lacks magic. She certainly foiled your plans, even when she had no idea what you wanted." His chest was bare, as was the rest of his body. Andrew stood back, checked his glorious naked physique in the looking glass Belinda avoided. While his form was perfection itself, on closer inspection, there was something not quite right about it, something twisted. It was as if worms festered against his skin, burrowing in and out, spreading a silent pestilence. He was slightly aroused. Thinking of Lori often did that to him, and he found no shame in it, instead he gloried in his masculinity. He pulled his shoulders back, straightened his spine. Belinda didn't watch him. Her concentration remained locked on the blood splatter on the sink.

"Jan could've killed you."

"She hasn't the ability."

"The dragon could have."

Belinda shook her head. "I don't think the thought occurred to him. Besides, he would not release his prowess in front of the girl. They keep her ignorant."

"They won't much longer, if you continue to play the fool. It will be easy enough to cause Lori to forget, more convenient, I believe, than allowing you to live."

"There is sanctuary at Reptile's Roost."

"Not for our kind. Besides, even acknowledging sanctuary, if he let you into the expanse he could have his way with you. Not much of a feast for a dragon, but you wouldn't be the first witch he's eaten."

She laughed, without mirth or pleasure. "Maybe he wasn't hungry."

"Fool. A dragon is always hungry."

Their powers were different, and overall, his were greater. He could crush her, for this foolishness, for her rash actions, but she might yet be of use. Andrew turned his back, proceeding to his room, where he began to dress.

When Belinda was certain he was gone and wouldn't be coming back, she lowered her head and lapped the blood coagulating on the sink.

Lori only took one step forward, but it was enough to bring her over the threshold. That small movement was enough to tilt her world so far off its axis she doubted she'd ever be able to right it. She stopped rock still, her mouth agape. Her eyes darted, scanning for seams, or nails or anything to indicate what she witnessed was a set, suitable for the big screen.

She glanced to Byron, but he made no comment, not even a "Well, what did you expect?" hiked eyebrow. She turned toward the interior, then back again. She thought he hadn't moved, but he had, in a significant way. He had curled the corners of his lips up, and his too-long teeth were completely visible. He looked arrogantly pleased at her confusion.

"What the—" she said, not to him, but to the environment she faced. Disoriented and enthralled, but definitely not terrorized, she moved forward. One shaky step, another, then another. She supposed it was a miracle her knees held her.

"A cave?" Her words echoed, for although the grotto was small as such things are measured, it was extremely large. The stygian blackness, a total absence of light not possible to the same degree anywhere above ground, would have been complete except for randomly spaced torches shoved in sconces which, although they burned cheerfully and almost smoke free, only added to the impossibility of what she witnessed. There was no ceiling and no sky. It might have felt less bizarre, more rooted in reality, if she saw one or the other.

"How high?" she asked, pointing with a quivering index finger.

He didn't find the question unusual. "It varies. Where we're standing, a little over thirty feet. It's higher in some places, lower in others."

She twitched which he took to mean he should continue. She didn't lose sight of his teeth when he spoke, for they seemed iridescent, brighter than normal, and longer than she expected.

"There's an exit, that way." Byron pointed to a part of the cave cloaked in the black, for the torches didn't reach that far, adding to the surrealism surrounding her, the immensity she couldn't comprehend. "Where the ceiling slopes down, I have to crawl on my belly to get through." He laughed, finding humor in a joke she could not understand. "I doubt you'd even have to bend."

Lori studied her feet, an unconscious survival mechanism: when all is chaos, find something to root yourself in normality. Her heels were pressed together tightly, another method of coping, she decided, trying to keep herself small, compact, less likely to implode. In another second she'd be muttering "There's no place like home. There's no place like home."

Recognizing her mounting hysteria, she moved her feet apart, gave herself a firmer foundation to stand on. She bent down, touched the ground, seeking to pull in more data for analysis. "I'm a scientist. I have a PhD."

"And a university degree can explain everything?"

Lori knew he mocked her, clearly understood the sarcasm in his tone.

She would not give in to fear or hysteria. What she saw couldn't be real, so it stood to reason if she collected enough data, she could unmask this hoax, get herself to a safer location, mentally, physically, perhaps even spiritually.

"This is not a cave."

He tweaked a hand out, a "Please continue" movement.

"When I bend down I'm going to touch linoleum, or something painted to approximate bedrock."

"We'll apply the scientific method if it makes you happy."

Her heart almost stopped beating when her fingers met stone. It was cold, it was damp, and most assuredly bare rock.

"If you leave now," Byron said, folding himself down beside her, so he met her gaze eye to eye, "you won't be hurt."

Even squatting, with the long bones of his thighs thrusting forward, he was so massively tall she had to look up at him. Although menace dripped from his words, the hint, or perhaps the threat, of pleasure existed. His eyes had turned gold and his teeth, always a shade too long for his mouth, seemed longer still. Whatever this place was, real or imagined, he was perfectly at home.

Her earlier trace of fear vanished without fanfare. She didn't think to miss it, although Lori knew instinctively she should be afraid not only of the unexpected cave, but of Byron. She realized what was different about him; he no longer pretended to act civilized. It was as if all those times she had met him in the kitchen and in the forest where he kissed her, he was playing a role, and here he reverted to his true self.

As unexpected as the cave was, the very danger he radiated drew her. She rose, smelled her fingers, hoping to add another sense to the unreality surrounding her. She inhaled the dark, damp, moldy smell all around her, and something else, which might have been ocean seaweed washed upon the shore, decaying slowly in the dark.

She met his gaze, stood transfixed under it for longer than she felt she should. "I'm not leaving." Lori felt the need to stamp her feet in childish rebellion. "And you can't make me," remained unsaid. They both knew he could make her do anything he wanted with little effort.

"I'm not leaving until I get some answers." Then she added, almost as insurance so she wouldn't be hurt, "and I don't think I'm in any danger."

He laughed and it was darker, deeper, and more primal than any sound he'd made before. "That's right," he said, sidling closer, sucking all the air from around her, "you don't think."

There was no need for him to mention the danger. She felt it radiating from him in waves.

Lori straightened her spine, rubbed her hands across the seat of her jeans, as if to deny both what her fingers had felt and what they would feel. She walked fifteen feet, until she reached a column located near one edge of the cave, situated between two brightly burning torches, the kind created when a stalactite and a stalagmite join. The air smelled of wood smoke and burning oil, the former sweet, the latter leaving a sharp stench in her nostrils. Both scents were added to the stagnant dampness of the cave she had first detected. It was already starting to smell familiar.

The column was slick, dripping wet and cold. For whatever reason, her teeth chattered. Lori would have been happier if her fingers had met steel, paper Mache' or plywood.

"The monster…" She had no words to finish the sentence, and had no desire to have him complete it either. As an academic, she'd never had much use for the "ignorance is bliss" cliché, but in the darkness of the cave, Lori thought it might be the only comfort she would find.

Her sister Brenda had been afraid of monsters. Every time the light went off: monsters in the closet, monsters under the bed, until she needed some serious counseling before anyone in the family was able to sleep through the night. Lori didn't believe in monsters. Never had. She had felt Brenda's fears groundless, childish.

Now, recalling his statements, even if she had no point of reference, she questioned her conviction. Depending on your definition, there were certainly monsters. The evening news and the local newspapers were filled with current stories of monsters. The true crime section of any bookstore was chocked full of them. Not Steven King fictional monsters, but the kind who lived next door, often appeared friendly until some kid went missing or some young woman was found nearly unrecognizable stuffed in a culvert.

The question was if her Aunt Jan positively and absolutely knew Byron was a monster, why did she let him in the house? Would she have been so amused when Lori gave the complete verbal rundown of the forest kiss? Her aunt had made some odd statements, had dropped some weird innuendos, but never did she warn Lori away from Byron, nor was there any question their relationship was friendly.

"I climb six, maybe ten flights of stairs, going up," she added for clarification even though the climbing verb should have made it obvious, "and come to a cave twice as big as Grand Central Station on the top floor of my aunt's house in the middle of upstate New York?" She hadn't meant to make it a question, but her voice rose with inflection toward the end. Maybe if all that were true, believing in monsters wouldn't be much of a stretch.

Byron's answer was nonverbal. He started slowly, provocatively, unbuttoning his shirt.

Over a mouth suddenly gone dry, she decided she would try sarcasm. "I suppose this means you're feeling better?"

Another button ceased its hold. Another inch of naked male chest exposed. One of them was definitely feeling better. Lori felt ready for a heart attack. She could ask for mortal tea and broth to be consumed in the red living room, but would not for three very important reasons: first, he had said a particularly grisly murder had been committed there. Second, he told her there was a secret passageway from the dungeons—or the depths of hell—which she didn't feel like chancing. Lastly, her feet had for all practical purposes grown roots. She couldn't move.

Although fascinated with his taunting strip-tease, she couldn't watch so she forced herself to turn away from whatever devilment he was up to. She had to ground herself in reality before facing the complications which would surely arise when he succeeded in removing his shirt.

"A cave," she said it aloud, the words only for herself as she walked deeper into the blackness, toward the place where he said he would have to crawl on his belly. She might like to see that. Her steps brought her no closer to a hint of light at the end of the tunnel—by any definition of that cliché. She detected no scent of fresh air from the outside. Wherever the exit was, it was a fair distance from where she stood. She tripped, almost losing her balance. The floor was uneven, not surprisingly, as if created by rushing waters or retreating glaciers. Something chittered above her, ear splitting squeaks, then a small shape as black as the dark flitted past without touching her.

"Bats?" she asked, and as her voice escaped, she barely recognized it, for the pitch was higher than normal, and the 'a' elongated, as if spoken with a foreign accent acquired in the dark.

His chuckle echoed. "It might be safer if you think of them as bats."

That wasn't much of an answer. Was it possible it was something worse than bats? Then she remembered him removing his shirt, wondered without turning around, how much progress he'd made on that task. Yes, there easily were things worse than bats.

"This is a gorgeous cave." Lori spoke as an exercise, like morning sit-ups, to keep her muscles functioning. It certainly gave the impression of a cave, every sense she owned indicated cave: sight, smell, sound, touch. Water dripped and it wouldn't surprise her to come upon an underground river, ice cold and darker than pitch filled with pale white eyeless fish. It was equally likely she would meet trolls, dwarfs or other creatures of fantasy which legend said lived in caves. There were probably fissures, places where if she dropped, she would fall straight down past all those landings she mounted as she climbed, through the kitchen or the red living room, clear to the center of the Earth ... if this were still Earth.

She could accept this as a cave without reservation if she'd been walking a deserted hillside and discovered an open crack in the fieldstone, half-hidden by brush. Perhaps if she'd taken some subterranean elevator down the equivalent of a five story building, led by guides holding flashlights, and following clearly marked glow-in-the-dark signs it would be more believable.

Lori turned back. She had been walking too far, too fast, in what was becoming deeper dark, with no end in sight. She looked up; her eyes well acclimated to the stygian darkness now, and screamed. There, toward the front of the cave, standing freely a la Twilight Zone, was the door where she had entered, and beside that, the staircase, with the same hand rail, the same red patterned runner-carpeting, heading further upwards, to who knew where.

When Byron noticed where her gaze rested, he shrugged, offered apologetically: "When you said this cave was at the top of your aunt's house, you weren't entirely correct."

"There are more floors above?"

He chuckled again, and with a swift, arrogant movement, pulled his shirt off his shoulders, and negligently threw it away. "I think you've gone as high as you need to today," then he placed his hands on his narrow hips, and continued, "or at least as high as you can get by climbing."

Byron shifted his hands to his belt buckle. Torchlight burnished his naked skin a brilliant copper color, reminiscent of the dragon teapot. His chest was broad, heavily muscled, his arms corded. She watched his breathing, as his chest expanded slightly in a controlled cadence, which had her breath tripping. He had looked untamed in the forest, when dripping sweat without his shirt; now, he looked unrestrained, feral. He had been as a tame wolf in the forest, used to people, but still a wolf. Now, the wildness, in his eyes and his grin indicated he was no one's tame anything.

Lori continued her perusal. His chest tapered down to his narrow waist, his long legs planted firmly apart. She couldn't help herself. Her interest centered above his legs, below his belt.

Lori found herself salivating, at the same time she found her throat dry, an odd juxtaposition. Since the rules seemed to have changed, she crossed her arms against her breasts, tapped one impatient foot as she tilted her head. "What do you think you're doing?"

Byron shook his head, not in negation, but in Alpha-male supremacy. "You bed a dragon in his lair, you pay the price. I've told you twice now to turn around and you refused, so now you're in my domain and under my dominion. Perhaps too I want revenge. You are the mage's servant, so I will extract it."

"Revenge?"

The belt opened, but he made no movement toward the zipper. "I will make you scream."

"Scream?"

"In pleasure. Although I don't know why, when you spy for Andrew."

"I do not spy for Andrew." But she had no doubt the rest of his statement would come to pass. Based on dreams alone, she had no doubt he would bring her mindless pleasure. Already, without him having touched her, she was aroused, almost throbbing for a climax she knew would be possible in his embrace. If kissing him set of fireworks throughout her body, she could only anticipate what their lovemaking would be like. She suspected something on the order of a nuclear explosion.

"I'll send you back to him after I have been buried deep inside you, after you have felt my power. Then you can mourn the wrong choice for the remainder of your life. When you chose for yourself a man of power, you picked the weaker."

"You might be a man of power," yes, with his shirt off, he definitely had power over her, "but you haven't been listening to a word I've said. I am not going back to Andrew. Not now. Not ever. The last time I left him I called the police to tell them of his blood sacrifice. I would imagine I am not on his favorite-person list. He probably wants to see me destroyed with at least as much intensity as he wants to destroy you. Is it so hard to believe he used me?"

Byron stretched, a slow pulling of muscle against bone, highlighting the perfection of his physique. "In that case, you won't mind if I use you." He preened, and if she hadn't been so entranced, she would have kicked him, for his arrogance, for his assurance she wanted him, and that he would use her, then discard her.

He bent, showing his firm rear, a calculated display while he removed his boots. He couldn't be feeling half the desire she was, if he could move that precisely. Lori wanted to scream, then rip her clothing off, but not until she got him to understand. "What can I say or do to make you believe he was a grad school infatuation, a diversion? I want more than the blue towels or anyone else can give me. I want you."

He stood, his feet bare, his toes long, clean. Byron wore only low slung jeans now, and the belt around his narrow waist hung open. Who would have thought she could be attracted to a man with this degree of passion?

"I intend to take you, if only to show you what you have so thoughtlessly set aside in your quest for power. No one puts a leash on a dragon. We're not like a gargoyle you can chain."

Her pulse leapt and Lori found this invitation—or threat—delightful. It was far more desirable than thinking she'd lost her mind.

His nostrils faired as if he caught her scent. "It's been a long time since I've tasted manflesh."

"Manflesh?" she questioned back. She rubbed her forearms through the sweater she wore, felt goosebumps. She thought of a fish, seeing a worm, knowing there was a hook there, debating for a second whether the price of giving in to the temptation was worth the cost of freedom. She decided yes, stepped closer, prepared to bite.

"Human," he corrected, "mortal," before he grinned, lightening his face. "No, I misspoke ... and I apologize. It's been a long time since I've tasted a woman's flesh."

"How terribly romantic." Lori snorted, no longer amused but suffering a spiking anger. Too much was too weird and this maniac was threatening her? For even if he meant it only as a proposition, it was a threat.

Something dark flew past her low, about a foot above her head, something she couldn't see, couldn't feel, could only sense the flapping of its leathery wings, approaching then vanishing just as quickly. It helped root her in the unreality of her situation. Lori inched closer still, knowing Byron himself as unusual as anything else surrounding her. "This is not right."

He cocked a hip, snorting. "You want wooing? Then you've chosen the wrong venue."

He moved, shifted his weight and she discovered two things simultaneously: first he stood between her and the door; second, a pallet waited only a few feet away. She couldn't use the word 'bed'.. It was a mess of blankets and pillows raised off the cave floor a good two or three inches by what looked to be pine boughs. For some reason, she hadn't noticed it as she made her unsuccessful attempt to find the exit, the place where he would have to crawl.

She looked again at the pallet, swallowed, thought of taking a hook between her teeth. She thought of the fish, fighting capture, giving the angler a good run for his money. Although she had never thought of it this way before, she would bet the fish too felt it worth it, the five or ten minutes of glorious battle, which made it feel far more alive than swimming placidly, unmolested in the river.

Byron saw where her eyes traveled, then laughed. "You'll be comfortable soon enough."

For all her temptation, perversity was in her nature. "And if I refuse?" She had to deliberately force herself not to wipe her moist palms on her jeans again.

He moved closer, cupped her chin with two very large, very warm hands. He looked deeply into her eyes, not so much seeking her agreement as establishing his dominance. "Should you want to run, little coward, there's the door."

His breath was warm on her cheeks, and she noticed highlights in his eyes, sparkles of gold, riches she never would have expected. The hook he was tempting her with might be one of the most precious things in the world, but it was still, as far as she could tell, a trap.

"I'm not going anywhere," and she underlined the last word by giving it deep vocal inflections, "until I get some answers, about this cave, this house and most especially about you."

He nodded, as if bowing to her superiority, a servant to a master, but he must have misinterpreted her demands, for instead of giving her verbal answers to her query, his fingers worked the zipper of his jeans. Her eyes widened as she watched while he pulled his pants down. She didn't see him step out of them. He stood tall, magnificently naked, and incredibly aroused. In the otherwise silent cave, his breath was loud.

"What I meant ..." Lori started, but watched him, and realized it didn't matter at all what she meant, not when he looked like that. He didn't give her the opportunity to finish her sentence, even if by some miracle she had the ability to think coherently. Byron silenced her by inching toward her, laying his lips on hers. The kiss started gently, tentatively as if he were unsure whether or not she would break, before it deepened and grew out of control. His lips, she decided, were some potent kind of incendiary device.

Lori feathered her lashes down, for it was easier to get lost in his kiss if not distracted by her unbelievable surroundings. With her eyes closed, she didn't find it much darker, but the other sensations were heightened a hundred fold. The kiss of the forest and the kiss of the red living room were preludes, experiments, preliminary work. This, here, now, with this naked man in this fairy tale cavern, was the real thing.

For a long moment, she stood still, letting the experience ripple through her, letting her body adjust for his invasion and eventual victory. She didn't twine her hands in his hair, she didn't wrap her arms around his waist, or even touch him lower, pulling his buttocks forward, so he would press against her. The kiss wouldn't be enough for long, but at that moment, savoring all her senses while her universe shifted, it was all she needed.

He smelled musky and a tad sweet, exotic like the tea she had drank in her aunt's kitchen. Tea she had enjoyed in her bedroom, where she felt safe and cherished. Lori tried to grasp onto that lifeline. She didn't feel safe and cherished now: she felt ravished. His assault would be gentle, and he would leave no lasting scars, but she had no control over the situation.

It would be easy to think herself a victim, or a reluctant—yet—not unwilling—participant with no say in the outcome. Easy, but wrong. The conclusion was foregone. It was no longer a matter of submission or fighting. She wanted him and knew he would let her escape if she chose that avenue.

Oddly enough, Lori found the fact that she retained power an incredible aphrodisiac. This wasn't rape, no, she was too willing, but it wasn't seduction either, for in a seduction, she could say, "Yes, I like that," or offer instructions like "lower," or "harder," or even, "no, don't leave me yet." A seduction offered some measure of control, even if it were only perceptual. This encounter between them was inevitable. When something was this inevitable, you just hang on for the ride. When she got her arms to move, she was going to hang on, indeed.

She opened her mouth, letting his tongue mate with hers. The sensations of sensual teas heightened with his taste, and she liked it. His mouth was hot, his lips firm. She moaned softly, with pleasure, the only verbal response she could make.

"Ummmmm," it was as expressive and effective as any words she could have offered. His response was a low growl, issued from deep in his throat. If she had been a cornered rabbit, she would have been terrified with such a sound, but she was no rabbit. She had no idea what she would be long term, but at the moment she was his mate, and that was desire itself.

While his lips plundered, his head kept shifting angles, this way, then that, seeking perfection in movement, in the love match of tongue against tongue. He was so tall, so she stood on her toes, but that rubbed some hard part of him against some soft part of her, and she almost swooned. He reached out, pulled her against him, cocooned in his embrace, her feet dangling a good foot from the cavern floor.

With his free hand Byron sought other territory. He mussed her hair, fondled her ears, rubbed her back and grasped her buttocks, all seemingly simultaneously, all making her mindless.

Finally her passivity broke. Under the force of his caress, she could not remain still. His skin was hard and soft, and hot and inviting, all at the same time. Lori found his spine, his shoulders, his ribs, her hands as restless, as inquisitive as his. His chest was very smooth; there was nothing to impede her investigation of his skin.

He set her back down, holding her against any stray impulse to escape, even when she had no intention of going anywhere but where he led. Buttons popped as he opened her blouse, then he ripped it and the sweater, off her shoulders, his hands caressing the length of her arms as the material all but shredded. She swayed, unsteady on her feet, wondering what was happening, why it was happening so fast, and why it hadn't happened days ago.

"I," she said, the first word she had managed in a long time. Lori found it odd when she spoke, she thought of herself, for under his kiss there had been no 'me', no 'you', only 'us'. As with her earlier attempts at communication in his broad cave, Lori had no idea how she would have finished the sentence, if he let her.

"We," Byron corrected, reading her mind, or perhaps shoving his thoughts into hers. His kisses merged down her neck, had the hint, the threat, of those too-long teeth. She moaned afresh, liking the sensation, this feeling out of control, being ravished. She wondered which of them had taken the bait.

His hands moved to her belt, to the snap of her jeans, to the zipper, while Lori explored all of him she could reach, his magnificent shoulders, the length of his incredible back, his firm, tight buttocks. Each a new pleasure, each a piece of a whole she labeled paradise.

Her zipper lowered, he lifted her effortlessly, carried her the three feet to his bier where he laid her down and returned his mouth to hers continuing his seduction.

She lifted her hips for him when he returned to remove the impediment of her jeans and found her panties vanished in the same action. The cavern air was cold against her exposed flesh, but she doubted catching a chill would be a concern in the next few moments.

Byron sidled above her, between her legs, his weight on his hands, and she met his glare of possession. His eyes shone, a brilliant copper mixed with gold, and the corners of his lips twisted up, radiating not so much his dominance this time, as his pleasure.

Lori reached out, gently cupped his jaw. With quivering fingers, she gave a slight tug down in her direction. She opened her legs wider, grinned when she realized she wasn't as powerless as she'd suspected.

Her body complied, ready with a moistness and a trembling and foreplay hum that created desperation. She raised her shoulders and her chin, looking between her naked breasts, the length of his exquisite chest, to the juncture where they would join. He was so very big, almost terribly engorged. She had time to wonder if he hurt, then moments later, he abandoned that distance separating them making them one.

His possession was so complete, so invasive, she gasped, before she realized it wasn't pain she was experiencing, but pleasure so intense she hadn't recognized it.

Lori wrapped her legs high against his back, holding him tightly. Her hips met his, matching his rhythm, his mindless pace. His kisses returned to her neck, her forehead, and finally her breasts. She could not respond in kind, only ride out her roller coaster madness, and accept the sensations sweeping through her, wave after wave of blinding pleasure, with a building force, reaching a crescendo.

She'd climaxed before, felt that powerful little death, of course she had, but nothing even approaching the devastating magnitude of the one she neared. She was certain when it hit, her heart would stop or the sun implode. She wasn't certain she would live through the experience.

"Byron…" Her voice begged and thanked at the same time.

The coil tightened, centered where they joined, but running all through her. The wave peaked and broke. She screamed as her climax and his merged into one explosive whole.

He hollered too, and the cave echoed with the violence of his roar. She'd seen lions mating once, and it was a noisy affair. This was similar: possession and release and completion all merged together.

He collapsed against her, and she had enough strength left in her arms to wrap them around his back, touch lightly, and caress.

He shifted, so his weight no longer pinned her, their bodies were no longer intimately connected. Loath to be separated, Lori spooned against him, resting her head on his chest. While her breathing had regulated she flicked out her tongue, tasted the fine sheen of perspiration on his skin.

"Next time I'll listen to your warnings," she promised. Her voice was shaky, not yet recovered.

"You should," was Byron's response, although she could tell it was a general answer, and not to any specific warning. His eyes were closed and he might have been asleep except where his hand wrapped around her back it gently caressed her skin.

"You did say if I entered I would be attacked." Lori watched him, and while he didn't open his eyes, a self-satisfied grin possessed his face.

"By a monster," she finished.

"So you were."

She nodded, pleased with the way the morning had progressed. "And you have tasted woman-flesh."

"Indeed. It was an experience I have waited centuries for."

"Centuries?" She liked the idea.

"Eleven," he answered, "minus a decade or two."

"That's a long time to go without …" she blushed, but it had been a liberal education she'd gotten at her university, "… without being close to someone."

"I was waiting for the right woman," he answered. "There was always the possibility that if I chose the wrong partner, she could be crushed—or eaten."

She shivered with no idea how this conversation had gotten so far off track. "Well, I hope you don't have to go another eleven centuries before it happens again."

"No," Byron responded, with his eyes still shut, raising his head to find her lips. "It probably won't be long before I'm interested in trying this again. I am selfish. I will never give you back to Andrew."

Her response was a lazy, honest "Who?" that had him laughing.

"You are mine now, and what a dragon captures, he keeps."

She was languid and replete, but she was also curious to know every inch of him. His skin was smooth, hot, and hard, tempered by his loving, and the lack of spare flesh on his bones. Her fingers on his shoulder blades felt something curious, and she investigated two raised knobs equidistant from both his arms and his spine.

"What's this?" she asked, frightened by the unexpected. Not lumps like tumors, for they were very hard, but definitely abnormal.

"That's where my wings sprout," he said, shifting one shoulder, then the other, a stretching twist, as if in exercise and the knobs vanished. "They have a habit of appearing when I'm feeling frisky."

"Frisky." She liked that image so much she forgot all about questioning him further about bumps on his shoulder blades or wings springing forth unannounced. His kiss heated, and her body flamed under his touch. Where he found the stamina she had no idea, but she spread her legs, and let his possession renew.

CHAPTER 18

The knock on the back door was unexpected. Anyone who came in the back door was well certain of their welcome and waltzed in. No one tried the back door with a knock.

"Oh, for heaven's sake," Jan answered, dropping the green beans she held. "As if I haven't got enough to do."

The knock returned, more insistent, almost invasive. Jan had no idea where Brew was, but she was not defenseless. Whatever catastrophe was occurring at the back door, she could handle. She only wished she had gotten more of the green beans pickled.

"What is it?" She opened the door, holding out in front of her a hoe, like a drum majorette held a baton. "Oh, it's you."

Arthur stood there, shuffling his feet, his hands entwined. "May I enter?"

"You have the power to enter. You don't need an invitation, unless of course you're not who you appear."

The black cat twirled around Jan's ankles, figure eights, while a half-dozen little kittens slept in the box, wrapped nose to tail, nothing more than soft balls of fluff.

"Genevieve," Jan said, bending down to scratch the animal between the ears because it was simply too painful to look at him, to talk with him without anything more happening between them.

"I wish you hadn't named her that."

"Yes, you're who you appear," Jan said, resolving her identification. She opened the door wider, set the hoe aside. Arthur looked at the farm implement, shivered a bit, almost imperceptible, but she knew him and how he would react.

"You still love her. It's been how many centuries and you still love her, mourn her."

"No," he said.

It was a lie, she knew, but under the circumstances, it could also be considered a kindness. "What do you want? I've got tea on, and there's fresh scones if you're hungry."

He entered easily, passing through her wards, another confirmation that he was who he appeared. She poured tea, two mugs, and brought out the scones, clotted cream, lemon curd. The English tastes were peculiar, but not all their cooking was horrendous.

He sipped the tea, leaning forward. "There's trouble."

"When isn't there?"

"This, I don't know—"

"Tell me what you do know."

"There's a new mage in town. Very powerful, at least that's the aura he projects. He's aligned himself with Brenda, and they've hunters with them."

"Hunters?" Jan asked, capital h, "or hunters?" lowercase.

"Hunters," he responded, upper case. "I think they're after fangs."

Jan took a sip of tea, hoping to find relaxation in it, realizing as she gripped the mug handle her hand shook. "Byron can take care of himself."

"Easier if warned. Also the faeries are up in arms. There's something about this mage they don't like."

"They rarely like a mage." While true, it wasn't the whole truth. For faeries to complain about a mage loud enough for Arthur to hear indicated extreme distress. Generally faeries dealt with their own problems.

"Jan, I'm going after them. I wanted you to know."

"After them? How convenient." She set the mug down roughly, splashing the tea onto the table. "I won't mourn."

"You will, and I don't want you to."

"You're a fool. More than anything in this universe, you of all men have been blessed by your god." She stood, paced, but her kitchen was filled with bushel baskets filled with green beans, with kegs of cider vinegar, with heavy bowls of pickling spices. "You don't trust women. Betrayed once, curse forever."

"It was more than a betrayal."

"Ha!"

"And I don't hate women. I could love you."

"Fine. After all these years you tell me, then go mindlessly into the forest to kill yourself? Go!"

"Jan, I would stay, if you needed me. But you've never needed anyone or anything. I suppose in that, we're opposites."

CHAPTER 19

Lori had no idea how much time passed before she stirred, not that the passage of time mattered to her. It seemed to move differently in this cave, as if time itself were not a dimension accepted here: a three dimensional world, instead of four. She liked the idea. Decided she could live with that. She could stay here, making love with Byron through all the long days and the endless nights without fear of time encroaching, making them late for something, or even making them older. They would have eternal youth here, but more than that, endless passion, stamina, isolation.

Her love, if love it was, would need that isolation to survive. If she didn't have to face the real world, whatever that was, she could concentrate on Byron, accept what he was and her role in his life.

She felt a smile spreading, encompassing more than her lips, including her eyes, the remainder of her face, if not her whole body. It was that kind of smile.

"You look pleased with yourself."

Amusement rippled within his words. With her eyes closed, but her grin growing broader, Lori shifted, and found him by touch alone. His muscular, nearly hairless chest was warm beneath her questing fingers. He felt as comforting as a flannel blanket in the coolness of the cavern. Bold, she caressed the strong, rippled muscles of his chest, migrating lower, down his abdomen, to the softer skin of his belly.

"If you could have one wish, no, don't open your eyes," his fingers gently tapped her lids closed again. "If you could have one wish, right now, what would it be?"

"No consequences?"

"Darlin' there's always consequences, but let's assume there are none. What would you wish for?"

She stretched slowly, enjoying the muscles working through her complete relaxation. Then she shifted her head until it rested in the gap between his shoulder and neck, a comfortable position, made just for her.

"Could I take a rain check?"

"No gold? No wealth?"

"Although I will admit I ooohed and ahhhhed over the jewelry in your shop, I'm not much for bling."

"No one calls dragon gold bling."

She giggled at his indignation. "All right, I've not much use for treasure. I suppose dragon's gold should be slept on?"

"Actually, that's the best use I've found for it."

"See? I don't need it. You're much softer."

She opened her lids and sighed.

"Something the matter?" He ran his index finger from her forehead, down her nose, to her lips, where ever so lightly he circled, he caressed, he teased.

"I almost thought it was a dream. The cavern, the way you made me feel." Lori caught his finger, thought to nip, but instead she pulled him deeper in her mouth, her tongue suckling.

His eyes turned molten again, liquid gold.

She looked lower on his body, below where her fingers had traveled, noticed the resurgence of his interest. He dipped his eyebrows, lowered his eyelids half-mast. Both, an "I'm game if you are," statement. She was having no trouble reading his body language.

Lori forced the smile from her lips, tried for a sultry pout, found her happiness dominated. Her smile wouldn't be subjugated. Her pleasure required recognition as it resurfaced. She caressed him slowly, down the length of his muscular legs, liking the tingling sensations she experienced as she touched him. She avoided the hard part of him, for there was no need for the urgency of a little while before.

Hoping she wasn't living a bad cliché even as she thought it, her mind continued to assert he wasn't like other men. Testing the theory, for she was an anthropologist and she had dedicated her career to studying primitive man, she ran her fingers down his nose, across his lips, his chin, and along his neck to his chest, a provocative action that increased his breathing rate and brought a sharp flash of wildness back to his eyes. It brought images of possession, impressions she was certain brought a flush of deep color to her face.

"How long was I asleep?" her voice was raspy, felt unused, or rather, used too roughly. She had screamed when she climaxed in his embrace—both times. The cave was large. The sound had echoed a long time.

He grasped her hand before it could travel to more inviting territory, brought it to his lips, where he gave it not the sweet kiss she was expecting, but a nip, which didn't hurt at all, from his long canine teeth. It was only after marking her, possessing her again, Byron spoke. "Not long, only a few minutes."

Subliminally it bothered her that he spoke of minutes, when she had already determined time didn't exist here in this stolen dominion. Her fault, she supposed, for bringing the subject up. She reached out, boldly brushed her fingertips across the sharp edges of his teeth, as if taunting this beast in his own lair.

"Long enough for you to study me?" she asked, hoping to make the question sound casual.

"Ja. Long enough for that." He snapped his teeth together, for although it was playful, he didn't make contact with her flesh. It was not so much a bite as a warning or a statement of identity.

Then she remembered something she had discovered while he had been deeply embedded in her body, while they had rocked, forging this fire-bred passion between them and she shivered. "Roll over," she ordered, giving him a gentle two handed shove. "Right now, roll over. Lay on your stomach."

"Why?" He hiked an eyebrow, stretched, naked and glorious, flexing muscles along his chest and shoulders. His legs were long, corded with muscle, and his toes, she decided, were exquisite. One day, when the newness of their romance didn't pressure them so, she would go over his body, inch by inch, getting to know him. His eyes were going smoky again and his breathing had increased, just a bit. Byron looked concurrently prepared to be indulgent and on the defensive. "Are you planning on attacking me? Here, in my own lair?"

Lori slowly brought her gaze back to meet his. Under her quick perusal, his lower body reacted, hardening. He thought she might attack him? While that did sound like a good idea, she didn't think she could survive another intimate encounter with him, without time to pull herself together.

"Are you going to do it?"

He laughed, supreme, masculine, aroused. "I would rather you make me."

She gave him another shove, using both her hands and her forehead, a push with the initial success of moving a brick wall. When he shifted, rolling easily over onto his stomach, he caught her off balance, making her splat across his back.

Byron looked back at her over his shoulder. "I would be more comfortable if you were under me."

She straddled him, starting at his neck, working her way down, rubbing her palms across the broad expanse of his back as if giving him an impromptu massage. What she was doing was a shade removed from that.

"I was certain there was a knob here, small, but hard."

His body trembled, tiny laughter she felt more than heard. "Ahh, my wing ridges."

"Yes, that's what you said. There's nothing here."

"I don't feel the need for my wings at the moment, or for any major transformation. I like the form I'm in right now."

He stretched his arms. She watched the byplay of muscles and she felt hungry. "There was something here."

"I'm not denying it," Byron answered, then he moved quickly, too fast for her to respond, shifting to his back, with her still straddling him, their position quite a bit more intimate. "But I think I am in enough trouble with your aunt already, without compounding the problem by showing you the monster I really am."

She wiggled her hips, splayed her fingers against his pecs. "I don't think you a monster."

The smile vanished from his features. "You would if you knew me."

Lori laughed, suspecting he was being facetious. She had hoped he would match the infectious giddiness she felt, with a answering laugh of his own. He didn't. Suddenly she felt embarrassed at being wanton and naked on top of him. Lori pulled up a blanket to cover her breasts, even as she could not forget the feel of his lips suckling at her nipples, the touch of his hands over every hidden recess of her body. She hoped the darkness was enough so he wouldn't notice her blush. Still, for all residual pleasure from their lovemaking, she had questions in need of answers.

"Byron, how did I get here?"

The devilish glean in his eyes returned. "Here, on top of me?"

"Here, this pallet, this place."

His laugh curled her toes. "I carried you, from about three feet over there. See, where your blouse is?"

A part of her wanted to accept his foolish evasion, surrender reason, allow her to bend over, clamp her lips against his, and renew the fires which had seared both of them. But it was only a small part of her. The rest of her studied the cave, too huge to be a simulation, and knew she couldn't be happy with his passion, if she didn't have his honesty.

"Byron, I'm not in the mood for games. I want to know what is going on."

He ran his hands though her hair. His fingers looked longer, much longer than she remembered, yet her body still remembered his caresses, the tenderness he was capable of with those expressive digits. She slid off him. They were too close, too intimate for the conversation to continue. She sat cross-legged beside him, still wrapped in the blanket, all she had for a shield.

He stretched out, casually, his feet crossed at the ankles, his hands folded under his head, still completely naked and clearly aroused. There was a dark thatch of hair at his sex, intriguing because he was nearly hairless on his chest, arms, and legs. His breathing was controlled, even. Lori watched his chest expand, then retract, in controlled cadence. For the beginning of his confession, he sat up, faced her.

"No one comes here accidentally. Even your Aunt Jan cannot find this place any time she wishes. Don't get me wrong, it's always here, but the path here isn't always obvious."

Annoyed, Lori pulled the blanket tightly around herself. "Is that supposed to make sense?" She was not in the mood for games of this nature. While she relished sexual teasing from him, at this point she was certain she wouldn't accept any belittling frivolity. There might be more than one way to get from Point A to Point B, but the route shouldn't be arbitrary, susceptible to a change in the wind or fortunes.

"I took the stairs," she growled. Stairs were stationary, not prone to being there one minute, gone the next. Stairs had no say in who they allowed to pass, or their destination. Stairs could be considered well-behaved, following all standard laws of physics without question.

She studied his naked chest, remembered the weight of his body as he pressed her against the bier, the feel of his hips rocking powerfully against her own and the pleasure he brought her. She remembered too, the nubs at his shoulder blades, he had said were his wings starting to sprout, when now there was nothing there.

To the far side of the cave, in the blackness and far out of sight, something skittered. "Do you believe in magic?" Byron asked.

"No." She wanted to, but at the moment she needed answers, not evasions. Magic was slight-of-hand, misdirection and specialized equipment with hidden pockets or mirrors or sedated bunny rabbits. Magic, for all intents and purposes, didn't exist. Yes, there were people who wore long robes and went about muttering ridiculous chants at midnight, but they were looking for justification for their hobby, or, remembering Andrew, their depravity, and not magic at all.

"No. I don't believe in magic."

He scratched the stubble on his chin. "How about alternate physics?"

The blanket, though soft, had a coarseness to it of natural fibers and hand weaving. It had a slight scent, not of horses, but some other animal: a clean scent, but earthy all the same. She would have been more comfortable had it smelled of fabric softener or laundry detergent. Her mind throbbed. She thought of wing ridges and Byron lying on the couch in the red living room, without enough strength to hold his head up, speaking of secret passageways and blood on the carpet.

She looked around at the vastness of the cavern, black at all the edges, lost in time, space, or imagination. She shivered involuntarily. Caves were notoriously cold, and she didn't like the direction this conversation was heading. "Let's not quibble over semantics. I read science fiction. For all it is delightful supposition, and makes for fascinating reading, there is no invisible parallel world."

He shrugged, a mere lifting of his left shoulder which had her hungry all over again.

"If you believe that, it will be impossible to explain to you how you got to my lair."

She pulled a deep drag of cold air into her lungs, a stalling tactic while she considered her body's reactions on different levels. "You drugged me."

"No. The only thing I have given you which could be described as a drug is the dragon tea, and while there are frequently mind-altering substances within it, there hasn't been any in the tea I've given you. You have my word."

Her mouth was very dry as she picked up the phrase he had used so cavalierly. "Mind altering drugs?"

He had been sitting, cross-legged as she was, now he moved, getting to his knees, reaching out to clasp her shoulders. "Lori, I have never drugged you. This I promise."

With a simple twist of her torso, she broke his hold. "Yet something has skewed my perceptions."

He reached over, recaptured his pants, spoke with his back to her while he fitted them, without underwear, over his narrow hips. "Your perceptions were based on faulty data. Physical laws of Earth do not work here."

"Here, this cave?"

"The cave, yes, and your Aunt Jan's house, any place you find by exiting the back door off the kitchen, and many places you can reach from the front door."

Lori felt cold icy fingers around her throat, felt a foreboding shiver curl down her spine. She wondered if the artificial trappings of civilization, her clothing, would bring warmth, perhaps help ground this miserable conversation in reality. "Byron, I'm not in the mood for jokes."

He straightened, and although half-dressed, and therefore half-naked, he looked tall and regal. She could easily imagine him wearing burnished armor, astride a battle-trained destrier, riding off to battle.

"I am quite serious. Your aunt should be able to explain better than I can, since this is normal for me, but she fought it, as you are fighting it, for the longest time before she came to understand the majority of the established laws of Earth-based physics don't hold here."

He slid into his flannel shirt, worked on the buttons, the action, oddly enough, making him look less civilized instead of the reverse.

Lori curled her top lip. "I only want some simple answers."

"Unfortunately, there are no simple answers unless I can get you to accept the basic premise: magic exists."

"Magic exists. Sleight of hand?"

"True magic. Not deceit and misdirection. You may prefer the phrase 'powers beyond your control'."

"But not beyond your control?" she asked sarcastically.

"Actually there are many magical powers beyond my control. No dragon likes to admit that, but it is true."

"What are you talking about?"

"Honesty." He bent down, pulled on a boot. "You may not recognize it yet, but it is what I am offering you."

Lori felt she was going around in circles, and she was starting to feel dizzy. She hoped if she asked her questions with simple words, he would give her answers she could accept, drop his façade. She felt too naked, vulnerable. "Tell me about this cave. Do you stay here, alone?"

His eyes flashed, dark and wild. "I am not alone now. I like having your company."

"Byron, just answer the question."

"I stay here alone. It's safer. I slaughtered and ate the previous tenant, but so many years ago, no one but me remembers. Until you arrived, except for the creatures you call bats, and an occasional brave foray by your aunt, there hasn't been another living thing up here in longer than you can comprehend. As I told you, there is an entrance, that way." He pointed, but it was ineffectual, for she was securing her bra, so missed his action. "There are villagers in the valley. They could climb up, I suppose, if they wanted, if the trail manifest itself. In all the centuries I have been here, they haven't. Not once. Perhaps the trail is hidden, like the staircase usually is, but I think the explanation is a bit more simplistic. They fear the dragon, and even with the flawed promise of treasure, they are correct in thinking it wouldn't be worth the risk."

"Treasure?" Lori liked the thought of jewels and rings and broaches stacked ceiling high. She didn't want to have the treasure; she wanted to imagine it, a telling distinction.

"Actually, no. Do you see any treasure? I do have a cache of gems I use in my work, but I don't keep them here, and as for accumulating piles of jewels, I try not to. I really don't wish to develop hobbies which tempt knights to sharpen their spears—or whatever the modern equivalent might be—and coming looking for me."

"I agree. Knights can be pests." She spoke dryly. She wondered if he understood sarcasm.

"You don't know the half of it," he said with a long-suffering sigh.

She exhaled slowly. She had a decision to make: she could continue this pointless conversation and drive herself mad, destroying whatever was developing in their fledgling relationship, or let it ride, enjoy being in his presence, accept what he offered.

She chose middle ground, leaving the bier, where she had found pleasure, and reached for her panties. "You're not making any sense you know." It didn't really matter. Rubbing her breasts, tender from his suckling, and remembering the passion he had brought her, Lori decided she'd never been happier.

"That is an axiom you know: 'conversing with a dragon will never make anything clearer'. Many people try to obtain dragon wisdom, but it is never obtained by listening to the answers we supply."

Lori rubbed her eyes, feeling the start of a tension headache. She set her teeth. "And is there such a thing as dragon wisdom?"

"Many of us like to think so. But then, we believe in magic."

"Byron, enough of your games. Say something right now I can build a hypothesis around, test and believe."

He thunked his bare foot into the other boot then thought for a moment, as if her question was not as easy as it sounded. "You must admit that it would be unlikely, using accepted Earth physics, to find a cave of this magnitude accessible by a staircase a few flights up from any normal house."

"Given that premise, yes," she admitted, grudgingly.

"Corollary, if you were to exit from this cave, from any other point, except the stairs, you would find yourself in a place far different than the place you expect. You wouldn't be in New York, or even on Earth."

"So you say."

"I do say. Actually, I insist. Different types of alternate physics exist all over this house. Haven't you noticed?"

She didn't answer even to sneer, so he continued. "There are other entrances to this cave than the one you stumbled across. Each utilizes a portal, a door into another dimension. All of the creatures Jan welcomes to her house know better than to enter my lair without permission."

"I suppose that makes me the exception."

Byron adjusted his pant leg inside the knee-high boot. "In more ways than one. I should get you back. I am certain she must be frantic wondering where you are."

Lori raised her wrist, tried to get her eyes to focus in the dim, flickering torchlight. "This miserable watch seems to have stopped and it was a new battery." She thumped the face with her index finger. "What time do you have?"

"The watch is probably fine," Byron said as he sat, cross-legged, and handed across clothing of hers he had been hording. "No need to blame it, when the odds are it will work once I decide to allow you return to your aunt."

"You're going to let me go?" For all she didn't have a clue what was going on, staying forever wasn't necessarily an option she wanted to pursue.

He hiked an eyebrow. "Of course. I think you learned your lesson. And there's no food here. If I were to keep you, you'd eventually starve to death."

"No food at all?" Now that he mentioned it, Lori remembered she hadn't had any breakfast and she'd been here, trapped for hours, if not days.

"I could fly down to the valley and kill something," he said, "but I really am trying to keep a low profile. It would be best if the villagers didn't band together and petition the overlord to have me slaughtered. I doubt they could, mind you, but I wouldn't want them to try. I do like having a place where I can stretch my wings with impunity."

Her stomach growled, and Lori realized it had been making noise for some time now. "No food at all?" she repeated.

"I could probably round up some halchits."

"Purple halchits?"

"Yes, certainly. It's the only type your aunt grows, although I've told her often enough there are other sub-species and I could use some variety. But don't get your hopes up. There's only a handful, if there are any at all, and they're last year's crop, so they might be a bit moldy."

She giggled, forming an image in her mind. "Moldy?"

"Mold doesn't actually hurt them, and like your Earth cheese, it even improves the flavor, but it makes them too soft for my pallet."

"So the only thing to eat in this entire cave are some moldy, mushy purple halchits?"

"I'm afraid so. I could eat you, which would satisfy my hunger, but wouldn't do much for yours."

"Eleven centuries you go without tasting human flesh and now you want to eat me?" She tried to act indignant.

"I'm not really fond of the idea of eating humans, as they tend to be a bit mushy too. Except for the bones, of course, and you haven't got enough bones to give me a good, solid crunch."

"We may have to head downstairs then," Lori answered with a giggle. "I suppose after I've eaten you can give me some more logical explanation of this cave, especially how you made it look so realistic. It must have taken you a long time."

He sighed, and she thought of his axiom that dragons made no sense, whatever that had to do with the current conversation. "Well," Byron said, "I could explain the cave now, if you'd like." He grinned, reaching for her sweater, finding it hopelessly torn. He held it out from his body, with a quizzical look on his face, as if he had no idea how the damage occurred.

She reached down, scratched the floor, finding it bedrock, cold, a trace damp, and oddly enough, smooth. "The cave?" Lori questioned, hoping to keep him on tract.

"It did take a long time." His smile returned and it was predatory. "It was formed by waters melting as the last glacier in these parts retreated. Is that long enough ago for you?"

"This whole conversation is ridiculous," Lori said, standing, stamping her feet which had grown tingly as she sat, "and I'm hungry." She started rooting around the cave floor for the remainder of her clothing, pleased when he located her other hiking boot.

"How'd it get way over there?"

"I'm afraid I was a tad impatient to get your clothing off. I might have thrown it."

She slipped the boot on, worked on tying the laces. "This really is a marvelous simulation."

"I'm glad you think so," he answered dryly.

Dressed, Byron reached out. Hand-in-hand they walked toward the free-standing door.

She released his fingers, made the complete circuit around the door before he thought to stop her. Her world, which had been rooted with his loving, twisted and turned.

CHAPTER 20

"It's actually more effective if you go through the portal," he said with a chuckle. Then he turned the handle and opened it and Lori stopped, stunned anew.

"It's not—" she said and started to stutter. "It's n-n-n-not a simulation, is it?"

"The cave? No. But I think you'll feel better once you've eaten."

She grew lightheaded, a combination of low blood sugar and trying to conform the round peg of reality to the square hole she'd witnessed, but before she thumped to the floor in a dead faint, he grasped her and tenderly carried her down all those flights of stairs.

"What did you do to her?" Jan demanded. She set aside the gallon jug of cider vinegar she held.

"Do? Me?" Bryon responded, while in his arms, Lori started pelting his chest demanding: "put me down."

Jan reached out, felt her forehead, a normal reaction of concern on a day anything but normal. "Are you all right?"

Lori shook her head, half expecting to hear brains rattling, like seeds in a dried gourd. "I suppose so. I'm not really sure. But I had the strangest dream." She wouldn't grant it the dignity yet of calling it an experience.

"Dream?" Jan question, but when she spoke, she looked to Byron. "What did you give her, more tea?"

"No tea. Through providence, or just misfortune, she found my cave. I simply proved to her she could not intrude without consequences."

Jan cupped Lori's face, looking deeply into her eyes for signs of trauma. "What consequences? At least she's still breathing. What did you do, Brew?"

He smirked, boyish and unrepentant. "I think you would be more comfortable getting the story from her, but you should feed her first. The possibility exists the only thing wrong with her is an empty stomach."

Lori slammed her palm on the dining room table. "I wish you two would stop talking about me like I'm not here." She growled at Byron, showing teeth. "But I am starving." The entire kitchen had that primal, almost irresistible scent of pickles, and it had her salivating.

"Why didn't you say so? Breakfast is ready." Jan turned her back long enough to grasp something from the counter behind her. "Here are some waffles, and I've got maple syrup to top them." Jan handed Lori a plate still steaming. "The syrup is fresh. It's been boiling for a couple hours while I was getting to these beans."

The waffle was an airy, light slab, at least three inches in height, filling a dinner plate, a delightful, golden brown. The syrup was sweet, rich, and completely unlike anything in a bottle whose main ingredient was high fructose corn syrup. She drizzled the warm liquid onto her waffles and decided the two of them could talk about her all they wanted, for she had all she needed.

"And you, are you hungry?"

"Famished. Do you have anything in there for me?"

Jan rolled her eyes in clear histrionics. "I swear, Brew, you become more troublesome every year."

He grinned, obviously enchanted with her statement. "In that case, I think I'll feast, then when I come back you can yell at me. You'll probably have a full head of steam by then."

"Undoubtedly you're correct. Go while I get the story out of Lori. And I did have your promise, you old monster, the moment we knew she was coming, that you wouldn't hurt her."

He shrugged, shuffled a foot in faux innocence. "That was before she entered my lair."

"Then I suppose you'll have to move it?"

"How many times have I told you dragons can travel through the portals, but we cannot make them?"

He walked to the back door and opened it. "I'll be back after I feed."

"Ancient One," Arthur said, "we need to talk."

Lori swallowed quickly, surprised to note half the huge plate of waffles had already disappeared. "You're not going to yell at him for using that door?"

Jan picked up a long handled spoon, then dropped it in the sink. "Brew comes and goes as he wishes and perhaps he should spend the rest of your visit making himself scarce."

"You never let me use that door. You always make me go around."

"Promise me, Lori," Jan said, taking her hands, making her meet her gaze, "you'll never go through that door. Never let him talk you into leaving the house that way. I want your promise."

"But why?"

"You'll come across enough monsters if you head for the forest by the front door. Those you'll meet out the back door are considerably worse."

The word 'monsters' rang around them, and she doubted Byron would contradict that statement. He'd been calling himself a monster all day. "Nonsense. It's just the long way around."

"No, it's not. Remember the witch who was trying to kill Bryon? She wanted to go out the back door. That should give you an idea of the kind of creatures who live there. Promise you'll only leave through the front."

In the face of her aunt's vehemence, Lori could only agree. "I promise I won't go out the back door," unless it's absolutely necessary, she finished to herself, looking out the back door, realizing the forbidden was always more enticing than the allowed.

Jan picked up another spoon and tapped it into her palm, as if testing the heft of a weapon. "Now tell me what devilment Brew has been up to, but first, whatever possessed you to go up the stairs? I suppose I should've warned you." Jan turned back toward the counters, returning almost instantly. "Now, here's some tea," she said, the blue teapot appearing, a small whiff of steam escaping the spout. "Mortal tea. Drink up and tell me everything."

Nothing was making sense, and even her senses were unreliable. Too much of what she saw, felt, tasted, smelled, couldn't be true. It would be easier to accept all this if her brains were rattled.

"My watch is working." She said it as if that was the most unusual thing which happened this morning.

"Shouldn't it?" asked Jan, back to the stove, shifting something which scraped, as if a caldron were being dragged over stone. Annoyed, Lori looked around. Hadn't there been green beans and pickling spices over every inch of the kitchen? Kettles bubbling, jars in canning baths or resting on the counter, fresh, whole green beans ready to be cored and chopped? The kitchen she saw now was completely transformed. Not a trace of beans remained. Instead, the kitchen was jammed with about fifteen to twenty bushel baskets filled with strawberries. Lori was willing to swear in front of a judge there hadn't been a single strawberry anywhere in sight a moment ago.

"What...what happened to the green beans?" Not a dirty dish, not a gallon of vinegar appeared.

Jan shrugged. Lori would have screamed if her aunt had responded, "Green beans, what green beans?" but instead she said: "I was just finishing up when you appeared. How do you feel about helping me make some preserves?"

She pushed the plate from her, suddenly not hungry, although it was a moot point, for it was empty, and who knew how that happened. Lori stood, faced her gray-haired aunt who was busily stacking bushel baskets as if nothing untold had happened. "I want some answers about the cave upstairs, and who—or what—Byron is, and where all those green beans went."

"And I'd like to hear what happened to you in the dragon's lair. I suppose I should be thankful he didn't eat you."

"He threatened to," Lori spoke without thinking, then she shifted around a bushel of strawberries, and looked into pots, all empty, and drawers, filled with standard kitchen utensils. Not a sign of a freshly canned jar of beans in the entire kitchen.

Jan gasped. "Were you frightened?"

"Of Byron? No. Once he took off his shirt, I didn't think of anything at all."

"Yes, I have seen him without his shirt often enough to see how that would happen. You better start from the beginning." Jan removed the plate Lori had eaten from, and in a single, swift motion, upended an entire bushel basket of strawberries onto the table. She handed Lori a small paring knife, shoving her back into her seat. Taking a chair beside her, Jan started coring the strawberries. Lori held the knife as if uncertain what to do with it, then followed her aunt's lead and started coring the plump, succulent fruit.

"Was it because your watch wasn't working that you went upstairs?" Jan prodded.

"Why would I do that? No, as far as I know, the watch was working fine when I was in my room, and while I was climbing the stairs. How many floors are there to this house, anyway?"

"How many would you like?"

Lori ignored her aunt's quixotic response. "I lost track counting as I headed up, but there had to be at least ten." She remembered the strain in her thighs, the fact that she recalled walking upwards for a long time, "perhaps twice that many."

"Ten sounds about right." Jan shifted a pile of cut strawberries into a huge metal bowl, one large enough to be used as a bathtub for a Great Dane should the need arise.

"My watch didn't work upstairs," Lori wasn't comfortable saying the word 'cave'. "I thought the battery died."

Jan continued her rhythmic cutting, the knife smooth and even. "Well, there is an explanation." When Lori hiked an eyebrow, Jan continued. "Sometimes in the worlds Brew inhabits, mechanical things don't work."

Lori eased a pile of cored strawberries off her cutting board into the bowl, not that her contribution made much of a dent. The work was easy. She didn't mind cutting. After the confusion of trying to pull answers from Byron, Lori found dealing with the tangible activity of coring strawberries relaxing. Still, she gave a sigh as she studied the kitchen, realizing the magnitude of the task. It would take her all day to fill the pot once, and looking around her, at the stacked bushel baskets, she decided she could easily be trapped here all week.

Digesting her aunt's last comment, she swallowed, wondering why she hadn't questioned the things she saw before. Beyond the gas stoves and a refrigerator which ran by elves pedaling bicycles for all she knew. She didn't see a single electrical device, not a coffee maker, blender, mixer, or toaster. Lori thought of the places she had been within the house. There were lights in her room and the bathroom which turned on with a switch, and a plug for her hair dryer, but she had yet to find a television or a radio, a computer or a phone charger.

She started feeling cold, wished her sweater hadn't been destroyed, although the kitchen was exceedingly warm. Oblivious, her aunt continued to make headway against the encroachment of fresh, luscious strawberries. "Have you been to any of the worlds Brew inhabits? Have you been to the cave?"

"No, I haven't been to any of the worlds Brew inhabits. How much free time to you think I get here? But to answer your second question, I have been to the cave. Once.

"I got caught up early with the tasks I had set for myself and I thought I'd clean his living quarters. I knew the cave was there, and I'll admit curiosity had a large factor in my venturing up the stairs. I know this house pretty well now, so I don't give into those impulses anymore, but I was new here, anxious to serve, and intrigued with the idea of a cave on top of the house. It wasn't much of a hardship, after all, I do clean all the bedrooms. I was under the impression, from snatches of conversation he dropped, that Byron was quite the slob, leaving carcasses all over. I went up there, holding my broom and a mop, with my determination firmly in mind. I am the caretaker, and even though the cave isn't by most physical definitions 'in the house,' I'm responsible for it. I got up there, and while dusty, it wasn't particularly messy. He must swallow the bones when he finishes, for there was nary a one to be found. Then I decided I have more than enough work in the house, I don't often get out of the kitchen—especially this time of year. I came back down. There are other rooms in the house I have never been in, and that's for the best, as far as I can tell."

Lori continued slicing. "I didn't see any gnawed bones either, but he did say he had some moldy purple halchits up there."

"Purple halchits are actually better once they start to mold. Don't stop coring, or I'll be here all night. Now, do you feel comfortable enough with what happened up there to tell me?"

"Sure." Lori moved a large pile of strawberries closer to her, pleased. She needed time to think though some things, particularly what happened on that bier, and talking them over with her aunt seemed to be the best way.

* * *

Power, for a sorcerer was measured in two distinct ways: the first:

innate ability, the second: experience. Based on the latter, he was only slightly beyond a low-level apprentice, coming new into his art. He had been practicing independently, without his mentor, not three years yet. He knew the truly powerful sorcerers measured their power in decades. His was a cut-throat profession. Only the best survived. The others lost their minds—or their lives. No one retired. No one, after taking up the robe, set it aside to concentrate on a more mundane hobby like collecting stamps or growing orchids.

But based on raw talent, he had great power indeed. His master had been nothing short of amazed at his abilities. Those with his level of talent were usually detected early. This type of power manifested itself in youths as early as five, not easily hidden by children, and therefore was easily recognized. That he was unknown, coming from parents without magical ability, yet with the potential for almost limitless ability was significant.

His master had been frightened of him. He was raw and undisciplined and craved power with an intensity most did not develop until taking lessons for a score of years. His master felt his student would not live long enough to mature into his abilities. He found Andrew too rash, too impatient. This was a vocation where the only virtue with any validity was patience. The other traditional virtues were not sought by sorcerers.

His master pleaded for restraint and had tried to force him to learn the basics by rote before tackling harder spells. Endlessly his master spoke of discipline. Andrew grinned in remembrance. His master died with that thought on his lips, his first kill.

Walking through the forest, his robe swishing at his ankles, power crackled around his feet. Power strands followed him like trained pit bulls, eager to do his bidding. He wouldn't be held back by anything, or anyone. But with his master dead, he had a significant problem. His education was unfinished and he no longer had an instructor. The witch he had joined up with was worthless, as witch spells were based on female powers. She could teach him nothing. Still, she had her uses. Without her, he wouldn't have known about the dragon, wouldn't have found his former lover, a woman his master had suspected was an enzyme—something which facilitates experiments, but remains unchanged in the process.

He made some mistakes there too, thinking her mesmerized by his abilities, having no idea she was not under his spell and would run the first chance she got. He wasted half a week trying to find her, not a lot of time in the scheme of things, but significant since he had a locator spell he'd been assured was flawless, but had failed.

He rubbed his hands together, hoping to feel the warm rumble of power his master had promised when he learned control. Perhaps he had been too hasty in taking his life. His master had had his uses. Now it was extremely unlikely he would find another sorcerer to teach him.

Andrew believed he was the most powerful wizard alive and wanted his reputation to say so. He needed some major success to prove to the others he was a force to be reckoned with. So while the witch was out perusing other avenues of destruction, he recited the spells he'd been taught, calling on the dark powers he believed in, but had never seen.

It wasn't easy. He felt resistance as he continued, gravity increasing until it pressed down on him, making it difficult for his lungs to fill with air, making his words sound flatter, lower. He saw this as success, a sign he was approaching his goal, so instead of running scared, what he would have done even a few months before, he increased his concentration, speaking the words of the spell with more authority. It wasn't a question of integrity. He doubted he had any integrity left. It was a question of dominance, and he knew greed, so he claimed the power for his own. He felt no fear, for to be afraid an organism has to be aware of repercussions.

Then the universe started tearing, a rift through the cosmos, into the fabric of four dimensions: length, width, height and time.

He knew terror.

CHAPTER 21

Byron felt the wing ridges form at his shoulders and as he always did when his wings sprouted, he felt the joy of returning to his true form. He ran from the house, needing movement and the distance speed provided. He would tell her. He almost told her upstairs, when as a result of loving her, the wings had started to grow spontaneously. They did sprout spontaneously when he was feeling frisky, but in centuries he had lived on Earth, while in the presence of a mortal, they had never arrived without his summons. He had more control than that. Still, he wanted Lori to know him as he was born, wanted no more deceit between them.

His wings grew broad and sturdy. He flapped them as the transformation continued, his fingers turning into talons, his body mass increasing, his spine elongating until he became the flying reptile he was. With a bound he was airborne, before the change was completed, finishing the alternations as his wings caught an updraft and he bellowed his dominance.

He liked being a man, never more so than that morning, burying himself in her receptive body, sharing her passions. He never spent much time in his human guise but in this land of humans, he could not continually maintain his original form. There were advantages, and he had just discovered a primary one. He would love her every day of her life. Nourish her with his tea; sate her body with his loving. They would both find pleasure, release, and something more he had never dared hope for: completion. Perhaps, eventually, there would be a child. He had always wanted a child.

Arthur had spoken of increasing danger. Andrew needed to be dealt with first.

Byron soared above the tree-line, working his wings to lift his solid body. As a dragon, he was too heavy to glide with the grace of a hawk. He stayed aloft only through exertion, but like a hawk, his eyesight was excellent and he sought prey. He grew amused as rabbits and squirrels fled in terror at the sight of him. Not enough meat to bother with. Not worth the effort. He was after larger bounty.

He was hungry, yes, but his body relaxed in the decadence of flying and the residual from his morning's activities. He banked on an updraft, cherishing different sensations, the coldness of the air, the strain from his shoulder muscles. It had been centuries since he'd made love, but now, with that enforced fast broken, he was eager to feed and see if he could recapture the pleasure he had experienced while buried deeply within the secret passage of her body.

Acres of the garden he had tilled spread below. He had dug into the rich earth with his back claws, harrowing up the clods until nothing remained except perfectly turned soil. He smiled internally for dragon's facial features weren't conducive for that action. He might never complain about tilling again. It was, after all, the first time he kissed her, the first time he realized there might be more possible for him.

The fields were planted in halchits, the vegetables immature, although the plants were large, many already in flower. Dragon tea was good for so many things. The beast tried to smile again. That day he fertilized the plants, had been the second time he had kissed her. He might think more kindly of halchits from now on.

Before he realized what was happening, Byron was knocked aside by an invisible passing power wave. He tumbled, taking long seconds to right himself. Ripples crashed around him, bouncing him like a ball, waves of heat, gravity, magnetism, sound and light so intense it seared his flesh. His wings flapped instinctively, but he dropped, unable to find the purchase he needed to stay aloft. There was no wind, no air, no support. His jaws opened, seeking to scream his defiance, to breathe.

The atmosphere had been sucked away, leaving a poisonous void. Falling, he saw the cause of the destruction. A door. A new portal into another dimension opened, ripped through the universe, a painful, destructive birth. Of all the magics, some were forbidden, so evil and destructive, that no mage would attempt them. Opening a portal was one such supernatural skill. Yet some sorcerer had broken the ban, for this was definitely wizard-created.

Controlling his fall, Byron dropped lower, cautious now, to see what manner of devil had opened the door and to determine if he could stop the creature from wreaking any more havoc, but the trees were heavy in new leaf, and his vision was obscured. Around him, devastation continued, uprooting trees, tearing branches asunder, rocking the very foundations of the earth below him. All his senses were affected. A deafening roar, enveloped him. The stench of ammonia stung his eyes and lungs, and the power waves rippled around him, through him, trying to destroy him.

Dragons were nearly indestructible. Nearly. Which is to say, facing the proper opponent, he was vulnerable. He didn't see the arrow in flight, didn't hear its song of resistance against tainted wind, didn't notice it at all until it embedded itself deep in the soft unprotected flesh of his shoulder, under his wing. Not a mortal wound, but a significant one. Byron lost altitude quickly, screaming his defiance as he did so, scattering the wildlife

for miles. Pain stabbed through him, and with it thoughts of Lori.
And thoughts of death.

CHAPTER 22

It was the second arrow, imbedded deep in his chest, which caused the reptile to fold his wings and fall the remaining distance to the forest floor. Over the centuries, Byron had become a seasoned fighter. He had known pain from a dozen wounds, but never had he experienced anything this intense, this debilitating.

The pain was dichotomous: both centralized and general, spreading burning fire through his nerve endings as if his blood vessels were etched with acid. The torturous poisons mutated internally, touching every organ and cell. For a long minute he lost awareness of everything but agony.

He struggled to maintain consciousness, but more importantly, to sustain his shape. There were other options open to him, other changes, but with each he became more vulnerable.

Byron pulled a tortured gasp in through his nostrils, and analyzed the scents originating from his own body: finding, among others, cinnamon and ginger and a rich, intoxicating mint. He thought again of tea. It would be so easy to give up, to surrender to his pain and seek oblivion. He had lived far too long. He was an anachronism. With no soul he was promised no afterlife. This existence was all he had. If other dragons had found heaven, there had been no way for them to share that information.

His left wing shattered on impact, the long bones breaking when he twisted, trying to keep his wound upright and prevent the arrows from being thrust deeper into his body. He knew even if he somehow found the strength, he wouldn't be able to fly. That avenue of escape had been cut off. Any transformation he attempted would make things worse.

He owed himself a last measure of raw defiance so he raised his long snout, pulled breath into his burning lungs and bellowed his identity into the night. His high pitched warble of pain and dominance echoed into the darkness.

The only response to his roar was the continued violence of the ground tearing asunder: no birds chattering, no wolves howling, just utter destruction as worlds were created … and destroyed. He belatedly realized he should have kept his silent, been more circumspect, although realistically he knew a full sized mature dragon falling to Earth was not the easiest object for assassins to overlook.

Byron slipped into oblivion as poison seeped into his bloodstream. Massive internal bleeding weakened him further, paralyzing his wings, draining strength from his rear legs. He doubted he could lift his snout a second time to vent his anger, even had he wanted to. His lungs filled with his blood. His eyesight failed, for everything he saw appeared surrounded by an ethereal halo, a glow in greens, purples, and magentas, punctuated with occasional sharp lightning strikes of white.

He knew how the arrow had pierced his scales, normally considered impenetrable, including, he suspected, to a nuclear blast. The arrow tip in his chest was a venom filled dragon fang, one of the four each dragon had. He tried to analyze, determine which of his friends—or enemies—had died before him to inadvertently become the cause of his death. There were too few left. There was at least one less. Considering his helplessness, the toxins in his system, the weakness in his muscles and the assassins closing in, a great possibility of two less.

He arched his neck, tried to position his mouth to pull the arrows free, digging, because it was the most accessible, for the one under his wing. It would hurt, and cause additional damage, but that pain was infinitely preferable to leaving it fester within his body. He couldn't reach it, couldn't manage the angle necessary to wrap his teeth around it. His foreclaws were basically useless, mere vestiges of arms, as his strength and most of his musculature were in his wings. The best he could hope for would be to die alone, preferable to his carcass falling into the wrong hands.

He realized that wasn't going to happen. He heard the hunters closing in, smell them over the cinnamon and acid stench of his own wounds, the ammonia reek from the uprooted land. He pulled himself to his feet, left wing a definite liability, hanging useless. He roared again. Let them find him. There was fight left in him. He would die, but so would some of them.

Before the hunters broke through the cover, Byron thought of Lori. How tragic after centuries of being alone, he had found someone to love forever, only to lose his life now.

***

In the kitchen, over the continually refilled canners and the rhythmic chopping of broad bladed knives, there had been a "what were you thinking," response from Jan, as Lori told of her adventure upstairs. Jan's tirade was directed more at Byron, a safe target, since he'd vanished, than at Lori. Still, Lori had suspected she was in for a long lecture on propriety: dealing with strange men in even stranger surroundings, but her aunt seemed to have accepted their relationship, and apparently approved of it, for all she held Byron responsible. Her cryptic comments had Lori wondering what was going on. Statements like "Eleven centuries of living on this planet and now he finds a mate?"

That wasn't the only obscure utterance. Under her breath, Jan had been almost continually mumbling, statements that made little sense, "I should find some way to set a gargoyle on the second floor landing, so no one goes up," and "those stairs should have known better." Other comments too, "I knew there would be trouble letting a dragon in the house. Really, how could he not cause trouble?" and "with all that time on his hands to choose a woman, why did he have to pick an innocent?" She sounded like those harmless people who loiter around park benches and bus stops, talking to themselves, interrupting conversations, then including total strangers, as if they knew what they were talking about.

Lori was about to tell her aunt she was no 'innocent' when she decided that was a conversational thread she didn't want to introduce. Instead, as if putting all her concentration to coring the strawberries, she asked, "He will show up after he's eaten?"

Jan chuckled. "I doubt anything would keep him away tonight. I suppose when you think of it, he must have been unconsciously calling you."

"Calling me? He'd never met me."

"I've heard it said Byron can let out some fairly strong pheromones when he's in the mood. I suppose I'm lucky. There could have been hundreds of maidens pounding on the front door, if not thousands, reacting to him."

"You're not really making sense, you know."

"No, I suppose not," Jan agreed. She looked around the kitchen, with brows knitted and intense concentration, as if there were other maidens somehow hidden, and she only needed to squint to see them.

Arthur stayed in the corner, nodding, apparently approving of everything Lori confessed. He said nothing, and Lori wondered if like Byron, he feared being conscripted into kitchen duty.

Lori set the knife down, rubbed the blister on her palm caused by the repetitive motion of cutting the strawberries. Jan worked at the stove, measuring sugar, adding pectin, making jam.

There were still over a dozen bushel baskets of strawberries lining the walls. It didn't appear there were any less than when she started hours ago. Still, time had passed quickly, while her anticipation grew. Every second was a moment closer to when Byron would return to her. Then she would find out more about the cave, about the stairs, about the tingling she still felt deep within, where he had been.

She rubbed her palms down her arms, remembering the pleasure and intensity of his touch. There had been magic in that cave, and she was willing to try to find it again. "I think I could easily fall in love with him."

Jan lowered her brows, creating all kinds of road-map wrinkles across her face. Lori needed no Rosetta stone to understand her look: Keep coring, you can talk and chop at the same time. Her mother had perfected it, but with a fraction of the power of Aunt Jan's.

Jan didn't respond, at least not directly. She upended a basket of strawberries on the table, and shoved Genevieve away with a "there's nothing here for you or your kittens," push. The cat flashed her tail, sashaying toward the baking powder box. Genevieve turned back, raised her whiskers, as if hopeful her entreaty this time would meet with success. "I took care of all the darveni myself this time. There's none left for you."

Darveni? Lori wondered. It was something in strawberries the cat was fond of, apparently.

With the mother cat out of the kitchen, Jan sat down, rested her elbows on the table. She wiped sweat from her forehead as she hooked a loose strand of hair back behind her ear. A moment later, she looked directly at Lori. "If I told you getting involved with Brew would only bring you pain, would you believe me?"

Lori looked away, tightening her eyes against a sharp prick of mental anguish. She knew her aunt had her best interests at heart and hoped her confession of lovemaking would meet with Jan's unabashed approval. The knife slashed, coring the strawberries. Their fresh scent reminded her so strongly of tea. They were plump, bursting with moisture, and Lori was certain, vitamins. They exploded with flavor when she stole one, bit it, relishing the garden fresh sweetness. They were so fresh they had to have been picked only hours before.

Slowly Lori raised her eyes. There was only so long she could ignore that question. "Pain?"

Jan stood, went to the canners, did something when a timer dinged, as if Lori's question had been synchronized to the sealing of pint jars.

"Then he has a wife?"

"No."

"Someone he is promised to."

"No."

"A terribly painful disease for which there is no cure, and I will spend the next year at his bedside, watching him taken from me, one gasping breath at a time." The image of Byron, on the couch, too weak to even hold his head up reasserted itself, and she thought of cancer, or any number of hideous diseases, recognized only by their abbreviations.

"No. Lori, don't make yourself sick." Jan was back, not coring strawberries, but shoving them, by the handful, into giant pots where she would add more sugar, more pectin. "The odds are very good he will outlive you."

She liked the thought, laying, as an old woman, her wrinkled hand holding his wrinkled hand, her deathbed surrounded by their children and their grandchildren, and their great grandchildren. "I won't mind."

"Maybe he will mind. Did you ever think of the pain you would cause him?"

Jan switched from her pain to his. It was not necessarily a comfort. "Your logic is faulty." She reached out, shoving past the tipped bushel basket on the table, pulling a pile of rotund strawberries within the range of her knife. "You think I should not get involved with him, forget I love him, because I might cause him pain fifty years down the line?"

"Lori, it is not up to me to give away Byron's secrets. Those are his, and what I know is not meant to be shared, but it is vital you understand he is not like you."

She remembered his naked chest, the rapid response of his body as she caressed him. She would not deny that. "Isn't that the spark which brings spice to a relationship?" Funny, she had meant to say marriage. One night in his arms and she was already planning white lace and promises. "I don't want him to be exactly like me. I want to be continually surprised by the things he does—"

"Oh," Jan interrupted. "If you want to be surprised, you will be." From the corner, Arthur laughed.

"He's a nice guy, isn't he?"

"He is nice," Jan stated, leaving her sentence oddly unfinished, and Lori almost heard the words she hadn't said, "but he is not a guy."

Genevieve returned, figure-eighting around Lori's ankles, meowing. Lori bent down, ran her fingers through the animal's luxurious fur. Once the cat had her attention, it turned tail, headed for the back door, then stepped back toward Lori, repeating the process a couple of times. From decades of watching Lassie reruns, Lori knew what the cat needed.

"Can I let her out?" Lori asked.

"Sure."

"The back door?"

"Of course. She can take care of herself."

"And I can't?"

Lori didn't wait for her aunt's response. She let the cat out, standing in the open doorway, examining forbidden pleasure. It was the same horizon she witnessed when she left through the front door and walked around the side of the house, a wide yard, ending abruptly at the start of a forest, continuing up the base of a mountain. Yet, above the treeline, there was something huge but indistinct, something copper colored which dropped from sight before she could analyze it. A hot air balloon, perhaps?

Jan came up beside of her, placing a warm hand her shoulder. "Why don't you sit? You've had a busy morning, and are likely to have an active night."

In the forest, out of sight, something let out a high pitched bellow of pain. She shivered. Monsters, she thought, churning up her childhood fears of closets and under-beds and autumn wind shifting leaves against gravestones in invasive patterns. She had no idea why the idea should frighten her so now. She felt a chill to the marrow of her bones.

She forced a lighter image into her mind, smiled as she imagined Byron comforting her, his hands caressing her, bringing warmth and a palpable excitement. She felt a flush rise to her cheeks.

"Then you don't mind that Byron and I—?" she didn't know how to finish the sentence, although she had confessed everything. Too much between them was too unsettled, too confusing to know what they had, except that they had a beginning, a start of something which might be wonderful.

"Of course I don't mind. The things I said earlier, I was just rambling on. As an old woman, I am entitled. He's a good man," she put an odd reflection on the final word, which had Lori raising an eyebrow, before she continued. "He deserves happiness. He's been through a lot. Maybe one day you can sit him down long enough to get his life story."

CHAPTER 23

Wind howled, a harbinger of a blizzard, perhaps, except it was April and even this far north, most winter storms were a thing of the past. Lori thought of the last vestiges of the season, refusing to cede to spring. Winter had always seemed more than a season to Lori. She never thought of it as something controlled by the calendar, instead she envisioned it as a monster, gaining prominence, then beaten back down again in a repetitive cycle.

It was late. She had no idea how long she'd been coring strawberries or how long she loitered upstairs beside Byron this morning, whether time moved differently there or not. Dusk was starting to strip all the color from the scenery, taking the greens and blues and muting them toward reds and purples and finally to browns, grays and blacks. There had been a flash of metallic copper in the sky, but it hadn't been sunset, though she had no idea what it was. The sun was setting, tired, ready to wake up some other locality and let this one sleep.

"If you're hungry, I've got seafood chowder on the burner. It will warm you."

Her aunt hadn't made the chowder, and Lori had no idea how it appeared, since it couldn't have been simmering on the burners the past few hours. Still, she had no doubt if she turned, there would be chowder, like there had been waffles earlier in the day, and the other meals that instantly appeared. Some foods were prepared and canned, some mysteriously showed up. Byron wasn't the only person she should be interrogating.

Instinctively Lori waited for her aunt to finish the sentence. There's tea too, good for what ails you. It will bring you pleasant dreams, warm your insides, but her aunt said nothing of the kind, and it almost left a hole she needed to fill. She suspected there was more than the ritual of tea drinking, more than sitting at a table and sipping the brew. She knew that much from Belinda, the woman her aunt had called a witch. Strange now when she wanted it, craved it, her aunt didn't mention tea.

What was it Byron had said? *If you want the dragon tea, you'll have to get the answers from your aunt, for I won't be around?* Well, he wasn't around now and she craved tea. Somehow just the thought of it brought the taste of Byron to her mouth, the taste she experienced as she kissed him, her mouth mating with his, her tongue exploring his chest, his neck and the slope of his ear with unbridled curiosity, while he buried himself so deeply into her body she only needed the taste of him to survive.

"It smells delightful, but I ate a lot at breakfast, so I'm not really hungry yet. Do you think Byron would mind if I went out to look for him?" She was feeling a tad lonely—or perhaps what she was experiencing was quite a bit more visceral.

On the tail of her words, booming shock waves rippled through the kitchen with the power of a fifty megaton bomb. Lori fell to her knees, her head snapping. She cried out in pain, and fear. She crouched, covering her head with her arms as dishes dropped from the cabinets, shattering into thousands of razor sharp shards. Baskets of strawberries danced around the slate floor in drunken splendor, hopping, sliding, bouncing off the pots and kettles which had escaped from lower storage cabinets. A din surrounded them, both low and rumbling and high and squealing. Through it all, there was definitely the sound of animals in pain.

"What's happening?" Lori demanded, crawling toward her aunt, screaming to be heard over the devastation which sounded like the entire planet was being destroyed. Jan had kept her feet using the door frame leading to the basement, grasping for dear life, her knuckles white, her fingertips already bloodied from the force keeping her upright. Jan's eyes were wide, terror struck, and blood trickled from a small cut at her forehead.

Lori had never been in an earthquake before, but knew from watching the news the way the ground became liquid, the complete loss of stability felt miles away. "Is it an earthquake?"

"Yes." Jan's pupils were dilated, and the word spoken had come after a long hesitation, as if she had to consciously decide if the lie was acceptable, and if she could fit the current disaster into its parameters.

"Lori, I need you upstairs." Swaying with the rollicking floor, Jan grabbed her niece, pulled her to her feet, and with a life-raft grasp forced her toward the landing. "Up. Go as far up as you can manage. Try for Byron's lair. You should be safe there." Her voice was shaky, raspy, but Lori had no trouble understanding.

The house continued shaking, rattling the walls, the floor, the ceiling. The noise was deafening. The roar grew louder, giving no indication it would abate any time soon. Lori shouted, her lips against her aunt's ear, trying to be heard over the rumbling. "Come with me. If I'm to be safe, I want you with me."

The slate tile in the center of the kitchen floor cracked, and a yellow, hissing steam with a decidedly noxious odor penetrated the kitchen, as if the ground had opened all the way to hell, and this was what it looked like, what it smelled like. The flaw with that argument was instead of hot, the mist surrounding them was bitter and bone-jarringly cold. Roaring surrounded them, as invasive as a dozen freight trains, throbbing, pulsing, raising in intensity and volume, lowering in pitch. Lori covered her ears, stood at the base of the landing, where the baking power box stood empty. The cat must have taken her kittens to some perceived safety.

"Go! Up!" Jan gave her another shove.

"Where are you going?"

"There are creatures in the basement who will be trapped," Jan said, her eyes wide, terror-struck. "It is better I allow them their freedom, rather than be responsible for their deaths. They are too valuable."

"The things chained in the basement?"

Jan didn't think to dissemble. "Yes."

"I want to help."

"There is nothing you can do. It will be worse for them, with a stranger. I promise they won't attack me; they'll be too interested in freedom. You would be another matter."

"Where's Byron? Can I go to him?"

Jan reached out, touched Lori, even over all the devastation, the disaster, her touch was comforting, offering sympathy and compassion. "I think I heard his bellow we heard a few minutes ago. And when a dragon yells with that much force, there is little a mortal can do to offer salvation."

Little of that got through, still, Lori fought being shoved up the stairs. "Then he's hurt?"

"He can take care of himself." The lie was real, bounced around the nothing a mortal can do to offer salvation statement. "Lori, I can't worry about you too. I have too much to do. I need you up."

"Oh praise the saints, I found it," Arthur said, rooting through the kitchen devastation, coming up with a long brilliant broadsword. "He left it here, with you."

"I've had it," Jan admitted.

Arthur stood, straightened, although the floor still undulated, the walls still shook. "I will go for Byron."

"Go," her Aunt said, pushing him toward the back door. He got one step outside, turned around, grasped Jan and planted a hearty kiss on her. Lori wondered if Jan would fight, but she swooned.

"If I am to die today, I did not want to go without telling you how I feel."

"You love another woman."

"Not for some time. Not since I met you, majesty."

"You've got your sword. Go."

He shook his head, and the look in his eyes was of wonder. "I thought I sought death, but now I realize it wasn't death I sought, but you."

Arthur kissed her again, this time lightly on the top of her head. "Majesty, I'll be back and we'll talk." Gripping his weapon two handed, Arthur bounded out the back door into the maelstrom of destruction, and after three steps, Lori saw him no longer.

"That man—" Jan said, and Lori, who was beginning to understand love, realized she could recognize it.

"Now you have to go," Jan said, stepping over bouncing pots and pans, covering her own head against raining bricks and mortar. "I've too many things to do to worry about you."

Lori allowed herself to be shoved toward the stairs. She gripped the railing, watched the walls dance like some macabre funhouse simulation. She stopped, turned, realizing nothing this whole day had made any sense, and this was only another facet of incomprehensible things. "In an earthquake, up is not the safest direction."

Lori had no idea of the truth, but decided if her aunt wanted her out of the way, she shouldn't argue. She had no idea where such perversity was coming from. She started up the stairs, made it to the second floor landing, before she turned around, noticed her aunt had finally stopped watching her and had left, apparently to unchain the things in the basement.

Her arms outstretched, holding onto both staircase walls for balance, Lori crept back down. The back door swung widely. The epicenter of this earthquake, although it felt directly under her feet, was probably some miles distant. The kitchen was obscured by the mist which had thickened beyond fog, and was now a pasty smoke, obliterating everything. She coughed, for it was hard to breathe, found, when she entered the kitchen, the split in the floor tiles had widened and there was now a chasm at least two feet wide. She thought of monsters, crawling their way up from hell, and shook her head, trying to erase the image. There was no such thing.

She held onto the table, trying to keep her balance as the floor suffered under the epileptic fit of an entire planet. The kitchen table, inexplicably, seemed to be an oasis in this sea of destruction, a sanctuary. She was glad the dragon teapot had not put in an appearance while she had been dealing with mountains of strawberries. She didn't want to take the chance it would be destroyed like the crockery shattering around her, although she wouldn't know how to save it. She would look through the cabinets, but it was her impression wherever it rested when it wasn't in use, it was not in a cabinet.

"Aunt Jan! Aunt Jan!" The roar surrounding her swallowed her screams. The tremors grew in intensity, seeming to tear the house from its foundations. An indistinct light came from no discernible source. Even the sun seemed to be affected by this worldwide devastation. Lori continued calling, but she got no response.

The door to the basement stood open. Lori took that as a good sign. She held onto the frame for balance, but she could not see through the stygian black. A sharp burning ammonia stench pushed back, her hand over her mouth and nose. With the liquid roller coaster the ground had become, she did not want to chance the stairs.

She made a silent prayer, 'Please, let her be safe,' adding the addendums, 'let Byron live. Protect Genevieve and her kittens. And let Arthur return safely.' Then, without thinking, without even debating whether she should head downstairs and help Jan with whatever crisis she was facing, Lori crawled toward the back door which swung drunkenly back and forth.

Timing her exit to coincide with the opening, she ran into the back yard and forbidden territory. It no longer mattered what was happening downstairs to things chained in the basement. The destruction of the kitchen didn't matter. Neither did the danger compounded by trees and falling rocks. It didn't matter she believed her aunt and the only safety for her would be upstairs in the dragon's lair where she was expected to wait patiently.

The only thing that mattered was her love for Byron. He needed her. Lori didn't know how she knew, or why she knew, she only did. Somewhere out in this nightmare, Byron was hurt, and only she could save him.

CHAPTER 24

Although dying, the dragon's hearing was acute especially since he forced his mind to lock on anything which distracted him from his pain. He could discern what was natural, if anything about this earth-trauma could be considered natural, from what was invasive. Byron heard the assassins closing, trying to make sure of their kill. He was too valuable a trophy to ignore.

Sound crashed far to the west as killers crept through the underbrush. Two, three. It was too hard to maintain focus, but at least three, one carrying a bow. He had the proof under his wing and imbedded deep in his chest. He ground his teeth, feeling his fangs. Undoubtedly one also carried an axe.

***

A tree, at least thirty inches in diameter, was uprooted, fell, taking branches of half a dozen other trees with it. The wizard was tossed to the ground.

Andrew rose to his knees, from there to his feet. His eyes were wide, rapturous. His face was split by a grin, evil in its intensity. "This is my doing. Do you know how many mages have tried to open a portal? I did it."

"Yes, you did it. Did you ever think the reason your kind don't open portals, is something like this could happen? You idiot! You fool! Why did you think you could find success when so many others have failed?"

"I opened the portal." While the statement was boasting and filled with dread.

The stench of things long dead barreled in through the invisible door, and the wizard knew there might be creatures slithering through the barrier, demons and monsters so vile that humanity had no concept of them, no names. But for the moment, there was only the reek of decay and the earthquakes undulating with increasing violence.

***

Lori stumbled, struggling to keep her feet. The ground continued to rumble, great shaking nightmares that made walking upright impossible. Still, every time she fell to her knees, she pulled herself back up, crawling when she had to, making her way deeper into the black forest.

She didn't know anything about earthquakes, but thought they only lasted a few seconds, a minute or two at the most. This one went on and on, releasing pent up tension, creating devastation. It showed no indication of abating anytime soon.

The roar grew louder with each step she made along the path. She heard clacking, rattling like a train, but that was the sound used to describe a tornado. There was no denying the roar. She tried to hold her hair back but it blew so wildly around her face she couldn't see. An earthquake and a tornado together. It wouldn't surprise her if a meteor had also landed.

Lori screamed, falling again and feeling a sharp sting of pain. She'd ripped her palms going down, skinned her knee, both injuries superficial but indicative if she didn't find safety soon, she'd be in worse trouble. At the thought, she realized it wasn't safety she sought, but only Byron.

Around her trees swayed, snapped, all but danced. Leaves and branches lay around her, many thicker than her thigh. If she were hit by one falling, it would be the end of her. She screamed as a tree beside her uprooted, twisted, then fell, into a deep, apparently bottomless pit. She ran forward, heedless of her direction, cursing herself for a fool.

Inside the forest darkness ruled, a black darker than the verdant canopy above her was responsible for. She couldn't see the sky, tried to remember what it had looked like as she tore out the back door. It had been sunset, not half an hour before she let Genevieve out.

She remembered seeing the sun specifically, remembered thinking foolish thoughts about making love with Byron having some universal effect—causing the sun to glow. No sun now. Her impression was highlighted as fat stinging drops of rain sizzled down, hissing as they landed, more than just wet: acid.

With the rain, she noticed the stench, the same one she experienced in the kitchen as the noxious gas crept up from the lower floors or from the Earth's broken mantle itself. She no longer smelled pine pitch, she smelled terror. If hell had a scent, it wasn't sulfur, it was this.

She ran quickly, blindly, tripping, stumbling, trying to hold on to the tree trunks bordering the path for their strength. While the path originally started out with sharp familiarity, because of the storm and her own rising panic, she quickly became disorientated. The more lost she got, the more she remembered the huge black monster that attacked Byron, and how she had been its target.

Lori raised her chin, took a deep breath, and set her feet down the left turn. The wind picked up, slashing branches with hurricane intensity, and as she moved forward, she had to keep her arms up, her hands shielding her face. The temperature plummeted.

She heard the shout of a large animal in pain, a screech of agony, mixed with the violent snarl of defiance. It sounded close. A wounded creature was bound to be deadly, and she doubted a faerie ring would protect her if it decided to attack.

"Byron!" She tripped, falling heavily, deep into the underbrush. She rested there, sucking her bleeding palm instinctively, taking the find strength, for she was breathless and terrified.

Seeing movement on the path ahead, her first impulse was to scream out, "I'm here," as if expecting a rescue party. Without knowing why, she held back, wondering if there were other terrors abroad. When she recognized who it was, she was glad she kept silent.

Belinda walked toward her, looking far different than she had in Jan's kitchen, scalier for want of a better word. Lori realized her form was steadier, as if this was closer to what she really looked like, and she did not have to try to maintain her appearance. The ground rolled beneath her, and the winds soured, but her footsteps were firm and her progress unhindered. Her face radiated anger and she yelled, and although Lori understood none of the words she recognized the violence in her slashing hand and snapping jaw.

Beside her, laughing joyously, as if this torment were all his doing, strode Andrew, her former lover. She almost didn't recognize him, for although it had been only days since she'd seen him, he had changed as well. He towered over Belinda, maintaining an unexpected height and assurance. On campus, he slouched, and she recognized the disguise had been deliberate, making himself look smaller. How he must have laughed at her those evenings when they walked together from the bus stop as she tried to entice him to straighten his shoulders, raise his chin. He was dressed oddly, wearing a long black robe which swirled around his legs, wrapping under the hurricane force of the winds surrounding them.

A third man walked behind, holding a long bow. His progress was hindered by the earthquake far more than his two companions. Perhaps too, he kept his distance to be out of sight of Belinda's torrential anger. Lori didn't recognize him, and doubted he would be welcomed to the Inn as a friend, if only by the company he kept. He was a big man and strong looking, dressed in rough work clothes with hands as big as footballs. There was something not quite right about him, for his forehead was too low, his nose and lips too broad. He looked like a creature stolen from the depths of antiquity, a throw-back. She did not doubt his aim with the long bow would be accurate.

Belinda stopped, only feet from where Lori hid. "Tonight," Andrew crowed, "I am invincible."

The witch spat. "And look what you've done."

"The portal will not bother us. It drew the dragon didn't it? If nothing else, it was worth opening the portal to obtain the prize. He wouldn't have come this close, wouldn't have been distracted long enough for the arrows to find him. The dragon is down. The spoils will be ours. This devastation should keep Jan and her protégé occupied, so they cannot come to his rescue. They will not thwart us this time."

Belinda snarled, showing small, stubby teeth. "I want the fangs. I don't care what you do with the rest, but the fangs are mine."

The wizard clenched his fingers, as if imagining what her throat would feel like under them as he squeezed the life out of her. "I want the head. The head isn't much use without the fangs."

"You idiot. The fangs are mine." Laughter finished the sentence, evil made manifest.

Andrew looked around, his gaze resting for a long second on Lori's hiding place, before passing over her, continuing on with his search. "I still hear him moaning. Dragons are not easy to kill."

The archer held up the bow. It was strung, the line taut. He notched an arrow. "They are with this tip."

Walking briskly, they were soon out of sight, taking a left turn, and Lori exhaled. She had been so frightened she held her breath. She wanted to follow, find out what dragon they had killed, wondering if there were anything she could do to help, and if so, who would she aid?

She stepped back onto the path, trying to determine if she would become more lost if she turned around and went the way she had come, when she realized something not particularly comforting. She didn't want to spend the night here, lost, with the trees whipped to a frenzy and something monstrous howling in pain, and with a woman her aunt and her lover considered a witch wandering freely. She would even have clung to Andrew, if he hadn't been with Belinda, if she wasn't so afraid of him too.

She followed them, terrified they would turn around and discover her, but they were too intent on their goal and fighting the elements. Lori hid, inching to one side, when the trio ahead of her reached a clearing. She struggled to get a good view, for what she saw was greater than fantastical: it was unbelievable. A dragon stood in the clearing, its left shoulder hanging low, dripping blood from at least two wounds. She wanted to scream to the witch and her companions, warn them, but she waited, biting her lips, to see what would happen.

It was a magnificent beast, gold colored, gleaming even in the indifferent light of the storm. Its head rose high, almost to tree height.

A dragon. How many times had Byron tried to tell her he was a dragon, had her aunt, had Arthur.

A dragon.

A dragon?

She dropped down heavily in the underbrush. Was it possible?

CHAPTER 25

Arthur swung the sword two-handed, bisecting the creature which had escaped from the portal and crept along the ground. There were dozens of them, maybe hundreds, creepy, slimy things with no discernible legs and arms, but with huge gaping mouths. They chortled when they saw him, but they must have been brainless, for they never ganged up on him, instead attacking one or two at a time, some waiting patiently for their turn, some wandering off to other mayhem.

When he killed one, they hissed, like stale, putrid air from a balloon, then vanished, leaving only a pile of orange dust. He was surrounded by dust now, found it coated every inch of his clothing, making his grip on his sword less secure.

Arthur had been looking for Byron, but come upon the portal first and had gotten no further. Whatever this door was it was incompatible with Earth and these alien creatures had to be stopped. He could not leave now, even though he bled from more than a dozen wounds. These creatures did not bite, did not tear when they touched his flesh, but sucked, pulling his skin and his muscle into their broad mouths.

Another one popped. And another. His shoulders were aching and the sword, his beloved, familiar sword grew heavy with his increasing exhaustion.

He could not kill them all.

And he could not leave.

***

The dragon struggled to position his feet, ignoring the pain from his useless wing, from the wounds which bled freely. As with most predators, he was far more deadly an adversary wounded than whole. He did not roar again.

The three assassins entered the clearing. The beast bent, his head low, his body crouched, instinctively protecting his broken wing. They were startled, clearly caught unaware. They had thought him dead. While not far wrong, he would make sure he did not die alone. Although his reflexes were slow and his stamina waning, he darted out, capturing the one with the bow.

Man flesh. He tasted man flesh twice in one day. She would laugh when he told her. But no, she wouldn't laugh for he would never tell her.

The dragon stuck his fangs deep into the flesh. The man screamed; the sound abruptly terminating as his life ended. Bones cracked. The dragon tossed its head, discarding the corpse. The wizard held his hands out, started an incantation, and the dragon dove again, this time his aim and balance off, for he was after the wizard's torso, instead he captured one arm, which shattered. The wizard fell, and beside him, the witch hefted the spear she was carrying. The weapon hit him, but did no damage. It bounced off impenetrable dragon hide. He didn't see an axe. They had not come as well prepared as he feared.

"I thought you said he was dead. This dragon doesn't look dead to me!" Andrew cradled his arm, struggling to get to his feet.

Belinda, for all her short legs, her round body, was surprisingly agile. She darted away from the beast's snapping fangs with seconds to spare. She hid at the tree line, camouflaged by the dense overgrowth. She could see into the clearing far easier than the dragon could see into the wood. Around them, the ground still undulated in a frightening tango of death where two worlds collided.

"He is wounded. We only need to stay away from his fangs until he bleeds out, and keep him occupied, so he doesn't change. This is the form we want him to maintain."

Streams of electric power coiled around the wizard's legs, undulating, dancing, feeding him. He twisted his arms, sent the power strands toward the dragon. But the lizard was experienced and deflected them. Simultaneously he slashed his tail, knocking the witch from her feet, sending her flying through the air a dozen feet, to crash into a tree, falling boneless, unconscious, into a heap, bleeding from a dozen scrapes.

The dragon snapped at the wizard, and the magic man darted, narrowly avoiding the talons and slashing tail. The beast, knowing itself dying, belched fire. The liquid caught Andrew, turning him into a flaming torch. Andrew ran blindly down the forest path, igniting everything he came in contact with.

The dragon felt himself separating, body from soul, although it was a well established fact, dragons had no soul.

***

Lori fell, huddled in a fetal position, her arms and legs numb. Her breathing quick and choppy, she felt lightheaded. She thought of dragon tea, and all of the references to dragons she'd heard lately, decided she was not surprised by the monster in the forest. Byron warned her there were worse than the garntz. But that wasn't all he said.

I am a dragon.

What she didn't know was if this dragon was good or evil. She had seen it kill. She turned, ran, taking random forks of the narrow path, climbing over any obstruction in her way.

Lori stopped, panting. Her lungs heaved from fear and exertion. It was then, gnawing on a thumbnail, a childhood habit completely broken except when she was lost, she noticed the fireflies. There were two of them, bright, and by their very nature, cheerful. Just seeing them buoyed her spirits.

Her vision blurred, grew fuzzy, then sharpened again as she looked at them. Her mind kept trying to fill in pieces left blank, as if she were witnessing only part of a whole, and a whole she knew intimately. They are only fireflies, she said to herself, needing the reassurance in this world gone insane.

They stopped a few feet in front of her, on a left hand turning. Nothing looked familiar, with images of the dragon killing, she doubted anything could look familiar. She had to be in Oz...or Narnia...or Shangri-La. It occurred to her quite rationally, that if she were in Oz, she was without her ruby slippers, and she could find no trace of a yellow brick road.

"I don't suppose you'd let me follow you?" she asked, clearly torn between ignoring them, and treating them like some guardian angel sent to lead her to safety. The unlikelihood of their appearance, in a blazing hurricane/earthquake didn't stop her appreciation.

The pair bounced up and down in unison as if in direct answer to her query.

"Will you take me back to my Aunt Jan's house?"

This time their response was different. Their light slid back and forth, not up and down, as they had the moment before. It looked for all the world like they were shaking their heads 'no'.

"You'll lead me to safety?"

They bounced again, then moved two feet down the path, and inched back, as if to ascertain if she followed.

"You don't think I'm insane, talking to fireflies, do you?" she asked, but there was a laugh in her voice, and she had already made her decision to follow, as long as they stayed on the path. If they veered off, or lead her to a bottomless abyss, she would head off on her own.

She'd been walking several minutes, only a half-dozen steps behind them, when she realized what she was seeing wasn't two fireflies in parallel but a single being, with what might be two glowing eyes and no other mass.

"You really are beautiful, you know," she said. Lori felt cheered, although it was nearly full dark and she had no idea which way was home, she was not alone. When it took a left-hand turn, she didn't think and continued to follow.

"I hope you're not leading me astray."

It bounced up and down, as if in answer, but never left the path, and never got too far ahead so she had trouble keeping up.

"Listen, firefly, I've really got to be getting back. By any chance do you know how to get to my aunt's house? It might be called Reptile's Roost, but I am not sure. It's a huge house, and my aunt's name is Janet Pikorski."

The firefly pair drew closer, then darted ahead. "Ok, I'll follow you. It's not as if I know the way myself."

It was then she heard snarling of what sounded like a pack of feral dogs, and so she picked up her pace, and followed even closer.

She almost tripped over Byron. She would have, if the fireflies hadn't stopped directly above him.

"Byron?"

He was lying on the path, in an odd position, his head turned away from her. "Byron?" she bent down, touching him, knowing he was hurt.

"Lori. Lori, you came." His eyes flicked open, filled with recognition, edged with pain. His voice was shallow, weak, and except for his eyes, his voice, she would have thought him dead. "I was hoping you or Janet would."

"I was led," she said, then nodded her thanks in the direction of the fireflies. "What happened? Can you move, get up?"

"I was careless," he said, his voice low as a small trickle of blood drooled from his lips. "It's been centuries since I was as foolish. I did manage to stop them, but as you can see, not soon enough to reach safety."

"What happened?" The paired fireflies darted closer, and in its wan light she saw a long-shafted arrow sticking out of his chest.

"You've been shot?"

"Yes. Lori, you've got to help me."

"I will. Anything."

"Anything?"

"Yes." Tears dribbled from her eyes. "I really want to help."

"Listen carefully. I can make it back by myself, so I don't want you to worry, but I need you to take the teapot to Jan. Can you manage?"

"The teapot? I don't understand."

"It's important to me, and I need your answer. I can't hold on much longer. Can you take the teapot to Jan?"

"Yes, of course."

"There is something else. You have to ask me for a cup of tea, and when it comes, you have to drink it." She was holding his hand, which had been non-responsive, but he found strength in his fingers, clasped her chilled hand in desperation. "You need to swallow at least a mouthful. It might be nasty. I can't guarantee the taste."

"Tea? How will that help you?"

"It will, believe me, more than you know. After you've drank it, you can throw it up if you have to. But you've got to swallow it."

"Byron, are you delirious? You're not making any sense."

"Janet will be able to explain it to you. Take the teapot to her. The chakra will guide you."

"The chakra?"

"This thing," he said, trying to point toward the insects.

"The fireflies?"

"Yes. Ask for the tea, please, then follow the fireflies. But before you do, there is one other thing."

The wind continued to whip around her, and the roar, from the devastation mutated, increasing in intensity.

"The door the wizard opened has to be shut before anything else gets through. Follow the chakra. It will show you the door. And Lori?"

"Yes?"

"The tea will probably taste off."

"All right."

He raised his arm, desperate. She clasped her fingers with his, listened to the rumbling from his lungs which couldn't be good. "If you ask for the tea and do not drink it, it will kill me."

"Byron, I don't want to take the teapot to Aunt Jan, I want to take you. Let me try to carry you, or make some kind of litter, or run back for the EMT's."

"Lori, please. Ask for tea, then take the teapot to Janet. And don't forget to shut the door."

"The tea. Aunt Janet said it has healing powers. You should drink it."

"I cannot. I've never been able to." The fireflies were bobbing up and down, as if desperate for her to follow. "You have to try and shut the door."

She kissed the back of his hand, then stood, swaying in the earthquake which showed no sign of abating. "Shut the door?"

She had no idea if any of this would ever make sense. Teapots, doors and dragons and death, for the witch lay in a heap about twenty feet from her, and the man's body, a little further.

"Byron, I'll be back with help, I promise."

CHAPTER 26

Jan moved down the stairway as quickly as she could, but they rocked as if liquid and there were no handrails. Finally, in desperation, she lay on her belly, slid down the stairs like a two-year-old uncomfortable with his balance.

The devastation was worse here than in the kitchen. Open fissures hissed cold, sour smoke. Rocks and building material lay, detritus from the earthquake. Still she knew moving downward, whispering prayers to herself, calling on powers of faerie claimed but never before used.

She heard the snapping, the battle being fought as she reached the lowest landing. Two seven-foot gargoyles, chained at their neck and one ankle fought.

"Stop! I've come to set you free. Milton, Longfellow, break it off!"

The gargoyles separated, only because they had a new target, one they would face together.

"If you've come to free us, you won't leave alive."

"Milton, give me your word you'll leave."

"Not with him free."

"I have to. The wards have failed. I can no longer in good conscience keep you here."

"In good conscience?" Milton mocked. "Is that how you keep us?"

She held her hands out, to show she was unarmed, as she moved cautiously closer. Their snapping jaws and hideous claws made even her small steps seem inadvisable. "You know why I keep you. But now I've come to let you go."

"Come closer to me," Longfellow said, a seductive slur to his voice. "And I will set you free."

She reached out, and a link at his neck snapped open.

CHAPTER 27

Lori stood above Bryon, knees shaking. "Go," he ordered, his voice weak, heavy with pain, "shut the door."

Her eyes misted and she swiped at tears, feeling desperately afraid. She crushed his fingers in her hands, but he had not the strength to respond. "Please," she begged, "let me take you to a doctor."

His eyes cleared. For the moment he looked at her and she knew he saw her. "You won't understand, but what I am asking you to do is far more important than getting me help. The door needs to be shut. All humanity is in danger."

As tears dripped from her eyes, she stared at his chest. Around the entry wound of the arrow, bright red air bubbles grew, popped. His lungs were damaged. Internal bleeding. He was dying.

"Byron, please."

"Lori," he gasped, struggling for breath. His eyes grew glassy, his breath labored. "I don't have time to explain, but do this for me. It is perhaps the greatest thing you can do with your life. If you succeed, they will write books about you, sonnets."

The ground continued to shake, undulating with a macabre fluidity. Darkness crept around them, evil, invasive and somehow thick, as if more than the absence of light, but gooey matter, inky black substance.

Tears dripped. She could not leave him. "I don't want my life, if you're not in it."

He twitched, spasms, perhaps death throes. "I promise the teapot will be here when you return. Save the teapot."

With knees shaking and her bones feeling less cohesive than sand castles, Lori turned toward the fireflies, instead, something caught her attention. In shock, she walked carefully through the trees for the earthquake continued, to a mass of clothing clotted in a pile. It was the witch Belinda. Lori bent down, put her fingers against the witch's throat, finding no response. The witch was dead. She turned, bile rising in her throat.

"Go, the door."

She stood from the corpse, faced the fireflies, looking beyond them. For a moment, in this spot, the tempest around her ebbed. She could still hear it roaring, knew the force of its fury hadn't dissipated, but at the moment stood in relative calm. The eye of the storm. An odd term for an earthquake.

This was the clearing. A huge dragon with a wounded wing, a creature from fantasy, had fought here. She couldn't be mistaken, but logically she didn't believe in dragons. Couldn't believe. A woman, regardless of what she was, lay dead.

She swallowed, drew courage. All she wanted to do was cry, panic, hold Byron, find some way to get him to an emergency room. She was intelligent. She could/would/should cope, but love had somehow muted things. Odd she should realize now that she loved him, when six months of being intimate with Andrew, she had never felt the smallest stirrings.

His lips moved, although she heard no sound. "Please!" he said.

The two glowing lights she called fireflies were only about a yard from her. If she reached out, could prevent her hand from trembling, if they, like the air, had mass, she could touch them. Lori looked back, but his eyes were glassy, and she remembered he thought her task important, and she had promised.

There was moisture in her throat, then too much, so she had to swallow again, and her cheeks were wet. "Alright, I'll follow you."

It/they didn't move.

Her voice trembled, shook, like the ground at her feet. It was high-pitched, didn't sound like her at all. "Byron said I have to follow you to a door he left open." They stayed where they were, bobbing up and down in perfect unison, but making no progress in leading her. On the path, Byron had passed out, his eyes not shut but they had glazed over. Bubbles of blood still popped at the wound in his chest, but fewer, smaller. She knew she would get no more advice from him.

"I really would like a cup of tea from the dragon teapot," she said aloud, feeling more than foolish. She bent over, and kissed him once on the top of his head. Lori was not a woman who believed in superstitions, even though she readily admitted she was enchanted with the ones her aunt came up with, so maybe she kissed him for another reason, because he was hurt, because she cared, because there might not be another opportunity while he lived. She kissed him, and whispered "for safety from evil spirits," then followed the fireflies who were bobbing up and down frantically, running to keep up.

"Here?" she asked them. They hadn't gone far, but far enough she had to catch her breath, far enough she couldn't find her way back to Byron without assistance. "The door is here?" She stood in the middle of a deep wood, night was thick around her like the darkness of biblical writings, born of evil. Ugly cold hung thick and she shivered. The wind whipped, knife-like and invasive. She couldn't stay here long, without freezing to death.

It seemed like an unlikely place to find a door. There was no cottage, no gate, no trap door to the gates of Hell which Jules Verne, C.S. Lewis or Stephen King would recognize. She stood, turning in circles, desperately seeking the answer. She could visualize nothing that she could shut. But the fireflies wouldn't move an inch forward or backwards. They stayed where they were bobbing up and down in increasing desperation.

"Lori?"

"Arthur?"

He moved closer, holding a massive sword, the hilt inlaid with precious jewels, covered in orange power, breathing heavily.

"What are you doing here?"

"Byron sent me. He's wounded. He said I had to shut a door."

"You can shut the door?"

"Since I was two," she answered flippantly. "Will you go back with me, help me rescue Byron?"

"I cannot. There is too much I have to do here. Evil has gotten in. I cannot let it run rampant, if I can stop it. But if you can close the door, it will be a miracle."

"This is stupid. No, it's more than stupid, it's criminally negligent. Byron is going to die!"

"And he will die in vain if that door can be shut and is not."

"I don't see it."

"And I cannot see it," he answered. "What are they?" He indicated the two lights, the ones she called fireflies, then he must have answered his own question, for he fell to his knees in supplication. "Ancient One—"

"What?" she asked. And something seriously bothered her, for she remembered who Arthur had called Ancient One.

"Lori, what you are doing is massively important. I will stand guard here and protect you, then I need to go hunt those who escaped."

"Tell me, what is this door?"

Arthur tried to explain as he fought things she could not see, as puffs of orange dust exploded around him and she sought an invisible door.

She reached out, fumbling, feeling like a mime, trying to close the door. Trying desperately to manage, so she could get back to Byron, find a phone, call the EMTs, get him the medical attention he so desperately needed. An arrow. Heaven forbid, in his chest and under his arm were arrows.

"Please, you've got to help me."

Arthur remained busy, swinging his sword and her fear multiplied for she felt creepy, invasive things touching her, stopping when Arthur was again coated in a fresh explosion of orange powder.

And then Lori felt it, something, she had no idea what it was, and the two parallel eyes, the things she had been calling fireflies, bounced up and down, pleased. "This is it? This is the door?" for although impulses from her fingertips to her brain indicated she felt something cold and metallic, there was nothing she could see. There was nothing there. Her eyes were unreliable, but her sense of touch was not.

She felt it. She raised her arms up and down, discovering the dimensions of the invisible item she faced, worked at it, until she discovered it moved, and it was possible to shut it. Not like a door, swinging on hinges, although she did try that first, more like sliding along a track. She pushed. It resisted, and she felt the fireflies trying to help her, give her inspiration or insight into her task, bobbing excitedly as she made progress.

She slipped, fell, when the door caught on something, an unexpected resistance. She landed awkwardly, heard something snap, felt the immediate stab of pain along her wrist. She yelped in pain, while the fireflies bobbed around her, silently screaming their desperation. And she remembered Byron, dying, so she pulled herself up, using the door she could not see. She put her weight against it, and again it moved, slowly, reluctantly, until finally it slid into place, and she could move it no more.

"Is that enough?" she asked. Arthur had gone, swinging his deadly weapon, chasing invisible monsters so no answer would come from him. But the fireflies weren't satisfied. If she understood what her invisible helpers were after, they wanted more. She pushed. She tugged. She rammed it with her shoulder, and a curious thing happened. As it slid into place, as it hit another obstacle, the roaring from the earthquake, the shaking of the ground and the devastation all around her eased until only a moment later, it stopped completely.

The roar had been going on so long, the shaking so intense, the silence which descended felt unnatural. She could hear herself think. The epicenter, she knew. Like turning off a switch she had stopped the earthquake. Foolishly she reached out, to touch the door, bashing her hand against the obstruction she knew was there but she couldn't see. The pain from her wrist was blinding. She'd never broken a bone before. She grew heartened as the devastation finally ceased.

"If I'm finished here, take me to Byron," she insisted. She tried to run, but the movement jarred her wrist too badly. Cradling her broken wrist with her left hand, she followed the fireflies back to the path where Byron lay.

Where Byron had laid.

He was gone. For a second she panicked, thinking he'd been carted off by some wild animal, or even died, then vanished in a puff of smoke, like fantastical creatures in movies she'd seen. But then she remembered. He said he would have the strength to get back to the house, if she took the dragon teapot back to Jan.

The teapot sat in the middle of the path, and Lori knelt down, carefully cradling her wrist, and looked at it. It was in a pool of something dark, sticky, and she dipped her index finger into the puddle, raised it, and smelled blood. Byron's blood.

If you ask for it and don't drink it, I'll die, Byron said, a statement which made no sense at all. The fireflies were still bobbing up and down around her, desperate.

"All right. I'll drink," she said. There was no cup. She would have to sip directly from the spout. She lifted the pot, finding it light. There wasn't much liquid within. And it was leaking. From two small holes in the sides: one on the broad chest of the dragon, the other under a wing. "It's cracked, broken." She would have discarded it, for what would her aunt want with a leaking teapot, but she'd made a promise.

She raised it, holding the teapot single handedly to her lips and sipped. It was warm, and had a sharp, copper taste to it, thick and disgusting. She almost spit, almost vomited, but forced herself to swallow, forced herself to take a second taste.

"Thank you," she told the teapot, using politeness since it had appeared once when she had needed it, had comforted her when she had been scared and lonely. Although it was only a leaking thing, she felt she owed it that much.

"I'll take you to my Aunt Jan now."

CHAPTER 28

She kept a running commentary of what she was doing, more to keep herself moving. Her adrenaline from the earthquake was wearing off, and the pain from her wrist increased. She wanted to lay down on the path and moan, wanted someone to comfort her. She found she couldn't rise to a standing position while holding the teapot. She was dizzy, sick to her stomach from the tea—or whatever it was she drank, and her knees wouldn't hold her. But the creature, she had given up of thinking them fireflies some time before, wouldn't leave. Their desperation kept her moving until the house came into view, and she was able to push herself along.

"You're going to let me go in the back door?" she asked, following the eyes, what else could the two parallel dots of light be, but glimmering eyes? Then she remembered, she had left from the back door. If she went in that way, Aunt Jan was likely to beat her, but she doubted she had enough strength to make it around to the front. The door was shut, and she couldn't manage with her damaged wrist while holding the teapot, so she set it down awkwardly, almost dropping it. The eyes danced again, frantic.

"I'm sorry," she mumbled, adding a sharp curse. It wasn't as if it wasn't already leaking. She put her left wrist to the doorknob, tried to turn it, but found she couldn't. She always lacked strength in that hand, not from any injury or illness, but because she was so dominantly right handed. She kicked, pounding on the door, feeling the need to cry. She grew lightheaded, dizzy, and the need to retch increased.

"Let me in," but no one heard her cry, except the black cat Genevieve, who twirled around her ankles. Seeing the cat somehow gave her strength to continue. She tried the knob again, this time using both hands, although, because of the pain in her right, she had very little strength. The door opened. She entered, relieved, calling out.

"Aunt Jan!"

The kitchen was a disaster. The opening in the floor still hissed some kind of noisome gasses, and the dishes and pots which had crashed to the floor from their cabinets were still scattered. There were dozens of overturned baskets of fruits and vegetables: peaches, grapes, and green beans; fat things (slightly purple but not at all moldy looking) and she wondered if they were halchits.

Jan was nowhere to be found. The back door was swinging shut before she remembered the teapot, ran, stopped the door before it closed and crushed the fragile teapot into a thousand shards.

She bent down, picked it up. The eyes danced. "Are you coming in?" she asked.

They bobbed back and forth, a clear 'no', then slowly made their way back toward the forest.

Lori carefully set the teapot down on the only clear spot she could find on the table, cradling her arm, running down the main hall yelling.

"Aunt Jan, I need you."

"Land sakes, child, what's gotten into you?" Jan said, coming down the stairs holding a pile of red towels. She was disheveled, her hair a mess, covered in some kind of sticky mire. All over the kitchen floor were piles of red towels, some torn, some whole, all of them used. "I have a crisis on my hands down here..." but she didn't have to finish.

"What have you done to the teapot?"

"The teapot isn't the issue here. Where is Byron?"

"Byron you say? Have you seen Byron?"

"Yes. He was wounded, two arrows in his chest. He told me he would make it back here, if I could bring the teapot. Aunt Jan, I'm frightened. He didn't look good."

She spoke to her aunt's back, for Jan was cradling the teapot, speaking to it with cooing assurance, as if it would respond. "So, what trouble have you gotten yourself into now, Brew?" she said. Gently she swirled the teapot. "There isn't much left."

"No, there's not."

"Lori, this is important. Tell me everything that happened to Byron."

"I don't know what you mean. I did nothing to Byron. Aunt Jan, I think he was dying."

"This is vital. Especially in light of what happened here this morning, with the ..."

"Earthquake?" Lori finished for her.

"Yes, the earthquake. I need the whole story." Jan cleared devastation from a chair, then put her hands to Lori's shoulders, forcing her to sit. "Anything you can remember."

Lori swallowed, panting. Oddly enough, she was more frightened now than she had been carrying the teapot back to the house. It was as if now that she was safe, didn't have to cope, she could give in to her panic. "I was scared. I went out the back door. I know you told me not to, but I thought if I could find Byron, I wouldn't be as frightened any more."

Jan set the teapot gently on the table, then busied herself around the kitchen, frantically shoving debris this way and that, obviously desperate to find something. "What happened to your wrist?"

"I fell. It's broken. I heard the bones snap." Lori cradled it, watching it swell. Already a dozen different colors vied for dominance against her pale skin.

"You keep talking. I'll wrap it for you." Jan found what she was looking for and pulled a basin from a cabinet Lori had never seen her use before, a big round cauldron with steep sides. The pot was an odd color, a dull burgundy, and looked none too clean. Jan poured water into it from the sink, stirring carefully as she did so, as if there were more in it than water, and whatever was there was extremely delicate.

"Stick your hand in there. It might be better if you don't look inside."

"The wrist is broken," Lori said. Her mother used "soaking it" as a general cure-all for everything from headaches to bone tumors. "Soaking isn't going to help."

"You're not soaking it, dear. You're wrapping it, immobilizing it."

"What if it needs setting?" The bones felt like they needed to be set, but someone should X-ray it, should have some professional let her know for sure. It had been a hard fall.

"Stick your hand in."

When her aunt took that tone of voice, Lori didn't think to disobey. The water was shockingly, blindingly hot, almost boiling. "Don't pull it out. It must stay in there at least a few minutes."

"It's hot, and it stinks."

"That's how you know it's working."

Lori gasped, in addition to the heat, and the vile stench, it felt like something was alive in there, swishing against her skin. She was certain of it. "There's something in here."

"They will make you feel better. Don't move your arm." Her "You might feel some discomfort," came a second too late, for something had definitely bitten her, a sharp needle-like sting.

"There's something alive in there!" How it got in the pot, Lori had no idea, for it had been in the cabinet, and, as far as she could tell, Jan only added water.

"Don't remove your hand," Jan reiterated, holding it in the water, when Lori fought her. The things which felt slimy, like eels, were tightening from her knuckles half-way to her elbow, and she was bitten, stung, at least five or six additional times.

"You did do a number on your wrist," Jan said.

"What's happening? It hurts."

"It won't hurt you. Now stay silent while the bandage sets."

"Bandage?"

"I told you, a broken wrist needs to be immobilized."

While the water stayed hot, Lori felt her hand acclimating, so it didn't feel so overpowering. After a while, Jan was able to let go. The pin prick bites she had felt earlier didn't repeat, and while her hand was being wrapped, it did feel better. She could wiggle her fingers and the wrist itself felt stable.

"You still should soak for another ten minutes at least. Fifteen would be best."

Jan ran out the back door, was back in minutes with a shallow, long tray filled with dirt. She brought the tray to the table, shoved something Lori couldn't see into it, then set the leaking teapot on it. "The tea is too precious to waste even a single drop. There's nothing I can do for what spilled while you brought it here, but I can make sure no more is wasted."

"Will you concentrate on Bryon!" Lori screamed. "I'm telling you he was hurt!"

"I don't doubt that for a minute. I am doing what I can. Healing is not one of my callings, but I know a thing or two about Brew, and Lori, if he lives or if he dies, this must be done right. You did a very good thing bringing the teapot here. A brave thing. There must have been danger."

Her eyes flashed, as she remembered the epic battle between the dragon and the witch, the wizard and the man with a long bow and the orange puffy things Arthur fought. She had no idea how Byron came to be hurt and she suspected the others were dead.

"Now while you're soaking, you can finish the remainder of your story. How did you find the teapot?"

"I was lost in the forest, and I came upon a dragon."

"The old beast was there?"

"You're not surprised there was a dragon?" Lori asked. Jan was busy, she had rinsed her hands from the soil, then rooted around the mess on the kitchen floor and found the blue teapot, miraculously unharmed in the disarray at her feet. She washed it at the sink, the same sink where she had filled the caldron with hot water Lori was soaking in.

"There was a battle. The dragon fought." She gave a brief description of what she witnessed.

"The dragon was already wounded."

"Yes. I ran, frightened, but a pair of eyes, I thought of them as fireflies, brought me back. I thought they were leading me to safety."

"His chakra," Jan said, but the word left an unpleasant taste in her mouth, for the older woman almost spit.

"I found Byron lying in the clearing where the dragon had fought. He set me off to do something," she wasn't certain she wanted to admit what she had done, "and told me when I finished the teapot would be there, right where he was."

"Makes sense."

"Then I had a sip of tea, and I brought it directly to you."

"You drank the tea?" Jan screeched.

"Yes. It was nasty."

"You foolish, foolish child," Jan spat, her eyes venom filled as she stared her. "Can't you see this is all that is left of him? He needs his strength. You could have killed him. If you'd drained this teapot …"

"The teapot?" she asked, wiggling her fingers. She could use a fresh cup, to wash the miserable taste out of her mouth, but the kitchen was in shambles, and Jan obviously was concentrating on saving this teapot.

"If you drain it, or all the fluid leaks out, Bryon dies."

"He said he would die if I didn't take a sip of the tea. It was awful," she continued, answering her aunt's unspoken question, expressed only with a raised eyebrow.

Then Lori remembered something she had noticed before. When Jan had been feeding the seedlings using the teapot forfertilizer, she had been extremely careful, and the one time she had accidentally spilled a drop in the greenhouse, had been exceptionally thorough in wiping it up completely. When Lori wasn't directly looking, she took the rag she had used and buried it near the pile of soil Lori had been using to fill the pots. She had also put two seeds into the hole.

"Oh, heavens. I haven't been able to round up those things I let go, and now this."

"Things you let go? The monsters chained in the basement?"

"Yes."

"We're better off without them."

"That's not true. Lori, I need to take care of this for Byron. Can you get yourself upstairs? You should be finished soaking. It might be better if you got some sleep. It's been an eventful day, and tomorrow I'll need your help to get this kitchen put to rights again."

"I want to look for Byron. He has to be here. He said he would be here."

"I will take care of Byron."

"I am tired." With her aunt's suggestion she rest, Lori realized she was exhausted. "My wrist…"

"It won't hurt you any more. We'll have the cast off in a week or so, and you should be as good as new." Lori removed her hand from the burgundy pot, and water sheeted off her hand as if drawn away like metal filings to a magnet. Her forearm was completely covered in a cast.

"Where did this cast come from?"

"You'll have to trust me to explain later, as I'm going to be busy tonight. Lori, before you go?"

"Yes?" she was out of her chair, half way toward the stairs.

"Did you see what had wounded Byron?"

"Arrows. He had two arrows, one under his arm and another in his chest."

"Yes, I see. Did he say what caused it? His hide is usually thick, unless he was caught in manform."

"The witch was there. She was dead. I saw Andrew, my old boyfriend. Another person with them was carrying a long bow."

"Did they see you?"

"No. It was during some of the worst of the earthquake. I hid off the path."

"Good. If I can prevent this teapot from leaking any more, maybe I can save Byron's life."

* * *

Sunset painted the backyard an artist's pallet of colors, swirling, changing, like northern lights, Lori assumed, but there were too many mountains and the forest was too close to be actual aura borealis. Aunt Jan had made herself scarce over the past week, appearing only sporadically in the kitchen only to offer food and tea from the blue teapot. No huge cooking projects, no quiet chats while Lori pitted bushels of cherries. When Aunt Jan did appear, she was frazzled, looked tired beyond exhaustion, had no energy or breath to make any attempt at conversation.

Tonight, as Lori arrived at the kitchen, she only found a covered plate poised above a slowly boiling pot of water, with a note stating it was her dinner, and to enjoy. A plate over boiling water, Lori laughed, thinking that was undoubtedly how leftovers were kept hot for late arrivals in the days before the microwave. She looked around, seeing nothing resembling a microwave. Nothing electric. Intrigued, she started looking in cabinets and on high shelves. No crock pot, no electric can opener, no coffee maker, no blender.

After spending the week at Byron's sickbed, able to do nothing more than hold his non-responsive hand, Lori finally heard her Aunt Jan's words. "Take a break, get some sleep, shower, get some fresh air and exercise." It hurt to know her aunt could dismiss her so completely when she felt she had to do something, even just be there.

She'd been incensed, spitting mad at Jan's refusal to call an ambulance, to take Byron into a state-of-the-art emergency room and from there to an operating theater, but Jan was resolute; she would tend him at Dragon's Roost and if he died, well he died. Lori had thought to overrule her, had searched the house or at least as much as she could access, for a telephone without success, cursing that her cell phone had been left at Andrew's.

Rooms on the main floor were locked, cutting off access and once, when she was denied Byron's bedside, while her aunt did who-knows-what, she sought to find the cave, or cave simulation, as she liked to think of it, only to find she couldn't get above the second floor.

The stairs were still there, she saw them without difficulty. They allowed her to go only down from the second floor, not up. She wondered if the day she'd made her great discovery of Byron's lair, she'd caught them off guard, but now it/he/they were alert, and nothing was allowed to pass. She was losing her mind. Now she was anthropomorphizing stairs.

Lori spent two days cleaning the kitchen, while Jan kept her banished from the sickroom. The kitchen remained painfully vacant, lonely without Aunt Jan and the perpetual canning. Lori wondered if people would starve this winter without the canning, wondered too if there were huge piles of food going to waste now that the ranges were quiescent.

Still, on the rare occasions when Lori left his bedside, there had been a plate, kept hot over a pot of gently boiling water, a vegetarian lasagna one night, a meatloaf with baked potatoes and steamed sugar peas another. Breakfast, lunch, dinner, one bowl or plate kept waiting for her. Who knew what Jan ate, as there was never any sign she ate at all. The same went for Byron: no bags of IV fluid suspended over his bed, no bowls of half-eaten green Jello abandoned on the bedside table, no cloth filled with chipped ice to moisten his lips and tongue.

Lori was no medical doctor, but she strongly suspected Byron wasn't getting the best medical care. Still Aunt Jan insisted anything else would kill him.

Lori removed the plate, ate at the table, not tasting or even recognizing what she was eating, thinking instead of sitting across this table and unabashedly flirting with Byron while listening to him extol the virtues of dragon tea over what he called mortal tea. The man never did make sense, but he could kiss, and she shivered in delighted memory: there was nothing better than his lovemaking.

Lori finished, laid down her fork, trying to remember exactly what she had swallowed, coming up clueless. Judging by the fact that it was an empty plate before her, not a bowl, she discounted stew or soup, and not enough of a trace remained on the plate or caught between her teeth to give her a clue.

"I'm really going to have to start paying more attention to what I'm doing," she said aloud, the words swallowed in the huge silent kitchen instead of echoing as she feared they might. She showered before she ate with no idea how many days had passed since she had last done so. She left her long hair down her back, slightly scented of strawberries. She hadn't taken the time to blow dry it, and it was still damp. Clean, it made her feel alive, something she was beginning to suspect she hadn't while spending days at Byron's bedside.

"Get some fresh air," Jan had admonished, making it an order. "I haven't got time to tend you if you get sick," so leaving the kitchen table Lori stood and made her way to the back door.

She stood at the threshold a minute, remembering her aunt's warning to always go around, before she dismissed the memory with one of Byron, looking jaunty, not a care in the world, after their lovemaking, exiting this way. She refused to connect the position he was in now—laying near death, with him using the back exit. That was simply ridiculous.

Lori didn't grab a jacket, forgetting how cold the nights had been, even though by now spring should be getting a good toehold everywhere else in the state. A crisp breeze ripped through the knit top and cotton sweater she wore and she turned to go back inside, only to get a jacket, when she found the door locked. Was the back door always that color puce? She had thought it brown to match the window trim.

Lori thought she would walk as far as the stump where she left the caramel apples. Aunt Jan could accept she was safe as she got some fresh air, for there definitely had been an implication of danger if she used the back door. After a quick walk, she would get back inside the house and to Byron's side before she froze.

She didn't see the stump.

It couldn't have been more than fifty steps from the back door, but she didn't see it. She walked deeper into the yard, toward the encroaching forest. The stump should be right there and although twilight was fast approaching, it wasn't dark yet. Her vision remained in no way impaired.

It had been such a particularly broad stump, solid and waist high. It would take a dozen men and a back hoe to get rid of the thing. Even if it had been devastated by the earthquake, there should be some indication: a hole or a messy pile of mulch. Lori stepped further into the yard, annoyed.

Her next conclusion was equally as startling. As Lori looked down, she realized the ground she was walking on wasn't lawn. It was low brush, overgrown weeds, thistle, and unrecognizable wild flowers, with no sign of greening grass.

"This is too weird," she muttered, needing sound, particularly her own voice to root her in reality. She still hadn't located the stump.

She noticed off to her left, not two dozen yards, a pond, or perhaps depending on width, a small lake. As often as she'd come this way, and it had been several times, she didn't recall seeing it there. Choosing that as her new destination, she headed for the water.

It was further away than it looked and correspondingly larger. She was almost breathless when she reached the shore and definitely chilled. She had halted a dozen times, thinking the journey foolish, but she kept going, without knowing what drove her.

The land dropped down about three feet the entire circumference of the pond, enough to make getting down an effort, but not a challenge. As she approached, Lori noticed a small shore, not much wider than a foot, of moist soil, undoubtedly slimy slick mud, which would suck her feet down so she'd have to pull herself out. She decided not to go down the steep embankment. The water would be cold. This wasn't wading weather.

To the far side, directly across from where she stood, reigned one of those massive weeping willows, the kind that often grew at water's edge, and could hide an invading army under its narrow branches. This was the kind of willow perfect for an afternoon assignation with a handsome boyfriend: a place to bring a picnic, a book of sonnets and a bottle of wine. A place of stolen kisses. She looked at the tree, saw its potential, and thought of Byron, not laying near death in the red living room, but laying beside her, relaxing after an intimate encounter. For a second, the thought made her warmer.

Lori rubbed her palms down her forearms. She still wore the cast which had formed itself around her wrist in the burgundy pot. Since it had been applied, (by who or what it had been applied she had no idea), she felt no pain from her wrist. She often thought of asking Jan about it, but when she saw her she only thought of Byron, pale and unresponsive, and how important it was to get him to an accredited hospital. There had to be one somewhere.

She brought her long-distance gaze back in from the willow, as she decided to walk the perimeter. It would give her a destination, but more, it would give her a chance to investigate the willow, without it being the focus of her journey. There was nothing else to do.

As she approached the edge, perhaps a dozen frogs plopped into the water, pinging like randomly dropped stones. As she moved further down the shore the diving continued. She never actually saw a frog sunning itself, and only had the impression of frogness in the movement, before the splash. The air was cold, the sun warm. Rings circled out from the amphibian's point of entry, but other than that, the surface of the water remained smooth.

She approached the willow, and reached out, touching a handful of branches, preparatory to pulling them back, wandering inside.

"It might not be the best idea to go in there, at least not without an armed escort."

Lori looked up, startled, she'd thought herself quite alone, and saw Byron walking toward her. She smiled in spontaneous pleasure and started to run to him, thinking to leap into his arms, shower him with kisses when he held up both his hands in warning, palms out.

"No! Don't touch me!"

"Why not? I'm so glad to see you."

He stepped back, keeping an artificial distance between them. "I am not fully here. To touch me would be … unpleasant …for us both."

"I don't understand."

"Of course you don't, but at the moment, I have no explanation to give that you would accept."

"Can you stay and talk?" she asked, her emotions roller coasting between extreme joy he was alive and out of bed walking, and hurt he would not allow her closer.

Byron shrugged, moved a bit nearer to the willow. "I can stay for a while at least. He doesn't have the strength to call me back."

"He?" Lori questioned, but Byron shook his head, closing that line of inquiry.

She stopped and took a good look at him. She shook her head again, trying to sharpen her vision, for something was distinctly wrong.

She could see right through him.

CHAPTER 29

Shock built up around her, brick by brick, until her teeth knocked together and her bones grew weak. Every Halloween urban legend she had ever heard, every horror novel she had ever read, twirled inside her. Pieces started to fall into place, making a puzzle she could almost understand but with a picture not only monstrous, but taking on a life of its own.

The wind picked up, the eerie, hollow moan of a creature in pain she felt as well as heard. Lori shivered, holding her cupped palms in front of her face, using her own breath as the only available source of warmth. She stepped, stumbled, righted herself, then stopped. As she moved through the maelstrom, it became clear the knife-edged breeze carried with it not only cold but misfortune and an increasing morbidity.

"Are you a ghost?" Lori asked when she discovered her voice. She found it distasteful how many things she didn't believe she considered plausible considering the circumstances. She shivered uncontrollably, backed up, trying to impose a distance from him or it, whatever this thing was which looked so much like her lover.

"Halt!" he called, his voice bellowing with power, his hands outstretched as if he would reach out and touch her. Obeying blindly, Lori stopped as if paralyzed, her eyes wide, her heart thumping to a bass drum cadence too rapid for jazz.

"Turn around," he ordered.

Petrified to take her eyes off him, Lori did as she was told, to find if she'd taken even the smallest half step backwards, she would have slipped down the embankment and fallen in the black-water lake. It wouldn't have killed her, but it certainly would have been unpleasant. There were enough uncomfortable things around her, and she'd rather not add more to the list.

She exhaled a sharp breath of relief, turned back to face him again. Byron her heart said, but her eyes were saying something else. She was trained, used to seeing beyond the surface of things, checking the most minute details for validity. As a researcher, she had always considered her sight the most reliable of her senses.

He shimmered, as if trying to become more corporeal, ending up appearing slightly more solid than when she had first seen him. He tilted his head, indicated the pond. "It's very deep there, and the water is so cold it would probably send you into shock. I wouldn't be able to rescue you and he would be shattered if he eventually recovered only to find you drowned."

"He?" she asked.

"Me," he responded, adding a sheepish shrug, as if embarrassed to be caught using the wrong pronoun.

She moved away from the edge, where the ground was spongy and the grass slippery. She shifted from the willow tree as well for it suddenly looked too possessive. She was also careful not to move any closer to the creature which might be a ghost.

Her breath felt real. It wafted up in streamers from her nose and mouth. Her heart felt real. It thudded and thumped and was altogether uncomfortable. Her hands felt real, she knew this because earlier she dug her fingernails into her palms, to be certain she could still feel pain. She was awake, but could not rule out hallucination.

"Am I drugged?"

He was quick to reassure her, even if he didn't come any closer. "No. Using your terminology, not particularly apt for describing the situation, your body is working within normal parameters. What you see is what is."

"You didn't answer my question," she said, listening now to her teeth chattering, as she sought any indications she could detect from his body, such as there were no streamers of cold breath coming from his mouth and nose. "Are you a ghost?"

He gave that grin, so totally like Byron, and a long shank of his hair fell into his eyes, something she had noticed on Byron, the real Byron a dozen times. "The answer to your question is dichotomous."

"Yes or no?" she demanded.

"Yes and no," he agreed, offering no more explanation.

She held herself tightly, cupping her elbows, in a desperate attempt to keep warm. "Could you tell me what's happening?" Lori did not like the desperation she felt flooding her life-support systems. She wanted to be casual here, prepared for anything, even sophisticated. She didn't want to quiver, act like a little girl terrified to be out at night.

"I will answer any question I can, if you understand much of what I would say you have no basis to comprehend."

Anthropology had taught her that lesson early. It was easy to judge a culture, to put your perspective on their rites and customs, but until you understood the whys of any number of other seemingly unrelated topics, you could not have the answers you needed. First impressions were frequently absolutely wrong.

"Can you start with something easy, how Byron ...you... got hurt?" She didn't stop, for dozens of additional questions were bubbling up inside her. "I would like to know why I can see through you if you aren't dead, or why you're here if you are? What caused the earthquake? Who were those dead people? I know one of them was Belinda, but who was she, or what was she? I don't understand anything about the door I shut. Not how I shut it or why. What was Arthur fighting, for he was definitely fighting something? Finally, I want to know why I had to carry the leaking teapot to my aunt when it was obvious you were the one who had taken two arrows to the chest."

She desperately wanted to touch him, even as she found she was having the exact same problems with pronouns he was. And she wanted to scream in frustration, perhaps pull her hair out. The only viable option Lori could foresee was checking herself into a mental institution for years of therapy involving padded walls and extensive drug treatment, maybe punctuated with delightful afternoons spent finger painting. Nothing made sense. She very much suspected even with his answers she still wouldn't understand—or believe.

Fifteen feet away, the willow branches stirred almost in Halloween parody—as if they were reaching out, trying to grab hold of her. Byron shimmered, grew considerably more transparent. Whatever he was, he wasn't all here. "I don't know how many answers I feel comfortable giving you, but first would you do something for me?"

"Of course." She hoped she hadn't agreed too readily. Still this was Byron, it had to be Byron, who else could it be?—and she would do anything for him.

"Find about a dozen stones about this big," he said, holding his hands apart as if holding an imaginary football. "And put them, sides touching, in a circle."

It wasn't a difficult task, as the stones were plentiful, but her teeth chattered in staccato rhythm and her hands grew numb from cold.

"Good, now find some dried brush for kindling." He hadn't moved while she had sought stones, hadn't offered to help, and it was on the tip of her tongue to berate him for it when she turned and looked right through him again. She wasn't sure if he were more transparent now than he had been, for there were times when she looked and saw a flush and hearty Byron.

She brought twigs, branches, small logs, most of which, coincidentally or not, seemed to have broken in shapes that fit easily into her makeshift fire-pit. "Enough?"

"It will do. Now stand back," he ordered, and with a roar the wood she'd collected burst into glorious flame. He had made no movement she could discern, no match striking a cover, no clicking of a lighter, no flame emitted from his mouth (which wouldn't have surprised her much more than she already was), but she was certain he was responsible.

Lori jumped back, then saw the flames settle into a well-behaved pattern, and held her hands out and moving in closer. The fire burned hot, blue at the base, and brilliant orange and red at its fingers, with yellow blazing nearly five foot high. It was a beacon. The warmth felt heavenly.

"How did you do that?" She turned now, her back to the flames. The coldness which invaded her bones dripped away, like icicles on a spring day, and a fullness wrapped itself around her and through her, as if the flames were food she were feasting on.

"A dragon can always make fire, in any guise," he answered. "Now, sit as close to the blaze as you are comfortable. I needed to get you warm and this seemed to be the most expedient way."

Lori found a round, flat topped boulder, and perched herself on it, then held her hands out, reveling in the blanketing feeling of warmth, as the sting as the cold in her nose and fingers retreated. "Isn't spring ever going to come?"

"Not where we are," he corrected. "It's much warmer at the house."

"We could go there," she said, in an effort, perhaps, to be perverse.

He stood in the shadows, and looked more solid because of it. With the sun's retreat, it had gotten dark very quickly. "No. I wouldn't be welcome. Not in this form. Your aunt would yell."

"I suppose she would." Lori breathed deeply, enjoying the rich scent of pine and apple, which reminded her of comfort, of fall, and on some level, security. She was an anthropologist. Wherever there were humans, there was fire, and to a real degree, the social and economic development of a society could be graphed to correspond directly to how intricately they tamed and controlled fire. "Would it bother you if she yelled?"

He didn't sit, but he did shift, foot to foot, his hands behind his back, then clasped in front of him. "Yes, it would, because she is a friend to all of faeries and I don't want to hurt her. I cannot yet go back."

I cannot yet go back. There was shock, like a physician telling you your mother or your husband or your child had malignant cancer and the treatment options didn't look good. You could never go back with such a diagnosis. You could go forward, resume your life, live, for whatever time you were granted but your old life, your innocence would be gone.

"But you have to go back." She put no emphasis on the words, mainly because she was not sure where to put it: But YOU have to go back. But you HAVE to go back. But you have to go BACK.

He shrugged again, but made no comment. His hands were restless, buried deep in his pants pockets. It was odd, really, to think of a ghost with pockets, but he was dressed as her Byron would be.

"You have to go back," she repeated, because if he were here, maybe he was looking for something from her, and she had advice to give. "Byron will die if you do not," she supplied, surprised at how deeply she believed this was only a part of Byron, an essential part, perhaps, but she knew the real Byron lay unconscious in the red living room and she had been holding his near-lifeless hand for days.

"Not die," but amended, "from your point of view, yes, die. Cease to exist, pass from this realm. It is not a thought I care to dwell on."

She set her teeth. She wanted to scream or shake him. She couldn't be rational when nothing around her was, but she intended to try. "Explain to me your definition of 'not die'. I want to get the terminology correct."

"He, I, have no soul. Death, in your comprehension is the separation between body and soul. There are religious implications, of course, and nearly every established religion has some type of resurrection, a reuniting of sorts." He stood beside her, close enough for easy conversation, far enough she would not accidentally touch him. He existed deep in shadow, but she cherished being near him, for this is what she had been praying for at his bedside: another chance to be near him, to talk, if he were incapable of giving her anything more.

"So he, you, will cease to be?"

"Yes."

"Forever?"

"Yes, as we both understand the word."

As if there were other definitions of the word neither of them understood.

"In the form you are now, will you remain as what I might call a ghost?"

"No. If Byron dies, his chakra will vanish."

"And the teapot?" Lori had no idea where that question had come from.

"I have enjoyed the teapot." He said nothing more, and although curious, Lori felt she wasn't ready for his explanation of enjoyment, and exactly how the teapot fit in to this mess which surrounded her.

"The witch is dead."

"Jan told Byron, so I know."

"You killed her?"

"Yes. She wanted something of mine I wasn't ready to relinquish."

"Fangs."

He raised an eyebrow, an unspoken question.

"I heard her talking. Andrew wanted the dragon's head. The witch wanted the fangs."

Lori had no idea how she had shifted to her belief to Byron killing the witch, from the belief the dragon killed her. She still wasn't certain she believed in the dragon.

"Yes. In a witch's hands, the fangs are a powerful weapon for evil. It would be worse if Andrew got them."

She remembered Byron's too-long teeth, how he had nipped at her while they made love in his lair, and knew the fangs had power to bring her pleasure. She was not willing to venture in, not speaking to this shade while Byron, the physical manifestation of her lover, lay near death.

"What is this place?" she held her hand out, indicated the pond, the willow, the land.

"It is best described by mathematics, but that is not a skill I possess. The mages have terms for it too, and from what I have seen, none of them have any use for numbers."

"Are you hedging the question?" she asked. It was the first time this evening she had been charmed. Her fear seemed to have vanished with the chills.

"Yes. With certain exceptions, it is best if mortals don't know too much about the portals."

"Certain exceptions?"

"Your aunt is one."

Lori brought her left leg up, setting her heel at her buttocks, so she could wrap her arm around it, resting her head on her knee. "Then my Aunt Jan is a mortal?"

"Of course. Never doubt that. She has special abilities, given to her by the Faerie in return for her work, and she has learned to incorporate a lot of the powers around here into her life. Though she is mortal, frankly, there are hundreds of us who wouldn't survive without her."

Lori thought back to her encounter with him in the cavern, when they had been intimate, but that wasn't where her thoughts strayed. She thought of kissing him in the forest, of talking with him in the red living room while he was exhausted, of the times they had spent together, sharing bits of each other. He was inside her. She didn't know how it was possible, but she knew she had drank him, his essence, his—what he would not consider his soul. She knew him. Beyond their love-making, she loved him. There was no doubt. "Maybe you won't survive without me."

He inclined his head, a ritual, respectful bow. "That much is true. You rescuing the teapot is certainly case in point. I would have died had you not brought it to Jan."

She grinned, brushed hair from her forehead. "I don't suppose you're going to explain?"

"There will be time later, and if there is not, Jan will tell you when she buries my remains. She knows what to do and by then she will have no need to keep my secrets from you."

She would have asked about the burial, but he must have read her mind, for he continued. "It is essential that the evil ones do not gain control of my body—in any form."

"Then tell me about this place."

He looked around, smiled. "There are many analogies I could use. Think of the door you shut. This place is through another door, one that always remains open. The house skirts several, the main reason going out through the back door is usually not recommended for mortals."

Lori heard another splash, something jumping into water. It was too dark for her to see what it was. "Are those frogs in the pond?"

"Frogs, yes. There is also a creature there, who calls himself Baby Slimy. He has no idea what he is, and in all the land of faerie, none other knows what type of creature he will become. He is maturing slowly, and growing in mass. He is older than I am."

"Twenty," she thought, "thirty years old."

Byron laughed, reading her mind. "I myself am many centuries old and he is centuries older than me. He has seen the Teutonic plates shift, the rise and fall of the dinosaurs. In all the time he has lived, he still doesn't know what he is."

"What is he like?"

"Kind," Byron answered. "He is learning wisdom, and many of the faerie creatures speak with him, hoping to learn, but faeries mainly are creatures who like a good joke, and they use him for the brunt of their humor, and yet he is always kind."

"One day I would like to speak with him."

"I hope one day you shall."

"Do I need to put more logs on the fire?"

"No. I do not require warmth in this guise, and the dragon flame does not burn wood as quickly as you think it might. What is there will provide all the warmth you need." He grinned, looked young, and a hank of unruly hair dropped into his eyes and he swung his neck, to clear his vision, a movement so totally Byron she couldn't believe the thing she was talking to wasn't him, complete, hale and hearty. "Should we add more fuel at this point, there will be a bonfire that could easily burn a hundred years."

"But it won't spread beyond the rocks?"

"No. It won't spread beyond the rocks."

"Dragon fire?"

"A form of dragon fire. It is one of the talents we take the most pleasure in. It is particularly useful for burning knights to a crisp."

"I'm sure it is," she said, tongue in cheek, and hoped he was joking. She remembered Andrew, engulfed in flames as he fled. She shivered and the flames beside her could not warm her. In the dimming light, she thought he looked familiar, not as Byron, but as someone, something else.

"We've met before." The brilliant flames died back a bit; they were not so hungrily reaching for the stars. Now they were content to burn with less intensity, but the heat was far more profound. She was happy to be there, under a broad panorama of stars, which might or might not be familiar, taking to a creature, she could not call it a man, who by many definitions, might be a ghost.

"Of course we have met before." He was prepared to be amused.

"No, you are, were," talking to him she seemed to have a problem with her verbs as well as her pronouns, "the fireflies which lead me to the door."

"Yes."

"While I was following you, first to Byron as he lay wounded, then to the door, I pretended to believe you fireflies, knowing it wasn't those I followed."

"I was relieved when you thought me fireflies. It made my task easier. I hadn't wanted to frighten you, but even more than saving Byron's life, I needed that door shut."

"I still don't understand the door." She took a stick, poked at the burning embers, watched sparks cascade into the heavens.

"Maybe one day I'll explain it to you, too."

"Perhaps. Did you open the door?"

"No. It is not an ability I possess, in any form."

Outside of the halo of the fire she saw only impressions of things, not the item itself. The willow lost most of its 'tree-ness' and looked like a huge hulking monster, dressed in robes swinging idly around its feet.

"Could you tell me how to convince my aunt to get Byron to a hospital?"

"That is not in his best interest."

"You would say that," she said, her ire rising, "because you like being free, don't you?" That last statement was something of a gamble and Lori had no idea if it were true.

"Yes, I do like being free, but I also need the body. Oddly enough, many things are impossible without a body. I like being a dragon, and I cannot be a true dragon like this."

"I hope one day all these conversations will start to make sense."

"Perhaps one day they will. I really couldn't say."

"Is Byron going to die?"

CHAPTER 30

Lori shifted, sought for the word, "pass away, whatever term you want to use?"

"Yes. He's fighting it, and he has a lot of power, but there really isn't enough of him to save."

"Is there anything I can do? I really want to help you." You, him, it. Miserable pronouns, but she needed reassurance she was talking to Byron, a living, vital Byron.

"No, but he … I … appreciate the offer."

"I really want you in a hospital."

"This much I can tell you: hospitals are for mortals, not for creatures of faerie."

"And you are a creature of faerie?"

"Come now, Lori, you know I am. There has never been any doubt, has there?"

She wanted to argue, and the hackles at her neck rose, for they had made love, and he was enough of a man for her then.

"Your aunt is doing everything humanly possible."

"Is there something … not humanly possible? Something only another creature of faerie could accomplish?" She thought of her cast, how it had felt like eels circling her wrist, tightening against her skin. It might be eels she wore now, creatures which had swam in the cauldron, dried to a hardness as she raised her hand from the water. Nothing else could have formed the cast. Like the faeries and the caramel apples, she should find some way to thank them for setting her arm.

"Perhaps. There are options. I know your aunt is not ready to give up hope." He raised his chin, listened sharply to something she could not hear, his eyes hardening as whatever he heard solidified. "I must leave. Please forgive me for not escorting you back through the portal. Trust me when I tell you I must no longer be here, but before I go, I leave you with a warning. Go, as quickly as you can back to the Inn, and enter through the door you exited. This one particular time, do not go in the front door. Then I need you to promise me you'll never leave through the back door again."

She stood, needing her feet under her as she faced this conflict. "Ever?"

"If Byron recovers, you may go with him. He is strong enough to protect you. Your aunt has enough of the aura that she is rarely in danger, but she doesn't have enough ability to secure your safety too. There are things out here you don't want to meet. Now, I'll have your promise, not to go out the back door again."

"I went out the back door the day of the earthquake. I found you..." It was all she could manage for justification: because she had exited that way, she was somehow available to shut his door, to take his teapot to her aunt.

"Did you think, perhaps, he was wounded because he was trying to protect you from the evil which roams this land?"

Lori swayed, sat awkwardly down on her bolder. "Then I killed him? He was protecting me?"

"No. No. Not this time. He was out hunting, didn't know you were out until after he had been shot and I brought you to him. My statement was unkind."

The creature, the ghost, shifted, looked poised to run. "What is the house?" she asked. She would do anything to keep him a few moments longer, and she saw he was anxious to escape.

"A sanctuary which spans worlds, although the word you might use is dimensions, although the term is not entirely correct. Not that 'worlds' is correct either. I don't have time to go into lengthy explanations."

"Involving mathematics," she said, and he bowed again, granting her the point. "And the doors?" Lori continued. "They're different, aren't they, the front and back door. Before you lie to me, I mean in a metaphysical sense."

"Yes, they are different. Generally I would not have you cross the portal—but there is danger to you in the forest tonight. And I cannot protect you. The gargoyles have been freed, and there is no faerie ring available this night. I must leave. I do not care to be vulnerable."

He moved, quickly heading for the forest, giving the willow tree wide berth. The darkness skittered around him, as if it were puppies, eager to chew on his feet.

"Wait!"

"I cannot!" he said.

"Will you give me hope Byron will live?"

"I cannot, for his wound is grievous, but do not worry. Your aunt knows how to dispose of the body so it will not be used for nefarious purposes. She has done so for others. Evil must not be allowed control of his carcass. You can be proud. You did not let the black forces have his body."

After he finished speaking he disappeared. He did not vanish into the forest, but disappeared, fading first into the two intermittent flashes of light, then even they were gone.

Something of his panic, his desperation, got through, for Lori stood, intending to run all the way to the back door and the comfort of her aunt's kitchen, when she found her way blocked by a large, hulking presence she bounded into.

She screamed, her arms pinned to her side, and she fought her captivity, yet found it impossible to escape. Lori struggled, blinded by her hair floating around her, in full terror until the words her captor spoke finally got through.

"Is this any way to great an old lover?"

She capped her panic, flipped her head to get her hair out of her eyes. "Andrew," she gasped. "Andrew."

"It's good to see you too." He grinned slowly, and she wondered how she could have been so blind not to see the evil inherent in his features. His eyes were dull with it, and his pallor, she refused to think of it as a complexion, filled with it. She wondered if she had been so desperate to find a bed-mate she was even willing to slink so low, but it was only since loving Byron she had begun to understand the true nature of things.

"I thought you were dead. I saw the dragon burn you."

"I will get my revenge against that beast yet. I am recovered. My magic is stronger than his."

"What are you doing here?"

"Would you believe, searching for you? I wished you had called, told me you were leaving the university. I've been so concerned." He held her hand, far too tightly to be comfortable, pulled her back near the fire, she hadn't gotten more than a dozen steps from it, forced her, with his free hand, pressing her down on her shoulder to sit.

Her teeth resumed their chattering, this time far more to do with her terror than with the cold night.

"Well," she snarled, "I wasn't certain I was leaving myself, until I saw you dissecting a dead body in your attic. It was a human body?"

Andrew's grin this time was sardonic, and the evil emulating from him increased in visible waves. "Oh, he must have taught you much for you to ask."

"Then do me the dignity of answering it. If you have any left." Lori spoke so forcefully, spittle flew from her lips.

"You may not believe this, but through the forces I worship and the Vows I have taken, I have great dignity. I prefer to call it majesty."

Lori rubbed her arms, facing the flames, rather than the monster talking with her. "I doubt you know the meaning of the word."

Andrew pranced around the firepit, trying to catch her eye, but did not touch her again for which she was silently grateful. "You are, of course, welcome to your beliefs. But to answer the question, yes, the corpse in my attic had been human. He is serving me well now, so at least his life was not lost in vain. Think of that, if his passing brings you grief."

The moon and the residual starlight had completely disappeared, the only light as far as she could see, coming from the fire. Blackness surrounded her and she was certain the worst of the darkness arrived with him.

"Serves you, as part of your evil incantations?"

"Yes."

"Andrew, what did you need with me?"

"The dragon hadn't told you? I should have thought he would."

"Dragon?"

"I don't know what he calls himself ... Bryce, Bruce, Billy—"

"Byron?"

"Byron." The name on his tongue sounded soiled. "He's not mortal. I suppose he told you?"

"Not mortal? He is in the house dying now." She bit her lip and cursed herself for a fool. She hadn't wanted to admit that.

"Ahh, then the arrows did fly true. I thought they had. I don't suppose when he dies, you'll let me have the head?"

"How sick are you?"

Lori pulled back her hand, preparatory to slapping him, but he was quick, and aware of her aim, and grabbed her cast which was so comfortable she could forget for days at a time it was there. Andrew screamed, fell to his knees, releasing her, cupping his right hand in his left.

"Damn stupid witch."

"Witch? Belinda?"

"Your aunt. I went to a lot of trouble researching Jan Pikorski, and found she had a weakness, a family, and you did not disappoint, running directly to her when you ran from me."

Lori was only half listening, for her cast felt weird, coming apart on her, when nothing had affected it before: she showered with it on, and when washing Byron, soaked her hands in a basin, rinsing out a face cloth. But now she felt a tingling, and she moved to scratch the rising itch, and the cast separated into six wiggling creatures which fell to the ground and scampered off. While she watched, they dropped down the small embankment and dove into the pond, their entry into the water not making a splash. She thought them eels or snakes, until she realized they walked on tiny legs, and the needle pricks she felt along her wrist as they had been forming the cast might have been nothing more than their sharp little claws digging into her flesh.

"Now I suspect Aunt Jan's going to kill me," she muttered to herself, forgetting for a moment she was not alone. She rubbed her forearm, finding it not the slightest bit tender. There were red spots, tiny dots of injury she knew would heal scarlessly, but her wrist felt good, and her range of motion was unhindered. "I've lost those things," she said, seeing the last one dive, "as I caused her to lose the things chained in the basement."

Andrew's ears perked. "The things in the basement are gone?"

Lori didn't want to give him any information, and had no idea what he would do with her statements, but she nodded, almost in spite of herself. "Yes. Jan let them go the day of the earthquake, afraid they would die wherever it was they were. She was looking for them when I came in with the broken wrist." And the broken teapot, but Andrew undoubtedly knew that as well.

"Ahh, so the Reptile's Roost is unprotected?"

She stuck out her bottom lip and prepared to be obstinate. She had given too much away already. "I don't know what you mean."

"The reason ..." he paused, looking for the term, "... my kind cannot enter the house is it is protected. We can deal with the wards. The gargoyles bother us. If you haven't seen them, you probably don't need to know what they are, but they are powerful. It is the main reason I was hoping to get invited inside as your date. If we had a wedding to plan, I figured I could convince you I wanted to meet all your relatives. You, in your ignorance would be pleased to invite me, and Jan would be caught off-guard, little suspecting you had aligned yourself with a wer-wizard."

"You'll never get inside now."

"Ahh, but I will. Not as your beloved, perhaps, but there are other avenues, now the gargoyles have disappeared. It really was quite nice of them to be so accommodating. Considerate, too, of your aunt to release them. They have been there ever so long."

"I'll never marry you."

"There was never any danger of that," he said, still cupping his wrist. "It was only a ruse to get inside the Inn. And relax, I'll never touch you again, not with his stench on you."

"His stench?" she asked.

"The dragon. Although I am a bit surprised he touched you after I left my impression on you."

"The only impression you've left on me is one of revulsion." She stood, strong enough she felt she could overpower him, if she caught him off-guard.

"Come," Andrew said, making it an order. He grabbed her wrist, where the cast was no longer there to protect her, and pulled her to her feet. "There are places we need to go. Perhaps, in a few days, when I get through with you, your aunt will be willing to make a trade."

And Lori grew scared, for she knew her aunt loved her, and would do anything in her power to keep her from harm.

"What do you want, the gargoyles?" his word.

"No, I want the teapot."

"It's leaking. What good could it possibly be to you?"

"Ahh, yes, it is leaking. It is, to my kind, still priceless beyond measure. And to set the record straight, since I always did try to be as honest with you as I could, it is the dragon I want. Should I get the teapot, I should be able to rile him enough to shed his disguise and revert to his natural form. Then I will chop off his head, and with a dragon's head in my possession, nothing will stop me."

CHAPTER 31

Without touching her, Andrew idly moved his hands in some form of sign language Lori couldn't decipher, but a second later, it was as if all the nerve endings she possessed had been plugged into an electric socket. Liquid pain surged through her: flames and acid and torture merged until she only felt pain.

She screamed long and hard, until she had no breath. "What are you doing to me?"

He looked down his nose as she crumpled to the grass. "It's an ancient form of persuasion. I've become quite the expert at it. It's so much more useful than a traditional weapon, and has the added bonus it doesn't leave any marks. At least none a non-adept can find."

She tried to straighten, tried to see him though the waves of agony blinding her. "I bet Byron can find them."

"I'm sure he can. He can see them, but he cannot manipulate them. That's one difference between us, and one which will see he and his kind always defeated by me and mine."

After the pain ebbed, Lori straightened, tightened her eyes as she wondered how she could fight him. "It hurts. Don't do it again."

Andrew nodded, then twisted his head, indicating she should move. Aware he could renew his attack effortlessly, Lori followed him slowly, for her muscles still suffered from spasms, and her mind couldn't forget the intense pain.

"After what he did to me, hurting you is my pleasure. But don't worry. I need you alive for a while longer."

"What did Bryon do to you?"

"All but killed me. I thought with two arrows in him he would be weaker than he was. I barely escaped with my life." He tugged her, this time using no more lethal combination than his hand at her elbow. "We're going this way." He shoved her toward the willow.

"Byron will kill you," she said through clenched teeth.

"Byron hasn't yet realized he's dead," Andrew responded. "When he finally does die, I'll have the body."

She hissed and tried to kick him, but he laughed. Andrew continued to drag her, when she wanted to both crumple and whimper and fight and to victory. Being a victim was never pleasant.

His eyes changed. Not the shape or the color, but the pupils had an eerie cast, cloudy and insidious. Evil was no longer just a concept. Lori realized she was now looking at it made manifest. He held himself differently too. She remembered how he walked so arrogantly in the forest during the earthquake, as if all of God and nature could not hurt him. He had that swagger still, only it was harder, more perverted. She thought of slime and rotted garbage when she saw him.

"I can't believe I ever loved you."

He laughed again, a predator's laugh of evil, when he knows his prey is paralyzed, and only waits to savor the anticipation of the kill.

Lori shied, but he was strong and under his grasp, she was helpless. The tree reached out, long tendrils which approached menacingly, as each an independent strand of Medusa's snake-like hair.

"Not tonight," he said to the tree, speaking with his hand manipulations as well. "Until I am through with her, this one is mine."

Branches with narrow, sharp-tipped leaves rubbed against her arms, leaving her feeling violated. She pulled her elbows in, unconsciously leaning closer to Andrew.

"Back!" Andrew ordered, speaking to the tree. "Don't make me reveal myself here. There are too many of the faerie around." Then he laughed, as if the tree had said something particularly witty, which Lori didn't hear. "There are possibilities there I will definitely consider. But I have plans for her tonight."

Andrew kept pulling, and she passed through something, a door for want of a better word, which she could not see, only feel. Lori felt one step was normal, then she was falling, dropping down a black hole. Before she could scream, she landed on her feet, Andrew pulling her along, keeping her upright. Whatever happened, she was no longer where she was a moment before. She couldn't explain it any better than to say she was somewhere else.

"What happened?" she mumbled, finding so many of her senses unreliable. A minute before, a step before, she had passed beneath the willow's hanging canopy, had the campfire at her back, knew she could find her aunt's house. Now, she was in a totally different land. She was no longer on Earth.

Darkness enveloped her, or more than darkness, for it had a tangible thickness. Beyond the dark, there were distant scatterings of stars in the sky, those two things, the dark and the stars, were the only points of continuance. She faced a long flat desert, which went on for miles in every direction. A desert, but not of sand. It had a multi-colored gloss, a shimmer, which made it look like streams of glass or perhaps something molten, not yet formed. In the far distance, a range of mountains rose, steep, craggy affairs, with snow on the peaks but kaleidoscopic transformations visible along the sides. Lori rubbed her eyes, wondering if her vision was unreliable, or if she were completely insane.

"What?" Lori said, rubbing her eyes. Cold shivers rumbled through her and she feared she had lost her mind for everything around her was so alien, so completely different, she could not even form words.

Lori concentrated on the mountains, looking past the undulating desert, hoping to find something normal within the panorama. She got dizzy and had to close her eyes, hoping to find comfort in the blackness behind her eyelids. But she was a scientist and beyond the rising terror, she was curious, so she opened her eyes, took a step, then another, deeper into unreality.

The colors shifted, reds, golds, blues, and greens, mutating, as if metallic, the way mercury picks up colors and reflects them back. She could discern no pattern, just ripples.

"Just there," Andrew said pointing toward the closest mountain, a distance which looked extreme, "there is a stream. Anything which bathes in it is immediately healed. I came here after the dragon set me on fire, more dead than alive, and in more pain than you could possibly imagine. I was completely well in two days."

Lori looked at it, trying to remember why healing was so important. "Is this a nightmare?"

Andrew's sides rolled with laughter. "It is for you."

"Everything is …" she struggled to find a word, her mind not functioning. "… twisted."

"Twisted," he said, nodding. "As good a word as any."

Her eyes adjusted slowly, for the panorama no longer seemed quite so unexpected. The strands of light around them pulsed, and on more than one level were stunningly beautiful.

"What is that?" she said pointing to the undulating floor of the valley which separated them from the stream. If a pit containing a hundred million squirming snakes composed of neon lights of every imaginable shade and hue were allowed freedom of movement, what she faced would be no different than the expansive foreground before her. The valley was comprised of tubes of color, radiating an almost painful brightness, no one color dominating, no one shade confined to a single location.

"That," he said arrogantly, "is my power."

"Your power—" she said, then gasped, when she noticed something else so unexpected, so frightening she tripped, and from her knees could only look up and stare.

The glass desert and the kaleidoscope mountains were not the most significant difference in this unknown world. Above her, hanging ten, or a hundred times bigger and brighter than a full moon, was a planet, an Earth for want of a better word, blue and green, with oceans and swirling cloud cover, and continents which bore no resemblance to her home world.

"Yes, Dorothy," Andrew intoned, mocking and malicious, "we're not in Kansas any longer."

"I ... um ..."

"Speechless, are you? Well in this scenario, you are not alone. The first time I arrived, it took me days before I found my voice. It's impressive, isn't it?"

"Unbelievable." Literally. "There are more things in heaven and Earth, Horatio..."

"Except this is neither heaven nor Earth. If you hadn't shut my door the day your lover was hurt, you would have seen a dimension even more bizarre. Alas. It took some of my best magic to open that portal."

He pulled her back to her feet, tugging, to get her moving.

"Oh, dear," Lori responded without sincerity. It hurt to look up into the sky at the planet suspended in thin air. Subconsciously she kept trying to impose continents she knew into the landscape, as if it were a globe or a hologram, but she suspected it another world entirely, a place where the physical laws of her Earth didn't apply.

"We've quite a long walk ahead. I hope you're up to it."

"I'm hungry," she said, to be perverse. She was hungry. It seemed as if it days had passed since she had eaten.

"Whoops! The nearest McDonalds is a world away. I can feed, but nothing here will help you."

She bent down, rubbed her calf, a delaying tactic. "I am tired. I want to rest."

"No rest for the weary. Or for the wicked either," he added with a laugh. He pulled her, snapping her shoulder, for his movement was abrupt and meant to be painful. "Follow me."

He stepped down, two, three natural stone stairs, the only thing in the panorama which looked real to her. Pulling her, he stepped directly into the undulating morass of shimmering lights. The neon snakes coiled around his ankles, wrapped around him, crawling up his legs. Andrew closed his eyes for a moment, the expression on his face one of sexual ecstasy.

In the same miasma Lori felt things around her ankles, like snakes crawling, but the feeling, once she got used to it, was neither pleasant nor uncomfortable, just there. Nothing seemed to move up her legs, and it looked like the intensity of the neon things was less around her feet, as if as many as could manage, were willing to give her wide berth.

"They won't hurt you," he said, moving forward, his pace hindered by the swirls, by the obvious pleasure they were giving him.

"What are they?"

"What are they?" He tapped a forefinger on his chin. "How to put it in terms a human can understand, without a fifteen year apprenticeship? Let's see. Do you believe in magic?"

"No." She hadn't. She wouldn't admit her change of heart to this creep.

"Well, I'll be sure to tell your lover, before I hack off his head. Anyway, getting back to the subject at hand, this is the physical manifestation of magic. On Earth, to the uninitiated, magic is invisible. When it looks like a true magician is waving his hands aimlessly, he is actually manipulating these strands. On Earth, where the specific density of the planet is much less, these strands have the ability to float invisibly in the air. A magician could," and here he moved his fingers, as if tying a large, imaginary bow, "manipulate these things to do his bidding."

"Magician?" she asked.

"I am not referring to a hack, a showman who knows slight of hand. The word magician is for your benefit alone. The title I prefer is mage, or more specifically wer-mage."

"Sorcerer?"

"No, sorcery is something else entirely."

She watched the strands crawling up his legs, reached out, touched one beside her. She felt it, it had mass, was made up of some kind of matter, but what, she couldn't determine. Normal words didn't apply to it. It wasn't hard or soft, rough or smooth. "And what do they do?"

"Absolutely anything. Think of it as living electricity you can call to obedience the way you could put a trained Doberman through his paces. It is fire and light and power and weaponry and pleasure, all wrapped in one. And, because I am an initiate, I can feed here, and never need organic food or drink. This can sustain my body indefinitely. Which won't help you, as I mentioned. And, sorry to admit this, there isn't a lot of available for you to snack on. Nothing really. If you're hungry now, you're liable to be a lot hungrier when we get through with what we're doing."

"How did we get here?"

"You don't know, do you?"

"Know what?"

"About the portal."

"I have no idea what you are talking about."

"The dragon had you shut a portal. I thought he would have taken the time to explain to you what one is."

"Portal," she said, struggling for vocabulary. "Door."

"Exactly."

The willow had vanished, literally. There was no fire, no possibility of finding her aunt's house. Andrew continued walking ahead of her, and shocked, Lori followed without him having to pull her. Since she didn't know where she was, one direction was as valid as any other.

"That portal is like any door. When it is open, anyone or any thing can go through it. It is exactly like the one you closed the other day. However, this one has been opened for centuries, and over the years, this land has eroded, so the door is for all practical purposes in the middle of the sky. It takes some getting used to."

She felt her shock fading, and the emotion which replaced it was anger. She rubbed her wrist where he had grasped her, showed her teeth, thought about the dragon. "Then why don't you move it?"

He gave a sigh of exasperation, as if he had been repeating the obvious over and over to an idiot who refused to grasp the concept. "Doors don't move. I've recently learned to open them, but I cannot shut them and I cannot shift them." He tilted his head, looking at her with new expectation. "Unless moving them is one of the talents you possess?"

"I don't know what you're talking about."

"The dragon wouldn't tell you." Andrew smiled, more in his element, and he was definitely chatty, as he continued walking. "Since the beginning of human kind, there have been only fourteen people who had the ability to shut a door. Fourteen documented cases, but all the same, there can't be more than one or two undisclosed cases."

"I don't—"

"I'm explaining. In all those cases, it was a woman who shut the door. And in all those cases, the woman was associated with a man of power."

"Byron."

"Yes, in his own right, Byron is one. But so am I. It is important for you to realize this. Your dragon cannot open nor close doors. He can see them, and obviously can go through them, but he cannot alter them in any fashion. I only learned the day of the catastrophe how to open them."

"That destruction was your doing?"

"Yes, it was mine. The problem with opening a door, and it is a significant problem, is there is no way to determine where the door you are opening leads. As far as all the educated mages can determine, it is completely and strictly random. If there is a way to control location, no mage or wer-mage has ever located the spell."

"You were telling me about women who can shut doors."

"Yes. The last recorded instance of a woman with the ability to shut doors was the year 1421. Portugal. She was unfortunately crushed as a witch, so there is no telling how powerful she might have been. Her career was short-lived, but the documentation as to her ability is solid. I studied it myself, going over the data time and time again, to determine if she and the others like her had any factors in common: early childhood trauma, a tattoo, born under a full moon of a mage parent. I've found no unifying characteristic, not that there is a lot of extant data on the other women. On most there is only a scribbled notation in the lore. And there hasn't been another woman who could shut a mage portal in almost six centuries. Not even a hint of a woman with the ability. Then you come along and casually shut the door."

"There wasn't anything casual about it."

"Trust me; it will get easier with time. What is so funny is, I didn't know you had this priceless ability. I saw you only as a way to enter the Inn, as a way to approach your aunt. She is an extremely powerful witch, for want of a better word, although I doubt she would consider herself as such. But even she cannot close an open portal. I'm not even sure she can see them, although, obviously she uses them on a daily basis, probably using signs for alignment."

"And you need me?"

"Yes. There are fortunes to be made, unbelievable billions of dollars, for a wizard who can discover a new world. Believe me; I would only have to find one. Conclaves of wizards have been trying for centuries, for eons, without success. The problem is, once a door is opened, it cannot be closed, and sometimes the door doesn't react well to Earth."

"Doesn't react well?" Lori asked. "You call the devastation I witnessed not reacting well?"

"Not all alternate worlds are based on the same physics. Mistakes like what happened the other day are extremely likely. I was willing to take the chance, and obviously I wasn't lucky my first time out. But with you beside me, and in a place like this where the magic is available for the taking, I could open a hundred portals, or a thousand. In one of those, there should be one with the economic potential to be of benefit to mages."

"Or to mages with money."

He laughed, liking her insight. "Of course. If I open a door which leads to a place I would not wish to travel, you can close it, and I can try again. I have infinite patience."

"I'm not going to do anything to help you," Lori said, but she remembered the pain, and knew she would.

***

Jan trudged up the stairs, her legs leaden, her hands filled with a large tray too heavy for her to manage comfortably. She blinked as sweat dripped into her eyes and cursed herself, for she should have made two trips, but she was in a hurry, and time was of the essence.

"Jan—"

She jumped, dropping the tray. It landed loudly on the kitchen table, scattering the contents. "You're alive."

"I think I've killed all of the creatures that entered in through the door. I haven't been able to find another in days."

"Arthur," she said and without thinking, just responding to relief and the stress she'd been under, she hugged him.

"You scared me," she said. "I've been so worried about you."

The hug, which started spontaneous, shifted, subtly, insidiously until passion bloomed. "Would you believe me if I told you I've loved you for years?" Arthur asked.

Although loathe to do so, Jan broke the hug and rubbed her eyes. For some reason they had gone all misty. "No."

"I know the day it happened, the exact minute."

"No," she said again, although this time it was probably agreement. Who could tell? She was hugging one of the most powerful heroes of mythology, a man who had the sword Excalibur belted at his waist. "No," she said a third time, although clearly she was thinking about the hug, the rising passion and that in all her years she never expected this.

"You named your idiotic cat Genevieve."

Her bottom lip trembled. It was massively embarrassing. "I was trying to get a rise out of you. Get you to notice me. Oh, I know who you are and what you've done. Brew wouldn't let me forget, but I was so miserably attracted to you. Hormones at my age. Can you imagine?"

"Jan, for all you like to complain you're ancient, you're not that old. What are you, fifty-eight, fifty-nine? Barely middle age. Now, in the Middle Ages—"

"Which you remember—"

"Of course I do."

She laughed, and the moment, which was starting to grow awkward, lightened. "I think when all this is dealt with and we have a few minutes, we should talk."

"I'd like that," he said.

Jan noticed something hadn't been there a second before and she brought her knuckles to her lips. "What are you doing here? He's not …"

"He's not gone," the Byron shade said. He bowed respectfully, once to Jan, once to Arthur. "And I know I am not welcome."

"Go back where you came from."

"I cannot. He is too weak to hold me."

"Then help me, you fool! Tell me what I can do to save him."

"There is nothing. But you have another problem."

Jan surveyed the damage caused by dropping the tray. Some of the items had spilled, but nothing was broken, and nothing irretrievable. "What now?"

"The wizard has Lori."

"What!"

"She went out the back door. I warned her to hurry home …"

"And…?"

"I may have delayed her long enough she couldn't get back safely. I only thought to answer her questions, and I wanted to be with her. My heart …"

"Your dragon heart right now lies in a dying body. I doubt you have a heart at all."

"True. I was speaking metaphorically. I love her. I did not wish to be parted from her, and I find having her grieving by my bedside hour after hour extremely painful."

"Find some way to heal."

"I cannot. Such a miracle cure does not exist in this realm. I think you know I am dying. I am appreciative of all your efforts, and wish to thank you."

She looked at him, through him, seeing Byron, and not Byron. "I don't want your thanks."

"Nonetheless I offer them. I would ask a favor, although where I was raised, it is considered bestowing a blessing."

Her hackles were up, and she was willing to refuse his request just to be perverse. "What?"

He waited a beat, let the import of his statement sink in highlighting it by silence. When he spoke, the words were slow, deliberate. There could be no misunderstanding. "Drink the remainder of the tea."

Jan reeled, leaned against a chair so she wouldn't fall. "Never!"

"Let me pass. I beg you."

She clamped her eyes shut, grasped the edge of the chair, her hands lifeless. "Do you know what you ask?"

"I know. It is an accepted practice that those of my kind when they are wounded beyond salvation, go to someone they trust, someone honorable and beg this blessing."

"Never."

"I would offer it to Lori, but she is under the wizard's control now."

"And wouldn't understand what you were giving her."

"Would you tell her, after I'm gone?"

Jan busied herself, straightening the objects on her tray, to avoid looking at him. If Byron's chakra noticed the quiver in her hand, the hesitancy, he was polite enough not to mention it.

"Tell Lori? I don't know. I don't think so. I wanted to tell her when she told me what happened in your lair, when her eyes were wide with promise and confusion, but I didn't, for it was your secret. Now, it's different, Brew." Her breath hitched as she pulled air into her lungs, clamping her lids shut, for a minute, trying to put all manner of fear into perspective. "What purpose would it serve to tell her after you're gone? She would not be able to accept and would think me a fool."

"I would like someone to grieve for me."

"We will all grieve, Brew."

"Then I will leave the decision in your hands and as I have so many times in the past, I bow to your wisdom. But if Lori questions in a few months or a dozen years about the things about me which did not settle, I would be honored if you would explain to her the majesty of the dragons, and that I did not wish to ever leave her."

Jan stared at the devastation on the table, the ruination from the earthquake which still hadn't been cleaned. All she witnessed were wisps stolen from the past: a jaunty Byron sitting beside her, complaining about mortal tea, flirting with her niece who had no conception of what was happening beyond a handsome man's interest in her.

"We would be honored to fulfill your request," Arthur said.

"I will tell her. I'll make sure Lori knows everything that was good about the Superior Dragons."

The shade nodded quickly. He was far more insubstantial than even a few minutes before. "And drink my tea quickly, for I hurt." Hurt. Sad really, how much love hurt.

"You have done so much good." The words were spoken over a lump in her throat and came out ragged, as if she had been crying for days.

He shifted, but he was a shadow, not a living being, so he did not sit, did not reach out to touch her, to comfort her, as his spirit yearned to.

She growled. She could be perverse when she needed to. "Then you know what to do. Find some way to heal."

He ignored her or tried to, for his eyes tightened momentarily as if in pain from wounds she inflicted with only a tongue. He was a dragon. If he no longer had a dragon's prowess, at least he had a dragon's pride. "If you drink the tea now, to the last dreg, it will give you powers, abilities, which will aid you in your effort to provide for the creatures of faerie."

Her legs would no longer support her. She pulled out the chair, slumped into it, her head cupped in her palms, momentarily blinded, except for visions of the past, as clear now as when she had lived them. "Yes, I know."

He stood still, exhibiting bravery, valor. Dragons, on the whole, were not creatures known for self-sacrifice. It was a new emotion for him. "It is all I can give you. Jan, you have been a good friend."

She shook her head, taking all the strength she had left. "I don't want it. I do what I can with the powers I have been allowed."

"I am offering you more."

"At the expense of your life."

"I die anyway. You take nothing from me that will not be done in the next few days. The tea is being wasted."

"It is not being wasted. Every single drop I am using for my plants."

"I know my friend." He reached out, nearly touching her. It was a gentle motion, one filled with devout friendship. "The jewelry shop will be yours, as will all the wealth I have. You will know, when you drink the tea, where I have hidden my gems and how to get to them."

"Nothing can be done?" she asked, annoyed she was now looking at the shade through a heavy mist covering her eyes.

"On this Earth, nothing. I only beg you let me save you instead."

Jan swallowed, swiped at her eyes with the back of her wrist. "Let it be as you say. I will get the teapot."

CHAPTER 32

Lori looked back over her shoulder, and not watching where she walked. Her feet caught on some obstruction and she tripped. Cursing, Andrew pulled her upright.

"What are you doing?"

"Trying to remember landmarks. I'm going to get away from you somehow, and when I do, I want to know how to find the exit."

She thought he would mock her, deride her ideas as foolishness, but he did not. "That is an important lesson. You are wise to do so, even if it will not help you. In this world, in many worlds like this one, there are no maps, no way to navigate, except by landmarks. The stairs are easy to find, and the door, there, shimmers a bit differently than the rest of the sky. Should you ever need to return, the only advice I can give you is keep the mountains to your right."

"Have you ever been lost here?" she asked, getting to her feet, following him.

"Many times. If I hadn't been able to feed here, I would have died of starvation more than once trying to find the exit. Beyond the mountains to our left, there are no landmarks, and distance cannot be judged with any degree of accuracy."

"Can you use that—" she said, indicating with a twist of her neck to the planet hanging suspended in the sky, "as a point of reference?"

"No. It has an oddly elliptical orbit, and if its location can be determined, I haven't been able to manage it."

"You should bring down a surveying team."

"I wish that were possible. Their equipment would not work, and I doubt there is anything magnetic to determine the equivalent of longitude and latitude."

Andrew kept walking, stopping periodically to wipe his brow, for he was sweating excessively, although, the temperature was moderate, and he was only walking, not engaging in strenuous activity. And she noticed, even though he could maintain a conversation with her, he was counting, something she only suspected was his footsteps.

True to his statement there were no landmarks, he would weave occasionally, as if looking for a specific place which had moved, turtle fashion, since he was here last. Although Lori kept a sharp lookout, for she was interested in finding her way back, she found no house, no castle, no cave. How he knew he reached where he was going, Lori had no idea, for the swirling power strands, his words for the undulating neon snakes, still surrounded them, and they were no closer, nor further away from the mountains. It was a spot like any other. They could have stopped two minutes before, or walked on for another two hours. What difference would it make?

"We're here," he said, settling down, but not sitting. He squatted, his rear low but not touching the ground, his heels together, his feet flat.

"What are you going to do?"

"I'm going to open a door. This world is a good place to experiment. While nearly all mages know of this place, few travel here."

"Unless they are in need of healing," Lori said, cursing herself for a fool. She didn't wish to keep reminding him she knew of the magic stream.

"I suppose. As a group, generally we can only be hurt by another of our kind, and traditionally when one of us assaults another, there isn't enough left to heal. Your dragon should have been certain he killed me."

"I'm sure it's a mistake he won't make again."

Andrew shrugged, but most of his attention was devoted to knotting strands of varying hues into a complex whole. "He was busy dying at the time. He should accomplish that goal at any minute, don't you think?"

"Yes," she agreed, "he is dying."

"I wish I could have tried the tea, even once. Dragon tea is wasted on mortals."

"It is delicious."

"My point exactly. One of the most potent fluids in all the known galaxies, and you treat it as an afternoon ritual for replenishing fluids and catching up with random gossip with other brainless idiots like yourself. You know what I could accomplish with one cup of dragon tea rushing through my bloodstream?"

"No, what?"

"No matter. It is his head I want, and I doubt there's even a drop of tea left, especially if he is as weak as I think he is."

She watched as coils of power curled around him, up his legs, around his torso, down his arms. The silently hissing, lifeless snakes had a deadly beauty, merging with him in a symbiosis of destruction. Andrew worked his fingers in fantastic patterns, knotting strands, red and blue and green and yellow and a dozen other brilliantly descriptive colors, forming a sculpture both magnificent and frightening.

"I'm going to open a portal. It will take some time, but power is plentiful, and I should eventually get one open. If it is a good one, you won't have to do anything." He grinned, but he looked as evil as any monster she had ever imagined, this human-like creature, coated with blinding neon, "but the odds are not in our favor."

Lori looked away, toward the healing stream at the mountains, but she didn't want him to know where her thoughts strayed, so she turned back, met him eye-to-eye. "And what will I get for helping you? You'll get millions, you said, or was it billions? I want a cut of the profits."

"My greedy little lover. Sorry to disappoint you. You won't have much use for wealth here, as there is nothing to buy. But, I will let you live. You should be grateful."

She sat, and since the power bands were interested in him, they gave her wide berth. The ground, when it cleared around her, was dark and there was soil of a sort, the kind her aunt could use to plant purple hatchets. Her mouth grew dry. She would die without ever tasting them, not even the fresh kind, the ones that hadn't had opportunity to mold and turn flavorful.

She kept her eyes averted from the planet, suspended in the sky, although she did look up periodically as the hours lengthened, to see it was setting like the moon. It was smaller now than it had been when she first arrived, farther away. She hoped it would be gone soon, below this alien horizon. Things would be a lot less weird without a planet hanging boldly in the sky, where her mind kept telling her it had no right to be.

And, while she waited, she took the time to grieve, for she knew Byron was dying, and the ache within was intense. Loneliness, sorrow, regret, and memories of happiness merged with the ten thousand questions she had. But the answers no longer seemed important. Only her love mattered, and his life. She would remember him every day for no matter how many years were left her.

Andrew moaned, drawing her attention back to him. Sweat beaded on his forehead, huge droplets, but they were consumed by small buttercup yellow asp-like powerstrands. If he fed on them, apparently the reverse was true, they fed on him as well. Tiny scrapes opened up along his skin, at his forehead and his cheeks, his chin, his lips. They bled freely, but like the sweat, the blood vanished, consumed, leaving dry scars. Andrew would twitch with pain, for what he was doing obviously hurt, but he would not be turned aside.

The knot he was building was huge, as big as a closet. He had to move, stretching, reaching, pulling the components he needed from the morass surrounding them, setting them where it was required they go, into a pattern only he could see. The snarl, it was too knotted to think of it as anything else, was composed of all the colors surrounding them, in, from what she could determine, a completely random arrangement.

They held their form. That was the greatest significance of his creation. When Andrew placed a strand, it stayed put, stiff, without the undulations of the free strands. It gave his knot structure, form, all the more diabolical because of it. After a few hours, the powerstrands were harder for him to capture, as if sentient and realizing what he was doing, wanting no part of it. He roared, his voice spilling words in a language she could not decipher but only a few would come to heel, the rest he had to chase.

The structure continued to develop, now as big as her bedroom at the inn. No doors, no windows, no structure apparent beyond the knot, but it was substantial. She had no idea how this twisted morass could be a door, even if it did possess a breathless horror.

It reminded her of a car wreck, or perhaps a dozen, piled haphazardly one on another, pieces so intermeshed from the destruction they would be impossible to separate.

Oddly enough, for her disgust at the car wreck sculpture, there was also incredible beauty. She didn't understand it, but the blended colors were breathtaking.

"Are you ready, my dear?" He looked over his shoulder at her. She had been mesmerized by his actions, almost hypnotized. Lori had no idea how much time had passed. It could have been days. She had been hungry, but had passed into a type of lethargy where hunger was no longer an issue. In response, she struggled to her feet, found her legs tingling, almost unable to hold her weight.

Her mouth was dry. She had to pull moisture from under her tongue to speak. "Nothing I say can stop you from completing this madness?" She had no idea what it was, or how it was, she only knew this blister he had created was wrong, and the strands, although obeying blindly, were being used for evil.

"When I am this close to success?" Andrew asked. He held his hands out, a victory celebration, fingers splayed, arms raised over his head. He had to be exhausted, for all he was feeding off the power strands, but he did have energy for self-glorification, probably the worst of his sins.

"Don't" she screamed. "It's wrong!" Lori had no idea if she meant any door was wrong, or this particular portal opened into a place where he would not want to go. She was dizzy from watching an undulating surface she had no ability to comprehend, scared spitless for Byron, who could be dead by now. This door wasn't right. She knew that.

She looked around, noticed things she hadn't been able to discern before. Other attempts at doors, none as advanced or as complex at this one, all abandoned for reasons she could not fathom. If these were Andrew's earlier attempts or those of generations of mages or wer-mages, she had no idea. They were all wrong. Whatever these powerstrands were, they sought—or deserved—freedom.

He spoke in some obscure language, one she knew instinctively had no source in Earth lore, words she suspected meant, "I am the Great and

Powerful Oz!"

With her stomach twirling, Lori thought back to all her anthropological studies, to primitive cultures and their worship of magic and their spirit guides. There were probably mages throughout history, their powers belittled by those educated in her generation, because no scientist could believe what she was witnessing. Over how many generations had this magic been forgotten, except by those sons and grandsons and great-grandsons, let in on the secrets, or more correctly, the partial secrets. Magic did exist. Andrew had mastered it, even if his purposes were evil.

He twirled his hands and a door opened.

CHAPTER 33

The portal opened into a realm of evil. This she saw, physically, spiritually, emotionally. The door she had closed for Byron she had found by feel alone, aided by the fireflies. Whether because this was a different realm, or because since here, she had become more sensitive, Lori had no idea. It opened a crack at first, a mere sliver into a gruesome zone of terrors. She remembered the earthquakes, the stench of ammonia, the tremors and the approach of Armageddon. There was nothing similar now. Only an eerie disappointing silence.

Andrew leaned forward to check his handiwork, and without wondering about potential consequences, Lori shoved, dropping him through the door. She heard him drop, a wail of unexpected surprise he could not control. With him vanished, she realized the action wasn't as mindless as she thought. She expected resistance, that she would fight him and he would hurt her, but he had been off balance, and it had required very little effort on her part to thrust him through.

Bravely, for it did require courage, Lori hitched her breath and making sure she was balanced on the ground, looked through. Andrew was no longer visible. A second later, she saw him, twenty feet below her, bobbing in an ocean of water the color of ripe olives, no landmass in sight. She grinned, the action spontaneous. She had done it. It was empowering, this success. She had fought a mage, and for the moment, she was the victor.

She thought of escape, of Byron and Jan and mindless running, but she forced herself to be logical, then giggled, bordering on hysteria, for nothing in this realm could be, or perhaps even should be, based on logic. Lori searched until she found the door frame and shoved and tugged until she got it mostly shut. She found closing the portal easier this time, for at least a half dozen reasons. She could see the door, there were no earthquakes, no sulfur, no terror, and, as important as any of the others, she had done it before. Surprisingly, there was little or no resistance. The door, for want of a better phrase, wanted to shut.

Terrified, she grew disorientated, until she remembered what Andrew had told her. Gathering her courage, she ran back the way they had come, keeping the mountains to her right. She wasn't certain she would be able to find the door she had entered, but as she started panicking, her breath coming in deep gulps and her thoughts out of control, she noticed a mass of snake-like power strands concentrated in one area. As she looked, they formed what she took to be a staircase. She climbed, more afraid than she'd ever been in her life, and made it through the door.

The willow grabbed her, wrapping a million tentacles around her, squeezing a bit too tightly, making it impossible to breathe. She found herself growing light-headed, then that starved for air.

Although she struggled, Lori realized she could not fight the tree, or whatever it was. She had no weapons. A dozen small cuts opened along her arms and her legs, not deep, but painful, and each bled profusely.

Andrew was evil, but he was an evil she understood. He wanted power, revenge, money and self-glorification. She didn't understand his vocation, could not condone his complete lack of morals, but she could understand him. He was evil, but he was human. This tree was something else entirely. She had no idea what, except it was hurting her, and somehow it had communicated with Andrew, and as she thought back, he had been frightened of it. Even Byron, the Byron she could see through, hadn't wanted her near the tree.

Then she saw the dragon fire, burning steadily in the small carne of stones she had created. Not knowing what she was doing, Lori filled her mind with thoughts of the dragon fire burning the tree. Surprisingly it felt like the tentacles holding her were loosening. She struggled, keeping up her thoughts of fire until it let her go. She had no time to stem the bleeding. She ran. Time was running out.

Byron might be dead already.

She raced to the Inn, barging in the back door. Jan was pouring tea from the dragon teapot, holding it up, shaking it, as she mentally judged the remaining liquid.

And when she saw what her aunt was doing, all the pieces fell into place for her. Statements Byron had made which others alluded to finally made sense. She knew what he was, all three of his physical manifestations, four, if she included the chakra which had spoken to her more than once, and had started the dragon fire, for dragons can always make fire in any guise.

Byron, a man of power, but beyond that, not a man at all. A dragon. And, heaven help her, a teapot. She had been taking internally his essence, and while she did so, he had felt it was his honor to provide it.

"Give me the teapot!" she ordered.

Jan was startled. For all her eyes were dry now, they were red, swollen, and her face was ravaged. Her grief was tangible. "What?"

"I need the teapot. I've found a place where I can heal Byron. If I repair the teapot, he lives, doesn't he?"

Jan's shoulders sagged. "Lori, it's too late. There isn't a drop of tea left in here."

Lori grasped the cup from her aunt's hands. She stared at the tea within it, black and thick and less than a cup.

"I can pour it back."

"That's impossible."

She indicated the teapot. "When this is empty, he's dead, isn't he?"

"Yes."

"Why? Why did you do it? Did you think to kill him?"

"He's suffering, Lori. We have to let him go. There was poison in those arrows, which causes him incredible pain."

"I can save him."

"It's too late. Give me the tea."

She did not respond, at least not vocally. Lori lifted the cup, as if offering an invocation, then drank it down. The taste was bitter, acidic, worst by far than what she drank at the closing of the door. But she felt the power traveling down her throat, knew it was Byron inside her.

"The curse of the dragons," Arthur said, "if one finds a mortal to love, somehow she will drink all his essence until he is gone. I always thought it a curse, but in this case, it is a blessing."

A blessing. Somehow Arthur's words and the tea inside her empowered her. "Now I'm taking the pot."

"It's empty. I emptied every single drop. I made sure." It was a confession of sin, of guilt. It had been Byron's final gift, his blessing, and Jan would feel the pain of this betrayal the remainder of her days. "I'm sure he would rather you had the tea," Jan finished.

Jan turned around, then shifted back, faced her niece. "There is something you must understand. What you drank, wasn't just tea—"

"Yes. It was his life force."

"Yes. But, it will change you, alter you. Give you powers."

"What powers? Power to save him?"

"No. I don't know what power. To everyone a dragon's life force reacts differently. But you won't be the same, Lori."

Lori lifted the pot gently, swirled it around. She heard distinctly, liquid inside the pot. Not a lot, a tablespoon, maybe less, but liquid nonetheless.

"He's alive," she said because she had to believe it. Anything else was unthinkable.

"Then he's not dead," Jan said, and she reached out to grab the chair, in relief, in guilt, missed her aim, fell, painfully to the floor still covered with shards of glass she hadn't had time to clean, from crockery and cookware, shattered in an end of the world disaster. "I emptied it, but he's not ready to die!"

"I have to go."

"Lori," Jan looked up from the floor, making no motion to right herself, "take the tray."

There, on the table, a tray, filled with dirt. Beside it, an apple, not eaten, but ravaged. "I put apple seeds in there. They will germinate, I promise. They were the only seeds I had in the house. One apple, in this entire house. Just one apple. But it should be enough. No single drop of dragon tea should be wasted."

She remembered the long, rough drop from the portal. "I only can carry the teapot where I'm going."

"Carry the teapot in the tray. It is still leaking. Promise me you won't waste a drop. If he dies…"

"He's not going to die," Lori insisted, and she took the tray two handed, and set the teapot delicately in it. Already nine pale green shoots were appearing, apple trees germinating, when they had only been planted moments before. This she knew, because the apple, on the table, had not yet started to brown.

Arthur helped Jan up, and she folded herself into his arms and she kissed him, and Lori had no time to wonder about their relationship. She ran out of the house, Genevieve, the black cat, following. She stopped only once, to pick up a branch and stick it into the dragon fire long enough to have a burning brand to protect her from the willow. She found the door, dropped down, almost dropped the teapot and the tray. She apologized. The cat sprinted ahead of her.

"Byron, I'm so sorry," she said. She ran, following Genevieve who seemed to know the way. The powerstrands swirled around her. It felt like walking through mud, for the walking was hard, but she gave it no thought as she continued, with single-minded intensity for the stream. It was entirely possible Andrew had lied to her about its healing powers, but she didn't think so. He gloated over how he had survived the wounds inflicted by the dragon. He wanted her to see how clever he was. Perhaps for the only time in his life he would have spoken the truth.

Still, she had no idea if the stream would heal the teapot, if Byron was too far to recover fully. She might bring him back as only a shadow of what he was, some brain-dead victim in an irreversible coma. That would be worse than letting him die, honorably and with dignity. She didn't know anything about dragons, wasn't even sure she believed in them, but she believed in him.

"Don't leave me," she begged, trying to run, finding the mountains no closer, the stream vanished, for she could no longer see it.

Even Genevieve had disappeared, far ahead of her, when she had been bounding on her light cat feet through the powerstrands, the manifestations of Andrew's evil.

No. The powerstrands themselves were not evil. They could be used for evil, bound and perverted and abashed, but they themselves were not evil.

"If you help me," she whispered, knowing it part irrational hope, part prayer. "If you help me, I promise I will not leave here without seeing that monstrosity torn down." She did not know how to manipulate powerstrands, but she needed some lure to keep her moving.

And she felt the tea within her, giving her added sensitivity to her environment. Her eyesight was sharper. Her strength almost limitless. The thought curled inside her as intimate as loving him in the cavern.

Her tears dripped, landing in the soil, moistening it even as it continued to be fed by the dripping teapot. She prayed there was still fluid remaining. The tray became unmanageable, increasingly heavy. The apple trees were now over eighteen inches tall, starting to develop branches, and the leaves were growing as she watched, this high-speed time-lapse-photography of growth and development. Nine apple trees. They too had Byron inside.

She saw the river now, a pale silver more than blue, translucent as if the light were below it. There was no sign of the huge Earth-like planet in the sky, but she had no time to look. She only saw the stream.

"I will free you," she vowed to the strands, and they separated, making it easier for her to run, and then they did something else miraculous, they wrapped around her ankles, forming some kind of vehicle, and she effortlessly glided over their surface. She drew closer to the river, her shoulders aching, the tray was unbearably heavy, the trees double in height over the last few minutes. She feared for the teapot. If the trees were growing that rapidly, they were being fed too much. She wished now she hadn't drank so much or her Aunt had not been so diligent in trying to empty the last drop.

"Byron, hang on." If she had a free hand, she would caress the teapot, rub the dragon's wings, feel it shudder, as it had under her touch before. Her hands were occupied, but her hair was long, and it brushed the ceramic. She wanted to kiss it, make promises of forever. She kept moving forward, propelled by the powerstrands.

They stopped, unexpectedly, and she flew forward, landing hard, rolling from her knees to her side, head over heels. She dropped the tray, and the trees bounded out. She gasped, watching the teapot catapulting, until it reached the river. It hung suspended, floating for a second until it began to sink.

She jumped in, finding the stream icy cold, but doubted what flowed in the river was water. She had no idea what it was, but it wasn't water, or more specifically, not solely water. Miraculously her own wounds healed, but she didn't notice. She only saw the teapot, and the potential there.

"Live, Byron," she said, and she reached the teapot, and with two hands, she held it under the water, as if she were trying to drown it, as if it would fight her, as a cat or a child would. "Live!" she ordered. "Byron, I command you to live."

She remembered something her aunt said once, although it might have been Byron, her mind was so confused. She didn't understand it at the time. While a mortal was holding the teapot, no dragon would appear. She had to let it go.

The stream was powerful, forceful, moving off to some undisclosed location as if in a race it could not lose. Slowly she forced her fingers to open, to allow the teapot to be carried away. She prayed and cried. She even would have screamed in frustration and powerlessness, as the teapot floated away, except there was no time.

Around her the stream started bubbling, boiling, churning, and before she could react, in front of her stood a full sized dragon, about twenty feet high to the tips of his ears, probably twice that in length.

He was magnificent, with a rich gold color reflecting the many colors from the powerstrands, absorbing them, and strengthening because of them. His eyes were copper, like Byron's, and like her lover's, they were ringed with gold.

Lori, you can't know how much I love you.

She stepped back, frightened, terrified. She had suspected he was a dragon, the teapot merely one of his manifestations. But this was a dragon, full bodied and huge. He was more frightening than anything she could imagine.

She forced her fears into a tight little box, remembered the tea within her, remembered the passion and the exhilaration she felt when he kissed her. "Are you all right?"

I am.

"There's a wizard, Andrew. I can show you where."

Climb aboard. I can fly.

She felt the joy he felt, of life and health and being reunited with his entire self. He was whole.

He spread immense glorious, brilliantly copper colored wings. He looked like the teapot, a million, a billion times larger and more animated, but the colors were the same. There was a feathery growth at his eyes, greens and teals, appearing delicate and feminine. She noticed his claws, long, sharp talons, and he opened his mouth and she recognized three layers of teeth, each one longer than her fingers, but four longer still. She was no longer afraid. This was Byron and she loved him.

You knew?

"About the dragon and the teapot? How could I? You tried to tell me.

Right now, everything you said is beginning to make sense, when it didn't before. I didn't truly know until I saw Jan holding the teapot, willing to drink down to the last dregs. Then I realized what I'd been denying."

She rubbed her stomach and her womb. There was more there than the tea. More … although, at the moment it was only potential for more. She would love him tonight, when they got back to Earth, when they finished this one last distasteful thing they had to do. She knew it would be a very good thing she and this creature could create together.

She studied his wings, his broad shoulders. She very much wanted to ride a flying dragon, but she didn't know how. Fantasy, reality, she had no idea where one began, another ended. "I don't want to hurt you."

You could not hurt me. I will bend my foreleg. Climb there, seat yourself in front of my wing ridges.

She had no idea what a wing ridge was, but she pulled herself up on his knee, then swung her leg around, as if she were mounting a very large horse. There was a spot which looked made for her to sit, so she did.

Take-offs and landings are rough, to those who are not used to dragon flight.

"I'll hold on." She screamed in fright as he took off, and screamed again as he gained altitude, this time in pleasure, in ecstasy and completion. The planet in the sky had moved, well toward the horizon, but now there was something different hanging above the swirling morass below, a golden dragon and his long-haired rider.

Here, he said. There was no need for her to give him directions.

He landed, and it was not as rough as she feared, although it might be already she considered herself an experienced dragon rider and had compensated for his movements instinctively, jostled less than she might have been.

She jumped down, stared at the huge knot, maleficent and snarling. "Byron—"

"I am here, my love." She turned, and it was the man Byron she faced, familiar to her as her own heart. She rushed into his arms, weeping and crying, loving him with all of her being.

His arms were warm, wrapped around her, and she felt his passion. She kissed his chest, laid her head back so he could kiss her neck, her eyelids, her ears. She broke from the embrace, before she could not. Although she wanted to, she could not make love to him in front of this monstrosity.

"I have to shut the door for good."

Gently, firmly, he pushed her away. "Destroy this thing."

"Can you help?"

"I am forbidden," he said. "Even if I was not, I could not help. It is not something I have the ability to do."

"Blow fire on it."

"Fire would not destroy it, and again, I cannot interfere, even if in interfering, I am only attempting to bring it down, and not succeeding."

"How do I do it?"

"I cannot say."

"Cannot, or won't?" She grew angry. This door was an eyesore, a festering blister. She had made a promise to the powerstrands she would destroy it, and she wanted to. She needed to, for it was evil, a structure built by Andrew.

"Does it matter? Lori, if it is to be destroyed, you will have to."

"I am no wer-wizard."

"True. You are not. But you have the ability to shut doors. I have seen you."

A woman, associated with a man of power, who had the ability to close portals. One of fourteen. Fifteen, when she considered herself. The ground under her feet started to churn, rumbling, and she remembered the destruction from the first door Andrew had opened, and she did not wish a repeat of the devastation here, where, although it was not her world, things did have a pristine beauty. After all, this world had healed Byron when he was all but dead. She owed it something in repayment.

She reached out, pulled a strand, hoping to loosen it, to grant it freedom. There was a low level shock, stinging throughout her whole body, a chewing-on-tinfoil pain. She gasped, pulled back her hand.

"I am forbidden to interfere," he said, but she clearly heard the "But—"he did not vocalize.

"Tell me what I need to know."

Byron shifted … man … dragon … teapot … back to man again. "You will not be able to succeed until the door is completely shut. You are trying to do one thing while the thing you work on has properties in two separate dimensions."

"I see." And she did. If the door were shut, she would be in this land only. But a frightening possibility asserted itself. The door was open. Far wider than it had been after she had shoved Andrew, after she had run for the other portal.

Her eyes widened, and her voice shook. "He got out. He got free."

"I will fight him again, then," Byron said. "Or someone else will, one of his own kind, for we will have our own trials. But for now …" he let his sentence drip off and she wondered why he was forbidden to interfere, and by who.

"For now," Lori said, liking the idea she could do something this magnificent being could not, "I will shut the door before something else comes through." She reached out, squeezed his hand, for he was in manform, and she liked touching him, whole and healthy and impossibly real.

"Could this be a good door? One it might benefit humanity to leave open?"

"I do not know. The longer it stays open, the more impossible it will be to destroy. It can become permanent."

Lori remembered feeling evil through it, evil beyond what Andrew had said and done. She had a promise to the powerstrands. Whether or not they were sentient, they had helped her. She would help them.

"I will shut the door," she said, "although I wished I had made sure of locking Andrew inside."

"He is evil. He will be destroyed."

"But not until he causes more heartache."

"Yes." How Byron knew, she had no idea, but she knew it too. His evil was tangible and was loose on Earth. There would be heartache in the future because she had left a door open, concerned with rescuing a teapot.

Byron brought her hand to his lips, kissed her knuckles, running his tongue against her skin, lightly, provocatively. When he released her, Lori knew it was time. She bent, strained, tugged, pulled, swore, tore her knuckles, and the door wouldn't move. "Help me, Byron."

He backed up, one step, then two. The powerstrands gave him wide berth, but by the same token, Lori believed they honored him, with what looked like many of them standing at attention, on their ends. "I cannot even attempt such a thing. Do not forget, I am a dragon. I can only do the things I can do."

She set her back to it. It should be easier now than the door she had shut back on Earth, because she could see its dimensions, knew its depth and breadth, where before she only had sensations from her fingers. "Am I doing it right?"

"I do not know."

"Byron—"

"Lori, it might be you are so full of dragon tea, you are, temporarily, a creature of faerie yourself, and therefore forbidden to interfere. I do not know. It might be the wizard put a spell on it, so this door cannot close. I do not know, and I cannot say, even if I did know."

She leaned against the door, slithering down, until she sat on the ground, until a few small, brave powerstrands sniffed at her feet and legs, blue ones mostly, although a pink one was in there somewhere. "I don't want to leave it open. Whatever it is, it isn't good, by any definition." She held her hand out, let a narrow, yet brilliant orange strand come closer, wind itself around her fingers. This one was soft, like kitten fur. It wrapped around, a bracelet, not living, yet somehow sentient. The strands had done the same for Andrew.

"Should I pull it off?"

"I cannot say."

"Do you know?"

"Yes." As a dragon, he could lie, but as her lover, he wouldn't.

"Byron—"

"Do not ask me. This is too intrinsic to what I am. If I break this commandment and tell you, it would be far better, if I had died from the arrows and fallen directly into the wer-wizard's clutches. I have already interfered too much in flying you here. I can fight a wer-wizard on his terms and on my terms, but this is magic, and I am forbidden."

He turned his back, started walking away, and she gasped, crying out, but she realized he was doing what he had to do. If worse came to worse, she would leave the door open and return to him, but she wasn't willing to concede.

"Tell me one thing before you go, if you can," she said, calling out.

He stopped, but did not turn around. She missed his jaunty swagger, that male supremacy he had exhibited when he took the left turning, leaving her by a faerie ring. But he waited, and she knew he would answer if he could.

"Did you know I could shut doors when you asked me to?"

"In the forest, when I was wounded?"

"Yes." The orange strand slithered higher up on her arm, still worn like a bracelet, but now nearly to her shoulder. The blue strands were closer to her feet, but no others touched her. There were strands swirling around Byron, but none touched him either.

"No. I had no idea. I was desperate, dying. There was a wer-wizard loose, and I knew Earth could be destroyed if that door were left open. You were available."

"Could it be, do you think, I had the ability all along, I could do it because you asked, or because there was desperation within me, or because I had been with men of power?" She had meant to say man, a man of power, cursed silently to herself because she had said men. His back was to her, so she couldn't see his expression, knew, though, by the way a shiver ran through him, he caught her mistake, and understood it. She had a wizard lover before she had been intimate with a dragon.

"I do not know the answer to your question, but this too I am forbidden to answer."

"Byron—"

She waited, hoping for some response, some acknowledgment, but although he stood still, without going forward, neither did he respond.

"Byron, I love you. With all my heart and soul I love you."

"And I love you," he responded, but he had no soul, so he could not answer in kind, and she wondered how their love would find completion, when she was human and he wasn't. At the moment, it didn't matter. It was only important he loved her.

He stood there, his confession ringing in her ears, the most beautiful words she'd ever heard. Byron stood far enough away he would not be a distraction, close enough she knew he would be there for her if he could. He was walking a fine line, and Lori knew their marriage, for she would settle for nothing less, would be the same, each doing everything he or she could for the other, knowing there were impossible things and beautiful things.

She studied the door. It had no hinges, but it would slide, if she could figure out the obstruction. She spoke to the power bands in English, although Andrew had not when he had manipulated them, she needed to focus her own concentration, and keep a running commentary for Byron, who, although he could not help, could listen and share her trials.

She noticed a small orange strand, where it didn't belong. How she knew it didn't belong, she had no idea, for all the colors were to her, randomly juxtaposed. And she knew each color meant a different thing. Although she had no idea their inherent natures, that orange one, for whatever reason, needed to be moved.

She pulled and she tugged, but beyond a slight electric buzz, could not shift it. She was human, not mage, and felt powerless. He was dragon, and wouldn't move a strand, even if he could.

She rubbed her arm, where the strand remained, although she liked it there. It was somehow comforting. "Can you help me?" she asked it. "Or is this beyond your nature?"

She bent down, and the orange strand uncurled, an inch, then two, still wrapped around her arm, but it undulated, and the obstructing orange strand wiggled, stretched, becoming thinner and longer and freed itself. It slithered off, into the morass, vanishing completely into the shifting colors, invisible, as if it had never been there.

"Thank you!" she called. She bent her back, realized the door would move, and it moved so easily when she tugged, she fell, screamed because she was startled, then laughed because she was not hurt. Lori rolled in pleasure, and around her she felt the strands approved.

Byron moved when she screamed, then stayed when he realized she was all right.

"The door is shut," Lori said.

As it should be, he responded, still not turning around. Instead of Byron the man, now, with its back to her, was Byron the dragon. She wondered why he had changed, if something had precipitated it, or if he could only hold onto human form in this realm for small increments of time. She would ask him later. Then, the dragon lowered its head and roared, loud enough the ground shook, and all the long powerstrands backed up. A flash of brilliant colored lightning hit beside her, exploding in sparks of fire.

She screamed, rolled away from the knot, rising to her knees, thinking to run to Byron, when Lori noticed Andrew. He rode, five feet in the air, flying in a chariot made of the powerstrands. He looked majestic, powerful, almost god-like, although she knew, this too, was a facet of his evil.

"Stay away from the door!" his voice boomed, shattering the silence, echoed, although there was nothing it could echo against.

In her fear, she had forgotten the door, but with his order, she reaffirmed her resolve to destroy the knot. Andrew straightened one of his hands, forming a glowing lance. He threw it, and she realized what the lightning was that had shattered beside her only seconds before. The dragon roared again, and his teeth snapped, and Lori shivered, for she had seen Byron wounded, dying, and she hated Andrew with a passion. Defiantly she stood, returned to the portal, pulled, randomly at a powerstrand, without success.

"Do not destroy my portal!"

Her teeth rattled and her knees quaked. She turned back to face him. "You'll have to get past my dragon if you want to stop me," Lori yelled back.

"He is forbidden to interfere."

"With the powerstrands," she said, "not with protecting his mate. I imagine there is no law on any plane which says a dragon cannot protect his mate."

You are right. There is nothing to stop a dragon from defending the woman he has claimed as his own.

"She is not your kind," Andrew said, but a strain of desperation infused his words, as if he now realizing his mistake. "You should have stayed dead. You seemed willing enough when you begged the witch to let you."

How did you know?

"I occasionally have ways to hear inside the Inn. Please let me die, you begged. How I cheered. However, this battle between us might turn to my advantage. I do so want your carcass."

The dragon roared again, but this time, it was tinged with what might be laughter. *When you scream, Please let me die, I just might accommodate you.*

The chariot, formerly suspended above them now swayed, as Andrew displayed his confidence. "In a battle between a fully vested wer-mage and a dragon, fought on a plane loaded with powerstrands, who do you think will emerge victorious?"

"There is one other variable you forgot to take into consideration," Lori said, grasping a powerstrand from the knot, and pulling. This time, for some reason, it loosened, and she gained about three feet. Like pulling yarn from a knot with fifty thousand ends, it was a start, but not enough.

Andrew screamed. He had changed. He wore a long robe, the robe she had seen him wear when he passed her in the forest, during the worst of the devastation.

"You don't know what you tangle with. And only a mage or a wer-mage can manage what you attempt."

"A mage or a wer-mage or perhaps a dragon's mate," she answered, feeling brave. She knew little of mystical creatures, most of her information obviously false, stolen from anthropological studies, but Lori knew she was not a witch or a creature of faerie. She pulled another, but this one only tightened, so she left it, chose another at random, hoping for a flash of insight, like when she determined the role of the orange strand. She liked that idea. She had had luck with the orange. She let go of the strand she held, sought an orange one and tugged. There was a moment's resistance, then the entire strand pulled free. The morass reformed, seemingly as impenetrable as ever, but she was heartened, for she sensed success. Ignoring Andrew, she sought another orange. Maybe they had to be released in order, although not how they were built. Maybe if she freed all the oranges, she could choose another color, red or indigo or violet or some other hue, and this house of cards would tumble down.

She dropped the orange and it slithered, but not to freedom, like the first orange. This one found another orange, and nosed it, like a puppy meeting a littermate. Lori needed no second invitation. She would have gloated to Byron, showed off for Andrew, but their battle was joined, and dragon claws slashed out, powerstrand lances flew, and Lori had no time to watch them, for she knew what she was doing was vital. She pulled another orange, and then another, although the last was redder than true orange, deeper and longer.

Andrew yelled, and a lance hurled past her, and Lori screamed, dropping the strand before it was pulled free, and it coiled back inside the knot. Another lance flew, then another, and Andrew was beside her, struggling to pull open the door she had shut bleeding from a dozen open wounds. The dragon snapped at his heels, but did not approach the portal.

"Bryon—"

I have to let him go.

The door didn't slide open, it tore open, with a ripping sound, and

Andrew jumped, vanishing.

She had never been so angry or empowered. "I can keep destroying this. He won't get out a second time." She continued pulling, and strands came out in clumps. Not only orange and red, but the blues, the greens, the yellows. It was easier, and it was exhilarating. Fifteen women. She bet not one of the others had ever been able to destroy a door they had closed.

"Enough?" she asked, when she had the knot almost unraveled.

But he did not answer, so she continued, until no two strands remained together, and the entire portal vanished.

"Is he trapped for good?" she asked.

I could not say. If there is no other portal from that world to this one, perhaps. But I would not count on it.

And she remembered Byron had said there would be a final accounting with the wer-wizard, and that fight was not necessarily theirs, and she knew the battle which had raged around her while she was pulling strands was not his final end.

"Let us go back. Jan will be glad to see you."

Byron faced her, male and human-looking, and so welcoming she raced into his arms. "Jan will be glad to see us both. We will invite her to the ceremony. Actually, we have to invite her to the ceremony, for she will officiate."

"Marriage ceremony?"

"Yes."

"Is my aunt a witch?" Lori had been through a lot, was not sure how she felt about this one thing, but she was in love with a creature of power, a dragon, so she supposed her aunt being a witch was not as significant a thing as she might have thought, even a few weeks before.

Byron could be diplomatic when he chose. "Your aunt is a friend to all who are creatures of faerie. She is a caretaker and an administrator to the Inn."

"The Dragon's Roost Bed and Breakfast."

"Yes, where many wondrous things have happened, and where many marvelous things are yet to happen. But as for calling her a witch, like many words, it is a term which can be taken two ways, depending on how it is spoken, and I am not certain it is a term your aunt would embrace."

He would not help her locate the portal, and she was not certain he could not, or was as blind as she was to locating the stairs. She remembered enough to keep the mountains on her right, but they looked different. There were nine tall things there, as big as buildings, which hadn't been there before. She became afraid, and thought of monsters, until she realized they were apple trees, and this land would never again be a place where a human could find no food.

"I hope Aunt Jan doesn't want her tray back."

"We will find some way to buy her another," Byron said, but his eyes twinkled, and he looked at the apple trees, as if it were a very good thing they had done together in planting them.

CHAPTER 34

It was with trial and error, and several long minutes of desperation while she feared they would never get out, before she located the staircase. With Bryon beside her, Lori climbed through the portal, back to the land under the willow, were she saw the dragon fire still burned. The long sinuous branches of the willow approached only once, but Byron roared, a man-roar, and the branches kept as far away as they could.

She stopped for a moment beside the fire, put her hands out, warming them. She understood why when she'd been here, talking with the chakra, she felt so comforted. The warmth from this fire was Byron's, the warmth she felt laying naked beside him, the scent of their loving still fresh in a massive cave.

"Have you been reunited with your chakra?"

"Yes. It followed while you carried the teapot. I am not whole without it, nor it complete without me."

"But you are strong enough to hold it now."

"I am."

They passed the pond, where fat green things, frogs, she had thought, but now she wasn't sure, plopped into the water, leaving only ripples in the glassy surface. "This part is not Earth, is it?"

"Actually, no place you can reach from the back door of the Inn is Earth."

"But we're closer?"

It was dark, no moon shown, no stars glittered, and Lori ached, for she found she missed the colorful swirling morass of powerstrands, but by the same token, she decided she could live happily ever after if she never saw another.

"'Closer' is a term which does not apply."

She was used to Rand McNally road atlases, and landmarks that stayed put and meant something. Lori folded her arms under her breasts. "We have to pass into this realm to get back to the Inn."

"Perhaps."

"I think dragons spend too much time being inscrutable."

"So it has been said," Byron agreed. But they entered the Inn through the back door, Jan hugged them both. She cried, for she was certain Byron was dead, and with the wer-wizard on the loose, Lori was in danger. She was so relieved she promised brownies, and Lori, who was happy, refused to ask if she meant a heavy chocolate cake treat to eat or if she meant small creatures of faerie known to be mischief makers. Byron clearly said "Later!" and picked Lori up, as if she were weightless.

"I am weak, but if you would like a cup of tea, I am sure I could arrange it."

Lori ran her fingers through his hair, for it was long, and had fallen down into his eyes. She remembered what the dragon looked like, and looking at Bryon the man she saw both, knowing his strength came from his ability to be all three, man, dragon, teapot. Four, if she wanted to count lover, for that was a role he would play every night for the rest of her life, and it too would become crucial to his being.

"I want to sleep, and I want to hold you, not necessarily in any order, and I want to taste a purple hatchet, and I don't even care if it is moldy."

"A purple hatchet?" he said, and he laughed. There were so many other things she could have asked of a dragon.

"Yes. I thought, while you were dying, I would never get to eat one, and I realized I would regret it for the rest of my life."

"I may never understand you," Byron said, but he wrapped his human arms around her, and carried her up the stairs, past landing after landing, until they reached, inexplicably, a huge cavern. One day too she would ask him how this cave came to be at the top of the Inn, although she knew the staircase went further, and so the cave couldn't be the top after all.

"I will feed you purple hatchets, but I can guarantee you, they would grow, even without me."

"But not as well," she insisted.

"No," he agreed, "not as well. They do particularly well with dragon tea."

She reached up, worked on the first button of her own shirt. "As I do well with dragon tea. But right now, I think it is time for you to taste human flesh again. It's been too long since you have done so."

And his grin spread and he set her ever so gently onto the pallet where they first made love. "Yes. It is time I tasted human flesh again." His grin flashed, showing the whiteness of his too long teeth. "And you will scream."

"I look forward to it," Lori answered, tugging at his clothing, for time pressed her too much for any elaborate, seductive strip-tease. If there was no time dimension here as she once suspected, then it was love pressuring her, or the primal need of a man and woman, or even more likely, the residual of dragon tea deep within her body, where she had impressions of a miraculous creation.

Byron reached down, his teeth nipping on the tender flesh below her ear, not gently, but without any pain. And she did scream throughout the night, but it was only in pleasure.

The End

Betsy J. Bennett's author's page

My name is Betsy J. Bennett and I write fantasy/paranormal romance. I often tell people that I write because my characters are far more interesting than the people I know, and that's true, but there are other reasons. I write because I see these people. I know their stories, their problems, their search for love and I have to tell it so readers can see it. I also write to avoid depression and possible homicide charges. When I write I'm happy with the world around me. I can not always control my worlds, but they always lead me to fascinating places and take unexpected turns which always turns out happily.

Betsy J. Bennett's Books

The Dragon's Roost Bed & Breakfast Series
Book 1   **A Dragon's Tea**
Book 2   **A Gargoyle's Vow**
Book 3   **A Wizard's Spell**
Book 4   **A Ghost's Chance**

Santa Takes a Wife
Yes, Virginia.

The Frog Kiss

Her Puzzle

Strangers in the Night

Left Star of Orion's Belt

All books are available on AMAZON.com